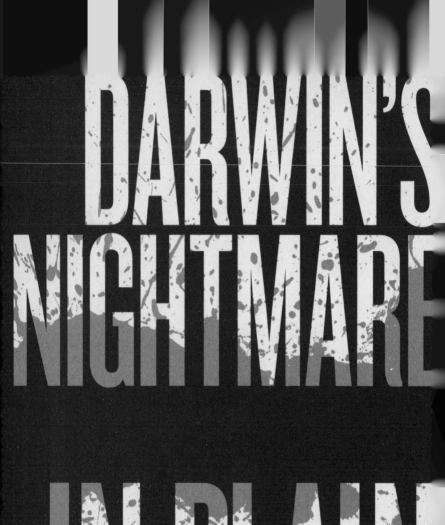

DARWIN'S NIGHTMARE

IN PLAIN

THE WILSON MYSTERY OMNIBUS

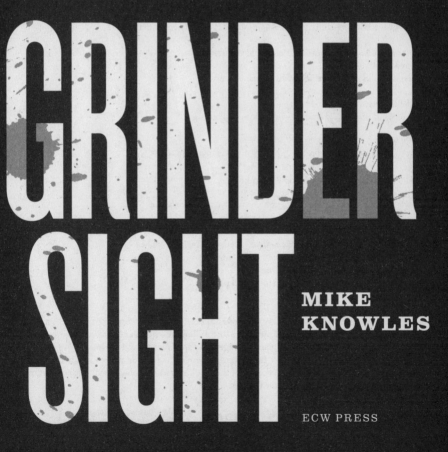

GRINDER
SIGHT

MIKE
KNOWLES

ECW PRESS

Published by ECW Press
2120 Queen Street East, Suite 200, Toronto, Ontario, Canada M4E 1E2
416-694-3348 / info@ecwpress.com

This is a work of fiction. Names, characters, places, and incidents either are the product of the
author's imagination or are used fictitiously, and any resemblance to actual persons, living or
dead, business establishments, events, or locales is entirely coincidental.

Library and Archives Canada Cataloguing in Publication
Knowles, Mike
Wilson mystery omnibus / Mike Knowles.

(A Wilson mystery)
Contents: Darwin's nightmare — Grinder — In plain sight

ISBN 978-1-77041-047-3
also issued as: 978-1-77090-241-1 (PDF); 978-1-77090-242-8 (ePub)

I. Title. II. Series: Knowles, Mike. Wilson mystery.

PS8621.N67W54 2012   C813'.6   C2011-906947-4

Originally published in hardcover as *Darwin's Nightmare* (2008, 978-1-55022-842-7), *Grinder*
(2009, 978-1-55022-895-3), *In Plain Sight* (2010, 978-1-55022-948-6).

Cover and Text Design: Ingrid Paulson
Cover image: blood spatter © itchySan / iStockphoto
Printing: Webcom   5   4   3   2   1

The publication of *The Wilson Mystery Omnibus* has been generously supported by the Canada
Council for the Arts which last year invested $20.1 million in writing and publishing throughout
Canada, and by the Ontario Arts Council, an agency of the Government of Ontario. We also
acknowledge the financial support of the Government of Canada through the Canada Book Fund
for our publishing activities. The marketing of this book was made possible with the support of
the Ontario Media Development Corporation.

 Canada Council   Conseil des Arts
for the Arts   du Canada
 Canadä   ONTARIO ARTS COUNCIL
CONSEIL DES ARTS DE L'ONTARIO

Printed and bound in Canada

FOR ANDREA.
IT COULD BE FOR NO ONE ELSE.

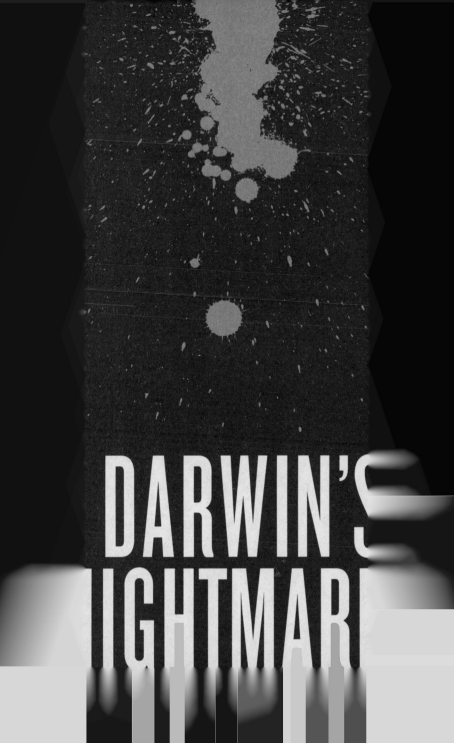

CHAPTER ONE

Watching for the switch was the easiest part. This guy was such an amateur that he drew attention to himself just standing there. The bag, the object of my interest, was being held by a young kid with blond highlighted hair and several days' worth of dark scruff growing on his face. His small mouth was chewing gum, hard, and his head was looking around one hundred eighty degrees left then right. If he were capable he would have spun his head in a constant rotation, taking in everything in the airport. He couldn't even dress the part; he was wearing a long beige trench coat — unbuttoned with the collar turned up. The only thing missing was a fedora. I was sure he watched spy movies to pump himself up for the deal.

The deal itself was the only thing hard to figure. I had been paid to steal a package from an unknown person, and I had no knowledge about the courier, size, contents, or nature of the package. I knew only the location, Hamilton International Airport, which made any tools I wanted to bring pretty much useless. The airport was small in comparison to its counterpart, ninety minutes away in Toronto. The Hamilton airport ran about three hundred flights per week. Only one third of those flights were international. Most of the passengers who used the airport were businessmen on domestic flights to Ottawa or Montreal.

It was eight in the morning in mid-October, and the airport was in a lull. The passengers who had arrived on the red-eye had collected their luggage and gone outside, leaving only a hundred or so customers in the terminal. I had to intercept the bag before it got to a plane, and that meant I might have to follow it to a gate. So I came in light.

There were only a few minimum-wage rent-a-cops working as airport security near the entrance; there was no need for more. The crowds were sparse and half-asleep, and the real action took place after you bought your ticket. The blond kid moved around the terminal looking at brochures and the candy on display in the convenience store. I watched him and everything else in the terminal from a seat near a row of pay phones. No one else seemed to be watching the kid, which made me think the deal was going to happen on the other side of the metal detectors. Every so often, my gaze would catch the boy's blond hair, and I would focus on him. He was young, no more than twenty-five, and under the trench coat he wore a black Juventus soccer warm-up suit. The flashy labels on the casual clothes under the coat made the kid easy to spot. His light olive skin put his ancestors around the Mediterranean; the warm-up suit narrowed the geography to Italy. His hair had been dyed blond a few weeks ago, judging from the inch of dark roots visible above his forehead. He augmented his faux blond hair with a lot of gel, making him taller and more colourful than anyone around him. Everything about his outfit, his features, and the way he carried himself screamed, "Look at me!" He made no effort to be anonymous, to be invisible, like me. It made me wonder what I was doing involved with this kid, and it made me wonder about the bag. What could a kid like this be trying to move? And why would it be important to my employer?

Just when I thought it couldn't get any better, a watch started beeping. It was the kid's watch; the beeping startled him, and he shut it off so he could complete another full scan around the room. He moved toward a gate, and produced a ticket from an inner coat pocket. He would have to pass several small restaurants and stores to reach the double doors that led to the metal detectors. Only one of the doors was open, and there was a backup of ten or twelve passengers. I moved in behind the kid and took the roll of quarters from my pocket. If this guy was as amateur as he looked, it would all work out. I moved his coat to the side with my left hand and shoved the roll hard into his back right on top of his kidney.

"Turn around and walk to the bathroom *now*," I said, and shoved the roll of coins harder into his back like a gun barrel.

"What?...What are you doing? W...w... why?" he stuttered.

"Too bad, kid. If you didn't know, you would have screamed," I said into his ear. "Move out of line and walk to the bathroom. If you don't I'll just clip you here. The gun is silenced. I'll be in the car before anyone figures out you've been shot."

The kid didn't question me; he moved away from the line and turned toward the washroom as though he was being pulled by marionette strings. As we walked, the back collar of the beige coat became brown with sweat. The bathrooms were down a long hall, and we had to weave around several people to get to the door. If this poseur had been anyone else he would have shoved off and been mixed into the people before I could get any shots off. But he wasn't anyone else.

"Stop here," I said as we neared the handicap washroom. I pulled down an out-of-order sign I had taped to the door and ushered him in. I eased up on his kidney, and he made his move, just like I hoped he would. He pushed back, trying to trap me against the door, and spread his arms, ready to take the pistol. If I had a gun he might have taken it, though more than likely I would have put a bullet in him. My foot found the back of his knee, and his body shifted down until his knees hit the tiles on the floor. I drove my forearm across his jaw, hard, and heard the sound of it coming out of socket; his mouth must have been open. Both hands had risen up near his face when I palmed the roll of quarters and went to work on his back. Two hooks to each side of the kid's body put him flat on the floor gasping. I lifted the bag. It was light, lighter than I expected, almost as if it was empty. I got over my surprise and got back to the task at hand. It was time to go. I eased the blond kid back onto his feet and laid a tight uppercut into his jaw using the quarters.

CHAPTER TWO

On the drive back to the office, there were no flashing lights in my rear-view, and no dark cars following in my wake. Even though I was sure that I had no tail, I manoeuvred the streets using random turns and sudden bursts of speed, keeping my eyes on the mirrors. No cars stayed behind my old Volvo, and no one on the street looked at the car twice. Its exterior was well worn, like most cars in the city, but I kept the guts in shape. The car was unobtrusive until it had to run; then you couldn't help but notice it — while it was still in view. The bag I had picked up was locked in the roomy trunk, unopened.

When I got to the office, I went right to the safe. I put the bag in and pulled out one of the ten prepaid cell phones that were arranged neatly inside. I closed the safe and took the phone over to the desk. The hard wooden chair groaned with my weight, but it held me without collapsing. I powered up the phone and dialled a number I had committed to memory.

"Yeah?"

"It's done," I said, and the line went dead. I knew from experience that I had an hour or two until pick-up — after that I could eat. I pulled my Glock 9 mm out of the top right desk drawer and set it in my lap, propped up against my thigh.

I waited, staring out the window, the chair leaned back and my feet resting on the windowsill so that I could see the street below. Across from my fifth-floor window was a worn-out high-rise, home to a number of small businesses like legal aid, a free clinic, and a blood donor centre. I spent an hour and ten minutes guessing which service each person entering would use. After ten minutes of inactivity on the building steps, I saw a woman in a fitted business suit make her way up the stairs. Each step bounced her large shiny purse off the back of her skirt. I imagined her at first to be a lawyer or doctor, but her bag was just a bit too shiny to be high-class. I pegged her for a working girl stopping into the clinic. Most of the working girls I knew tried to pinch every penny. No one wanted to work under men forever, and hookers needed condoms like offices needed paper clips. The sound of the door opening brought me back to reality. I swivelled in the chair, hand in my lap, to face the door.

"Morning, Julian. What's new?" Julian hated me and I knew it. I asked him questions because I knew it drove him nuts. He never had to answer questions to anyone but his boss, and I was certainly not him.

My pleasant, offensive good-morning was answered with a grunt as Julian moved toward the table. My hand instinctively tightened on the gun just as someone's hands would tighten on the wheel of a car if a bear walked toward the driver's side window. He was six foot four and at least three hundred pounds, but he didn't stomp; he glided to the desk and sat down. Julian was solid like a tree was solid, but he had some flab on his stomach and face. He wore grey cotton slacks and an untucked blue linen shirt. On the street people might think he was trying to be fashionable, but if you looked closely you would see that the shirt concealed an angular bulge at the base of his spine. The bulge was not a wallet; it was a gun, and judging by the size of the bulge, which I had seen on many occasions, it was big. The two of us enjoyed a friendly relationship; he showed up every once in a while and always left within five minutes. When he spoke he was pleasant, but under the pleasantries hid a killer. I had seen the real Julian once before, up close, and he had come out the winner. Julian had humble beginnings as a childhood friend and protector of Paolo Donati. He spent years looking out for the man who would one day be king of the streets. Julian was with Paolo for every step of his ascent. He went from being a leg breaker to working as the right hand of the most powerful mob boss in generations. He was the only person I saw when I worked for Paolo.

As Julian's ice-grey eyes stared into mine they momentarily lost their congeniality, but it returned as quickly as it had vanished. He was a pro, but there were some feelings he couldn't keep completely bottled up. His hatred slipped out like steam from a pipe ready to burst. He hated me and what I did, and he could never let that go. I stood, leaving the gun in the chair, and walked to the safe. I opened it and took the bag to the door. Julian rose without any indication of discomfort, placed a stack of bills on my desk, and moved to the door.

"What is it? In the bag, I mean. Did you look inside?" Julian always seemed unsure if anyone caught his meaning so he worked hard to make himself as clear as possible; he repeated himself over and over in different words, all meaning the same thing. It was an annoying habit, but I was sure no one told him that. I was also sure there would be a time when he wouldn't try to clarify his thoughts to me. When that happened, there would be trouble.

I opened the door, and he took the bag and walked out. He always asked the same question in some form or another. I never responded; I just held the door and let him walk. Julian knew I was a professional and that I hadn't looked in the bag. His question was a reminder that he beat me once, and that to him I was just an amateur. He used more syllables to say "fuck you" than anyone I knew.

After he was gone, I sat and watched the street again. I didn't see Julian leave — I never expected to — but I watched all the same. I thumbed through the money Julian had left on the desk; I didn't count it because I knew it would all be there. After a time I felt hungry.

I walked out the front door of the building, my own angular bulge in the back of my shirt. I walked down the street from the office, passing different windows that advertised sandwiches with more meat and less fat, some grilled, others toasted. I breezed past the advertisements until I came to a Vietnamese restaurant I frequented. The place was not a chain, and by no means a dive. The restaurant catered to Vietnamese people. Everyone who worked there and most of the people who dined there were from Vietnam. The menus were in Vietnamese with numbers and pictures for any interlopers who chose to stop in. The dining room smelled of spices and was heavy with steam from the kitchen. I took a seat in a corner of the dining room in a place where I could watch the street and the action inside. The lunch crowd was eating like it was Thanksgiving at the soup kitchen and no one looked my way—until a man stopped at the window.

He didn't slow and then stop; he stopped at the window, and put his face up to the glass. When his eyes found me, he was startled to see me looking back at him. He regained his composure, looked around for another ten seconds, then left in a hurry. I was surprised. It seemed the amateur from the airport had amateur friends who had identified and followed me. I ordered a number fifty-eight—the chicken soup, which was so much better than it sounded, and rice. I drank the cold tap water left for me out of a small glass half full of ice and contemplated how I had been followed to the office. No one had tailed me from the airport, so they had to know who I was. My thoughts were interrupted by the arrival of two steaming plates. The soup was a dark broth, and in the centre was a piece of chicken still on the bone. The rice was light brown and smelled heavily of green onions. I stared at the food and had more of my water. I knew that the food was far too hot and that I had to wait at least five minutes before I could even try to eat it.

After I paid the bill, I left the restaurant and walked three blocks up the street to the gym. The whole way there I used store windows to look around me, and made several trips across the street to see if anyone followed, but no one did. There were no scruffy kids in tan trench coats reading newspapers under lampposts or lurking in alleys.

The gym was like a time warp back twenty or thirty years. There were no treadmills or flashy machines; there was only iron, tons of it. No one manned the front desk, and there were no trainers in neon outfits spotting out-of-shape housewives and businessmen. The place was old-school and hard-core. Just inside the front door was a sign: "Train or leave." It wasn't the club motto, it was a command. If you weren't there to work, you weren't there at all.

I had a permanent locker at the gym, stocked with several pairs of pants, shorts, shirts, as well as a shaving kit, and a knife. I kept several places stocked like this because I rarely went to the house I had spent my adolescence in, even though it was all mine and I was the only one living there. I showered at the gym and lived out of the office as much as possible.

I changed into old unwashed sweats, locked all my things in my locker, and made my way to the brightly lit workout floor. The room was well lit because it was a windowless box hidden deep in the concrete. It had a musty smell, like old shoes, which had developed over the past decade. There were only a handful of people there, not one of them talking over the loud thundering music. No one acknowledged my presence; they just kept on lifting. The majority of the people in the gym weren't large by bodybuilding standards. The men here didn't lift to look good — they lifted for strength. These men were like ants. They easily moved twice their body weight with just arms and legs. I found a spot and got ready to dead lift. I spent half an hour moving weight off the floor to my waist and back down again. Once I finished, I moved the bar and weights around and devoted my time to the clean and jerk. The gym was full of cops, firemen, and people like me. All of us worked here to be better. There was an unspoken truce in the gym. Everyone knew what everybody else was outside the doors, but inside the walls of the gym it didn't matter. It wasn't uncommon for cops to spot career low-lifes while they pushed hundreds of pounds above their necks. Letting the weight fall would have saved blood, sweat, and countless hours of manpower, but no weights ever crushed anyone's throat. The gym was time off the battlefield. Time off that everyone was grateful for.

It had been more than a decade since I was first shoved in the door by my uncle. He dragged me to the gym and told me if I wanted to work in the adult world with him I had to be able to pull my own weight. No one would work on a job with a kid in his late teens who looked like a target for any bully wanting to kick sand in his face. Since that day, I had never stopped coming. I trained every day; it was that or go home to the empty house I hated so much.

After the workout I showered, staying long under the spray, letting the heat wash away the stiffness. Once I was back in my street clothes, I sat on the bench and began to consider my situation. I did a job and was paid. The only hang-up was that the owners of the bag had found me; that face in the restaurant window could only be a tail. I had a few options: I could lay low; I could call my employer; or I could handle it myself. I wasn't going to run, and I was pretty sure my employer wouldn't give a shit, so I decided to handle it. That brought on another set of questions — how to do just that? Do I nab one of the amateur trackers or do I wait for their move? The narrow bench began to dig into my ass, so I made a decision. I would go about my business and wait to be followed again.

CHAPTER THREE

When I left the gym, I navigated the streets in the same way that I had after leaving the restaurant. I crossed the street several times and used the bright storefront windows to see what was behind me. I moved through the city entering different stores and shops so that I could look out and see if any faces looked familiar. After two hours the exercise seemed futile — I couldn't find a tail, and the sun was lowering into the west. I needed to rest, but I didn't want to go back to the office — it would be an obvious place to pick me up again. I decided to leave the car there, and took a cab to Jackson Square, a downtown mall that shared its lower level with a farmers' market. I moved out of the cab and paid quickly, using a ten for a four-dollar fare. I moved into the market and let the crowds wash over me. I followed their pull and moved with the throngs of people looking for fresh food to bring home at a price better than the supermarkets. At six in the evening, the market was perfect: there were dozens of exits and hundreds of people. It was a nightmare for tailing someone. I randomly made my way through the market until I saw a bus pull up at a stop just outside one of the exits. I walked casually out the door and on to the bus just before its doors closed.

The bus lurched ahead and the damp musk of the people hit my senses like a sucker punch. My nose was flooded with the different smells of people and the wares they had bought at the market. I found a lone seat and sat reading a bus pamphlet and planning my way home.

Home was a place I rarely used. It was mine in name, and had been my home for more than a dozen years. My parents had never lived there, and I had shared it with my uncle for only a handful of years.

When I was a child, three or four times a year my parents would tell me they had to work, and it was best I stay with family. I never knew at the time what my parents did. I never thought about why they only "worked" a few weeks out of the year. I learned about it all after the day they went to work and never came back.

During the "work" years my uncle watched over me at his house without comment or complaint. He wasn't an unpleasant or mean man; he was just quiet. He sent me to school, made my meals, and made sure I did my homework. He also left a book for me to read, every day, on the shelf beside the door. It was my job to come home, do my homework, and then read until my uncle arrived home to make dinner. The dinner conversations about books were the only way we developed a relationship. As we ate dinner, I told him about what I had read, and he asked me questions. He taught me the first lessons in my first real education. I learned to see beneath the surface — to look at what was going on under the current.

After a three-week stay in the fall, my uncle left me alone for a weekend. He said he had some work of his own to do and that he would be back soon. When he came back two days later, he had most of my things with him. I knew exactly what had happened when I saw him come through the door with two arms full of what I owned. My uncle told me there had been an accident, and that my parents had died on the way home to see me. It was here that the education given to me by my uncle first paid dividends. I looked through what my uncle told me; I saw all that was said in 3D. I asked questions, many questions, and all of them were the right kind: Where was the accident? Where is the funeral? How do we bring the bodies home? It was a moment I would never forget. My uncle stared at me for what felt like hours, and then the side of his mouth turned up in a cold grin. The grin scared me because of all it said, and how unable I was to decipher it. All of the questions and probing I learned from my uncle at the dinner table fell apart when I was faced with an unspeaking grin that told me I didn't know enough.

My uncle sat me down and told me for the first time what my parents did for work. "They took things that didn't belong to them," he said.

"They were bad? Like bad guys?" I asked, and immediately I hated myself for betraying my immaturity by thinking of things in terms of cops and robbers.

"They weren't bad people, but they did take things. They never hurt anyone. They only took from people with a lot of money and a lot of insurance. Do you know what insurance is?"

"Yeah."

"So nobody ever got hurt."

It was my turn. My mouth turned up at the corner just like his. I mirrored the grin until he got it. "Yeah," he said softly, looking at me. "Two people got hurt."

Weeks later, I got up the courage to ask my uncle the question that had been on my mind since the day he returned laden with all of my worldly possessions. "Uncle Rick, are you like my mom and dad?" I asked quietly across the dinner table. My mouth was dry with the paste of overcooked potatoes.

"No," was the only answer I got back at first. There was a long silence, and then the sound of chewing and swallowing. My uncle looked at me after he drank some of his milk. "Your mom and dad tried to be nice. They didn't want to hurt people, so they robbed businesses that had money and insurance. They had good hearts."

"But you steal things too, right? You're like them."

Anger flashed across my uncle's face for a second. "Damn it, Will! Don't you listen to me? They were good people. People can do the same thing, live in the same city, come from the same family. It don't make them the same."

My uncle went back to eating, and for a time I did too. I had made him angry. It wasn't talking about my parents that did it; it was asking about what he did. I ate more dry potatoes and decided to risk another question. "What do you do?"

There was no anger this time. "Kid, what I do is worlds apart from your mom and dad. I work all over, with different people, and I don't always do the same type of jobs. Now finish your dinner."

We didn't speak about the subject again for two years. I went to school and my uncle worked long, sporadic hours. Finally, years after I had moved in permanently, I spoke up again at the dinner table. As my uncle chewed a piece of leftover pork chop, I looked him in the eye and said, "I want to work."

My uncle didn't bat an eye at me or wait to swallow. "I know the guy who runs the Mac's Milk down the road. Maybe I get can get you a job as a stock boy."

"I want to do what my parents did. What you do," I said.

My uncle put down his knife and fork and looked me in the eye. "What the fuck, boy, you think it's the family business? Your parents weren't Robin Hood and Maid goddamn Marian. They were criminals. They did bad things, and it got them killed." He breathed deep in and out of his nose, and both of his hands gripped the table, his knuckles white. After a few moments he relaxed, took a drink of milk out of his glass, and spoke. "Your parents didn't want this life for you, kid. That's why they went after big scores with big risks. They wanted to raise you right. They wanted you to live in a house, have friends, and go to school. They wanted to be the Cleavers and you were supposed to be the Beav. But all that risk caught up with them. No one can do that work forever; it just doesn't have longevity. No, that life isn't for you. You need to be what they wanted you to be — a normal kid."

"I need to know," was all I could get out at first, in a weak voice. "I need to know them."

My uncle looked at me, and his face softened almost

imperceptibly. "Kid, they were your parents —"

"No," I interrupted, my voice gaining strength. "I didn't know them. I didn't know what they did, or why they did it. They never let me in on that, and now they never can. They raised me and loved me but they were never real. I need to know them. I need to know what they did. I want to work."

My uncle stared at me for a good long time, and just like countless times before, the corner of his mouth raised into a cold grin. The grin made me unsure of myself and what I wanted, but I held strong. I stared at the grin and said nothing; I fought every urge I had to turn away until he spoke.

"I can't turn you into them or what they were. They got killed for being themselves and doing what they did. The best I can do, kid, is show you what I do. You'll see the world they lived in, but you'll survive because you'll follow my rules. That's the best I can do."

"Okay," I said. I fought my lips but they moved on their own. I grinned at my uncle for about two seconds until his palm crashed into my cheek.

I was on the floor when the burning in my cheek was joined by a ringing in my ears. I looked up, and my uncle stood over me. "Smiling and laughing gets left in the schoolyard. You just left that all behind when you asked for a job. You're not going to like it and you're probably going to hate me for it, but I'll teach you. You're in for a rough patch, kid. Now get up."

I stayed on the ground for a second and stared at the figure above me. Then I got up, watching his shoes, then shins, belt, shirt, and finally his face. I let the grin I had seen so many times before form on my face. I knew it looked like his; I had practised it enough to know. My cold grin was not startling to my uncle; if anything it startled me when it was returned in kind. I was startled for about two seconds by my uncle's response — then his fist came into view, and the lights went out.

CHAPTER FOUR

After several transfers, I was a few blocks from the house. I walked towards it, conscious of the sounds created by the city and the night. In the glow of the streetlights I saw eyes watching me inches from the ground, but I saw no human eyes tracking my movements. I walked through the open gate in front of the house. Junk mail had been crammed into the mailbox by several companies that already thought I could be a winner. I unlocked the door, fighting the stiffness of the old mechanism. Its age made it turn with a groan, and I hoped, as usual, that the key would not break off. Inside the air was stale. The house had no real smell to speak of, probably because the house had no tenants to speak of.

I raided the kitchen looking for unspoiled food and found very little to choose from. I found crackers and an old jar of peanut butter that had given up its oil to the surface. I stirred the peanut butter with a knife and ate it with the crackers while I cleaned my Glock. When I finished with the Glock, I pulled my spare piece, a SIG Sauer 9 mm, from a compartment under the floorboards, and cleaned that as well. The amateurs I had met hadn't seemed like the fighting type, but then again they didn't seem like the type that would be able to find me, either. I decided I wouldn't let them surprise me again.

The next morning I used two buses and a cab to get me back to the office by nine. The Glock was in a holster at the small of my back; I placed the sig in a holster taped to the underside of the desktop. I made a cup of tea and rolled my chair to the window to read the paper. Between stories, I glanced at the street below, looking for things that stood out. After I had read a story about local rezoning, I looked down to see a car pull up in front of the building. Three men got out of the car; each was dressed in a trench coat and sunglasses. The car screeched away once the three were clear, its tires spinning until smoke poured out. The car disappeared around a corner amidst the screams of pedestrians and the horns of other motorists.

These guys were absolutely unbelievable. I pulled the gun from the holster at my back and racked a round into the chamber. I put the Glock, safety off, in my lap, and waited.

In two minutes, there was a knock at the office door. I didn't move. Thirty seconds passed, and I saw a face pressed to the frosted glass. Another knock. I put my hand on the gun in my lap and yelled, "Just a minute, I'm in the john."

Another ten seconds passed and then the door opened slowly. The first one through eyed my grin with amazement. He stood inside the doorway staring at me until I waved him in, saying, "Come on inside." He was regular height with black hair that stood up in the front. The hair was sloppy over the ears, and I imagined it had been some months since he had a haircut. His nose was pointed like a beak, and his face was unshaven. A belly created a bulge under the buttoned trench coat he wore. The other two men tried to enter together, the larger finally managing to squeeze through first. He was bigger than chubby, but not yet obese. He had close-cropped red hair with a goatee to match, and on his left hand skin cream had dried crusty white. The third guy was tall, well over six feet, rail-thin, with a ponytail tied loose. He had circular John Lennon style glasses on a small pointed nose, and an Adam's apple that protruded from his neck. I presumed that the one who entered first was the leader, because he was the one to speak first — unsurely, but first.

"Uh…" he said.

I cut him off. "There's no name on the door, and no office number, so I know you don't want anything honest. Just spit out what you really came here for."

The three men shared a look, and then it started. The two at the back pulled at their coats and began to produce guns. The whole process took several seconds because of the time the stubborn snaps on their coats took to open. I could have shot all three using either gun, but I let it play out. Two guns, big ones, were aimed at my face. On the right side of two guns, the talker lost all of his nervousness and began to question me.

"Where the fuck is the bag, you motherfucker? I'll kill your ass dead if you don't talk, fucker!"

Amateurs always thought hard-asses spoke like that. I

played along. "What bag?"

"You know exactly what bag. The one you took off Nicky at the airport."

"I'm sorry," I said calmly. "You must have me confused with someone else."

The leader fumbled under his coat, brought out a piece of paper, and slammed it onto the desk. I stared at it while the sweat from his palm dried off the surface of the glossy paper. It was a picture of me leaving the airport with the bag. The image was grainy, but it was me. The photo had several numbers in each corner, as though the shot came from a security camera. This was the first time I was impressed. They had a watcher, someone I didn't see, use the airport security cameras to get a shot of me coming from the bathroom.

"Well, it seems like I've been found, but you're late — the bag's gone."

"We know that, fucker! We want it back."

I filed the fact that they knew the bag was gone away in my brain, along with the name of the guy at the airport, which they had let slip. "Can't help you. The bag's been picked up," I said.

"By who?"

I knew something they didn't. It felt good to score a point against them after they had shown up knowing about me and the transfer of the bag. "You don't want to know. They wanted the bag. They got it. You candy-asses couldn't hang with them, so let it go. You lost the bag, but you're alive."

"Candy-asses, candy-asses, you fuck...fuck. I'll show you." The words sputtered out of his mouth as he twisted around to the fat one behind him. He wrestled the gun out of the fat man's hand and aimed it at my head from three feet away. His hands were shaking with rage, but at that range it didn't really matter; he could hit me no matter how much the barrel trembled. He held the gun with two hands and used both of his thumbs to pull back the hammer. I fought all the urges of fear and stared into his eyes. Time began to stretch; seconds felt like minutes, but everything snapped back when the skinny gunman with the Lennon glasses spoke up.

"Relax, Mike, we need this guy alive," he said.

Mike took a few seconds, and then pulled the gun away and gave it back to the heavier of the two men.

"We found you, you fuck. We know who you are. We want the bag back and if we don't get it, we'll get you," Mike said.

"I told you the deal is done. I'm a middleman, nothing more."

"You have a day. Let's go," Mike said, and the three of them turned their backs and left. Mike went first, followed by skinny, then fat. They took turns this time so no one got stuck. I sat there thinking about how they had turned their backs on me. I could have pulled out a gun from anywhere and shot them dead, but the amateurs didn't know that. One question rolled through my mind: how did these amateurs do such a pro job of finding me?

I sat in my chair and stared straight ahead. My whole lower body was damp with sweat. I spent twenty seconds like that, then I turned to the window. After a minute, I saw the three get into the black sedan they arrived in. As soon as they were in, the car peeled out from in front of the building. From the height and angle of my window, I only managed to make out an "H" on the far left of the plate, but I knew the vehicle: it was an Audi. The shape had been imperfectly copied by several American and Japanese automakers, but there was no mistaking the look of a real Audi sedan. I went to my desk and pulled a pad and pen from the second drawer on the left. I wrote down the information I had so far: the bagman named Nicky, descriptions of Mike and his two friends, the make of the car, and the "H" I saw on the licence plate. I tore the sheet from the pad, and stashed the information in a locked file cabinet with my paid bills.

I sat back in the chair and considered my options, which weren't many. The bag wasn't coming back willingly, so I could either try to find my new friends or wait for them to come to me again. I knew nothing about the bag or the people I took it from. I needed to know what I was up against before I made a move. In the end, I decided to make a call to the boss. Maybe he would give me an idea about who was on to me. I picked up the cell phone and dialled the same unlisted number I had called yesterday. It was the number for a restaurant, which it was, among other things. I waited, listening to the ringing tones. Promptly after the second chime, the phone was answered.

"Yeah?"

"I need an audience with the man," I said.

"I think you have the wrong number. This is a restaurant."

"Just tell him I delivered his bag and I just realized that

there's some other luggage that needs to be dealt with." I didn't wait for the guy on the other end to hang up first because I knew it was coming. The message would be automatically passed on and the right people would know what it meant. I figured I had some time before my question was answered, so I made a run to the deli at the corner. I picked up four large crusty rolls along with slices of pastrami, salami, corned beef, and turkey. I also got milk, a couple of deli pickles, and three pickled eggs. I took the food up to the office and set it in the small fridge I had in the corner. I pulled a book from a desk drawer and began to read with my feet on the windowsill.

I had finished two sandwiches and a pickle when I heard the steps. I dog-eared my page and gripped the SIG in the holster fastened under the desk. The room dimmed as a large shape blocked the light coming through the frosted glass of the door. I kept one hand on the gun and picked up an egg with the other hand as Julian walked into the room without knocking. He took a seat in the chair across from me and stared. I stared back at him and ate my egg.

"The job was done. You did what you were supposed to do. Everything was finished. Why the call?"

"This morning the bag owners were here looking for the bag," I said, in between small bites of the egg.

Julian stared. If he cared he didn't show it. "So? What's your point? How is this our problem?"

Julian's slow, repetitive style had a way of cutting through bullshit. "Point is, Julian, I need to know some things."

"So? What's your point? How is this our problem?" The

mastodon in front of me altered. His tone changed; he was no longer polite, no longer a pleasant associate. He was considering what would have to be done about me.

I popped the last of the egg into my mouth and chewed. After I swallowed, I took a sip of milk, never moving my eyes away from Julian's. "I want to know who the clients are, what they want back, and any other information I can get," I said.

Without a word Julian rose from his chair and left. I wasn't surprised he would go and consult with Paolo. Julian was important but he wasn't management. I made a third sandwich and cursed under my breath; I had forgotten to get cheese. About ten minutes passed before the same shadow loomed in the doorway. Julian came in without knocking, again, and sat in the chair he had just left. I held the sandwich with my left hand, keeping my right below the desk on the gun. I took a bite and returned the look Julian was giving me.

"Well?"

"The boss says he's disappointed. He's angry about what you've done. He's not happy. He says he used you because he didn't want any complications. I told him we should just cut off the contact point — you. You know, kill you. But the boss said to give you some time to handle the problem."

"How long?"

"Two days. Forty-eight hours."

"Two days. Fine. What can you tell me?"

"The owners of the bag were computer nerds. They were moving something the boss wanted."

Computer nerds. That explained the photo from an

airport surveillance camera. One of them must of hacked into the security feed. "Why use me? Why not you?"

"There had to be deniability. No one could know who was interested. It was supposed to be anonymous. But you fucked that up, eh, tough guy?"

I let his challenge go unanswered and continued to probe. "What was in the bag?"

"None of your business. You don't need to know. Next question."

"How did you find out about these computer nerds?"

"None of your business. You don't need to know. Next question."

"What else can you tell me, Julian?"

"Two things. The first is an address, twenty-two Hess. The second is I'll see you in two days." With that, the dinosaur was up and on his way to the door.

"Julian," I said. He turned to face me, his bulk erasing the door, and stared for a long minute. I put the last bite of sandwich in my mouth and raised my index finger and thumb. I felt a familiar grin pull at the side of my mouth and I dropped my thumb. It didn't scare him; he didn't even seem to notice. He stood in the doorway for ten long seconds, showing zero emotion; then he left. I went to the file cabinet and retrieved the notes I had taken earlier. "Computer nerd" and "22 Hess" were all I could add to the random details I had collected. I thought about the bag I had taken from Nicky. Paolo used me because he wanted to insulate himself. No one was to know about the contents of the bag or that he was interested in it. Since no one outside of Julian knew that I worked for Paolo, having me steal the bag was the best way to make it look like he wasn't involved. The contents of the bag had something to do with computers, which meant it was probably still around in some form or another. Software is worth something, but it's not like drugs or cash; it doesn't vanish, and it isn't consumed and can't be laundered. The information that was on whatever was in the bag must have been of interest to Paolo. But what kind of information could a bunch of amateurs have that would interest a man like Paolo Donati?

I leaned back in my chair and stared at nothing in particular. Whatever the contents of the bag, I had two days and few options. I could steal the package back from Paolo and spend my life looking over my shoulder, or I could get the amateurs off my back. It took only seconds to weigh it out: I had to visit 22 Hess and the boys who paid me a visit earlier.

It was still early in the day, only ten past one. I pulled a short-sleeved oxford-cloth shirt from the small office closet and put it on. The blue shirt had a faded pattern and it blended into a crowd well. I left the shirt untucked over my jeans and left the office. I got in the car, tossed the Glock into the glove box, gunned the engine hard, and drove fast away from the office, keeping a close eye on the mirror for a tail. As I made the different lefts and rights, I noticed a black Audi cut in front of me from a side street. It stayed with me until I made another turn, and a minute later it was ahead of me again. These assholes were unbelievable. They were doing a tail in front of me — which only works on long roads with few turnoffs — and they were using the same car they had driven to the office earlier. I pulled a pen from the glove box and wrote down the rest of the plate, H21 2T5, on my forearm. When I saw an opening, I made a U-turn from the far right lane to the far left. As I pushed the car through traffic, weaving tightly around other motorists, I heard the sounds of horns. I watched the Audi in the rear-view attempt a similar U-turn only to get blocked in the middle of the street.

I made my way alone to 22 Hess with little trouble after that. The neighbourhood housed pubs and restaurants, a dentist, a tattoo parlour, and other businesses. The road on this portion of Hess Street was brick instead of pavement, and each of the buildings was set back from the street; they all had ample front gardens or patios. The building I wanted was a two-storey walk-up that had no use for its patio, so the space had been converted into a small garden with a black iron fence and several benches for smoking employees. The building looked as if it had begun life as a house, but it had been recently modernized for a different type of clientele. The large window that faced the street had been re-paned with reflective glass that deflected the sunlight onto the garden.

I parked across the street and watched the building. For twenty-five minutes nothing stirred; no one went in or came out. The pedestrian traffic was light. Most of the crowds were probably going back to work after their lunch. The occasional person walked by my car but none of them were police or security. The length of time in which nothing happened made me think I would be able to meet with these boys without being disturbed. I pulled the Glock from the glove box and made sure it was loaded and ready.

I shifted in my seat and tucked the gun under my shirt into the holster at the small of my back. Once I was armed, I got out and fed the meter two quarters, earning me half an hour. I wasn't going to be long, but parking tickets lead to paper trails, and people can follow those trails. I opened the Volvo's trunk and pulled out a baseball cap, which I pulled low over my eyes while I waited for a break in the traffic. The second to last car before the light turned was a police car. I smiled at the cop in the passenger seat as he rolled by. He stared back uninterested. When the street was clear, I crossed and followed the path of the police car. The patrol car turned left at the next lights, and neither of the two men inside looked back at me. Seeing the police car didn't bother me. I had been on Hess Street for half an hour and it was the first sign of the law I had come across. I figured I had at least a half of an hour before the police would be back; that was twenty minutes more than I needed.

I doubled back up the street and walked through the garden with my hat still pulled low. When I opened the front door, I was greeted with the smell of recycled office air. Fifteen feet in front of me was a receptionist speaking into a headset. The woman seated behind the desk was plump, almost round. Her nose was pointed up in a slightly piggish way, and her round face was accentuated by a curly mass of short hair. She occupied her free hands with a bottle of red nail polish. I angled my head low so that the visor of the hat hid my features from any cameras above me. I couldn't be sure who knew me in the building, and I didn't want any new friends. I waited politely in front of the receptionist, looking at the counter, the floor, and the two hallways leading away from the reception desk. The hallway ahead had only one door I could see; its wood was polished and expensive. The hallway to my left contained several doors, each with plastic name plates beside them.

The receptionist finally told someone to hold on and greeted me cheerfully: "How may I help you today, sir?" It was said without any hint of sarcasm or feeling. It was an automatic response to a visitor.

I smiled pleasantly. "Hey, is Mike around?" I said, using the name the amateur let slip in my office.

She spoke again with congenial efficiency. "Just a moment, sir, let me check to see if he is available." She touched a button and spoke into the headset. "Mr. Naismith," she chirped, "you have a visitor who would like to see you." There was a pause and then the woman said, "No." She looked at me again, and I smiled before turning my head to look at the art hanging on the walls. I heard her say, "Not by me, sir," before ending the call with a "yes, sir."

She looked at me and said Mr. Naismith would be out momentarily to see me. I decided to chance it and asked the receptionist, "Is Mikey's office still around the corner there?"

The receptionist craned her neck, her eyes following my pointing finger down the left hall, and said, "Um, no. That is where our associates work. Mr. Naismith's office is the door in other hallway."

I thanked her and started down the hall. I heard a protest of, "Hey, you can't do that!" But I kept on walking. As I neared the door, I could hear a buzz and the sound of the receptionist calling from her desk to inform Mr. Naismith about my behaviour. I opened the expensive door without slowing down.

Mike was bent over his desk, his back to me, speaking into the intercom. It must have buzzed as he walked to the door, and he had reached over his desk to answer the call. He had just enough time to look over his shoulder and see me before I pulled his hand off the buzzer and punched him in the kidney. My arm was around his neck before he had a chance to slump to the floor.

I spoke into his ear calmly and clearly. "Tell the girl at the desk that everything is cool. Tell her we went to school together and I was trying to surprise you." When I said the last few words I squeezed his throat for emphasis. "Anything funny and you'll be dead before you hit the floor. The receptionist will be next, way before she gets from nine to one one on the phone."

I reached over and held down the speak button on the intercom. Mike laboured out, "It's okay, Martha, my friend just wanted to surprise me...I...I haven't seen this guy since high school. Please just hold my calls." There was a small grunt of pain in between breaths, but he got out what I wanted him to say.

"Yes, sir, Mr. Naismith." The receptionist sounded like she wasn't convinced, but she was in no position to question. She clicked off the line and went back to work.

I kept the choke on and squeezed until the man I now knew as Mike Naismith brought his hands up to pull on my arm. I seized the opportunity and let the choke go in favour of a wrist hold. I pinned him to the desk with his head beside a paperweight and his arm ninety degrees in the air.

"Now," I said, "it's time we had a talk without guns being pointed at people."

"How did you find me?" All the bravado and tough language from before had left when I hit him.

"Do you think it was that hard? You're an amateur and I'm a pro. Finding you is a slow morning. I want to know how you found me."

There was a long pause before Mike grunted. "We followed you."

I twisted his arm, feeling bone scrape on bone. "All right, all right," he said. "The bag had a GPS. We tracked it."

There was a new world dawning while I slept. A GPS tracker let these amateurs follow me home, and I didn't do a thing about it. I should have got rid of the bag right away, but I was told to deliver it. I assumed the bag was clean because, before now, every bag I delivered had been clean. I hated myself for five seconds, then I got back to work.

"Now, what did I take from you?" I figured identifying the package would give me some info on how bad the situation was. I had to find out how far these guys would go to get the bag back, and what it would take to persuade them to give up. Everything depended on the bag. Mike gave me no response, so I pushed the arm to ninety-five degrees and asked again. "What did I take?" I felt the last few degrees produce another grinding sensation deep in Mike's shoulder. His arm was so far back he was unable to offer any fight against the hold. Any more pressure from me and his shoulder would start splintering apart like old wood under too much tension.

"It was disks, that's all — disks. Goddamn it! You're breaking my arm!"

"What was on the disks? And who were they going to?"

I heard Mike breathe heavily in and out, and I listened to him groan. He was trying to raise his chest off the desk to relieve the pressure on his shoulder, but the position he was in gave him no leverage or muscle power.

"Answer me before I make you, Mike. Either way I win. If we do this fast you might even get out of a trip to emergency."

"It was the files we took; all of them. We don't have anything else."

Mike was starting to scream, and I was starting to realize that he had no idea who I was working for. I spun him around using the arm as a lever and laid my fist right into his stomach. Under his wrinkled untucked dress shirt was a soft belly, the kind you get from sitting a lot and eating at your desk every day. He wheezed like a balloon deflating, then slumped into a fetal position.

"I could do without the yelling. From this point on," I told him, "I want you to act like I'm new to all of this. Explain it to me step by step, or this will take a lot longer than you could ever want it to."

Mike lay like a fish pulled into a canoe; he gasped and struggled and before long he started to sob. I waited five seconds and then pulled him up to his seat by his greasy wax-styled hair. I showed a deliberate wind-up, and Mike gasped. I stopped the punch halfway to his face and asked again, "Will you tell me everything?"

"Yuh, yuh...yes." He sobbed. Snot ran down his face.

"What was it I stole?"

It took several seconds for the question to register. I had

to wait several more while Mike wondered how I couldn't know what I took. I decided to make things easy on us both. "I'm only pick-up and delivery, like FedEx. I don't know contents. I usually don't ask questions, but now that there are complications I want to know everything, and you are the only source of information I have."

Mike's breath came back during my little speech. His voice was less shaky, and the tears on his face had absorbed into his collar. "It was accounting records, all right?"

"Were they yours?"

"No. They belonged to someone else. We were selling them back."

I exhaled loudly and turned to the door. The turn masked my arm moving, and when I turned back I used my hips to power a left hook into the side of Mike's neck. My fist hit the meat of his neck — right in between where his stubble stopped and the hair on the back of his neck began. I didn't hit him too hard, just enough to shock and scare. The impact, and fright, drove him out of his chair.

As he sputtered on the floor, I crouched down beside him and said, "Listen, Mike, I don't have all day and I don't want you to keep holding out on me until I ask just the right questions. Tell me everything, and I mean everything."

Mike got out a, "You asshole," between sobs.

I put him back into his chair and asked once again, "Last time. Tell me everything about the disks."

He gulped in air. Then he began spitting out information almost faster than I could listen. "We repair computers here. One day an accountant, at least we think he's an accountant, came in with his laptop. He was totally freaking out.

I mean really losing it. He said he had lost some files and he needed them back pronto. He said he would pay anything — it just had to be done immediately. We took his laptop and gave it a full diagnostic check. Its hard drive still had copies stored from before the system crash. While we were restoring the files, we took a peek to see what was so important. It was all accounting files, with client names, company names, and bank account numbers. Some of the banks were offshore banks. Jimmy, one of the boys on staff, he was able to understand the information. He was an accountant before he came here. He saw…mistakes; he realized a lot of the information wasn't kosher. It took us a whole day to figure out what was hiding in the files. Once we had the scam figured, we made encrypted copies of the files, erased the originals, and then called the accountant to set up a trade. Heh, he said he'd give anything, right? We gave him a number, and he said he needed three days to pony up the dough. We said okay, and three days later we set up an exchange."

"At the airport. That was what I took off Nicky." I was beginning to see where this was going.

Mike seemed genuinely surprised that I knew Nicky's name; he must have not realized that he let it slip when we first met. The only part I couldn't figure out was how Paolo Donati fit in, and more important, why did he care about blackmailing an accountant?

"What's Nicky's last name?" I asked.

"Why?"

I pulled back my fist, and Mike barked a quick answer. "Didiodato," he said.

"Whose idea was it for him to be the bagman?"

"Bagman?"

"The guy who took the disks to the airport."

"Oh. He volunteered. No one here has ever done anything like this before, so no one argued with him."

I wondered why a kid who worked with computers all day would want to be the face of a blackmailing scam. Why would anyone volunteer to put themselves out there like that? I didn't allow myself to focus on any theories for too long; I had been in the office almost ten minutes. "Who did the accounting files belong to?" I asked.

Mike didn't answer. He shook his head twice, gritting his teeth, showing the first sign of backbone, or of a fear of something worse than me. I hit him in the stomach, and sound echoed off the walls. The sound wasn't my fist. The loud crack was something else, and it turned both our eyes to the door. Then the screaming started.

CHAPTER FIVE

Over the screaming, automatic gunfire erupted in the halls. Less than a second later, the heavy office door burst inward. The door was replaced by a more solid figure. I turned my hips to hide some of the movement of my arm — which was already reaching behind my back. But as I moved, the giant in the doorway raised a gloved hand. In his fist was a huge gun. He said only one heavily accented word. "Don't."

I didn't know why he hadn't shot me, but I didn't waste time on it. I locked eyes with the giant and waited. If he minded me eyeing him, he didn't show it. His gun was pointed at me, but every now and then he glanced to look at Mike — who was pretty messy from our conversation. He never asked Mike if he was okay, so I ruled out the giant being Mike's backup. The giant's glances were brief and allowed me no chance to move.

I stared at the giant and took in every detail. He was over six and a half feet tall, with short blond hair shaved close to his head. He had the shoulders of a man who swung a hammer all day. His face was young but worn, with the wrinkles and creases that come from being in the elements for extended periods. He was wearing a black nylon wind suit that he had zipped all the way up so that only a portion of the collared shirt he wore underneath peeked out. I stared at the outfit, intrigued by the contrast of a formal shirt with such a casual jacket. It was then that I noticed the gloves and shoes. The gloves were black latex. The shoes were zipped inside rubber covers — the kind used to protect leather shoes from the snow. The outfit told me all I needed to know. Something bad was happening here. The kind of thing that can't leave evidence, and I was in the middle of it.

I ignored all of my instincts. I would not let my brain entertain all of the questions forming in my synapses. I dismissed the thoughts about who the giant was, what was going on in the hallway, and whether or not I would soon be dead. I thought only of drawing my gun. I replayed the thought over and over, imagining the smooth draw I would have to make in a split second. My concentration lapsed when gunfire popped in the hall again. There was screaming, more gunfire, and finally silence. The smell of cordite snuck into the room over the shoulders of the giant. He hadn't flinched at the sound of gunfire, and his head didn't turn away in curiosity.

Fuck, I thought. *Why doesn't he look?*

I heard a thumping getting louder and realized that it was the sound of running — in heels. A blur passed the door, visible only in the slivers of hallway that showed from behind the giant. He gave no sign of realizing that someone had passed. He kept his head still and his gun level at my chest. I heard a voice shout, "Ivan!" The giant didn't move at first. The name was called again — with a much louder voice. At once, the giant sprang to life like a carousel being turned on. He turned at the hip, moving the cannon away from my torso, and fired once down the hallway. His hips turned back, but his gun was already on its way to the floor as the echo of my Glock bounced off the walls. My gunshot had mingled with his, making it inaudible outside the room.

The bullet entered his right shoulder at a point where there was minimal muscle mass. I was lucky with the shot because a few inches either way would have hit the dense muscle of a deltoid or a pectoral, and would not have done the job. Ivan acknowledged the pain with one small grunt and then he immediately began to bend for his gun, which had pitched forward into the room.

"Easy, big man, or the next one is in the head," I said.

The blood trailed down the nylon windbreaker, gaining momentum because it wasn't absorbed, and dripped onto the floor beside his covered shoes. He was still, bent slightly at the waist, staring at the gun on the floor.

"Leave the gun on the floor, step slowly into the room, and sit in the green chair, Ivan," I said calmly.

Ivan did as he was told, as though the idea was a direct command he could not disobey. He sat in the client chair in front of the bookcase; the chair angled toward Mike's desk and away from the doorway.

"Mike, take a seat behind your desk," I said.

"What the hell is going on out there? I can't stay here. I gotta go now. I gotta go. I gotta —" I smacked him hard with my left hand, and he staggered to his desk without any further complaint. I moved to the side of the desk, putting my back to the wall. It looked like I was watching a face-to-face meeting take place between Ivan and Mike. Mike's tears and Ivan's clenched jaw made the meeting appear extremely tense.

"Talk and you're dead, partner," I said to Ivan. If he heard me, he didn't let it show. Shock was probably setting in, or the monster was alive behind those eyes waiting, visualizing, just as I was. Mike looked back and forth nervously. Sweat had wet the waxed hair on the top of his head and it was starting to wilt. The shooting down the hall had him shocked and scared. His eyes looked at me as his head swivelled from the door back to Ivan. His mouth was open slightly as though his tongue was too big to fit into a closed mouth.

"Shut up, Mike," I said. "If you make this harder than it has to be, I'll put you down too." He sensed how serious I was, and his open mouth closed.

With Mike silent, I ran through ways to get out of 22 Hess. Mike's office had no windows to jump out of, and running down the hall had a lousy track record. I had to wait for an opportunity and take it when it came.

I picked up Ivan's gun from the floor and admired the size and weight of it; the Colt Python is only a bit smaller than a cannon. The gun was missing only the one round it took to kill the woman who ran for her life down the hall. I held the Colt down at the side of my leg with my left hand, out of fear that it would pull my pants down if I put it under my belt. I listened as the clock above the door clicked second by second one hundred eighty times. From the halls, I heard doors opening and closing, mumbled voices, and the occasional laugh. I knew the safety of the room would vanish when the voices down the hall called for Ivan again. There were no opportunities coming. I had to move.

"Both of you, get up and move to the door. Step into the hall facing right."

Ivan mechanically stood and moved toward the door, one arm immobile as he walked. Mike shuddered and stayed put in his chair.

"Get up, Mike, or I leave you here."

My words broke through whatever mental fog Mike was in, and he got up. He moved in Ivan's direction, but kept his distance from the big man as though he was afraid that the limp, wounded arm would come to life and strangle him. I moved around the desk until I was behind the two. I got close and pressed a muzzle into each man's neck while I spoke.

"Mike, is there an exit at the left end of the hall?"

"Yuh, yuh, yeah. It's around the corner at the end."

"How many steps?" I asked.

"What?"

"If you walked it, how many steps would it take?"

"I dunno, twenty-five or thirty."

"Okay, boys, we're going to back up twenty-five or thirty steps to the exit. Once we're there, Mike and I are out of here."

The giant moved as though he were a robot following a direct command. Mike moved beside him, dragged along by the giant's gravity. Mike suddenly realized how close he was to the Russian and tried to move back, but he changed his mind when he felt the muzzle of the Python in my hand separate two of his vertebrae. I moved backward, a step behind both men, down the empty hall to the exit. Ivan must have been sent alone to cover this hallway, which meant he was as real as he looked. As we moved, I whispered over Ivan's bad shoulder: "A bullet will drop you as easy as the girl. Remember that, big guy."

There was no response from Ivan — no twitch. He was waiting just like I had been, but I wasn't going to give him any opportunity to move. Using a low voice, I counted the steps back for each man. No one at the other end of the hall made any noise, and no one yelled down to Ivan. After fifteen paces, my heel touched the receptionist with the freshly painted nails. She wasn't breathing. The Colt had put a hole through the centre of her back. The exit wound left the white walls tinged with pink.

"Step lightly over the girl and don't look down. Mike, I mean it."

Both men took a large step backwards over the body. Ivan looked straight ahead; Mike stole a glance at the body. "Oh, God, Martha!" he screamed.

The sound of Mike's voice bounced off the walls with a boom like bowling pins falling down. A loud, "What the fuck was that?" came from the end of the hall seventeen paces in front of me. The voice was gravelly, and it sounded Russian — the *w* in "what" sounded like a *v*.

"Steady, boys," I said, before counting steps eighteen and nineteen.

"Ivan!" a voice called. It sounded like "Eevan" from

twenty paces away. I couldn't see who was speaking from the other end of the hall; I could only make out bits of images through the spaces between the two men.

"Keep moving. Don't stop." I shoved the guns hard into the two men as I said the word *stop*. We moved to the end of the hall as the voice repeated Ivan's name. After calling a second time, the voice clued in to what was happening and shouted something in a harsh language. We ignored the foreign command and kept walking.

"Stop!" The voice coming down the hall was loud and sounded like it was used to being obeyed. Out of instinct, all of us almost stopped. Ivan and I ignored the urge to comply and kept moving backwards. Mike, unable to disobey the voice at the end of the hall, stopped walking. He was falling before I heard the shot. It was low in the gut and it bent him over. Mike landed on his ass with a thump. His hands didn't break his fall because they were holding his stomach. I had five steps left. I raised both arms, pressed both guns into Ivan's back, and kept moving. I stopped counting out loud at twenty-seven, and after a silent twenty-eight and twenty-nine, Ivan made his move. He pancaked his huge body onto the floor, using his one good arm to break his fall. I dove left before a bullet could tear me in two at twenty-nine paces.

I hit the floor with my shoulder and rolled to my feet five paces from a grey metal door with a glowing exit sign on top. I pushed through the door and found myself in an alley. To my left were three metal stairs leading down to the pavement between 22 Hess and its neighbour. I leapt down the stairs and ran hard toward an overflowing Dumpster; I hooked around it, and kept running, invisible from the door I just exited. Once I was in the street, I crossed and entered another alley, which I followed to Queen Street. I went into the first coffee shop I saw and took a seat at the window. I waited for my breathing to slow before I got up to grab a newspaper and order a large tea. I flipped to the crossword and then scanned the room for a pen. I had to get up again to ask the girl behind the counter for something to write with.

"Do you have a pen I could use?"

"What for?" The girl's reply was cold, and she looked me dead in the eye as she said it. It was a challenge from a frumpy girl with hoops in her lip, nose, and eyebrow.

"I just wanted to do the crossword."

"That paper is for everyone, not just you."

I didn't think this meant no, because she didn't look away as though the conversation were over. "It's yesterday's paper," I said.

"It's still not yours."

"How much for the paper then?" I asked with a low, even tone. I didn't want any more attention than I had already gotten.

"We don't sell them."

She still didn't look away when she said this, making me still think we weren't done. "Did those hurt? The rings, I mean. In your face. Did they hurt?"

"No." Her voice was less sure; the conversation was getting away from her.

"Why three of them? Why not two? How do you decide what to pierce?"

"Why, you got a fetish?" Her tone was a bit more defiant.

She thought she had scored a point in her little game.

"I just want to know why you need to make something out of nothing. Why do you need to pierce a lip, or an eyebrow? Why do you make nothing into a whole production? What I'm trying to say is, why do you want to hassle me for nothing? Or did I just answer my question? You can't leave things alone — not even your chubby lower lip."

She threw a pen at me, meaning to hit me in the face. I moved my head, and she hit a woman behind me who was drinking a latte. I picked up the pen as she said, "Ma'am, I'm so sorry. I didn't mean to..." I heard someone call for a manager as I took my seat and started writing. The crossword would explain my presence in the coffee house for an hour or two. I had no interest in the puzzle; I instead used it to chart out what I knew and what I didn't. I filled in the boxes of the puzzle with everything I had found out at 22 Hess. I worked fast, filling in names, places, and information I had learned. I noted everything Mike had told me about their piracy, and what I knew about the team that had shown up to clean the entire building. To the passerby I was not a person who was almost killed less than half an hour ago. I was a person who was very interested in his crossword puzzle. Over the two hours I stayed in the Second Cup, I recorded all of the information I knew, and the questions I had. I also learned the local bus route. My uncle hated writing anything down; he said it was the start of something concrete. Something a person could follow back to you. Most in my profession would have agreed with my uncle, but ever since I had lived with my uncle I did it. He taught me to dissect books before I learned to dissect people, and those early lessons were hard-wired into my brain. Seeing things on paper started my mind turning. I could swim through the information, picking out important details like a pike among minnows feeding on the biggest fish. It wasn't my uncle's way to use pen and paper, but it was something he could accept because his most important rule was to use whatever worked.

The names and accents I had heard at 22 Hess made me think I had crossed paths with the Russian mob. They had been a growing element in Southern Ontario for years, following Russian hockey players and circus troupes to Canada. The Russians were violent, but they were pros; they would make sure what happened to the computer geeks wouldn't attract the attention of the law for at least another few hours. I couldn't go back: they would have eyes posted there until the cops showed. Eventually the eyes outside would settle on my car, parked across the street from 22 Hess. The car didn't have my name on it, but the right people would track it to me eventually. I went to the coffee shop's pay phone and made a call to Sully's Tavern. The phone was answered on the second ring by a voice that was clear and without distortion.

"Hello?"

"It's Wilson."

"What is it?" The voice on the phone did not sound interested or concerned, but I knew better than to think Steve wasn't paying attention; he heard every word.

"I need you to do me a favour."

"What?" Mr. Personality was laying it on thick this afternoon.

"My car is over on Hess. I need it picked up."

"Is it hot yet?"

"No, but the cops will be checking it soon, so it needs to be moved fast."

"Where are you now?"

I told him, and listened to Steve chuckle. He seemed amused that I was stranded so close by.

CHAPTER SIX

Twenty minutes later, I was in Steve's car, a beat-up, decade-old Range Rover. The SUV was uncomfortable in the city, but ready to run forever. I was driving so Steve could do the quick pick-up. Never once did he ask why; he would do whatever I asked. I did Steve a favour once, and he'd been ready to help ever since. I always felt a pang of guilt asking him for help because I knew he'd always say yes. He would always help me for what I did, but I hadn't helped him for favours. I helped him because he had become like family in a time when I thought I would never have family again. I owed him as much as he owed me.

"Who's tending bar?"

"Sandra. With help from Ben," he said.

Since the day Sandra had been kidnapped, Steve always had Ben at the bar when he couldn't be, just to make sure things were kosher. Ben was way over six feet tall, and well over three hundred pounds. All of his size made him look like the son of a farmer, one who didn't own any machinery. It didn't help that he was one of the only men in the city who had overalls on regular rotation in his wardrobe. I had seen Ben take apart groups of people at once, but the real menace of the bar was Steve. He was no danger to the regular customers — just to those who were there to threaten his business or family, specifically Sandra.

At one time, I had been no more than a passing customer in the bar. I'd check into it once in a while for information and the like. One night I happened to brace a junkie a little hard, and Steve told me to let him go. I didn't listen because bartenders are usually full of hot air and Steve didn't look like much — he only weighed about one-seventy, and he could barely see through the hair that hung over his eyes. While I was holding the junkie to the wall with my forearm, I missed the sound of the thin bartender moving over the bar. Almost at once he was behind me, tripping me backward over his foot.

I bumped off the ground ready to fight. The junkie saw that Steve was between us and rushed out the door. Steve tilted his head forward, and with a hard jerk he sent his hair flying back. He used a rubber band from his wrist to tie the hair up into some kind of shabby samurai topknot. I threw a weak jab before he was done with his hair as a setup to something much worse; he surprised me, pulling my arm tight — hyperextending it. Steve twisted and pulled the arm in front of him and began pushing against it like he was at the turnstile to get on a roller coaster. I grabbed the brass rail on the bar and pulled against my arm, interrupting Steve's momentum. He stumbled into my field of vision, no longer able to put me to the floor. My elbow drove back over my shoulder and connected with his jaw, but it did nothing to loosen his grip. I hit him five more times in the jaw and side of the head until my twisted arm was free. The fight went on for three more minutes. Steve tried repeatedly to take me down while I tried to knock him out. I used fast hard punches and elbows out of fear of getting a limb broken in a painful joint lock.

After three minutes, we both were slow to get up and Sandra had just come back from the store. She walked up to the fight, unafraid, and pulled Steve away by the arm. At once, his eyes softened, and he followed her behind the bar. The junkie was long gone, and my left knee and right arm were severely stretched. I staggered to the bar and did the only thing I was able to do. I ordered a Coke.

We weren't friends after that, not by a long shot, but I did my best to respect the bar, and Steve did his best to turn an eye every now and then when I had to brace someone a little rough. Three years ago that all changed — not because of some touching Hallmark moment, but rather because of something much worse. We both got blood on our hands together. Blood has a way of making two people stick together like nothing else.

The neighbourhood where Sully's Tavern was located was rough. No one lived there because they wanted to — they just had nowhere else to go. Every violent offender, addict, and pedophile was like a magnet dragging others like them to the area. Sully's Tavern was the eye of the hurricane; it was the one peaceful spot in a mass of human depravity. The only real order in the neighbourhood came from Paolo's men. It was mob turf, and everybody was expected to pay into the local protection fund. The hoods in charge of the collecting left Steve alone for the first little while because his bar didn't turn a profit, and he didn't care who came in with who so long as they didn't start trouble. But when the bar started getting regular customers, the neighbourhood boys became more interested in Sully's Tavern. The first visit was on a Tuesday, then every other day after Steve refused to pay. The boys just didn't understand, being so low on the food chain and used to intimidating everyone, that Steve wasn't going to be scared into anything.

I heard rumblings of what was going on and I talked to Steve about it. "Those aren't punk kids, Steve, they work for a dangerous man. Just give them a piece of the pie and call it the price of doing business."

Quietly, under his hair, he said, "It's my business, my pie, no tastes. You want another Coke?"

I came in a week later, on a Monday, to find Steve ramming a man's head into the brass footrest of the bar. Another man was on the floor, his left arm and leg at unnatural angles. On the floor between the two men were baseball bats.

"What's going on?" I asked.

Steve paid no mind to my question as he finished with the hood. The gong sound of his skull hitting the hard metal was replaced by the sound of a skull falling into blood and teeth. The sound was like raw chicken falling off a counter onto the floor. Steve never once looked at me or said a word. His wiry body rippled under his thin white shirt as he grabbed each man by a foot. He didn't even flinch when one of the men began shrieking because Steve was pulling on the leg that was obviously damaged. Steve walked right past me, dragging the bodies into the street in front of the bar. As he walked back in he ran his fingers through his hair, removing the rubber band; his face once again becoming hidden.

"Time to put out new peanuts," was all he said to me.

I found out that night, through the grapevine, that the two men were collectors. After Steve's repeated refusals to pay, they had decided to step things up by coming into the bar with bats.

The next day, I went to the office and found Steve waiting outside the door dressed in khakis and a white T-shirt. The veins in his forearms pressed out hard like overfilled balloons, and his hair was up in the topknot.

"Where can I find your boss?" was all he said.

I could see that he was ready to go through me to find out so I said, "Tell me."

Steve said he went for napkins, and when he came back Sandra was gone. A phone call came a few minutes after he walked in; it told him that to get his wife back he had to pay up all the "rent" he had missed. The kidnappers gave Steve three hours to get together all the money. Steve was no idiot; he knew that after what he'd done there was no way Sandra was coming back. He might get pieces of her, but she wouldn't be back as he knew her.

"The good thing is the time," I said. "They want the money so they'll keep her alive until they know they've got it. How much time is left?"

"Two hours." Steve's gaze was out the window; his fists were tight, clenching imaginary ghosts.

We left the office together and took my car downtown to Barton Street East; I parked in a public parking space, and we moved on foot over the pavement. The concrete had been repaved with chewing gum and cigarettes, making the rough surface smooth with urban grime. As we rounded the corner of an alley to Barton, its stream of people flowing by unyielding, I stopped and spoke to Steve. "This building around the corner — the barbershop — is the gate; Mario is middle management for some heavy hitters on the east side. Everything on the street goes through Mario. You do this and you are on everyone's radar."

Steve looked at me for about one second, long enough for me to see pure fury, pure hate. He turned and walked into the crowd, vanishing amid the faces. I followed, trying to keep up, but Steve moved fast, his thin body gliding through the human traffic. He entered the barbershop without hesitation. As I followed in his wake, I eyed the barber pole spinning. I took a breath and thought about nothing, relaxing so I could commit to what I was about to become a part of. I was helping Steve, and back then I never once thought that I shouldn't — never once. I took one last look at the pole spinning white then red, and got ready for a lot more red.

When I opened the door the chime didn't turn any heads my way. Two barbers were unconscious on the floor. Beside the barbers lay a man in a finely tailored black suit. Six feet above his body was a fine spray of red on the white wall.

I moved through the room and into the next. The door to the office had been torn from one of the hinges; it hung on like a loose tooth. In the doorway, face down, arms cradling his head, lay another suit, dead. I could see the defensive wounds that had leaked onto the floor — Steve had come in slicing high. The pool of blood was growing; so were the screams inside the office. Steve wasn't talking; he was taking off Mario's ear with a barber's straight razor. He must have taken the razor off one of the barbers when he came in. Steve was using the razor like a conductor's wand, making the fat Italian man scream a bloody aria. His pockmarked face was made even uglier in its agonized distortion. The ear came off despite the pawing of stubby fingers. Steve slammed it on the desk and started on Mario's nose. When it was half off he looked at Mario and demanded, "Where is she?" The question had an exclamation point in the form of a haymaker.

When there was no response he moved the razor back to the nose, and the answers came like water from a faucet. "Tommy took her! He did it! Talarese did it, all right? Just stop!"

"I know him," I said.

Mario saw me, and his eyes widened. "You fuck. You yellow traitor shit. I'll spit on your grave."

"Did you know?" Steve's voice was like a window breaking; it got everyone's attention.

Mario's eyes focused on Steve's, and he spit out hate camouflaged in English. "What did you expect when you acted like an animal. Everyone pays, everyone. Some just pay more than others." His last words were framed by a small smirk.

Steve stepped back and bent so that he was eye level with

Mario. "Where does Tommy live?"

"Why?" Mario's smirk vanished, and he looked puzzled. I knew what he was thinking: no one would go looking for Tommy Talarese.

The nose came off with screaming and pleading, and then, once again, answers came. Tommy's mother, wife, and son lived in a red apartment building on King William Street. Tommy had made his home in the centre of the city, away from his bloody work on the east side. I knew the area. The building was one of several luxury complexes in the heart of downtown. The city tried to create upscale buildings, like Tommy's, that would offset the rapid decay of the city. Each building that went up pushed more people out. It was the city council's secret hope that they could move every undesirable citizen out of the city a block at a time — a transfusion of wealth to revitalize the decaying concrete. The lobby furniture in one of the complexes would be worth more than a year's rent in any of the older buildings in the area. The new buildings also had doormen working twenty-four hours a day to protect those with money from those without.

The sound of Steve's foot hitting the bloodied face followed the answers. The kick knocked Mario from the chair to the floor, and then the stomping started. The sound was like boots walking in thick mud. Steve stomped Mario long after he had died on the floor behind his desk. It would take the authorities some time to decipher what the mess on the floor was, and even longer to figure out who.

Back in the car, I didn't question what had happened — no one needed doubt. We moved through the streets fast and smooth. Neither of us spoke for the first few minutes. I was thinking about what Mario had told us. Tommy Talarese was as scary a human as I had ever met. He was a man who had gotten where he was through nights of blood. He revelled in cruelty as though it were a religion. Tommy had butchered entire families, raped children in front of their fathers, and tortured enough people to fill a cemetery. Tommy was a maniac of all trades, but he was especially fond of taking limbs. The east side was like a little Sierra Leone in the eyes of those who had come up against Tommy. He was out-of-his-mind crazy, and now he was interested in Steve.

"This Tommy Talarese," I said. "He's a big deal. He's Mario's boss, and a scary fuck in the truest sense of the words. He's sadistic and violent on a whole other level. He got where he is fighting with the Russians on the east side. He killed and killed like it was eating or breathing. There were battles in the streets years ago — the Russians tried to keep up with Tommy, and they almost did. Eventually some boundaries were organized, and the Russians got a piece of territory. Tommy was kept on the east side as a reminder of the way things used to be; the way they could be again. The problem is you. Why the hell is someone like him interested in you? Why is he pushing so hard to get rent from a bartender?"

Steve didn't say a word. His face and shirt were speckled with blood, and he held the razor from the barbershop open on his thigh as he stared out the windshield. His voice eventually broke the white noise of traffic. "However this goes, you can always walk away. You try to stop me and I'll kill you." His voice never faltered. He never thought about it, or weighed out what he was telling me. He was saying what he was going to do; how it made me feel, and the problems I had with it, weren't going to change anything.

King William Street was lined with cars, so I double-parked outside number sixty-six, Tommy's building. Steve was out of the car before it stopped moving. I caught up with him at the front doors.

"Give me your gun," he said.

I gave Steve the Glock. He looked at it and asked if there was a round already in the chamber. I nodded, and we walked through the doors. Steve moved ahead, the gun hanging loosely in his hand. The doorman stood behind a counter protecting the tenants' mailboxes. He took one look at Steve's bloody face and reached for the phone. Steve walked behind the counter and kicked the back of the door-man's knee. The doorman slumped to his knees, his red trench coat becoming a dress on the ground. Steve turned the pistol around in one quick flip and hit the doorman on top of his cap.

I checked the doorman's book and found Talerese next to the number 5006. It was the highest number on the page. Talerese was on the top floor.

We got on the elevator and rode up side by side. I scanned for cameras, but saw none. The upscale building management must have thought the doorman was enough security. The elevator stopped just as a chime announced our arrival. We moved out and followed the direction arrow to apartment 5006. When we got to the door Steve knocked and waited. The knock was loud and authoritative.

A male voice said, "Who is it?" The voice was muffled, as though the man inside had his mouth full.

Steve knocked again. The voice barely got out, "I said who is —" before it was interrupted by Steve's boot kicking the door in. The door ripped through the lock and flew past the safety chain, knocking the owner of the voice to the floor. Steve fluidly moved through the door frame, firing a bullet as he crossed the entryway. Screams erupted like applause after the gun exploded. The bullet wasn't for the male voice; it was for the grandmother, the Nona, of the family. Mrs. Talarese — Tommy's wife — was shrieking as she rushed to the floor beside the body of the elderly woman. Steve quickly moved to the huddle of women on the floor and silenced the younger woman with a kick. The hard shin to the side of her head snapped her body onto the elderly woman already on the floor. The young man flattened by the door rolled to his feet and started to run at Steve. I grabbed him by the hair as he passed and yanked. His body, surprised and pained, straightened enough for me to loop an arm around his neck to hold him. Fuelled by rage, he strained against my body, pulling past the point of exhaustion. After forty-five seconds he was tapped, and his back slumped against my chest.

After the struggle was over, I had time to survey the situation. The son, a thin kid in his early twenties with a protruding Adam's apple, was hanging in my arms. Tears streamed his cheeks, and saliva hung in strands between his lips as he gasped for breath. He was like a mad dog surging against a chain on his neck, instinct forcing him to push against the yoke no matter the consequences. From the shape the side of his face was in, I could see he had already been worked over in a bad way. The other two occupants of the apartment lay huddled together. The grandmother was lying on her side near an overturned wicker chair and a toppled cane. Her white hair was thin and cut short. I could see her scalp through the strands surrounding her head. Her mouth was closed, and her chin sat higher on her face than it should have. She was old-world by the look of her. The old woman's toothless mouth would confirm her poor rural Italian heritage better than a birth certificate ever could. As she lay there unblinking, the centre of her blue dress bloomed a stain — one much darker than the light material of the dress. Tommy's wife moaned and held her rapidly bruising face as she recovered from the short kick she had received to the left side of her head. Her appearance was unlike her mother-in-law's. She was a petite woman, with a plain, unpretty face and large dark hair artificially expanded to twice its natural volume. The massive amount of jewellery on her hands and ears showed her to be far from the farm her mother-in-law grew up on a continent away.

Steve produced the razor from his pants and opened it slowly. The blade was black with the crusted blood that had pooled and dried while the razor was closed. The sight brought Tommy's wife to full attention.

"Where is the phone?" Steve asked.

No answers came from Maria's lips, so he slapped her hard across the face. When her head lolled back, Steve presented the question again, this time with the blade of the razor resting just under her nostrils.

"Call your husband and tell him what I have done."

Tommy's wife looked confused, but she did as she was told. She dialled the phone with shaking hands, softly whispering a prayer until someone picked up. "Tommy? It's Maria. Just listen. This guy just...just came here and shot Momma, and she's dead, and he hit me, and this guy he told me to call you. Help us! Please help us! I don't want to die, please, baby, please!"

The conversation turned into sobs and pleas. Steve took the phone from Maria. "Tommy, this is Steve. Sandra goes home now with you and she calls me when she's there. After she calls, you come home. Any tricks, and the boy and your wife die. You have twenty minutes."

The phone call ended with the beep of the portable. Steve looked around the large family room of the apartment. A dim light beside a beige sofa pushed away the dark from the corner of the room. The sofa was surrounded by wood furniture and encased by maroon walls the colour of dark blood. Steve told both mother and son to sit on either side of the couch.

Before I let the kid go, I asked Steve, "You know this one?"

"Came around the bar the other day."

It fit: Tommy was introducing his boy to the family business. The kid had been given a low-level muscle job to toughen him, the way his old man had probably been toughened. The kid tried to deal with Steve and came out with the short end of the stick and a swollen head. Steve had made an impact that no one could miss. The kid's face was like a billboard broadcasting the boy's ineptitude to everyone. The billboard caught Tommy's eye, and turned it to Steve and Sandra. The kid fouled up, and dear old dad was stepping in to show junior how to handle a tough situation. I grabbed the kid by the belt and heaved him to the couch. He had to use his hands to prevent himself from crashing into his mother. Once they were seated together on the couch, the rage began.

"You're dead, you animal. My husband is going to find you and your family, you greasy shit. You and him." The word "animal" betrayed her heritage; it came out as if there was an "eh" on the end of the word that wasn't there when I said it.

The son stared at me, burning holes in my chest, saying nothing. I leaned against a wall and watched Steve. This was Steve without Sandra. She could calm him down. She could reason with him. By taking her, Talarese had taken reason and restraint away from Steve. There was no one to stop him. No one to try to calm him down. It was like taking the bars off the zoo. The wild was loose in the city, and everywhere there was prey. He set the wicker chair beside Tommy's mother upright, placing it over her body, and sat in it. Her head protruded between his feet and he sat staring down into her open eyes. The curses kept coming from Maria, hurling at Steve like javelins meant to pierce his soul.

He stared at the dead woman between the legs of the chair and interrupted Maria. "You know what your husband is?"

"Oh, I know, and you're going to find out exactly what he is. You just wait. Just wait!"

Steve looked at Maria. Their hatred fought each other

in stares. Neither looked away; not even Steve as he raised the gun in his hand and wordlessly shot Maria in the knee.

As the two living family members huddled in agony, Steve went to the kitchen and grabbed a towel. He threw it at the son and told him to tie it around his mother's wounded leg. I stayed true to my word and did not interfere.

The gunshot had made the room quiet for ten minutes until a mechanical buzzing turned Steve's attention away from the two on the couch. Steve opened his phone and spoke. "Are you okay?...I know...It'll be okay now. Is he with you? Tell him to come home...It will be fine, I promise...I love you, too. Tell him to come home now." Steve disconnected and closed the phone. He had not let Sandra try to calm him down; he wasn't going back to his cage until he was done.

Ten minutes after that quiet conversation, the door opened. Tommy walked in, swearing at Steve about the nerve he had and where they would find his body. If he was fearful of two men holding his family hostage at gunpoint, he didn't show it. He moved across the room quickly like an overzealous prizefighter. He was so brazen that he walked past me without giving me a second thought as he continued his verbal barrage at Steve. Steve nodded to me, and I hooked Tommy hard in the right kidney. The punch drove all the air out of his lungs with a grunt that made the second hook, to the left side, only as audible as the dull thud of my fist against his soft flesh. He crumpled to the floor without another word.

When he raised his head he saw his family as if for the

first time. "Maria, what happened? Look at the blood…Oh, my God, Ma!"

He got off the carpet and ran to the couch to embrace his family. They sobbed together, holding each other tight. It was almost touching if you could forget why they were together on the couch. After a while Tommy pulled himself away from the embrace and stared at his mother for a long moment, then at Steve, and finally at me.

"You two fucks are dead. Dead!"

Steve raised the gun and spoke softly. "Is she back alone?"

Tommy screamed, "I'm going to kill you myself, you dirty prick. You, then that bitch of yours. Then I'm gonna burn that shithole down!"

Steve pointed the gun at Maria's other knee. "Tommy!" she shrieked. "Tell him please. I want him to leave. Please…tell him!"

She again broke into wordless cries and moans. Tommy stared at his wife for at least ten seconds. With each passing second his shoulders shook more and more. He finally erupted. "Shut up! Shut up!" he shouted at his wife. "Do you know who I am? Do you? Huh? No one does this to me! I made my bones. I'm made, and this piece of shit thinks he can do this? He's dead!"

"Tommy please…I…I need a hospital."

Tommy slapped his wife with a closed fist. She was trying to make him show that he cared, to make him show weakness. Tommy would never show weakness in front of us — it wasn't in him. Even with his back against the wall, he would never let anyone see under the hard skin he wore like armour. He hit her again and again until his son tried to intervene. Tommy didn't stop; his fists found the boy too. Both mother and son gave up and accepted their lumps. Tommy hit them both until he was breathing in heavy gasps. He turned to look at us once again and seemed to regain his composure. It was no wonder he was a made man and not just some strong-arm; he was trying to control the situation. He was trying to pass the events off like something that could never hurt him. Tommy was trying to show us that he was unafraid, and that it was us who should have been terrified regardless of the gun we held. He looked at us in disbelief, a look that told us we had made the biggest mistake of our lives. His look told us we should run and hide to avoid the fury of this self-proclaimed mob god. Tommy could have pulled it off too if we weren't who we were. He had no idea that there were others just as ruthless as he was. Other people who were capable of handling their own affairs instead of just passing them off to the many arms of the underworld.

Steve sighed and shot Tommy in the shoulder. The bullet hit him high on the right side of his body and spun him around, and down onto all fours. When he tried to get up, Steve kicked him hard in the ribs. Tommy flopped to his side, propelled by the foot and the crunching sound of his ribs. Steve stepped on the bullet wound and over the screams asked a third time.

"Is she back alone?"

"Yah, she's back alone. She's alone. Okay?"

Steve looked to me and said, "Check."

I went over to him, took the phone from his pocket,

hit redial, and waited. When Sandra answered, I had her check outside for cars and men. She told me the streets were empty. I told her to lock up and stay put, then I told Steve everything was good. He nodded and looked around the room. The fire in him seemed to slowly drain. He looked at me, and there was less anger and violence in his eyes.

"Is there any way out of this?"

Steve knew the mob wouldn't forget, and that they would keep coming until they were satisfied. Satisfaction would most likely involve the death of Steve, Sandra, and probably me. I had been working for Paolo Donati almost exclusively for a few years, and he owed me some favours. Unfortunately, favours from a mob boss are like Grandma's china — nice to have, but you never thought of actually using it.

"I'll do what I can."

The gun sounded three more times, and we were on our way out. I had Steve wipe everything he had touched before we closed the door. In the lobby, the doorman was still on the floor and the streets were still clear. I wasn't worried about the gunshots. I figured the neighbours knew who Talarese was and what he was into. That made them the type of people who would turn up the television to drown out gunshots rather than call nine-one-one.

I drove Steve back to the bar and let him out in front of the entrance. He rode back without saying a word and got out the same way. He began to walk away, but stopped and turned to stare at me. He came back to the car and sat in the seat beside me again. He looked like hell; his shirt was bloodstained, and his pants were dirty.

"I don't know why," he said, looking at me.

I stared out the windshield and thought about why. Why had I put it all on the line for a bartender and his wife? I wasn't one of the good guys. I was on the other side. Steve came to see me because he knew I would know who took his wife. But even though I knew the men who kidnapped Sandra, I never considered myself like them. There was a line separating what I was from what they were. I was independent; I chose the jobs I wanted to work. It just so happened that one person in particular used me for my skills more than others. Paolo recognized my usefulness early on and he used me for jobs that required the ignorance and secrecy that only an outsider could provide. I worked on the fringe and I made Paolo aware of where everyone stood, be they gangs, other organized outfits, even cops. Being an outsider, I couldn't use information I found to hurt Paolo: no one would talk to me or believe what I said. There were also the hoods he employed who would have been happy to kill me for no other reason than to relieve their boredom. I lived the life I was taught. I was off the grid to everyone. No one knew where I lived; I had no accounts or property in my name. I hardly had a name — just the one word I used for an identity. I was a ghost in the machine. No one saw me coming and no one traced me back to anyone.

I stared out the window, thinking of the why, unable to find an answer. "Go see her," was all I said.

Steve nodded and grunted something as he got out of the car again. Sandra opened the door as he walked away from me and ran outside to him. They hugged in the street and cried together, two people who refused to follow the rules.

I sat for a time watching the two forms joined together with arms and lips. I smiled and found myself thinking of my parents. All the years I had lived with my uncle had never shown me what they were. I learned what they did, but I never knew who they were. No matter how hard I tried to climb into their world, they were unknown. I could only hold on to their memories like the edges of dreams. I had parts and images, but no real recollection of them. I thought of them as I watched Steve and Sandra in the rain. I saw two people who fought the system to make their own life. Two people who went outside the rules to protect their small family. In that moment I felt closer to my parents, closer to two people who fought to give me a life I had no right to have as the son of bandits. Steve and Sandra refused to give in to the mob, refused to give in to their filthy pressure. They wanted a life on their terms, and I helped them get that — maybe only for a short time longer.

I pulled away from the curb and drove to a coffee shop around the corner. I found a spot behind it and parked, then sat in the car watching the streetlights fade into large blotches in the growing fog on the windshield. I got myself involved in a mess, and getting out was not going to be easy. I needed to meet with the boss before word got out — or worse, a contract.

I got out of the car into the glow of the streetlight and walked to the coffee shop to the beat of the gravel under my shoes. I used the storefront windows to check out everyone in the shop before making a move to enter. No one looked out at me. No one even looked in the direction of the doors. I moved through the pair of doors separating outside from inside and ordered a tea at the counter. I sat at a table for two against the wall and watched everything that was going on in the restaurant. The counter had stools lined up for solitary eaters at a red scarred countertop. Sugar, napkins, and ketchup were the only decorations in the restaurant. Four men sat in the red swivel stools at the counter and ate in silence. One waitress served them in her T-shirt and apron. She didn't move fast and she didn't move slow; she did her job with quiet efficiency amid the hum of the air conditioner and the clanging that sporadically erupted from the kitchen behind her.

The waitress came out from behind the counter and brought me my tea. After she had left me the water, a mug, and a metal container full of milk, I thought over the events of the day. I had witnessed the deaths of seven people who were connected in their own right. I hadn't killed anyone, but I hadn't stopped the killing either, so I was as guilty as Steve. If I didn't try to square this away, Steve and Sandra would be dead by tomorrow, and I would follow soon after. Steve wouldn't give me up, but they would make it hard on Sandra and she would — in the end. I had to try to mop this up before it spilled over into the streets.

I drank my tea slowly and turned a quarter in my hand. The only way it was going to work was if I had a sit-down with the boss himself to give an explanation. Tommy had kidnapped and threatened to mutilate Steve's wife for over-due rent. He went outside the natural order of things, and it had cost him. If someone doesn't pay up you beat them, or burn their place down. People don't pay when they're dead. Dead bodies also have the bad habit of attracting cops; no one wants cops. I had to make Paolo see it this way because the only other way to see it was two men decided they wanted to die in the worst possible way, so they picked a fight with a made man and his family. I finished the tea and left a few bucks on the table, then walked to the phone and dialled.

"Yeah?"

"It's Wilson. I need a meeting with the man."

"I'm sorry, sir, I think you have the wrong —"

"I'm coming now and I'll wait. Pass on a message that I have something important to speak to him about."

"You can't —"

I hung up the phone before the lackey could finish and made my way to the counter. I sat among the silent men and had another tea and a muffin to make myself busy for ten more minutes.

I finished eating, paid up, and drove. I got out of the car four blocks from the restaurant and walked the rest of the way. I wanted everyone to see me coming.

There were always four men out front discussing sports, food, or the women who walked by. The group changed members every couple of hours, but their purpose never changed. They were the first level of security, and if they didn't like the look of you, you weren't going anywhere. I crossed the street directly across from the front entrance and watched as the group of four men seamlessly shifted to block my way. By the time I stepped up onto the curb, I was on a collision course with the group as though that was my intention all along. The one to my left spoke as the others closed in around me.

"You got balls, Wilson, showing up like you call the shots."

I didn't answer because it was meant as a statement, not a challenge. One of the men to my right, shielded from view by his partners, began frisking me. It was a waste of time, I was clean; I left the gun in my car. When the frisk ended I was still in the middle. No one moved.

"I'm going in now, anything stupid and you're going to get hurt first," I said to the one who had spoken. He stared at me, and I let my face pull into a grin. It wasn't productive to do this, but I always hated being frisked. Even more, I hated being stalled by four idiots in a lame attempt at intimidation once I had been found to be unarmed. I brushed past the man to my left, making sure to edge him hard. I never turned back, not even when the four began hurling insults at me.

Inside the door it was immediately dimmer. On my right was a young woman behind a mahogany counter — another layer of security. The coat-check girl checked over whoever came in and called ahead with any problems.

"Check your coat, sir?"

"Maybe later," I said as I walked past the coat-check girl to a set of thick glass doors that led to the dining room.

"Everyone checks their coats, sir, house rules." Her voice had a hard edge to it; the word "sir" sounded as though it meant "you dumb asshole." I turned to the voice with my hand on one of the cold glass doors. She was short, maybe five feet, with long dark hair and eyes that matched. She was cute, not pretty, and that fact probably gave her a lot of attitude under her exterior. Knowing she would never be considered beautiful hardened her. She wasn't really cute at that moment because she was doing her best to give me a hard stare.

"I know what everyone does, and I don't care." The look in my eyes cut through her stare and for a split second she was scared. Her left hand moved under the counter — just an inch.

"If you're thinking of moving that left hand a little more, you should think of one thing first," I said.

She paused, wondering what I knew that she didn't. "What's that?" Her voice had no edge now, just a hesitant fear.

"I'll be through the door before you can get your hand above the counter." I never knew what she did once the door closed behind me.

The lights in the dining room were dim; they made the red walls a dark maroon. There were twenty tables below the five stairs in front of me. Past the tables was a hallway; on either side of the hall were booths. I walked down the stairs past the tables, each of which had a long tablecloth and four overturned chairs on top. Once I made my way past the tables, two men from booths on opposite sides of the mouth of the hall stood and approached me.

"Stay where you are."

I stood my ground. I could see that the two men in front of me had guns in shoulder holsters under their suit jackets. On top of that, the bodyguards were young and in shape. These two were first-rate newbies, immature and eager, like all before them. They must have had long and bloody résumés already, to be doing personal security for the boss.

"Turn around. Arms straight out."

I did as I was told and stared at the wall. The frisk was by the numbers, and more thorough than outside because this frisk was less about weapons and more about a wire. As by-the-books as it was, it was a slow job, something that didn't sit right with me. Too much time was spent on my upper body and arms. These guys were young, but they should have been good because the position they were in demanded skill. I kept thinking they should have been better than this. As a right hand moved slowly down my left leg, I realized what was happening, and my world exploded.

One moment I was standing, thinking only of the meeting and the frisking; the next I was on the floor forcing myself to breath as I tried to focus and forget that one of my kidneys just exploded. I lay sprawling for thirty seconds and then I managed to roll onto my back.

I saw Julian outlined by the light. His bulk was like the moon eclipsing the sun. All at once, he was massive and terrifying. He was made more so by the fact that I was laying at his feet viewing him only in quick flashes as I spasmed on the floor.

"You got a mouth on you. You talk too much. Always saying something. See what your mouth gets you. You get hurt. Maybe you get killed."

My mouth moved but nothing came out. A hard voice, cultured by years of smoke, alcohol, and acid reflux spoke out. "Get him over here."

At once Julian stooped and lifted me over a shoulder. I sloshed around watching the world reel. Inside me the anger was boiling, and for a moment I forgot why I had come. I should have been humble, quiet, and polite, but the rage pounding in my ears erased thoughts and rationality. My body was hanging so that I was chest to chest with the monster of a man. Despite the pain, I straightened my body so that Julian looked to be carrying a load of lumber on his shoulder. The pain in my back hit me and I almost buckled, but I managed to stay horizontal. I drove my elbow back hard, aiming at Julian's eye. He saw the blow coming, shrugged his shoulders, and tried to drop me. My elbow connected with his cheekbone before I was airborne

I landed behind Julian, on all fours, and saw that he had covered his face and turned away. I covered the distance between us in three steps and kicked him hard in the groin like I was going for a field goal. Julian dropped to his knees, and I kept coming. The next two kicks hit the back of his neck and knocked him down. The three stomps to the groin that followed should have kept him there, but he pulled in his knees and got up. He stood and smoothly extracted a large revolver from under his suit coat. I knew from the small distance between us that I was dead. No diving could get me out of range. I stared at him, but no bullet came. Julian waited. Even though he had me cold, he waited. He wanted the order, and it hadn't come yet. I knew right there that the monster in front of me would be a force soon. He didn't lose his head. As mad as he was, he followed protocol. I waited for a thirty-second year as the gun stared at me without flinching.

"Heh, he's like a dog, Wilson. You get into his yard, and he wants to fuck you to show you he's on top. Down boy. Let him sit."

Paolo was behind Julian in a booth — invisible beyond Julian's massive frame and his gun.

"I said sit!"

The gun didn't move, so I did. I walked around Julian and sat in a chair facing the lone man in the booth. Paolo was comfortable in the smoky dim light. He wore a tailored grey suit and tie, but he didn't look professional. The lines, the scars, and the ugliness in his face told his real credentials.

"You have nerve to tell me you're coming here. Like I need to wait on you, like you're somebody. This information better be important, boy."

I did the only thing I could do. I told him what had transpired. During my quiet retelling his face never moved. Only his eyes gave away his feelings. His eyes blazed, and his pupils violently shook. His expressionless face held eyes that forced out an anger that could not be articulated. Out of the corner of my eye, out of earshot, Julian stood smirking. He saw the eyes and knew the order would come. He was happy to be the hand of those raging eyes.

I didn't mince words. I told Paolo everything, but I never explained why I got involved; it would have violated every rule I was ever taught in my second education. My reasons were my own, and I wasn't sharing them with the burning eyes across from me. Paolo knew nothing of my life before I met him, and I kept it that way. I would never give him the ability to understand any part of me. Any understanding could lead to leverage. I focused on Tommy and the line he crossed to be a role model to his boy. Hassling, strong-arming, and threats were part of life here, but it never escalated to what Tommy had done. Every taboo was broken for money in Hamilton, but some rules had to hold so that anarchy didn't erupt. More important, the rules we had separated us from other organizations more than colours or territory ever could. Organizations from different parts of the globe who settled in the city didn't place any importance on rules. They wanted power and they were willing to push anyone to get it. Paolo and his crew looked down on the new gangs and their methods. Paolo's men saw themselves not as thugs and hoods, but as professionals in a business that had employed generations of families. Everyone who did business outside the law in a different manner was deemed inferior because they ignored the methods established over the years by true career criminals.

The story ended with silence. I stopped talking and stared straight at Paolo Donati. I didn't beg for mercy or plead for understanding. I told him part of what I wanted to say and I waited for the verdict.

"Rules," he said. "Fucking rules. You have got to be kidding me. We kill people all the time, with guns, knives, shit they force through holes into their bodies. Hell, we even put whores on the streets. Everything we do hurts everybody, and you want to tell me there are rules now?"

"There's always been rules. Some people forget them, but I don't. What Tommy did was out of line."

"Don't you say his name. He was family, you fuck. Family! You get that? And you, you're like some ungrateful stepchild. You get paid by me. What I do, what Tommy did, made the money you earn. And you have the balls to come to me and tell me you're following rules. Fuck your rules."

His hand stamped the end of his sentence into the table.

I was less worried. Yelling meant the situation was not cut and dried. If he wanted me dead, it would have been done already. The yelling made me think he knew the other half of what I wanted to say. My thoughts drowned out his rage until one sentence brought me back.

"Leave us alone."

Everyone, even Julian, slowly moved away, leaving Paolo and me completely isolated. "Why did you do it? And don't bullshit me with that rules crap. I know you don't believe in that shit."

"There are rules…"

"Bullshit!" he roared.

I took a second and considered the man who held my fate in his breath. "My reasons are my own. Now, do you want to hear the rest?"

The old man leaned back, his eyes dulled a fraction, and I almost saw a smile. "Tell me," he said.

"Tommy was more trouble than he was worth. All the brutality with the Russians cost you. He was so over the top that they banded together to fight him. He unified them, made them stronger. He's the reason you didn't take the Russians out. All his bloodshed brought public attention down on you. For a while there Tommy's work was regular in the newspapers. There had to be a truce."

I paused to see if he was listening. "Talk," he said.

"Now you have to live side by side with the Russians. You have lines between them and you. Tommy was the guard on your side. He was a reminder of how bad things could be again. Tommy was a guard dog, but he was always behind a fence. You never let him out to work anywhere else because you knew how destructive his presence could be. Now Tommy is dead, and so is his family."

"So how does your treason help me?"

"It's an act of war."

"You're right about that. You put a stick in a hornet's nest, and for what? Some greasy mick? This war will swallow you up."

"Not if I'm not the one blamed. If word got out that the Russians killed Tommy, you would have a reason to take back all the Russians have. You can do it right this time, without Tommy to screw it up. He'd be more useful in death than in life. He'll be a symbol now. He'll be the why. His death gives you a reason to break the truce. You couldn't pull him off the wall before; it would have shown you didn't trust him. That he was wrong. You can't show that kind of weakness to the Russians."

"Why would I want to go up against the Russians again?"

"They're into things you aren't, and they've already set up a system people are used to. All you have to do is slide in and take over everything they started." It was true, the Russians had come to town slowly, starting with the local hockey team. The team brought over two Russians to add speed to their second line. The players were given fancy cars as signing bonuses and were paid a good salary. Almost at once, the locals back home kidnapped the players' parents for ransom. After a successful payoff, the boys back home got better ideas. They blackmailed the players into using their contacts with the hockey team to ask for visas for key members of Russian organized crime. Once they were given access to the country, the mobsters set up companies using the hockey stars' names to garner capital and investors. These companies were fronts for gathering more work visas, and for money laundering. In time, we had our own Russian mafia cell in the city. The hockey team had brought speed to the team and even more corruption to the city.

The Russian neighbourhoods were reintroduced to the corruption they left behind in the motherland. The poor Russian immigrants had a hard-wired distrust for authority, and simply slipped back into the pattern of paying for protection. The gangsters called the protection "*krysha*," which means "roof." The people who paid were under the protection of a criminal roof — and everyone paid. It wasn't only money that was extorted; the gangsters had been known to become part owners of businesses, or the pro-bono clients of high-paid attorneys. The Russian mob was growing and soon it would branch out again.

"Crows eat their own. Did you know that?" Paolo changed the direction of the conversation at once.

"No, I didn't."

"Not all crows, but it has been shown that crows have been known to eat eggs and other chicks."

I said nothing, so Paolo continued. "The crows don't do this for enjoyment. No, far from it. They eat other crows' eggs so that their own eggs have a better chance to survive. They're cannibals. See, those birds kill their own for survival. That is a society without rules. That is a society where anarchy exists. That is the society you want to fucking bring to my doorstep. You want me to watch you eat my fucking family, my people, like I was a crow. I am no bird, you crow. I am the king of this fucking jungle." His hands gripped the table so tightly his knuckles were white with the strain.

"You aren't a crow," I said. "But Tommy is dead, and there is no changing it. You kill me and Steve and you get revenge, but then your symbol will be gone and forgotten. How long before the Russians come over the line? With the butcher dead, they will move out to your territory. Do you want that kind of message? People will ask who it was the Russians were afraid of. Was it you or Tommy? And soon in the back alleys and bars people will say, 'This never would have happened if Tommy was alive.' When that happens your teeth won't look so sharp anymore, and you'll have to fight your own people while the Russians watch."

Paolo said nothing; he just stared at me. His knuckles on the edge of the table were still white with strain. Slowly the white faded pink as the hands relaxed and the blood returned. "Listen up, crow. You're done with me. Out of business. I don't want to see you again. I'm not going to kill you yet. You've been loyal — more than Tommy, and that's something, since you aren't family like he is…he was." The boss let out a low laugh that ended in a small cough. "Ironic, isn't it? You're getting saved by loyalty."

"The business with the bar…is it finished then?" I asked politely.

"You got some nerve asking about a shithole bar like that. One word out of my mouth, just one, and I'd blow that bar down like the big bad fucking wolf."

"I know it and I understand, but I need to know if it's done."

"Caw, caw, little bird. You don't need to know shit. What I do is none of your business. None. Julian." With that one word the massive human frame just out of earshot came to life and moved towards me. I stood before he could get next to me.

I walked out past Julian. Neither of us said a word to the other, but I could feel the violence inside me slamming against the side of my skull. I winked at the coat-check girl at the entrance who eyed me, as I passed, with her hand under the counter. The four protectors out front gave a low whistle when I came through the doors. They were surprised to see me leaving under my own power. If they ever found out what I had told Paolo, they would hate themselves forever for not shooting me down when they had the chance. That was the difference between most people involved in the mob and Paolo. Paolo wasn't ruled by his emotions; he was cold, calculating, and educated. I had put together pieces of who Paolo Donati was from information I learned on the street. His father was the top of the totem pole before him, and he sent his kids to the best schools. Paolo grew up in the best neighbourhood, next to doctors and millionaires, and went to school with the other neighbourhood rich kids. Paolo's upbringing couldn't have been more different from his father's. He didn't have to fight and hustle every day to survive. Paolo had friends, girlfriends, and good grades. He excelled in math and science. People say he was studying to be a veterinarian, but that is probably bullshit invented because Paolo loved to talk about animals. He used them as metaphors to degrade a person. He spoke of the nature of the animal kingdom to show people how close they were to those lower on the food chain. Paolo never did anything with his science and math, except use it to intimidate. His schooling ended abruptly when he was called to the family business at twenty-three. There he encountered animals, but they weren't the kind in books. These animals were much worse, and in time Paolo ruled them all.

Paolo studied people as if they were locked in at the zoo; he analyzed details and missed very little. Nothing I had told him was a new idea to him. He understood Tommy, his behaviour, and the delicate balance his presence maintained. Paolo saw his empire as a vast ecosystem, and he would not allow it to become unbalanced. Unbalance meant he was not in control, and that chaos signalled weakness. For someone who thrived on being in control, being the king of his jungle as he put it, weakness was worse than death. If things were to spin out of control, Paolo would want to be the one doing the spinning.

I walked the four blocks, alone, back to the car. I drove, listening to the Volvo as it accelerated through its gears. I was forever connected to a maniac and his girl in the murder of seven people, and I was out of a job. I had pushed a group of very dangerous people toward another group of very dangerous people. There would be bloodshed for what I had done. I tried to console myself with the idea that war with the Russians was inevitable, and that the fight would be over quickly with the Italians rallying around the memory of Tommy Talarese. But I was wrong.

Paolo began a war with the Russians that raged for years. More lines were drawn, and the city became more divided than ever. I was wrong about being out of a job, too. I was working again less than a month later.

CHAPTER SEVEN

The dashboard clock read 4:23 as I slowed on the street where the Volvo was parked. Steve got out and told me he'd meet me back at the bar. I rolled Steve's Range Rover down the street and watched 22 Hess out of the corner of my eye. There weren't any squad cars yet, so Steve was good to go. I used the cell phone Steve left on the seat to call him.

"It's all clear," I said.

"I can see that. Let's meet at the bar."

Back at Sully's Tavern I ordered a Coke and waited for Steve. I made small talk with Ben and Sandra and went over the events of the day in my head. I showed up at 22 Hess to find out about what I stole from the airport and to figure out how to get those amateurs off my ass. The computer nerds stole accounting information from someone working for what looked to be the Russian mob. They blackmailed the accountant and set up an exchange at the airport. When the airport exchange didn't happen the accountant likely had to 'fess up to his employers about what was going on. The Russians had their own way of dealing with blackmailers that didn't involve airport handoffs. They came looking for the geeks and their property at the same time I did. So now I was in a Mexican standoff, with two big guns pointed at my head.

The first gun was in Paolo's hand. According to the dingy Guinness clock on the wall, I had just over a day and a half to get everything in order before Paolo decided to cut his losses. If I were viewed as a liability when Julian returned to see me, Paolo would turn him loose on me in an effort to keep himself insulated from the airport job.

The second gun belonged to the Russians. They were after their property and they had no problem killing a whole office staff to get closer to what they wanted. The Russians were real thugs, not amateurs, and they probably had my scent because Mike had not been dead when I left the office. They would gladly grind what they needed out of me to get to what had been taken from them.

I decided that when Steve brought the car back, I would go to the office. It was the only option. There I had a chance to pick up someone doing surveillance, or wait for the Russians to find me. I would be next on the Russians' list and I had no way of finding them without drawing attention to myself. There was no way the Italians would help me. Paolo had no interest in helping me when it was just the amateurs who were following me. There was no way he would help me deal with the Russians. I had to play defence — alone.

Steve pulled in twenty minutes after my second Coke and tossed the car keys at me as he walked to Sandra. He kissed her on the cheek and asked her questions in low tones. They both smiled and talked for two and a half minutes while Ben tended bar; no one complained about how slow service had suddenly gotten. When Steve finished talking to Sandra, he kissed her on the cheek and came over to me. He leaned in, resting his knotted forearms on the bar.

"They had guys at the corners scanning the cars," he told me.

"I never saw them," I said.

"They were around the streets. I saw one stop what he was doing to stare at me getting in the car. I guess I was okay in their eyes 'cause no one tailed me."

"You sure?" I asked.

"Yep," was the only response I got.

I told Steve I'd see him later and left the bar to make my way to the office. I found the car on a side street. It hummed to life without any problems, and the tank was full. I smiled at my friend's wordless act of kindness. As I drove, I tried to clear my head of all the thoughts I was having. I couldn't be afraid or hesitate. I had to walk head up into a trap and make it work to my advantage. This was the opposite of everything I wanted, everything I was trained to do. The situation also had no real plan to go along with it. I always planned everything or at least had an idea about how I wanted to spin a situation. I remembered the words of my uncle: "Planning separates the living and the dead, boy. Don't forget it. The morgue is full of guys who thought they could handle anything." I knew that deep down he was talking about my parents; they didn't have a good plan in his eyes and it killed them. The events of the past few days had left me without any control, and it pissed me off. I was struggling to keep ahead of people who all seemed to know more than I did about what I was involved in.

As I drove, I breathed deep and counted down from ten until my mind was empty. I turned off Duke Street onto James Street and circled the office a few times. I let my mind take in the area, waiting for recognition of anything that stood out. I didn't see people loitering in the shadows, and there were no strange parked cars concealing occupants hunched low in their driver seats. To be safe, I went up a block and parked on a side street. I turned off the ignition and checked the Glock. I reloaded the gun so that I had eleven in the clip and one in the chamber. I took off the safety and tucked the gun into the holster at the small of my back. I made sure my shirt was out over the holster, and got out of the car.

I didn't enter the building at first. I was bait, but I planned on surviving my predators. I wanted the Russians to take a run at me on my terms, in a place where I had control. That meant I had to make it past the front door and anyone waiting. I walked on the opposite side of the street, past the office, into a variety store five doors down from my building. It was the best spot I had to watch the street. I bought a paper and a coffee and walked over to the video wall by the door. I stared over the video rack of soft- and hard-core pornography through the window to the street. I spent twenty minutes sipping my coffee and pretending to split my time between the paper and the porn.

I left after the clerk started to cough a little louder than he needed to over and over again. I hadn't noticed a thing yet, but it had been less than half an hour — nothing in the grand scheme of things. I walked back up the street and used an alley to cross over James Street, the second-busiest street in the area. I hailed a cab and gave the cabbie a story about a cheating wife. I told the driver to cruise the area so I could catch her in the act. I told him I would pay whatever the fare came to, and settled in to watch the neighbourhood roll by. The cabbie spoke about his own cheating wife and how much he hated the bitch and *her* kids. I ignored the story, speaking up only to tell him where to turn. I watched the cars and the people as we cruised; I was looking for solitary figures sitting low in car seats, or random pedestrians who strode the sidewalks too long. In the hour I spent in the cab I saw no human forms in the shadows of cars or alleys. I paid up the cabbie when we ended up back on James Street for the twelfth time, and walked the streets again.

I carefully navigated the side streets and narrow alleys. The reek of garbage from the corners accented the putrid fumes being spewed by the sewers. I walked past the convenience store I had been in earlier, then I went past the office. No one looked at me twice, and no one stood out — yet. I knew deep down that Mike had squealed on me back at the office. People were coming.

After a few more strolls around the area, I went up the steps to the building. It was almost six, after office hours; the few other rented office spaces in the building were empty. I had the key ready, and I opened the locked door and entered the building without losing a step. No one shot me in the back; no one was waiting for me inside. I moved down the hall past the elevator and entered the stairwell.

I closed the door quietly behind me and waited. I waited for three minutes, listening to the hum of the fluorescent bulbs. I strained to hear any other noises above me, but there were none.

Before I started climbing the stairs, I took off my shoes. I held them in my left hand with my thumb and forefinger; my right was on the butt of my gun. Quietly I climbed the stairs. At first, my damp feet made quiet suction sounds, but the noise faded as my soles absorbed the grime and grease of the stairs. I passed each floor until I ran out of stairs at the sixth floor. No one was waiting for me on the top floor. I leaned over the stairwell and saw nothing below me, so I moved back down one flight to the fifth floor — my floor. Slowly I pressed the thumb latch on the door handle using the hand that was carrying the shoes. The first attempt was a little unsteady, so I put down the shoes and tried again. I opened the stairwell door and spied the dimly lit hallway for two minutes. Every office was dark, including mine. I didn't hear a single cough or shuffle of feet.

I picked up my shoes and moved down the hallway, making sure to stay low under each door so no one could shoot me in the back from a hiding place in one of the dark offices. I knelt to the right of my door and silently slid my key in. I turned the key, and slowly pushed the door open. I knew the score right away. The door moved too quickly; it moved open on its own and slammed against the door jamb because inside a window was open.

Behind my desk the blinds were up and the window was open. I kept low to the floor as I moved inside. Keeping the desk between me and the window, I pivoted to the blinds and released them. I didn't think anyone would shoot through the window at me; they would first want to find out what I knew. I was sure I had about two minutes until whoever was watching the window would be at the office door, so I got ready quick. I put my shoes on and went to the closet. The closet had a false back. I pulled out the painted wood piece that sat behind my clothes and took out a modified double-barrelled shotgun that I had sawn down to twelve inches. The shotgun was useless outside of ten feet, but up close it was like the wrath of God — scarring everything in its path. I stood, gun in hand, to the right of the door — out of the line of fire from both the hall and the window.

I was off on the time. The door was kicked open after five minutes. The bull who hit the door was a middle-aged guy with a beard, a beer belly, and scars around his eyes. He used a shoulder to hit the door, leaving his gun pointed at the floor. The grey suit he wore pulled at the buttons under the strain of his gut. He must have weighed two hundred forty pounds; most of it was flab. The crash through the door brought him into the room three feet from the shotgun.

I stayed where I was and waited for the man to catch sight of me out of the corner of his eye. His head turned to mine, and I watched the realization hit his face. I saw it in almost slow motion. Each muscle twitched, turning his face into a look of shock. He didn't say a word, and he didn't move; he just stood in front of me. We looked at each other for a quarter of a minute until a voice came from the hall.

"Gregor?"

The Russians had found me. I didn't speak because I wasn't sure I would be understood. I motioned down with the shotgun and waited. Gregor put his gun down and lowered himself to his knees. I moved his gun to me with my foot, never letting the shotgun drift from Gregor's centre. The voice called again, more sternly; it had the severity of a man in charge. I butted Gregor on the side of the face, and he went down the rest of the way to the floor. The noise was a sick wet bump, and the groan from Gregor's lips brought the hallway man into the room with his gun drawn.

As the welt on Gregor's temple grew, the second Russian and I waited with guns pointed at each other. I broke the silence. "You want to sit down?"

A heavily accented voice returned my pleasant invitation. "Not with guns drawn."

I'd had enough shit for one day. "Put yours down and we can talk — if you don't I'm going to do some terrible things."

I planted my feet and got ready. I began counting down from ten in my head. At one, I was going to kill him and risk the consequences. I figured the risk to be low: the shotgun blast would push him back and draw his shot wide. That was, of course, unless he was counting in his head too — with a lower number than mine. At four, he agreed to sit. He tucked his shiny gun into his pants and sat in the chair next to Gregor's body. I sat behind my desk and set the shotgun on the desk, the barrel pointed towards the Russian and Gregor.

"Now what do you and Gregor want?" I asked.

The second Russian was the new face of the mob: in his twenties, fresh-faced, dyed hair, gym membership. The new breed of mobster was unlike any of its predecessors. They were into their work for more than money, they were into it for a sense of identity. The lack of a war to fight in left many kids looking for a cause, and the mob was more than willing to let them enlist. These recruits served with a vicious devotion that would scare Germans from the forties. What these kids lacked in skill they more than made up for with brutality.

"Uh...money."

"You already snuck in once and left the window open. You went through my shit too. You tried to make it look like you didn't, but I can see that things are out of place, so don't bullshit me with some story about a robbery. You were here looking for something and you didn't find it. You waited for me to come back so you could ask me some hard questions. Once you got your answers, you were going to kill me. I want to know why. Who are you working for? And what do they want with me?"

He took a few seconds before he answered. "I do not know what you are speaking about. Now please, call police."

He looked unafraid of the prospect of involving the police. Handcuffs were better than death, and he knew deep down that I wasn't the type of person who would call the cops. He started to smile, probably thinking I would let him go. I felt my face pull to the left and I grinned at his smile. His eyes lost their mirth and his mouth formed a small, confused O. His gaze drifted down to the shotgun on the table, then back to me, and then again to the gun. He sprang from his chair, like he was shot out of a cannon, and grabbed at the barrel of the gun. He was lifting the shotgun off the desk when my hand came out from behind my back with the Glock. My grin didn't fade when I shot him.

The bullet hit him in the shoulder and put him on the ground. The bang was loud, but the offices were empty. No one would complain about the noise. I got out of the chair and moved around the desk. The sound of the shot had woken Gregor. He didn't make a sound when I kicked him in the temple; he just went limp and sagged to the floor again. His partner was still conscious as I picked him up off the floor. I took his fancy nickel-plated gun from his pants and pushed him over the desk so I could empty the rest of his pockets. Gum, cigarettes, a wallet, a knife, and a cell phone hit my desk in succession. I shoved the Russian back in his chair, grabbed a tea towel, and pressed it hard on the wound to get him to wake all the way up. His eyes focused, and we were back where we had started — minus a bit of his shoulder.

I sat back down behind the desk and put the Glock on the blotter. I didn't point it at him; I just let it sit casually.

"Now, what did you and Gregor want?" I asked. The edge in my voice told him I was serious. The hole in his shoulder proved it.

He stared at me, his eyes wide and shifting left to right. He was trying to think up a story.

"You've got thirty seconds to make me interested, otherwise I'll kill you where you sit. Then I'll start talking with Gregor. Seeing you dead will more than convince him to tell me what I need to know. The way I see it, you have a choice: are you going to be more useful to me dead or alive?"

The eyes shifted wildly again like a person drowning thrashes for air. After twenty seconds, his shoulders relaxed; he was ready to feed me the split. Most people under duress give you a sixty-forty split — sixty percent bullshit, forty percent honesty. People figure it's just enough to save them but not enough to do any real harm. I picked up the gun to speed up the split.

"Okay, okay, shit," he said in a voice that gained its base speaking an eastern language.

"Name, kid, then your boss."

"My...my name is Igor. I work for Sergei Vidal."

"Kid, you work for whoever gives you an order. Somebody else might sign the cheques, but your real boss is the one ordering you around. Now give me a local name and stop trying to impress me."

I could tell that this wasn't where Igor wanted the conversation to go. He wanted me to be terrified of the name of his employer and leave town as fast as possible out of fear and good judgement. He didn't know that I had played the game longer and better than him. A fact that should have been evident, considering he ambushed me and he was the one who got shot.

"I don't know who is in charge, I find out through..."

The sentence trailed off as I picked up the gun. I was so tired of amateurs and bullshit. It was getting late in the evening, and I wanted sleep — not more work.

"Consider that strike two. No bullet for that, but strike three gets you ejected from the game. And when that happens Gregor will be the next at bat," I said in a calm matter-of-fact voice.

Igor slackened in his chair while I waited patiently for the second split, the last split. "My boss... his name is Mikhail. He works in a private club on Barton."

"What kind of club?" I asked.

"It's a social club, for cards and drinking."

"Name of the bar, Igor. No bullshit this time."

He looked at his feet then the left wall. He was looking at it hard like it might open up so that he could dash through to safety. His eyes were glistening. The kid was realizing he wasn't going to become a powerful gangster. He now understood that, because of what he had failed to do, he would end up dead, and that it would be his friends and co-workers who were going to kill him. It's a hard realization the first time you feel it.

"It's called the Kremlin," he said in a low, quiet voice. It was the voice of a traitor.

I had a decision to make about what to do with Igor and Gregor. Killing them would be more trouble than it was worth. Disposing of bodies takes time, and it's hard to do unnoticed when you're in the heart of the city. There are too many people rushing out from each artery. Each person would bring with him complications I didn't need. Letting them go would be much easier; they were in too much trouble to stick around. They both fucked up. They didn't do their job, and they sold out their boss. They had to run far and quick before word was out.

"I'm going to the Kremlin, and I'm keeping your phone. If I find out you lied, I'm calling every number stored in the phone using your name to find out what I need to know."

Igor's eyes were glistening. He had just grown up in five

minutes, and it was taking its toll fast. He already looked older, weaker.

"I'm dead then," he said.

"You're not dead yet, but you've got a hell of a head start. You better start running. Both of you. When I show up at the club, everyone will be looking for you two. So you better run fast and far."

CHAPTER EIGHT

I watched Igor and Gregor help each other out of the office. I had their guns and a ruined rug. The blood on the rug was not a huge problem — in my line of work blood is a constant issue. Under the rug was a tarp cut to match its dimensions. I moved the chairs and rolled up the rug, pulling the tarp with it as a barrier. I used some duct tape to secure it and found a trash bag for the guns I took off the morons. Keeping guns is dumber than keeping a bloodstained rug. Guns have history, which can become your future for ten to twenty years if you get caught with one.

I stowed the shotgun in the closet and holstered the Glock behind my back. I also took the time to rifle through my desk for my credit cards. In the back of the drawer, stuck in the right-hand corner with a magnet, was a stack of clean credit cards and the item I was looking for.

Years ago I took a card off a small-time mugger. It looked like a platinum American Express card. In actuality it was a decorated piece of metal with a razored edge. The mugger I pulled it from used it to stick up guys in the bathrooms of bars. Once, he happened to hustle the wrong guy, and I had to remedy the situation. I took the card and used it to make sure everyone would see his face coming the next time he tried a bathroom stickup.

I pocketed the card, picked up the carpet and the guns, and walked down the darkened stairs to the basement exit. The back doors had no handle on the outside, just a push bar on the inside. I exited, listening to the click behind me as the doors resealed the building. I dragged the rug to the corner of the alley. The uneven concrete had developed craters over the years; the deeper divots in the corner were full of dark filthy water long after the rainstorms ended. I found the largest puddle and rolled the carpet in. The dirt and grime in the water soaked into the shag and added pounds of weight instantly. I towed the carpet to the nearest Dumpster and leaned it up against the side. The rug would dry black, hiding all of the stains inside, and would be on its way to the dump with the building's trash soon after that. The guns in the bag could not be taken care of so easily. I decided to use the alleys to dispose of them one piece at a time. After ten minutes, I had dismantled, wiped, and disposed of the two Russians' pistols in several sewer grates.

I had to make a stop before I visited the Kremlin. My watch read 8:33 p.m. when I opened the door to the variety store I had been in a few hours earlier. The wind chime that served as a warning bell let the clerk know I was there. He was a different man than the one who had shot me dirty looks earlier. This one was a short Middle Eastern man with close-cropped black hair. He wore the hair without gel, and its health was evident in the way it fought gravity above his scalp. His short, neatly trimmed beard framed tight lips below a large pointy nose. I didn't bother with a greeting. I moved through the aisles past jerky, corn nuts, cereal, and batteries until I finally found what I was looking for: a Trojan Magnum encased in shiny foil. I took the condom to the counter and bought it along with a pack of cigarettes, a lighter, and a lighter refill.

"Ho, ho. Big night, eh buddy?"

The smiling face across the counter beamed a conspiratorial wicked grin for three seconds, until it recognized that I wouldn't be replying. I gave him two bills and waited for my change. The clerk grumbled to himself about assholes and shitty jobs while he bagged up everything I bought. I took the bag and my change and walked out the door. The wind chime cheerily announced my departure; the angry man behind the register didn't bother with a goodbye.

I walked to the car and got in, leaving the engine off. I took out my groceries and used the plastic bag they came in as a trash bag. I tore the cellophane away from the cigarettes and opened the pack. I put a cigarette behind my ear and dumped the rest in the bag. I leaned across the passenger seat and rifled through the glove box for a Swiss Army knife I kept inside. I used the knife to work a small hole into the face of the empty cigarette pack. I tore the foil away from the Trojan and rolled the condom out. I used my finger to open the prophylactic up and then filled it tight with lighter fluid. I knotted the improvised balloon and then shoved into the cigarette package. The condom bulged at first, but I managed to work it into the confines of the empty package. I leaned across the seat and went into the glove box again. I found an old wet-nap from KFC inside, and used it to clean the condom lubrication and lighter fluid off my hands. The lemony smell of the disposable cloth erased some of the scent left by the lighter fluid. I stowed the cigarette pack in my pocket, put the remnants of what I bought in the plastic bag, and opened the car door. I got out and walked to the nearest garbage can, threw the bag in, and got back into the car. Once my pistol was stowed in the glove box, I drove to the Kremlin.

It took less than ten minutes to drive from the office to the Kremlin. Barton Street was a concrete Rolodex through the city. Every neighbourhood was connected to the street. I followed it through the Italian, Vietnamese, and Polish neighbourhoods until I found the Kremlin. I parked at the curb across the street from the club and scanned the front of the building; it was long and rectangular with a small sign that read "Private" to the left of the entryway. The door was made of heavy metal and looked like it would withstand a police battering ram. The two windows on either side of the entrance were barred with heavy black metal rods. It was clear that I wasn't getting inside the building unless I was allowed through the front door. I got out of the car and crossed the street. As I walked, I took the unlit cigarette from behind my ear and put it in my mouth, then I moved the pack of cigarettes and lighter from my pocket to my right hand. There was no doorman out front, and I expected the door to be locked. I was surprised when I pulled the door and it swung out on well-oiled hinges.

I walked inside and had to blink quickly to adjust to the lack of light. Two men in suits approached; they were similar, almost like siblings, but the resemblance wasn't genetic — it was in the scars they carried. Their noses were flat, their eyes had an abundance of scar tissue, and their ears were cauliflowered. My eyes became used to the dark enough for me to see two bulges under their suits; they had guns — big guns.

The man on the left greeted me coldly with a deep, accented voice. "I'm sorry, sir, this is a private club. You must be leaving."

His arm laced mine as the other man stepped behind me on my right. I didn't move. "Tell Mikhail there's someone here with business to discuss."

"You will be leaving now." The voice didn't rise in volume; it just mechanically repeated its command.

"Listen, I'm not moving. I'm going over to the bar and you're going to let Mikhail know that a friend of Igor's is here to see him. If he still doesn't want to see me, you can throw me out. I won't fight it."

There was only a fraction-of-a-second pause before the man replied, "You must be checked."

I sighed and put the cigarette pack and lighter on the nearest table. I held out my arms and waited while he patted me down. The search was thorough except for the fact that he left the cigarettes and lighter alone. The silent doorman never looked at me, nor did he look away; he had a sense of dreamy awareness.

After my search, the bodyguards went to inform Mikhail about my presence. I picked up my things and walked to the bar. I slapped the mahogany surface hard with my palm. "Vodka, comrade. Nothing cheap, either. Mother Russia's finest," I demanded in a happy tone. I wanted these men to think I was a joke — pushing them with North American ignorance would help.

The bartender killed me twice with his eyes, but he fetched the drink with robotic efficiency. Moments later, I heard the quiet footsteps of the returning doormen and watched them, out of the corner of my eye, take seats at a table ten feet from me. Their distance and looks of disgust meant I was about to meet Mikhail.

After a minute, I was joined at the bar by a sandy-haired man in his early forties. He sat lower than me on the bar stool. I estimated he was about five-eight. He seemed fit, and there was a U-shaped scar under his right eye. He had been a fighter once. The signs never left.

"Who are you?" Mikhail's voice had no accent but it seemed to command respect.

"You sent two boys to kill me earlier. I want to talk about it."

If my words hit a nerve or shocked Mikhail, he didn't show it. He turned his head slightly and looked closely at me. I put the cigarette pack on the bar and lit the only remaining cigarette.

"Was it the *boys* who told you to come here?" Mikhail put some edge on the word *boys*; the edge told me they would be dead by morning.

"I want to know why I'm on your radar, and I want to know how to work this problem out," I said.

"It is very admirable of you to try and parlay peace, but it is in vain. You were stupid to come here. All you have saved is the cost of the gas it would have taken to find you again."

Mikhail had confirmed I was on his shit list, and that I needed to get higher up the on the food chain before I could bargain. "Call Sergei and ask him what he thinks. See if my being here, and the fact that I'm not dead yet, changes anything. If not, I'll pay up, and we can settle this now."

"I will not be calling anyone. You made a huge mistake and I will not be doing the same." His hard eyes watched me the whole time he spoke.

I pulled out my wallet. The movement caused no alarm with Mikhail; he knew I had been frisked before I sat down. The bodyguards moved closer, about five feet behind me. One was to my right, the other to the left of Mikhail. I pulled the fake credit card free and put my wallet away.

I took the first drag off my cigarette and said, "I'll pay up and we can get started."

Mikhail smiled, as if my gesture was amusing. I looked into his eyes and felt the left side of my face pull into a cold grin — my uncle's grin. I took another drag of my cigarette and put the glowing tip into the hole in my pack of cigarettes. The package immediately began to expand. I had it airborne, on its way to Mikhail's face, by the time it exploded. His scream shocked the bodyguards, but they didn't draw their guns right away. The two men were street toughs; they never prepared for being attacked. They only thought they had to look scary. The fireball had confused them. They didn't know whether to protect the boss or kill me. The exploding condom set Mikhail's hair and coat on fire; his lips let out a shriek as he rolled, burning, on the floor. The credit card hung low in my right hand as I covered the five feet between the bodyguards and myself. The guard on the right saw me coming; he shrugged back his coat and reached across his body. I used my left palm to mash his gun hand against his chest, suppressing his draw. The card was edge out in my hand as I punched across the bodyguards shoulder, being sure to tag the side of his neck. The spray of blood that followed meant I hit the carotid artery. The second guard was faster and already had his hand across his chest. I took the first guard, now a crimson fountain, by his lapels and pushed the both of us like a battering ram into his partner. The second man had freed his gun from the holster, but the bleeding guard rammed into him and trapped the gun between their bodies. I dropped the card and took advantage of the guard trying to plug the leak in his throat. I pulled his gun from the exposed holster and shot through his body four times.

I kicked the second guard's gun away from his body and checked both men for signs of life. I turned away from the dead bodies when I heard a sizzle from behind me. The bartender had squirted water from his bar sink onto Mikhail to put him out. I shot the bartender square in the chest, sending water shooting up to the ceiling. Mikhail was the only one left; his curses and moans mingled with the smells of gunpowder and burning hair. I walked over to him and pulled out the cell phone I took off of Igor.

"Dial Sergei and tell him I want out of this."

"Sergei doesn't make deals. This ch…changes nothing." His voice had lost its tone of authority after the fire on his head went out.

"Look around, Mikhail. Everything has changed. Sergei might not make deals, but I'll float one your way. Make the call, and I'll move on."

I dropped Igor's cell phone on the bar and righted a stool. I took a seat and waited while Mikhail got up off the floor. Parts of his face and scalp were blistered, and a good portion of his neck was seared. He picked up the phone and dialled. I watched him press the buttons and committed the number to memory.

The feeling of the pistol on the burned skin of his neck froze Mikhail solid. "Put the phone on speaker, and keep it English."

Mikhail sniffed hard and spat out a glob of black fluid onto the floor. "I have to ask for Sergei in Russian or I won't be put through."

"Make it quick. This is not the time to get ideas."

I listened to Mikhail spit out a machine-gun sentence in Russian. I pressed the gun hard into his burned scalp, forcing him to keep the Russian short. He ended his sentence and waited nervously for a reply.

"*Da?*" The phone belched out a thick Russian voice.

"Sergei, there has been a complication."

"*Da?*" The same word, but a new meaning — something entirely different than yes. The quiet word spoke loud volumes, demanding explanation, apology, and appeasement.

"The two men I sent failed, and now the thief has killed three men here at the club."

"*Da?*" This last word was chiselled out of concrete. It was a short word, but its slow delivery made it seem like a harsh rebuke.

"Yes, he wants to know what can be done to . . . make this right."

There was no cryptic reply right away. The pause could be good or bad. It could be a thought or it could be the silence of a multitasker. The silence someone would need to send more men to the club.

"He is there with you now?"

"Yes, Sergei. He is listening."

"Something was taken… information. I want it back," Sergei said.

"The information is out of my hands now; it's been passed on and probably dissected," I said.

"*Nyet.* This information was… unique. The men who wanted it would not show it to many people. I am told the information was encrypted, and those who stole it will not be able to see what it is right away. It will take time, the proper tools, and expertise to make sense of it. You say you want this to be over. Regain this information you stole, along with any equipment used to decode it, and all will be forgotten. This must be done by tomorrow."

"Tomorrow is too fast."

"*Da?* What you want is expensive. The only way you can pay is through immediate results."

I had an opening. It wasn't much, but it was something. "If I get everything you want, we're clean no matter what?"

After a long pause Sergei replied, "No one will come for you again, and we will not look for you. But if you do not succeed, more will come and they will not be children. I know of one person in particular who would like to speak with you."

I remembered the huge Russian I shot, and the office that had been wiped out. "Whatever. Twenty-four hours and *all* will be forgotten?"

"*Da*."

My grin returned, but Mikhail didn't notice. The gunshot that came next filled the room. Mikhail's body was pitched from the stool.

"Mikhail?" Sergei's voice was louder but unconcerned.

"Dead," I said. "It doesn't matter, though. In twenty-four hours you will have forgotten him. *Da?*"

"*Da*," was the only reply I was given. I was sure it sounded more like "dead."

CHAPTER NINE

I powered down the small, now-silent phone and put it into my pocket. The phone would be my only untraceable way to contact Sergei again. I picked up a bar rag and wiped the gun I had used, and then I put it into Mikhail's hands. The scene wouldn't hold up as a murder-suicide when the police looked at the ballistics, but it would steer attention away from a homicide by an outsider for a while. I used the rag to wipe down everything else I had touched and then I went through everyone's pockets. I used the bar keys I found on Mikhail to lock up, as though it were closing time on a slow night. I wiped the keys with my sleeve and let them fall into a storm drain as I walked past my car. I did a small loop around the block to make sure no one was coming or already following me. When I was sure I was clean, I made my way back to the car and drove away.

The drive went nowhere in particular for a while. I had to weigh out my options. The Russian mob was a growing force; they had fought Paolo and his Italians for years, and they showed no signs of weakening. They were getting stronger, and the capital they had meant they could afford to bring in heavy hitters — much heavier than Igor and Gregor. They would find me again if I didn't come up with the disks, and it would be tough to walk out of an ambush a second time. The disks would be hard to find. If they were difficult to read, Paolo would need to outsource the job. It would take someone with the know-how, and with mob connections. There could not be many people who fit those criteria in the city. The only issue became who to ask. Questions are like wraiths — they take on a life of their own and they linger. Whoever I asked would understand what went on when they found out the person I asked about happened to get roughed up that very same night. If I had to ask someone for information, I would have to be sure it couldn't lead back to me. It occurred to me during the drive that, almost at once, I had decided to steal back the information from Paolo. I would once again bite the hand that fed me. I thought about how I had fallen into this situation, and it made my head ache. The blood pulsed hard in my ears, and red ate away at the corners of my vision. I had been given a job that was more sensitive than I knew. No one had told me I was going up against the Russians; it was a suicide job. Then it hit me — this was Paolo's payback for what I had done. Paolo was finally going to take the Russians down, and he was going to use me to do it. It was fitting, considering it was my fault that violence had resumed after Tommy's death. I had judged the Russians wrong then. They were stronger than anyone knew and they welcomed open war in the streets. The Italians had fought for years since I helped kill Tommy Talarese; dozens of made men had been killed, and millions of dollars had been lost. When I reached out for information, Julian said he wanted to kill me but he wasn't allowed. That was because Paolo wanted the Russians to kill me. He had Julian send me where they were sure to pick me up. Paolo used the Russians against me just as I had used them against him. I'm sure he had some kind of goose-and-gander analogy he found amusing. I wondered if I had been strung along for years by Paolo, or if the situation presented itself and he unleashed the anger he had held in check since I helped free Sandra. I couldn't tell and I wasn't sure I would ever know. Deep down the only thing I was sure of was that it had been a mistake to work for a man like Paolo Donati.

Because I had been so well prepared for this life by my uncle, I had no connections outside my work. My uncle never brought anyone near the house. It might as well have been a space station; it was inaccessible to anything that operated in his working world. He met people in a coffee shop. The shop was owned by the daughter of a very well connected man, so nothing happened there except conversation. It was a franchise shop with a comical robin welcoming all inside the yellow and brown interior. The air was thick with smoke and the smells of coffee and baked sugar. The coffee shop was used as an office and my uncle checked in often. I came along every time, even if business was going to be discussed. Learning how to operate and who to operate with was all part of my education. Some days we were there alone for hours on end. If I was lucky, we sat at one of the tables that doubled as a video game. The thick plastic tabletop was scorched with cigarette burns and covered in a thick layer of grease from food and skin oil from filthy hands. It was the kind of table that destroyed the myth about a three-second rule for dropped food. Anything that touched that table was instant garbage.

I remembered my slippery fingers as I gripped the joystick under the tabletop. I moved Pac-Man around the table under the coffee mugs and plates away from ghosts constantly following me. My uncle encouraged the game as though it were a poor man's chess.

"Rules allow you to win at this game," he said. "Rules. Knowing your rules and theirs — knowing them makes the difference. Once you know their rules you can plan around them. Make their rules work against them. You understand, Will?"

I nodded my response, not daring to take my eyes off the screen. "Yeah," he went on. "The ghosts, they outnumber you, they always will, and if you kill one of 'em word gets back fast, and they send more. They're fast too, faster than you, but they have to follow the same paths as you do. That's how you get them, boy. They follow your trail. You have to make them think they know where you're going. Once you can make them think the way you want them to then you're in control. It doesn't matter if they have more people, or if they're faster. If you're in control they'll be where you want them to be. How can they ever touch you if you don't let them? The plan separates you and them. It makes any situation work in your favour. You plan right, you'll live through anything."

I didn't bother to look up from the screen; he didn't want me to anyway. I thought of my mom and dad. They died — the ghosts ate them whole. I thought about them as I pivoted in a corner, moving back and forth, waiting to be surrounded. Seconds before the armless ghosts touched me I ate the large white ball in the faded corner of the screen and turned the tables. I didn't fight the grin as I screamed over the ghosts, watching their eyes run home. The ghosts were reborn again and again while I ran.

"You use confrontation too much, boy. You always want to fight. Why fight at all when you could be somewhere else? All that fighting slows you down. It makes you slow, predictable. Those ghosts have the numbers to lose to slow you down. They always come back, and soon you'll be in a corner without an advantage."

I didn't answer as I set up in another corner to wait for the ghosts. I pivoted back and forth waiting on them. I watched the yellow and orange spectres close in, moving as one, almost on top of one another. I watched the pair approach and waited for them to enter the corner until one ghost broke from the path and moved to the other side of the corner. Watching the unexpected advance, I moved one step too far. The yellow ghost collided with me, and I watched the mouth of my Pac-Man roll back clockwise into oblivion. I stared at the greasy screen for a second before finally looking at my uncle. He wore a grin on his face. It was cold and scary.

"You got predictable, and the machine made you pay. I knew people who got predictable and it cost them a lot more than a quarter. You know people like that too."

My hands gripped the sides of the game table hard. They slowly slipped away from the edges, sliding on human grease.

"Don't get mad. It's a weakness someone will exploit. You need to be able to think without connection to your emotions. You need to be unpredictable."

I didn't answer.

"Do you want more quarters?"

I nodded, and he slid one across the table. It left a trail in the grime. "I'll keep giving you money to play, but you have to play my way. I want you to avoid all the ghosts. Don't kill any of them. If you do, the money stops."

I played for hours that day until my eyes were bloodshot and my mouth tasted like the foul air surrounding me. I died over and over again at first, but the quarters kept coming — leaving trails in the grease as though they were snails. I watched the table and learned slowly to think ahead of one ghost, then two, then three. After too many hours I began to see the whole table at once. I followed each ghost with my eyes, learning how they moved. Soon I learned how they reacted, and then I survived them. They couldn't touch me anymore. I made a choice not to let them. They floated nearby, but they never touched me.

My uncle ate in silence as I navigated the tabletop universe. I finally looked up after logging my initials into the high-score position for a fourth time. My name was written in a vertical strip under the plastic tabletop. My uncle's face had no grin this time. There was only a smile. "You played them all. They went everywhere you wanted them to go. You controlled them. You were the one in charge even though it's their game and they had the numbers. You can manipulate any situation in your favour. You just have to play it without emotions — without connection." He etched my initials into the table grease with his thumb. Then he got up to leave without saying another word.

I learned to embrace living without connection or emotion. I lived my life disconnected, surviving the world by calculating every move. Then, in one day, I destroyed all of my work, following Steve across town on his homicidal visit to the Talarese residence. I did it because I saw two people connected. Two people who didn't fight to stay below everyone's radar. I remembered two other people who did the same. I refused to let the ghosts take two people who, despite my best efforts, I had connected to. Steve was the closest thing I had to a friend, the closest thing to human contact I had, and I couldn't let that go.

I had tried to manipulate the situation, to see every angle and fight the odds, but I hadn't escaped unscathed. Our violence took too much, and left little to barter with. We had our lives, but I lost my work and my contacts. I spent my life avoiding relationships and connections, and now that life was a prison. I was a ghost on my own, my education slowly killing me.

I never had a graduation. I always spoke of learning from my uncle as though it was an education, but there was no final commencement. There was no ceremony with cap and gown, just gunshots inside a strip club.

I had spent years learning from my uncle, training to be like him. I learned from him, and people he knew who were like him. He introduced me to hard men and women who didn't mind passing on what they knew to a young kid, and through them I developed. I learned from a small man named Rev all I needed to know about guns. He wasn't a man of the cloth; he got his name from the old revolver he kept no more than a heartbeat away in an ankle holster. The little man showed me how to clean, modify, and fire every type of weapon on the street. I spent years in a gym learning from an ex-prizefighter turned enforcer how to really fight — dirty without remorse. Ruby Chu taught me how to grift and steal for months until I picked it up. I had done work-study with anyone who would take me, and it hardened the boy I was into something else. Something unlike everything I came from.

I worked the jobs my uncle scored. No one knew me outside of the people I learned from, and they weren't connected to the kind of work my uncle and I did. I never knew who supplied the work. I just knew that we worked every few months and that the jobs were always different: armoured cars, stores, even banks. Every few months I was told about a job and the planning started. I was never clued into the who or why, just the what and how.

Robbing the strip club was just another new experience to me. I never knew why the Hollywood Strip presented itself as a target worthy of our notice, or why it had to be only the two of us. I was just told it had to be done, so I started getting things ready without question.

We hit the club on a Wednesday. The second night of the week the club was open. I wanted to wait to do it closer to the big money nights, but I was overruled.

The Hollywood Strip had a regular schedule. The club closed at two but the customers never rolled out until half an hour after that. Two weeks of surveillance told me the girls went next. They left through a series of doors coming from an addition built onto the side of the building. The girls came out scrubbed clean in track suits. They looked like they could be regular mothers and wives — if they weren't out at almost three in the morning on a weekday. After the girls came the bartenders and bouncers; they left out the front door. The boss came out last with a final bouncer. The bouncer worked the floor inside and was first on the scene to deal with problems. He was big, well over six-five. His arms and chest were covered in soft flesh, which concealed a powerful frame. He looked like he was unnaturally strong his whole life, the kind of person who was a starter on the senior football team when he was only in the ninth grade. His back was wide — the width of two normal people — and his shoulders were piled high on his back muscles, making him look like he was constantly shrugging. The bouncer was big, but he was out of shape. His gut hung over his belt as though he were concealing a beach ball under his shirt. His head was bald, making the skin tags and lumpy growths on his face and scalp stand out. He was beyond ugly, and most people probably shied away out of equal parts fear and revulsion.

The bouncer walked the boss out every night. Together they punched in the security code and locked up. The owner, a tall Italian man with brown hair combed high on his head, would pull the doors twice after he turned the key, taking the repeated sound of metal on metal as proof the doors were locked. I had seen the owner up close several times when I was working surveillance. His sharp nose and flared nostrils sat below a pair of crazed eyes. His conversations were animated with anger and volume. He spoke constantly about himself, the trips he took, his athletic past, and repeatedly about his growing up in the neighbourhood without a father. He didn't wear suits; instead he wore different warm-up coats adorned with international soccer logos and his name, Rocco, embroidered on the back.

After three weeks of watching, we made our move once the last bartenders and staff drove away. The exterior of the building was painted black, making our dark clothes blend in. We leaned into a spot, between two pillars, used by a hot-dog vender every night until twelve. The cart was gone by the time we got there, but the space concealed us both from the door. The bushes in front of the walkway, which shielded the identity of clientele coming and going, protected us from the road. I held a heavy sap in my right hand, and I had to restrain myself from tapping it against my thigh while I waited. My uncle held a gun pointed at the pavement. His, like mine, was a reliable piece with no history. Guns were part of the job, but we rarely used them. My uncle thought guns brought too much heat, and they let the ghosts know where you were.

We waited twenty minutes for the owner and his bodyguard to lock up. The mechanism on top of the door made a "ffff" sound, letting us know it was slowly pushing open. I heard the boss say in an angry tone, "I used to say what are those old fuckers complaining about? All they do is complain. But I tell you until you feel it you will never know. I can't do anything anymore — I'm too tired. I don't work out as much, and fucking — you can forget that."

A jingle of keys told me it was time to move.

"I went to the chiropractor yesterday and he's starting to

work things out. The pain is out of my ass, but now it's down my leg to my toes. I tell you it kills to move them, but you got to. You got to move them to get rid of the pain. Tonight I won't get to bed until six, maybe later. That's how long it takes me to relax so I can sleep. But when I was young like you I thought these old guys…"

Rocco stopped talking when he saw me club the bouncer behind the ear. The ugly man's hands dropped the gym bag he carried, but he didn't fall. His knees wobbled and he shielded his head. I hit him again with the sap above the fingers he pressed against the first wound. He staggered again but he stayed up — out on his feet.

"Into the club." My uncle's voice was calm; it made it seem like agreement was natural.

We moved into the club without another word. My uncle was in first, covering the two men as they walked back through the door. When the door floated shut, I sapped the bouncer a third and fourth time behind each ear. His staggering stopped, and he went down on two knees before landing face first on the soiled carpet. I turned around and checked the street for anything strange before locking the door. It was then that Rocco got into it.

"You two are dead." His body shook with rage. "You disrespect me like this? Me? You think you two little fucks can rob me and get away with it? Do you know who I am? Do you know how long I've been here? Do you even know who owns this place? You're gonna disrespect me like this? I'm gonna bury you."

"Let's go to the office," my uncle said, his voice still even and calm.

"Fuck you. I'm not going anywhere. You think —" I cut him off, swinging the sap across his jaw. The blow was hard enough to turn his head and break some teeth, but not hard enough to knock him out. I shoved him through the club as he grabbed at his face.

"This way," I said, pushing the club owner, who was dribbling blood on the floor, in front of me. The locked door to his office read "Private." We ignored the sign and the lock, opening the door with the keys the owner kept in his front pocket. Inside I saw several more locks and chains that would keep the door locked from the inside. I remembered wondering why this guy would need to be locked up so tight in this room. I guessed it was for entertainment. I found out later I was wrong.

The room was done in dark grey. The carpet, walls, and couch were all shades of grey. The only interruptions to the grey came from the dark mahogany desk and the art on the walls, which was vibrant and colourful. Each picture depicted great athletic achievements in soccer and football.

"Open the safe." My uncle's voice was still calm and even.

To my surprise Rocco bent and began to open the large safe on the floor behind the desk. He held his jaw in one hand as he clicked the dial left, then right, then left again. He mumbled something that might have been a death threat through his damaged face, then swung the door open. The safe was full of money — a lot more than two nights' take. I loosened the canvas bag on my back and got to work without being told. I worked fast moving the bricks of bills from the safe to my bag.

"Now open the other one."

I paused for a second. *Other one? What other one?* I looked over my shoulder at my uncle. He stared at Rocco, who returned his gaze with his mouth open a little wider than the injury made necessary. My uncle cocked the gun and asked again. The club owner said nothing. My uncle walked closer to him and put the gun to his knee. "Open the other one now or I take the knee. After that it's the other one, then your balls."

I had never known my uncle to do anything like this. Usually he hired a crew so that we never needed anyone to open safes for us. Tonight we had done everything strange. We came on a weird night, and we had no safe man when it was apparent that my uncle knew there would be two safes. Rocco shook his head, and the gun went off. I stared at the two of them until my uncle yelled, "Get the money, boy!"

I got back to work, moving less methodically than I would have liked. The club owner rolled on the ground, mumbling in Italian at us both. My uncle held the gun to the other knee as blood and cartilage spilled onto the floor.

"Obay. Obay. I'll do it," he said through his battered mouth. Rocco dragged his body across the floor. My uncle kept his gun against Rocco's knee the whole way. Rocco opened a mini-fridge in the corner and ripped out the shelving. Leftovers from the buffet splashed out from inside the fridge. The club owner had shrimp on his shirt as he worked his hand deeper inside the fridge. I heard a squeak, and his hand came out with a black bound book. My uncle took the gun off his knee and took the book. Rocco sagged onto the floor. His head stayed in the fridge. My uncle balanced the book on the gun in his hand; his left hand flipped through the pages.

"Motber fubber," was all I heard before my uncle's chest exploded red onto the ceiling. I threw the canvas bag at the fridge and drew the gun from behind my back. I pulled the trigger four times, putting bullets into the side of the fridge and the man's chest. I dropped the gun and ran to check my uncle. He had no pulse, and his chest was not moving. For half a minute I panicked, looking frantically around the room for help that was not there. Something caught my eye and challenged the panic. I looked into my uncle's face and saw that it was blank — completely without expression. I stared at him and realized that he had done something different; he didn't plan this out, and it got him. The ghosts caught up with him in this dingy strip club. I refused to let the ghosts get me too. They had killed enough of my family. I put the book that lay beside his dead body into the duffle full of cash and put it over my shoulder. I picked up my gun and used a tissue from the desk to wipe it down as I walked out to the entrance. I found the body of the bouncer where I left it — face down on the floor. I pressed the gun into his palm, waited five seconds, and then I walked back to the office. I put the gun down under the desk and stowed my uncle's pistol behind my back. I picked up my uncle's body and walked out of the club past the body of the bouncer still on the floor.

An hour later in a remote part of the city, I burned the car we took to the job with my uncle in it. Once the car had charred, I used the switch car to push it into a murky pond. It wasn't a proper burial, but it was much more than other members of the family had gotten. I drove home with the money, the book, and no idea what I was going to do.

I rose the next day and without thinking went to my uncle's coffee-shop office. The newspapers detailed the manhunt for the ugly bouncer who was wanted for questioning about a murder at the Hollywood Strip as well on several outstanding warrants. There was no mention of other blood at the scene or a ballistics discrepancy. They must have been saving that as a way to identify the real killer.

On my third day in the shop, an older man joined me at my Pac-Man table, sitting down with a coffee and a doughnut. I stared up at him from the newspaper and watched as he dunked his doughnut into the coffee. I glanced around the room and noticed that there were a bunch of empty tables, but this old guy had chosen mine.

"Help you, old man?" I asked.

Between bites of doughnut the man spoke. "I gotta tell you, kid, you are a hard one to find. That uncle of yours told me nothing of how the job was going to go down, and when he botched it like he did I thought he ran out on me. But I got wind of a partner he used, and a place they held meetings in. Lucky for me I know the owner so I just had to wait for you to pop up."

"Who are you?" I asked.

"I'm the guy you owe something to," the old man said in a cold voice. He went on without waiting for me to respond. "It's like ants. You know ants, kid? No? Well, ants bring everything back to the hill — it's their job. You found some tasty sugar and you're sitting on it. What're you trying to do, make your own hill?"

"I don't know you, ant man," I said, confused.

"I set up the job you pulled. I gave you all of the details. Now it's time for you to give me my cut."

"This is some grift. You figure me here alone means my partner is dead, so you try to move in. I don't know you, old man, and I'm not buying any of this. Who are you, anyway?"

He took another bite of the doughnut and looked hard at me. "I don't explain myself to anyone, ever, but you're young, kid, so I'll give you a heads-up. My name is Paolo Donati. The place you robbed was mine. I set it up."

The name shocked me. On the street Paolo Donati was all kinds of trouble. He was primed to become boss over the whole city. A red flag went up in my head. Something was off.

"If you are who you say you are, then why use us? You got plenty of people who work for you, why not use them?"

He put the last bite of doughnut into his mouth and looked out the window. He licked his fingertips and then spoke as he probed his molars with his index finger. "Like I said, it's like ants, kid. Most anthills have more than one queen. You know that? More than one? Well, if the ants see one queen is not able to function they will feed the other. Eventually it will die while the other takes over."

I didn't follow right away. It didn't matter because he continued, "That guy in the club was working for me, and it turned out he was trying to build his own anthill...without me."

I got it almost immediately. "He was screwing you out of money and doctoring the books. You used us so no one in your anthill would find out someone was taking advantage. Using us kept you secure in your position." I felt like an ass speaking about anthills, but the man across from me wasn't kidding.

"Yeah, kid, you got it. Now that we know who's who and what's what, let's get this straight. You owe me money and a book. I'm gonna tell you how much, and you're going to give me what I want. I'm going to pay you double for what you did because you killed that thief and framed that ugly bouncer. That worked out better for me than what your uncle planned."

"How much?"

He told me, and I looked out the window, screaming inside my head.

"Don't worry, kid, there's more money. I got lots of money, that is, if you want to work for it." That was the first time I went to work for Paolo. It would not be the last.

After Paolo had cut me loose for killing Tommy, I was left without a job again. I had spent so long living the way I had that there was little chance I could start over fresh. I only knew one kind of life, and that life gave me few options. I couldn't stay in the city — there would be no employment when word got out I was blacklisted, and solo jobs didn't have longevity. Working alone kept the jobs small and the risks high. No one retired from a career of working alone; coffins and cells are lined with cons who thought they could beat the system every time — by themselves. I needed to work my way into another network where I could find bigger jobs with other professionals. I knew of some names in Montreal, so I decided to scout out opportunities there.

I took a week and drove out to Montreal. I spent time in the right places asking for the wrong kind of people. After a few days of looking, the names I asked about sent a car for me. Some of the names I dropped from back home checked out, and I was told there could be work if I proved myself. Proving myself could have meant anything from murder to shooting up in front of an audience. There were all kinds of chest-beating rituals intended to sniff out undercover cops. I didn't trust anyone to set up a job for me, so I said I would think about it and let them know; they gave me a number to call when I had made a decision. I took a cab from the meeting and got out on Boulevard Saint-Laurent. The street, known as locally as "The Main," was full of bars, nightclubs, and restaurants. Even in the early evening the street was crowded with people trying to get a glimpse of the real nightlife of the city. The bloodbath in Hamilton forced me to operate with greater care because I had no idea when I could become a target for what I had done. A new city hundreds of kilometres away was no exception. I used the windows of every restaurant to check the posted menus, and to look behind me using the polished glass as a rear-view mirror. It didn't take me long to see that I was being followed by two men. The reflections I saw several times in the windows made me sure they were tailing me. Seeing two men at once usually meant trouble. One person is a good enough tail — if they're good. Sometimes two people worked together, leapfrogging after a target to lower the odds of the target recognizing a face. Two men together meant something else entirely; it meant there was going to be heavy lifting involved. If the two were pros there was probably a driver out there too, so the team could get away fast.

I stopped at a phone on the street and called the number I had been given at the meeting.

"*Oui?*"

"We just met. Do I have reason to think that there are *two* things you want to see me again about?"

The voice on the phone did not betray any emotion; it just shifted to accented English. "We are waiting for a call. That is it."

I clicked the phone down and kept walking, immersing myself deeper in the crowds. The men I met with denied knowing the two men behind me. It wasn't proof that the men belonged to some other outfit, but it was enough for me to know that they were there to start trouble. I moved quickly and entered the first mall I saw. I crossed the sensors of the first clothing store that appeared and picked a shirt, hat, and glasses from the nearest racks, tore off the tags, gave them to the cashier, and hit the change room. When I came out, I paid for my new outfit and browsed near the front of the store, using the window to look out into the mall. Through the spaces between the frosted letters in the glass I saw throngs of shoppers walking by. I could also see a man loitering by the mall entrance, cell phone in hand, meaning the other man was searching the mall for me.

I walked out of the store and went to the warm pretzel restaurant three stores to the right. I bought a pretzel and a Coke and sat at one of the tables provided out front. I was out of sight from the mall door, so I ate a few pretzels and waited twenty-five minutes. After the pretzels and Coke I got up and checked the door. No one was standing guard, cell phone in hand. I went deeper into the mall, found an ice cream shop, and ate for another half hour. When I finished the ice cream, I asked a girl at the information kiosk where the closest cabs were located. The girl behind the counter told me of an exit on the other side of the mall. On my way to the exit I spotted a mall rat. She was a teenage Goth kid hanging out by herself. She looked dirty — like one of the many homeless of the city. Montreal had a huge number of homeless teenagers who escaped their parents for the club life of the big city. I grabbed the girl by her arm, forcing her to join my pace.

"Hundred bucks if you leave with me."

"No way, loser. Get the fuck off me."

The crazy population of the city made sure nothing surprised this girl anymore. She didn't even seem scared of a strange man offering her money.

"No sex. No date. Just help me get out of here, and you can take the hundred bucks plus cab fare wherever you want to go."

"Why the hell would I go anywhere with you, asshole?"

"Either come or don't, but I don't have time to waste. One fifty, take it or leave it."

Her eyes lit up, and she licked her lips. "Fine. Where's the money?"

"You get it in the cab."

I didn't let her continue the conversation. We walked to the exit and got into a waiting cab. The watchers were looking for one man in different clothes. All they would see leaving was an unhappy man dragging his daughter out of the mall.

"Airport," was all I said to the cab driver.

"*Oui.*"

Two blocks into the ride, I told the driver to pull over. I got out and left two hundreds on the seat. I walked away without saying another word.

I wasn't sure who would be looking for me, especially in Montreal. If I had to guess, it would be the cops. Criminal organizations were big business in Montreal; the city had Italians, bikers, even Russians of their own. The organized crime guys must have seen me leave a hot spot and tailed me for an ID. I moved around the city for a few more hours, checking for a tail, but I never found one. After I decided I was clean, I took a cab back to my car. I had stashed it at an expensive city parking-garage a block away from the motel I was staying in. I travelled light so all that was in the motel room was a change of clothes in a duffle bag. I decided to leave clean, dropping the motel key down a sewer grate before paying up for the car and driving home.

When I got back into town I checked my office and found only one change: there was a plain unaddressed white envelope on the floor inside the door. The letter contained a piece of paper with a phone number on it. The digits indicated it was a cell number. Out of curiosity, I dialled it.

"I was looking for you."

The voice registered immediately — it was Paolo Donati. Our conversation was short — all that was said was a meeting place and a time. I had to haul ass to make it out of the city to a small-town restaurant that served all-day breakfast. I got there first and took a corner booth where I could eye the exit. The booth would also give me a chance to slip into the nearby kitchen if need be. Kitchens are always busy, and fire codes mean they always have exits. I checked before I came in — the kitchen exit was on the right. It was a standard door, which would open easily so the kitchen staff could get to the Dumpster with their hands full. I carried the Glock inside a folded newspaper into the restaurant. I could have cared less about the news; the paper let me blend in, and it hid my gun in plain sight. I looked like any other customer, but I was one who could pull a gun without making any grand gestures.

As I sat, I scanned the restaurant. There was no one looking my way, no one on a cell phone, and no one who suddenly got up to use the rest room. It was an odd choice for a meeting place, but it seemed clean.

Right on time, Paolo Donati made his way into the restaurant. He was an old man, but he looked fit. His hard, pointed nose showed signs of being broken several times. His dark eyes were hard, and they scanned the room, taking everyone in while simultaneously sending out a don't-fuck-with-me message. He wore green slacks and a blue nylon golf pullover. He looked like a golfer from a distance. Up close, he looked like someone who had just robbed and stripped a man on his way to the links. He wore a heavy grey wool cap, like the old-time golfers wore; it covered the immaculate haircut that framed his head in silver.

His eyes spotted me right away but went over the room twice more. A passing waitress saw him looking and said, "Just grab a seat, hon, I'll be right with you."

He didn't miss a beat; he gave her a sweet smile and said, "I just saw my friend. I'll be fine. Thank you, dear."

He didn't stroll with the languid gait I had seen on many occasions. He shuffled like a man his age should have walked.

"Nice walk," I said as he approached.

"It helps to blend in."

I shook my head. "You don't blend in. The golfer's outfit is wrong. You'd look better in a casual suit. Like a guy with money who still likes the simple stuff," I said.

All I got was a cold stare for a reply. We sat silent, waiting to order, then continued to say nothing while we waited for our food. Finally, after the food arrived and the waitress left, Paolo told me why we were there.

"I fired you for good reason."

"No argument here. It could have been much messier," I said.

"Everyone thinks you're out with me."

"I *am* out with you."

"You aren't out of shit, *figlio*."

I knew the word *figlio* meant *son*. I heard enough Italian over the years to decipher bits and pieces. Whatever the translation, he used the word like a boot, shoving me down into my place.

"I let you off. Never forget that. You didn't earn, justify, prove, or bribe anything from me. I decided your fate. You breathe because I had a single thought that you might be useful."

I took in the rant and thought it over. What he said wasn't false. The only missing part would have been the expense of killing me. It would have been hard, costly, and pointless. "The point is I'm out," I said between sips of tea.

"Fuck, you really are stupid, aren't you. You are what I say you are, and no one is going to hire you until I decide I'm done with you. Not even those bilingual criminals. Oh, don't look surprised, I know all about the little introduction you had. It's good you came home because I was ready to make sure no one would be looking to give you work."

I took another sip of tea. The man across the table controlled my immediate future; he could make things easy or very, very hard. I decided to hear him out.

"What's on the table, Paolo?" I asked.

He smiled then. It was the smile a cat would have on its face when the mouse finally gave up and stopped running. I hated that look and I promised myself I would remember it, and someday pay it back.

"We on a first-name basis all of a sudden? You and me equals now? What part of the city is yours? 'Cause I own fucking everything. Now shut up and listen. You're gonna work for me like before, but this time no one will know you fucking exist."

I had to admit I liked how this was going. It already sounded natural to me.

Paolo went on, "A man like me is always surrounded by people who are looking to take information and put it to use. Many people in my own organization would take me down if they could. I need someone no one would trust. Someone with no allegiances who will work jobs I set up. You'll get things for me, private things, on people who work for and against me, and you'll deal only through Julian.

That way I stay on top, and you stay employed. And if you get an idea to rip me off, to take from me? Well, I got an army who would love to know what really happened to Tommy."

"I'm not going to become a contract killer for you."

"I want information only. I don't need you to kill anyone."

"How much does it pay?"

"More."

Paolo didn't wait for me to say yes. He stood up. "Thanks for breakfast, *figlio*. Julian will be in touch." And he walked out.

I paid for breakfast. *What the hell?* I figured. *I have a job. I can afford it.*

CHAPTER TEN

I had a cramped timetable for getting back what I had already stolen. The Russian demand of twenty-four hours didn't give me enough time for finesse. I had no idea who Paolo Donati would contact to hack some encrypted disks. If I started asking around it would take longer than a day to find out, and word of it would leak up, leaving me blocked out or dead. My only option was to go at the problem head-on. I had to find someone in the know and grind what I needed out of them. I also had to get the information in a way that wouldn't leave any traces back to me. It would not be in my best interest to make things right with the Russians only to have more problems with the Italians. Paolo wanted me dead. I didn't know why he chose now to pay me back, but his intentions were clear. I had to weather the storm with the Russians so I could settle up with Paolo later.

I really only had one name to choose from — Julian. Julian was Paolo's second; he knew where all the bodies were buried. Julian would know who the disks were sent to and why. He wouldn't appreciate being squeezed, so I would have to make it hard on him. If I did it right, he would keep his mouth shut. If Paolo found out that Julian gave up information to me, he'd have the life expectancy of milk in the sun. Julian would have to keep quiet about what I did and wait for a time to deal with me privately.

After the business with Steve and Sandra, I had decided to find out where all of the major players lived. I knew where Julian lived, but there were few times when he was alone and unaccounted for. He worked whatever hours Paolo worked, and Paolo was a workaholic. The hours Julian spent at home in his condo were sporadic. Julian's condo also offered a high degree of security: there were guards in the building, in addition to whatever measures of his own he took to secure his home. I'd have to hit him between point A and point B. Point A was the restaurant; point B was his condo. I looked at my watch. It was 9:30 p.m. I still had time to do what needed to be done.

I took a cab from outside the office to the local hockey rink, which was always busy at night with games of shinny going on into the early morning. I stole an old Ford pickup with a large empty bed and headed away from the city to a garden centre on a back road in a quiet neighbouring town. It was still warm enough that a lot of the supplies were kept outdoors. I picked the padlock on the gate out front, drove in, and parked the truck beside a pile of garden stones. I piled as many of the huge garden stones as I could into the bed of the truck. Each stone pushed the shocks farther and farther down on the wheels. With the truck full, I drove out of the lot and onto the shoulder of the road. In the glow of the rear lights of the truck, I relocked the gate. I got back behind the wheel and headed back into the city. The truck lurched like a drunk, but when the odometer hit fifty the pickup was as solid as a sledgehammer.

I drove to the restaurant and parked in a lot on the corner; the dashboard clock read 11:23. I could see Julian's car parked out front. It was a Cadillac sedan, black, tinted, powerful, and fast. There was another vehicle parked out front: the black Escalade that transported Paolo everywhere he went. The fact that there were two cars in front of the restaurant told me Julian would be driving himself home eventually.

I spent the next two hours waiting in the silent truck staring at the two vehicles in front of the restaurant. At 1:13 there was finally movement. The lights went out in the windows, and the doors opened. Two men in suits came out first; they scanned the area before nodding towards the door. Three men left the restaurant and joined the two; among them were Paolo and Julian. Paolo got into the back of the suv with another man, and the two men in suits got in front. Julian waited alone in the street and watched the car pull away. He stood in the street for a full minute, waiting for something I couldn't see, then he walked to the Cadillac and shoved his body in. The car rocked from the impact of his huge body against the frame. I started the pickup and drove around the block.

The truck lurched forward, building speed slowly. After a minute, I was moving above the speed limit. I hung a left on a one-way street and used the road to connect to the street Julian would be taking. The truck slid a little as I rounded the corners, and there was a hard jolt when I pressed the gas pedal down to accelerate again. Pedal to the floor, I moved up the road looking for the black Cadillac. As if the heavens were looking down on me, I saw the car, alone, stopped at a light two hundred metres ahead.

As I approached the intersection I craned my neck to check the cross streets, saw no one coming. I yanked the wheel left and then hard to the right and swerved the weighted truck through the intersection like a right hook into the driver's side of Julian's car. I pulled my hands up to my face and shielded my head as the two cars collided. The impact shot through my body, and I felt ribs strain under the pressure of the seat belt. The frame of the old truck held, and I woke up after what felt like a long blink to find my legs still able to move, and the engine still clucking.

I pulled the emergency brake and kicked the dented side door open. I freed the gun from behind my back and held it with two hands as I approached the window of the Cadillac and looked inside. The window was shattered and the air bag had deployed, but no Julian. I bent to look deeper in the car and saw his body half out the passenger-side window. The direction of the impact and lack of seat belt had sent him flying sideways. The side impact beams kept Julian inside and the shape of the car somewhat recognizable, but the sheer force of the impact must have rocked Julian hard. Quickly I moved to the opposite side of the Cadillac. Julian's head and shoulders were out the passenger side window; he was semi-conscious and no good to me. He mumbled something in Italian through his bloody face when his glazed eyes saw me. I swore at him under my breath for not buckling up, then put him all the way out with the butt of the Glock. Killing Julian would let everyone know that the accident wasn't just a simple hit and run, and it wouldn't take long for Paolo to tie the hit on Julian to the disks; they would be gone forever after that. There were no cars nearby, but a set of lights approached in the distance. I reached in through the window and did a quick frisk. I pocketed Julian's wallet and a cell phone, and went back to the truck. I pulled myself in behind the wheel, leaving the broken door open. I released the emergency brake and put the truck in reverse. The engine chugged, but the truck made a choppy lurch back, slamming the broken side door into place. I moved away from the Cadillac and drove straight down the street. After a minute, I passed a car; the driver's stare at the wrecked front end of the truck was illuminated for me in the streetlights. I pulled a right as soon as I could and got off the main road. I found a parking lot a hundred metres from the road behind a closed Pizza Pizza, shut off the truck, and used my sleeve to wipe down the interior. I left the truck there and found a cab two blocks away. Police cars, sirens blaring and lights flashing, passed the cab on their way to the mess I left behind.

I changed cabs a few times to make sure no one was following me and got back to the office at 2:17 a.m. I put my gun, Julian's wallet, and the phones I took from Igor and Julian on the desk, then looked for whatever food I had on hand. I found some mixed nuts and a Coke. I ate and drank with relish before I even considered the phones. When I finished the food, I looked at Julian's phone. It was a slim model — modern and new. I pulled up the call history and clicked through until I found the date of the airport robbery. I checked the call log and saw that Julian had called a cell number minutes after I handed him the bag.

I took a deep breath and called the number. After six rings I got a sleepy, "Hello?"

"You done with the disks yet?" I asked in a gruff voice.

"What the fuck? Who is this?"

I asked again, and after another foul response I hung up. I went back to the call log and found the next number Julian had called that day. I tried the second number and got a much better response.

"Julian? I told you it'd take at least a week. Why are you calling me now?" There was a pause, then a hushed whine: "Aw, jeez, ya woke up Ma, now she's gonna be pissed."

I worked hard to make my voice deeper like Julian's and I tried to talk like him. "Listen, I got another disk with some things the boss said would help. Codes he said you'd need. Important information. But it can't be dropped off. These shits we took it from are looking hard at us. I need to hand it off to you. You need to meet me this morning. Now."

The whiny whisper took on a scared tone. "Look, Julian," said the Voice, "I don't mean no disrespect, but I can't get involved with that. I promised Ma I was clean now. Aw, crap. Hold on." His words were muffled under a cupped hand as he told his mother that the call was a wrong number and he was just hanging up.

When the Voice came back I decided to press my luck. "Fine," I said. "I got an idea that will work out. Something no one will expect. No one will see this coming. I'll FedEx the disk to you. Give me your address."

There was a pause. "Julian? You know where I live."

There was a hint of question in the words, so I turned up the volume. "Who the fuck are you? You say no to me and I let it slide. I don't even press you. I decide to help you out 'cause I feel bad for your ma, and you start questioning me? You gotta make a choice, A or B, it's up to you. You can either worry about your mother or yourself, because in a few seconds I'm gonna find someone else to do your job, and then I won't care so much about you...or your mother."

"Julian...I...Julian, I'm sorry I —"

"Shut the fuck up. Stay quiet. Don't say anything to me. Just listen. I'm not the fucking post office. I can't send shit without all of the information that they want on the label. I want the address, the postal code, everything. Now!"

It all came out as soon as I finished yelling. Once the Voice stopped pleading and gave me what I asked for, I was moving. I picked up Julian's wallet and Igor's cell phone off my desk and opened the closet. I pulled a black windbreaker over my untucked shirt and pocketed a black watch cap. I removed the panel in the back of the closet and put in the wallet and cell phones. I took the sawed-off shotgun out for the second time, sliding it under my arm. Then I went back to my desk and used a Swiss Army knife to cut two holes into the material of the watch cap. I pulled it on and checked my vision through the holes. After a little adjusting and finger tearing, I had clear vision through the hat. I rolled the cap and put it in my back pocket. I stowed the Glock behind my back and flattened the back of the jacket over the holster.

My shoulders were starting to knot from the collision. I was tired and wanted nothing more than to eat then sleep for a month. But I couldn't stop, I couldn't slow down. If I lost momentum, I would lose the element of surprise — the only edge I had. I did two minutes' worth of stretching to loosen my shoulders and back. The final stretch was to get a bottle of Advil. I put four of the sweet tablets into my mouth and chewed them as I walked out of the office.

In the car, I drove just above the speed limit. I didn't want to draw any cop's attention. I was just another poor schlub off a late shift trying to get home a little quicker. The address the Voice gave me was on the other side of town. I pushed my way through the sparse traffic towards the Voice and his mother wishing I could slow down, but knowing I couldn't. The call put the Voice on edge, and I had to get there before the whimpering fear I yelled into him turned into afterthoughts that would question the whole phone call. I found the building and circled it twice, looking for heads illuminated in cars by my headlights. Those types of heads are like alligator eyes above the water, watching in dark silence for anything to come too close. I saw no one watching, and no one waiting, so I parked around the side of the building and got out. I opened the trunk and hid from the streetlight behind the open lid. From under a blanket, I retrieved the sawed-off shotgun and slid it up the side of my windbreaker so I could hold it tight to my body with the side of my bicep. I closed the trunk and walked around to the front of the high-rise. My walk was odd; the bulges from the watch cap and pistol clashed with the awkward gait caused by holding a shotgun to my body using my elbow.

I eyed each car I passed, looking for anything strange,

but everything seemed clear. I took one last look around as I made a right off the sidewalk up to the Voice's building. Like most inner-city apartment buildings, this one had two sets of glass doors: one to enter the building from the street, another to the entryway that contained the elevators. The inner doors were sealed from the elements, and the old fan above pumped in the thick, untreated city air. I entered and simultaneous scents of cooked food, exhaust, and sweat filled the glassed-off partition like a gas chamber. There were no night watchmen or innocent bystanders in this building; the building was too poor and unsafe for either. I looked up and around and saw no cameras and no security system. The only sign of technology was the intercom, and that had a fist-sized hole in it. Through the smudges on the glass, I could see a stairwell and an elevator that would lead to the twelfth-floor apartment I was looking for. After one more look around, I made my awkward walk back to the car. I opened the trunk again and pulled a crowbar up from under the blanket. I shut the trunk and then wedged the crowbar under my left arm. I held it up pressed against my left side, forcing my walk to be even more constricted. Witnesses would remember the odd walk more than any other physical details. They would also not be concerned enough at the sight of me to call the police because they saw no evidence of a crime; they just saw another fellow resident afflicted by life in Hamilton's hard core.

The walk back was uneventful. Once inside the first set of glass doors, I let the shotgun slip down into my hand so I could place it on the dirt-caked floor mat. I let the crowbar loose next and forced it into the space between the inside doors. I pushed it in, wiggling it back and forth until I had it jammed far enough in to support some pressure. In one hard motion, I bent the metal door frame and cracked the glass, but with the destruction came a satisfying movement to the door. I picked up all I brought, concealed it once again, and hit the stairs.

On floor twelve, I opened the stairwell door quietly and checked the hall. No sound came through the crack in the door. The artificial ceiling light created the quality of perpetual midday. I waited a full three minutes in the stairwell, watching for any sign of life. When I was convinced there was none, I entered the hall and moved towards apartment 1207. I stopped in the hallway when I came upon the elevator. I pushed the button and waited, listening to the grinding of gears. Moments later, an artificial chime signalled the elevator's arrival. I stood off to the side and waited while the metal doors opened. No sounds came from the elevator car. I looked in and saw it was empty of people and cameras. I waited until the doors started to close; there was no sound letting anyone know it was about to happen, just an abrupt shifting of machinery and a scraping of metal on metal. I pushed the doors back open and used the crowbar to wedge them ajar. Satisfied that the bar would hold, and that no one would be using the elevator, I moved down the hall to 1207. At the door I listened carefully for any sounds from inside. I heard the faint sounds of a television, but I couldn't be sure if it came from inside or next door.

I stood a step away from the doorknob and moved my eyes over the locks. There were two locks: one standard mechanism above the doorknob, and a much heavier dead-bolt a few inches above that. There was no way to account for a door chain on the other side. I didn't think there would be one — usually the chains are only on doors with three or more locks. One extra lock means cautious, but not para-noid. Most cautious people buy deadbolts and self-install them to save money. This lock was more than likely self-installed because no self-respecting locksmith would put a deadbolt in crooked. It looked like a shit job, but the lock itself was a quality heavy-duty item. I couldn't waste time trying to pick the locks. The hallway was too bright for me to be inconspicuous, and the noise of the picks in the two locks might put the Voice on to me. I looked away from the locks to the door frame; it looked old. I dug into the wood with my thumbnail, and a piece came off with ease. The two steel locks were sitting in old rotted wood. Whoever put the second lock in never thought about how the door frame would handle the stress of being assaulted.

I stepped back from the door and took one last look down the hallway before rolling the watch cap over my head. I adjusted it with my one free hand until I could see clearly through the holes I made. I lowered the shotgun from under my jacket and rolled my shoulders to get the kinks out from the awkward posture I had been holding. Once I felt loose and my breathing was controlled, I stepped back until my back touched the opposite wall. The hall-way gave me only four or five good steps from one side to the other. I moved back and forth over the distance twice, working on getting a rhythm to my steps and my foot place-ment. On my second practice, I let my foot extend within inches of the door, aiming six inches to the left of the two locks. Then, crossing the floor for the third time, I hit it.

The impact of my foot drove the door inward. The bolts tore, like blunt claws, through the old wood frame. I planted my foot inside and used my shoulder to take the impact of the door swinging back on itself.

The room was dark, and the light from the hallway spilled in, illuminating the small tiled entryway I was standing in. In front of me was a closet. To the right the tile continued into a bathroom, lit only by a faint night light. A flicker from my left brought my eyes and the shotgun over to the television, which was casting soft light onto a couch where an old woman sat. The flickering glow of the television made the wrinkles on her frightened old face stand out.

"You must be mom," I said. "Sit there and don't move."

I used my free hand to push the front door closed. The exposed bolts caught on the splinters they left when they tore free, and the door stayed closed. The woman on the couch stared at me, unflinching. Ahead of me I saw an alcove kitchen and two doors. One of the doors slammed shut. I sprinted across the room and kicked the door open. Inside, staring at me, a young Italian man was frantically dialling a phone. I gripped the shotgun with both hands and drove the stock into his face. The blow knocked him off of his feet straight onto his back like he had fainted.

I scanned the room fast. A heavy desk lamp was the only light source. Two laptop computers were on an old brown desk set that looked cheaply painted, and an old stained futon rested against the left wall. There was no other furniture in the room. The only decorations were posters — Pacino as Scarface and a porn star staring out from the wall with seductive eyes. I looked on the desk for the disks but saw only DVD cases, paper, and a few photos in frames. I recognized a face in one of the frames and hesitated for a second. The face was with four others, all of them gazing out from a soccer field. The five young men looked sweaty, tired, and happy. One kid held up his finger, wordlessly telling everyone they were number one. I knew the kid and his face. I thought about the features, the dyed blond hair, the patchy stubble, and the small mouth. I had seen the features at the airport; they belonged to Nicky — the amateur bagman I stole the disks from. Before he and his co-workers had been cleaned by the Russians, Mike had told me no one knew why Nicky volunteered to do the trade at the airport. He said no one had done anything like that before so no one challenged him; they were probably relieved that anyone volunteered. It was clear now that the amateur had set up his own scam with Paolo and his crew through his friend the Voice. The bagman had been out for himself, and he had set up a deal with Paolo that cut his friends and the Russians out of the loop. The Voice was the link back to the beginning.

I spoke at the rapidly blinking eyes staring up at me from the floor. "Give me the disks now." The voice I used had a terrible Russian accent attached to it.

"I don't know…"

I kicked him hard in the groin, and he curled up tight, screaming. I used the shortened barrel of the gun to straighten him out. "The disks, or I take your foot, then your mother's." The accent was better the second time.

"In…in…in the desk," he told me.

I opened the drawer and saw several unmarked CDs. I had to be sure they were what I needed. I cocked the shotgun and turned to the quivering mass on the floor. I took aim at his foot and took a slow, loud breath.

"Okay, okay they're in the floor."

"Get," was all I said, hoping my surprise didn't leak through.

The kid slid onto his belly and crawled toward the futon. He yanked free a patch of flooring and pulled a worn and battered lockbox from a space below the floor. I smiled under the mask just before I spun wildly.

CHAPTER ELEVEN

My body whirled in a circle and I fell toward the futon. The bullet in my left arm made me a human dreidel. I shot back through the door with both barrels and saw the body of the old woman leave her feet. The revolver she held fell sideways out of her hands onto the floor. In my haste I had written her off, and as a reward she shot me.

"Ma!" The Voice screamed as he lunged off the floor. I couldn't stand fast enough so I grabbed his legs as he ran to the door. I pulled him to the floor and began clawing up his legs toward his torso. He was wild, and I was shot. Holding him was impossible, so I used my head. I rammed my head into the back of his skull, hard, taking away some of his spunk. The second and third head butts made his body slacken.

I got to my feet and grabbed a pillow from the futon. I used the pillowcase to carry the shotgun, lockbox, and the two laptops. I walked out the door without looking at Ma and found the crowbar still in place in the elevator; I got on and kicked it free. As I descended, I put the crowbar into the pillowcase. When I straightened up, I caught sight of myself in the reflective surface of the doors; the left arm of the windbreaker was taking on a wet sheen. My arm was starting to hurt, and I was starting to feel faint.

I managed to get to the car without passing out. I clumsily held the bag and the back of my left arm with my right hand the whole way. The blood soaked between my fingers and rolled down the nylon fabric of the jacket. I pulled off the watch cap and folded it over, then worked it up under the coat until it was over the wound. The placement made me wince, but I pushed hard on the wound, hoping to slow the blood flow.

The keys were slippery in my fingers, but I got the car started. After three blinks, which took twelve semiconscious seconds, I put the car in drive and watched the apartment building roll by the passenger window.

The driving was hard. I used my injured arm to hold the bottom of the steering wheel while my good arm held the dampening hat to the bullet hole. Every now and again I had to use both arms to painfully turn a corner. I drove, too slow, all the way to Sully's Tavern.

I pulled to the curb right in front of the door. It took me three tries to pull the keys from the ignition. On the third try I used my nails to get enough friction to pull the bloody keys from the steering column. I opened the door and took far too long to realize that the rhythmic beeping I heard was coming from the car I had just turned off — the lights were still on. I fumbled with the lights and got them off after two attempts with slick fingers. When I got to the tavern door the lights were off. Ten feet to the right was the door to upstairs. I walked to the door; it took sixteen small steps. I leaned on the buzzer for half a minute. When I released the button, it was red with blood. A voice greeted me, sleepy and pissed off.

"Huh?"

"Steve, it's Wilson... I need... help here."

The door buzzed, and I pulled it open. Steve was already coming down the stairs in a pair of boxers. His hard body, menacing in the stairway light, contrasted with his shaggy bed hair; he looked like a clown in a prison yard.

He helped me up the stairs to the kitchen. "You need to move my car and wipe it down, your door buzzer too. There's a bag and a gun on the seat. I need them... please."

Steve left wordlessly while Sandra, in a robe, pulled the windbreaker off me. It crinkled and cracked with caked dry blood. Sandra had seen cuts and bruises, but never bullet holes. She took a long look at me then stood and went to the phone.

"No doctors."

"But you're shot. I can't help you. You need a doctor. You could die."

"I know people who can take care of it, but not tonight," I said.

She took a deep breath and let it out slowly. "What can I do?" Her voice sounded defeated but also a little angry.

"Just tape gauze around it and cover it in plastic wrap. Try to clean me up so I don't look shot."

"You look like hell," she said. "You're pale, white as a ghost."

"Sandra, please, just help me. I'll be okay. I have a job to finish, then I'll get some help."

Pissed, Sandra left the room and came back with two washcloths, gauze, medical tape, and alcohol. She cut the shirt off me with kitchen scissors and used the washcloths to clean the blood off my upper body. Steve came in and put the pillowcase down by the door as Sandra was trying to tape gauze to the wound. The gauze had fallen off twice, and she kept having to start again. Wordlessly Steve understood. He pushed the gauze down hard and helped Sandra tape. I grunted with the pain of Steve's first aid, but he never let up.

When they had taped the gauze down I said, "Plastic wrap."

Steve went to the counter as Sandra spoke. "Why do you need that?"

"If you put it on tight and tape it down it will hold everything together and make it less bulky under a shirt. It will hide what happened," I said.

"Why would you want to hide it?"

"So no one else finds out it happened and tries to do the same thing again," Steve said.

His answer summed up the issue and it was good enough for Sandra. She used one hand to tilt my neck so she and Steve could wrap over my shoulder. This time Sandra wasn't as afraid, or tender. Nothing fell on the floor; she pushed hard with the plastic wrap, making sure the dressings would hold.

"Car hid?" I asked.

"Yep," was all he said as the box of plastic wrap went around and around my bicep.

The bullet had hit me high in the back of the arm. I couldn't see a hole in the front, so the slug still had to be in the meat of my arm. The nature of the wound meant that I could still lift my arm and move it in toward my body using my bicep, but any pushing movement was out of the question.

Steve spoke so quietly it was hard to hear him over the hum of the fridge. "The arm looks like shit. You can't leave it like this."

"It won't be like this long," I said. "Can I get a shirt off you?"

Sandra left the room without a word. Seconds later, I heard drawers opening and slamming. She came back with a high school sweatshirt.

"No good. People will know it's not mine, and it could be traced back to you. I need something like a plain long-sleeve shirt, dark just in case blood leaks through."

She left the room again without a word. "She's pissed," I said. Steve didn't respond. "Where's the car?"

"Around back. Beside the Dumpster. You can't see it from the road."

"It won't be there long. In the morning I need some pants, new ones, yours are too small. After that I'm gone."

Sandra came back in with a long-sleeve shirt. Its surface had a waffled pattern like long johns. The shirt was old and dark blue; it reminded me of the type of shirt a construction worker would wear under his flannel.

"Thanks," I said. "For everything. I just need to rest for a while. In the morning I'll be gone."

"Eat whatever you want, I'll get you pants in the morning."

Steve and Sandra got up to go to bed. Steve slapped my back as he walked by and chuckled when I gasped. Sandra was only able to manage a weak smile as she passed me. The bedroom door closed quietly. I heard the wood rub against the jamb and then a loud slam completing the seal. I could hear the sound of quick discussion going on inside the room, but there was no yelling.

With my right hand I pulled the Glock from the holster at my back and put it on the table. Quietly I got up and moved to the fridge. There weren't any leftovers, so I took an apple. I winced as I bent to get it from the crisper. I ate the apple silently as I looked through the cupboards. I pulled a box of strawberry Pop-Tarts down and took them to the table. I ate the rest of the apple and the entire box of high-calorie pastries without pause. The sugary crap went down slow, but I was suddenly too exhausted to get up for a drink. When I was done, I slept face down at the table.

At seven-thirty Steve slapped my head lightly, waking me up. I put the Glock behind my back right away and looked at Steve.

"Pants," was all he said.

"Thirty-two in the waist and thirty-four in the leg. Some kind of work pants, khakis, the kind that won't rip easy."

I stood up, shakily, and gave Steve three twenties. "Grab some of those caffeine drinks too."

Steve left without another word, and I had three more apples. I sat with my legs crossed, waiting for Sandra to finish in the bathroom. She must have gone in while I was face down at the table. Twenty agonizing minutes later she walked past the kitchen, hair up in a towel, dressed in a faded pink robe. I moved slow into the foggy, cramped bathroom and sat, because, shaky as I was, it would be neater. When I finished, I looked in the mirror at the shirt Sandra had given me. It was clean; no blood had leaked through overnight. The pattern in the shirt even made the bulge of the bandage less noticeable.

Steve came back half an hour later as I was stretching in the kitchen, using one arm on the counter to stabilize me. The car crash, gunshot, and nap at the table had left me aching in every possible way. He threw the pants at me, and I managed to catch the bag with my right hand. I put it on the counter and pulled free the pants and two four packs of Red Bull. I put the holster and Glock on the counter and dropped my pants on the spot. If Steve cared he didn't show it. The work pants were olive green and they fit fine. Steve left the room as I transferred my belt to the new pants, and came back with a blue button-up oxford-cloth shirt.

"To cover up the gun," was all he said.

The shirt fit a little snug, but left unbuttoned it was a good fit, and it concealed the Glock better than the tight blue shirt.

I chugged three Red Bulls without pausing and smiled as the liquid caffeine hit me. "Steve," I said. "Thanks for everything."

"What are friends for? Car keys are in your pillowcase."

I yelled, "Thanks, Sandra."

She screamed something back about a doctor. As I picked up the pillowcase heavy with lockbox, laptops, and shotgun, I caught Steve's eye.

"You need me, you call," he said.

"I won't."

"You need me, you call," he said again, and then he turned around and walked back into the bedroom to see Sandra.

I went down the stairs riding an artificial buzz. I didn't slip and I didn't fall. My car was out back where Steve had said he left it. When I opened the door a heavy smell of cleaning products wafted off the interior. Steve must have given the car a once-over. I thought to myself, a friend who will clean up dried blood for you is a friend for life.

I drove back to the office without any swerving or accidents, parked the car, and slowly walked up the stairs to the office. I moved cautiously, but there was no one waiting for me in the stairs or the hallway.

In the office, I made a strong cup of tea and sat by the window, letting it work its magic. Outside the city had woken. People scurried out of their holes and went frantically to their posts. They all wore the same uniform at this hour. The men were in pleated pants, pressed shirts, ties, but no jackets. The women all had skirts of sensible lengths accessorized with sensible heels. These were the middle-class urban go-getters. They were into the office first, coffee in hand, and out last, migraine in head. They would all be promoted by thirty, and dead by fifty.

The minutes clicked by, and each second was marked by a throb in my arm. I went to the bathroom and brought back the bottle of Advil, using one arm and my teeth to force open the child-proof top. Eight of the pills went into my mouth, and I winced at the bitter taste underneath the sweet coating. I couldn't risk trying to get anything stronger from the contacts I had in the city. It would be a dead giveaway to anyone looking for a person who was shot last night. The hard stuff wouldn't help me now anyway. I had to keep my head clear for everything that was to come.

I winced as I got up and went to the closet. I clumsily moved the invisible panel out of the back of the closet with my one good arm. I put the shotgun in, knowing that I needed to get rid of it as soon as possible, and pulled out the cell phone I took off Igor. Getting the panel back in place was a challenge, but I managed — dampening my forehead with exertion in the process. I powered up the cell phone, dialled the number I had watched Mikhail enter not long ago. After two rings, I was greeted in Russian.

"Get me Sergei."

"I am very sorry," said a voice that suddenly contained no trace of an accent. "There is no one here by that name at this number."

"Tell him it's Wilson and it's done."

"I believe you are confused, sir. I think…"

"Do you have call display?"

"Sir, you are…"

"Do you have call display?"

"Yes sir, we do, but I don't…"

"Listen, you tell Sergei I'll be waiting for his call at this number."

I hung up the phone without another word and waited. It was one minute before Igor's cell phone chirped. I let it ring three times before I answered.

"*Da?*" I said.

There was a long pause before I heard a response. "You

have what we spoke of?" It was the same calm, cool, heavily accented voice I'd heard before. The pause before he spoke let me know I had cracked the facade he was putting on.

"*Da,*" I said.

"Cut the shit. You are on thin ice as it is. You have done things no one would dare, and now you speak to me with a smart mouth?" The crack in his facade had burst wide open.

I thought of the death squad who attacked the computer geeks and decided to can the humour. "I have all of it."

"You are sure?"

"The disks and everything that touched them are here."

"You will bring it to the place you visited yesterday."

He didn't want to mention specifics, and that suited me fine, but in the shape I was in there was no way I could walk away from a meet with the Russians again. "No deal, Sergei. You will come pick it up at the same spot you sent those two shitheads to the other day."

"I told you to watch your mouth. You are testing my patience, boy."

"There's no way I'm walking into your house holding a bag that protects me right until I hand it over. You meet me. Come and claim your property, and I mean it like I said it. You claim it."

His voice got louder in the earpiece, and some of the *w*'s started to slip to *v*'s. "I will not come, I will send some associates of mine to collect my property. One of them remembers you, and demands to meet you again."

"When?"

"Soon. Stay put."

There wasn't much else I could do in the position I was

in. I was hurt and outnumbered. I didn't have the time or the energy to scout out a spot for an exchange with Sergei's men. The office was the best spot I had. Sergei knew that I made it through an ambush here, and now I had the advantage of being here first — it was the only advantage I would have. He would have to be careful, and whoever he sent would have to be better than Igor and Gregor — much better. I couldn't fight it out with Sergei's men in the condition I was in. I needed insurance, so I got up and went to the pillowcase. I reached inside past the laptops, and thumbed open the latch on the lockbox. Inside was a stack of disks. The CDs were unlabelled and encrypted, so I had no idea which ones contained the most incriminating data. I pulled a disk from the middle of the stack and walked to my desk.

I was already fucked with the Italians. The poor Russian accent I used with the Voice would put Paolo off my scent, but he would suspect me eventually. I had time with Paolo. He wouldn't let on his suspicions to his crew because it would be an admission that he didn't trust them to run the job on the Russians. That kind of admission of doubt would hurt him. He would have to take me quietly with someone he trusted. Maybe Julian, once he healed. Whatever was coming from Paolo would take time, and time was something I didn't have with the Russians. Once I gave up what they wanted, I would be on the wrong side of a bullet. I stole from them and killed men from their ranks. I had to rely on the idea that whatever was on those disks was important enough to keep me breathing. A kill squad hit the black-mailing accountants with no mercy; that kind of brazen effort meant whatever was taken was worth more than the cost of the heat the police would bring. Even more telling was the urgency from both sides. Everyone wanted me to finish the job quick. Paolo gave me a day before they would handle me themselves, and the Russians did the same. The short time frame from both sides meant one thing — war was coming. Taking the disks was an all-out declaration of war. But Paolo knew that the risk could be minimized if he could put the Russians off his scent and on to mine for a few days. That was all the time Paolo needed to decode the disks and turn them over to the cops or the media. The disks would decimate the Russian war party before it was mobilized. The Russians weren't going to let a coup like that go unchallenged, but they were without focus. They were working fast to get their property back, but the trail went cold with me. I didn't die as easy as the computer nerds. They couldn't force me to give up who I worked for so they had to settle for getting their property back; once they had it, they would find a way to make me talk. The disks were trouble from all sides, but holding on to one was the only way to keep me breathing.

I put the disk in an envelope and went searching, one-handed, for duct tape. The tape was with a number of other tools in the closet. I used the thick grey tape, tearing it with my teeth, to tape the envelope outside the window on the underside of the sill. The envelope matched the white concrete enough that it would be invisible from the street, and if the room was turned over fast it wouldn't be noticed unless someone held their head out the window. My life was taped outside the window, hanging in the breeze.

Once the disk was hidden, I got ready to meet the

Russians. I didn't think they would be long. The information I had was important, and twice stolen; they would want to get their hands on it fast. I put the Glock on the desk, then got the SIG from the closet. I took the spare gun out of the oily rag it was wrapped in, and put it in the holster at my back. It took three tries to get the gun behind my back, but I could pull it free from the holster without a lot of trouble. I was slow in my condition, so the idea of pulling a spare gun was better than trying to reload. I stopped worrying about the gun and went to the washroom to relieve the urge from the Red Bulls and the tea. On the way back from the bathroom I put the kettle on again. The tea would take my mind off how tired, sore, and battered I was.

I waited in my chair, Glock in hand, drinking tea, for forty-seven minutes. It was then that the frosted glass of my door darkened as though an eclipse had occurred in the hall. The eclipse was the man I had shot at 22 Hess.

Ivan came in with another man who was much shorter than his towering height. They both had on dark jackets, pants, and shoes. The dark jackets were open, and their hands were empty. I had shot Ivan hoping to put him in his place. Shooting him had done nothing but terrify me. His lizard brain was operating as soon as he was hit.

I stared at Ivan, watching the abyss behind his eyes stare back at me. The crocodile eyes looked and me with a carnivorous interest, but the rest of him stayed impassive. I moved my gaze slowly to the smaller of the two men and saw that he was taking in the room systematically, left to right, floor to ceiling. Once he finished, his eyes rested on me.

I had my useless left arm resting on the desk. Underneath

I held the Glock, safety off, in my lap. My palm was sweating against the grip, but there was no way I was going to wipe it off. I just gripped harder.

"Morning," I said. I got no response at all. "The stuff is behind you in the pillowcase."

The little one looked behind him at the pillowcase, and I understood the situation. The little one was the help; he looked at the bag because he was the one who was going to carry it. Ivan never looked. The stuff didn't interest him — I did. Ivan was here to kill me.

I made my play right away. "The bag has most of the data your boss wanted back."

The short one looked at me, blinked, looked again at the bag, and then to me once more. I brought the pistol up easy. The little one took a step back and moved his arm to his jacket.

"Put your hand down," I said with no menace in my voice. "I gave your boss back most of the stuff. Some I kept as insurance, a gesture of good faith. I gave some of the disks to … a friend, a friend I see every day. The disks I took are in an envelope addressed to a cop I know not to be dirty. If any of this deal comes back to bite me in the ass the disks will be passed on, and that clean cop will earn a huge medal taking down your whole organization."

"That wasn't what you were told to do!" The smaller Russian sounded petulant.

"I don't take direction well. I went as far as I was prepared to. Now I'm done. We're done."

"You were told what it would take to be done. This is not it." The little one was still petulant.

"This is how it works," I said. "There are no set rules in our game."

Ivan moved for the first time. He surprised me by turning away and picking up the bag. It wasn't his job to carry anything; the bag was a message. Ivan lifted the bag with the arm I shot, and opened the door with the other. The smaller man turned and left without being told. Ivan was the true heavy, the one in charge. He turned to me before leaving. "No rules in game," he said, and chuckled. His laugh was terrible. It was in the back of his throat, and it had the destructive sound of waves crashing on rocks. "Soon we be only game in town."

He left without closing the door behind him. I waited for ten minutes with my gun pointed at the open door. When my forearm started to ache, I got up and shut the door. I stumbled to the desk using any object I could to stay upright, and passed out at my desk face down with my gun still in my hand. My face had the idiot's grin of a survivor.

CHAPTER TWELVE

I woke several hours later. The angle of the sun through the window told me it was midday, and the clock confirmed it. My mouth was dry, but my body was clammy. The bullet wound had given me a fever, and I had sweated through my shirt. I got up from the desk and tried to stretch. My bad arm barely made it ten inches from my body. I scrounged for another energy drink, finally finding one in the pile of things I brought with me from Steve's. I popped the top and ignored the spray of warm liquid that went all over my hand. The drink was too sweet, and it had almost a medicinal taste as it went down my throat. When the can was empty I rubbed my hands over my face, feeling the stubble, as I staggered to the window. I used my reflection to confirm my suspicions. I looked like hammered shit.

"Damn," was all I said to myself.

There was no question, I had one priority now. I had to get the bullet out of my arm, and I had to do it quietly. I had to avoid any off-the-books doctors that had any relation to anyone I knew. That meant I had to avoid doctors who dealt with people. I knew a veterinarian. She worked on horses out in the country. She was also a drunk. For enough cash to keep her drowning she would work on almost anyone. I came across her while I was chasing Donny O'Donnell, an Irish gangster and local psycho who had been raping women in Corktown for years. Corktown was in the southeast part of downtown; it was a historic Irish neighbourhood, and much of the Irish blood had never drained out. The whole neighbourhood was terrified of O'Donnell and his crew, so he went unchecked, growing more brazen with each attack. For his last attack, he happened to choose a woman who lived about a block outside his neighbourhood, and who had been a waitress for a catering company owned indirectly by Paolo Donati. Word of the assault got back to him, and with it came tales of the nightmare of the small Irish neighbourhood. I was given the task of bringing the neighbourhood terror to Paolo. I worked my way through O'Donnell's small world and came, first-hand, into contact with his legacy. I met men and women whose lives had been obliterated by a big sick fish in a small pond. I finally managed to catch up with him and put a bullet in his gut, but he vanished on me. There was no trace of him in the city. The horror stories I learned searching for the bastard kept me on his trail. After a few days, I found out that he was convalescing in the country. Exactly where was hard to find; I only knew he was with a vet out in the boonies. At first, I thought he was hiding with a war buddy, but he was too young to have been in any conflict that I could recall. O'Donnell was never a soldier; he was too much of an animal. That was when it hit me — animals go to a vet all their own. After a day of grinding through the crew O'Donnell left behind, I was pointed in the right direction — Flamboro.

I went out to Flamboro Downs racetrack and planted myself there for a few days. I played the part of a degenerate gambler looking for inside information. I asked about the animals' health, diet, and where they were tended to. Each day I checked out vets and names I overheard, and the next day I was back asking more questions. I finally caught a break when an old horse broke its front legs a mile out of eighth place.

"That one is off to Maggie's," I heard a man say.

I found out that the owner was broke, and Maggie was a disgraced, unlicensed vet who fixed horses passably or put them down cheap. A little more digging got me an address and a life story the locals seemed to revel in. Maggie lost a kid, then a husband, hit the bottle, and then lost everything else, including her licence.

I found her place that night, and her Irish patient left with me, without a word, while she was sleeping. I made sure he stayed in good health — for a while. Now, years later, with the Irish gang gone, she was the only doctor I knew who was completely off the grid to the people I was involved with.

I kept money in a few different places around the city. Some of it in banks — more in safe spots where people would never think to look for it. It wasn't the most secure idea, but it was accessible at all times. Now was one of those times. I would pull what I needed for the vet on my way out of the city. I moved to the closet and used my good arm to free a bag and a change of clothes. I put the clothes in the bag along with some food for the drive. I didn't put in any identification or items that would give me a name. I wanted to be in and out, fast and anonymous. Packing brought with it a bit of dizziness, so I sat at my desk and waited for it to pass. I passed out again face down at the desk.

The sound of the door splintering off its hinges brought me awake. The frosted pane cracked and the door swung open, slamming against the wall. The door ricocheted back slower, one corner dragging on the floor. I was startled straight up from my sleep. I reached my closest arm towards the Glock still on the desk, forgetting that it was useless. The shooting pain my stupidity caused cost me seconds I needed. I moved my right arm and got my hand on the gun just as I heard, "Don't do it, Wilson."

The two men in front of me were middle-aged Italians. They had short dark hair, crooked noses, and scar tissue around their eyes. They were not handsome men. Their misaligned features were augmented with layers of fat that hung on cheeks studded with blackheads. They were brothers of the same ugly mother.

"Hand off the gun. Get up now."

I didn't move. I was still groggy and a bit out of it. My brain was telling me something I couldn't process. I blinked hard, and the speaker, the ugly guy on the left holding a snub-nosed revolver, spoke again.

"Hand off the gun. Get up now."

My brain snapped into focus. These were the Scazzaro brothers — Johnny and Pat. They were mid-level muscle, and they were probably here because Julian couldn't be. I looked at Johnny and played through my mind everything he had told me. While I was thinking, he again told me to get up. He never said he would kill me, and he didn't even threaten to hurt me. He wanted me up so I could go somewhere.

"I know you're supposed to take me somewhere, not shoot me, Johnny. Put the gun down."

He didn't move. The gun wasn't pointed at me directly, but that could change quickly. I shifted in my seat, moving my body forward so the 9 mm still holstered at my back was away from the chair. I put a little agitation into my voice: "I'm serious. It makes me nervous when you point those things at me. What are you afraid of? I don't even have my gun in my hand, you caught me sleeping. If you're not going to kill me, and I'm not armed, at least point the gun at the floor."

The two brothers exchanged looks, but their guns never moved. I pushed harder. "If you're so fucking scared I'll give you my piece. Here!" With one motion I used my good arm and both feet to shove the desk over. The Glock hit the floor along with the overturned desk. Both men looked at the gun on the floor; they never noticed my hand moving behind my back, or it coming back with a pistol. When their eyes left the floor and found mine, it took five seconds for them to read my grin and move their eyes down from it to the gun in my right hand. The room didn't fill with noise, and bullets didn't rip me apart.

My gun was pointed at Johnny. He was the talker, so I put him down as the one in charge. "Where am I supposed to be going?"

The two exchanged glances out of their peripheral

vision, unsure of the direction the discussion had taken.

"Boss wants to see you now," Johnny said.

"But he doesn't want me dead."

Johnny waited a second then spoke. "He said you crossed a line and he wanted your ass in front of him."

"Why send you two? Why not Julian?"

Pat sneered. "You know why," he said.

"No, I don't. Tell me," I said.

"Somebody hit Julian with a car. He says it was you. Boss wants to know what you got to say."

"You two are up to date on your gossip," I said. "Here's how we'll do this. You two are going to leave, and I'll go to the restaurant on my own."

"No. You're gonna come with us now. Like the boss said." Johnny's whiny voice let me know that he didn't like the sound of my idea. The gun in my hand meant things weren't going to go the way he planned.

"I'm going myself. Two shit button men aren't taking me anywhere. You want to see if you can make it otherwise, go ahead." The silence that followed told me they didn't. "I'll be along shortly, now fuck off."

Pat looked at Johnny for ten seconds, the two of them having a fraternal argument inside their heads. They both knew they were supposed to bring me in, not kill me, and the two of them weren't high enough on the food chain to make any executive decisions. They moved to the door, covering each other.

"We'll be waiting to follow you over, so don't get any ideas," was the only goodbye I got.

After they left, I ate everything I could hold down. I

drank a Red Bull with a handful of Tylenol, changing it up from Advil. I picked up the Glock from the floor beside the desk and tucked it into the front of my pants with my right arm, making sure I could draw it without wincing. Once I got it right, I practised walking across the floor. I tried to hide any awkward movement, but I moved like I was in a jacket that was too small. It wasn't ideal, but it was the best I could do. Before walking out the door I rummaged in the garbage for an old newspaper. I knelt and used the floor and my one good arm to crease the paper in half. I nestled the SIG I showed to the Scazzaro brothers into the paper, folded it, and put it under my left arm.

The broken office door closed when I left, but it didn't hold. I left it as it was — I didn't have time to worry about it. Johnny and Pat weren't waiting for me in the hall or in the stairwell. No one was waiting outside, either, but a minute after I pulled the Volvo away from the building I picked up an obvious tail. The two Scazzaro brothers were behind me in a black SUV. Their worked-over faces appeared closer than they really were in the side mirrors. Pat was in the passenger seat talking on a cell phone. They weren't taking any chances getting me back. They would guide me in, and any hiccups would bring backup — quick. Traffic was light, and I only hit a few red lights. At each one I caught sight of a second black SUV farther back. I thought it was the person on the other end of Pat's cell phone — I found out later I was wrong.

As I drove, I glanced at the newspaper hiding the gun. It was an offensive, stupid idea, but it was necessary. A gun in plain sight should get me in the restaurant without frisking, provided I used the right attitude. I double-parked beside the cars lined outside the doors. The four guards out front weren't talking about sports, food, or women this time. They were looking at me like wolves eyeing a lone fawn.

I put the newspaper on my lap and took five deep breaths before I reached across my body and opened the door. I stood and tucked the paper under my bad arm, feeling the reassuring weight of the gun. There was no pain as long as I kept my left hand in my pocket.

"Move the car."

I ignored the order and started around the front bumper of the car.

"Hey, asshole, we ain't valets. Move the car."

As I passed the final corner of the bumper my right hand moved inside the paper under my left arm. The dampness of my fingers caused a small bit of friction on the newsprint. The four guards tensed when they saw my hand move. Each man's right arm moved a second behind mine.

"Easy, boys," I said as I approached. "I have some business here today." I stopped in front of the group. "You know this place is watched, so keep your hands loose. If we start a gunfight no one leaves happy. I was told to come down and I'm here — on my terms. I'm going in, and you're staying here. Everyone watching this place will see me go in and everyone will see you stay out front as usual. You come inside and everyone watching will turn into everyone listening. When there ends up being something to hear, everyone will come in for a closer look."

I hoped my lies would play on the constant paranoia people in organized crime find themselves in every day.

The men out front glorified themselves in their own minds. In their heads they were important, dangerous men. They could not imagine a group of law-enforcement officials who would not fear them, and therefore would want to keep constant tabs on them. In reality no one watched the restaurant all the time. If anything it was bugged by recorders that were collected and transcribed later. The law wouldn't know I came for months, if at all. Who knew if the tapes were even checked.

Four hard faces looked at me. Four hard faces saying nothing. I didn't wait for a response; instead I moved to the left of the group. If they drew guns they would have to move them across their bodies to get to me. The extra milliseconds would be necessary if I had to draw on them from under my arm. No one moved as I walked a semicircle around the group. I went through the door of the restaurant sideways, my eyes never leaving the small crowd of men. Once I was inside, I turned, and the newspaper followed my gaze towards the coat-check stall. Cold eyes greeted me, and one manicured hand was already under the counter.

"We've been here before."

The coat-check girl said nothing.

"And you know what? I'll still be through the door before you draw."

"I'm faster than I was," she said, her hand still under the counter.

I looked at her and let the grin form on my face. For a second her lips separated and her eyes found my hand in the newspaper pointed at her. She was instantly unsure of herself.

"It's good that you've gotten better. Me, I've never slowed down."

Her hand stayed under the counter as I went through the second set of doors.

I walked down the steps into the restaurant. All of the tables had chairs up on them as usual. The only difference was in the hallway where the booths were located. Two men stood there with guns in their hands.

CHAPTER THIRTEEN

Neither of the two gunmen spoke to me. They took turns looking at me and at my hand in the newspaper under my arm. I took deep breaths and visualized shooting the one on the right and diving left toward the tables. I had to quickly re-evaluate my decision when I realized that my left arm couldn't take a bump on the floor; I'd have to shoot left and dive right.

"What in the hell did you do, *figlio?*" I heard Paolo before I saw him. He came out, empty-handed, from between the two men.

"The boys you sent didn't seem friendly. I decided I would come and see you myself. I meant no offence."

He stopped dead. "Don't you fucking lie to *me*, you stupid fuck. You took from *me* and attacked my people. You…you…fucked with *me*." Every *me* was emphasized like a sonic boom. Paolo was physically shaking. His rage dilated his pupils and made his hands shake. It turned him into the focal point of the room. No one could look anywhere else. "Then you lie to me like I'm worth nothing. Not even an explanation. I bailed you out when you should have been dead. I gave you work when I should have made an example of you, and to reward my generosity you become Judas? What did it take to turn you, Judas? How much money, *figlio?*" Paolo's voice had worn down into a whisper; he was now the grand inquisitor.

I said nothing. The man calling me *son* wasn't my father; he kept me employed because it helped him. He hung me out to dry days ago for the same reason. I didn't argue back. I forced myself to stop hearing Paolo so I could focus. At some point I would be told to drop the newspaper. In my mind, I visualized tossing it in front of me and using the movement of the paper and the heavy sound of the gun hitting the ground to conceal my drawing of the other gun from my waistband. I watched myself in my head, over and over again, until I realized Paolo was staring at me.

"Thirty pieces of silver, eh Judas? You have no loyalty. I knew that when you first bit the hand that fed you. When a dog does that they put him down because they know that he's got a wild streak in him that's no good for nothin'. I made a mistake there. I thought you were better than a dog. But you're not better than a dog, you're still a crow. You come in here with a gun and lie to my face. To me! You cripple a man, my man, and then lie to me about it. Take off that shirt and we'll see the liar. Take it off! Show me you're not lying and I'll apologize for the invitation that offended you so much. I know what's under that shirt. I know because you didn't kill that kid, or his mom. That was always your problem. You only killed people you thought deserved it. You never saw that you were living in the jungle and everyone deserves it. The lions take who they want; they don't weigh out the morality of the situation — they just act. Acting is what makes them king — not morality. I'm king of the fucking jungle. People die all the time because I say so, not because they deserve it — screw deserves. People die because I live. I'm what Darwin dreamed of at night. Top of the food chain, no remorse. Now take off your shirt."

"I did the job you wanted done. I picked up what you asked for. You lied. You never told me what I was dealing with."

"Risks, boy. Did you forget what you did for a living?"

"I never forget. I complete jobs that you need done. Jobs you want to be able to distance yourself from. I work for you, but I'm not your fall guy. You left me out to dry. You knew that the Russians would find me eventually. You knew they would have to work to find me and kill me, and you thought that in the time it would take them to do that you would be able to hurt them bad — maybe kill their organization completely. You set me up, and when that didn't work you sent men to bring me to you; to bring me to die. That's not how I work. My shirt stays on and I leave…for good."

"*Figlio.*" His voice was calm. "Do you know where you are? You don't show up at my place and tell me anything, and you don't quit — I fire you…for good."

Sensing the turn in the conversation, the two men raised their guns. The thug to my left said, "Put down the paper," in a cold, flat voice. I cursed myself for letting Paolo run the conversation and for getting me to talk. Since I had been shot I had just pushed forward, never stopping to plan. I was racing ahead while I was falling apart. My mouth let him get the better of me, and now I was at a disadvantage. Outgunned by two drawn pistols, I forced my knees to bend and my breathing to relax. I readied myself to shoot the man on the right. Two thumbs moved, and the guns in front of me cocked. The thug on the right repeated his order as the two men moved forward from the booths past Paolo, so that he was obscured from my view. We had fifteen feet between us.

I took one big breath and a step to the right table. "Okay, I'll put it down." My body started the turn, and I was about to let the paper fall when gunfire broke out.

I stopped and turned my head. Behind me, the sounds of gunfire popped again in the street. No one inside wasted time; four more bodies, armed with handguns, came out from the booths behind Paolo. The two men in front of me looked at Paolo for instructions; he had already decided what to do.

"Joey, go with them. Tony, watch Wilson."

Paolo went to the booths and picked up a revolver from a seat on the left. Tony, who stayed to watch me, had not moved his feet. He was looking to the door, back to me, then to Paolo.

"Get his shirt off," Paolo said. Tony looked at me, and I could see his eyes resist the urge to look anywhere else.

"Drop the paper," Tony said.

More gunfire sounded, closer now. It was automatic chatter, and it was replied to with single shots. I watched Paolo listen. Watched him realize he and his men were out-gunned. Paolo and Tony looked over my shoulder toward the sound of approaching footsteps; I moved a few steps right, toward the kitchen.

"Boss!" Joey yelled as he rushed past me to Paolo's side as though he were a child afraid of thunder.

"What the fuck is going on out there?" Paolo roared as I took another few steps toward the kitchen. Paolo's eyes found me. "Tony, you make sure he stops moving."

"I'm putting the paper down. That's all," I said, and I slowly took the paper out from under my left arm to prove it to everyone.

"Boss, it's the Russians. They're in the street. They're killing everyone!"

Tony had his eyes on mine as I moved my arm to toss the paper toward the tabletop. We ignored Paolo and Joey's voices as they went over what was going on outside. I tossed the paper high and it landed with a loud thump. The sound interrupted the conversation and pulled everyone's eyes to the newspaper. No one watched my right arm move.

Three quick shots sounded; they were followed by a woman screaming, "No!" More automatic gunfire rang; its volume let us know it was just outside the dining room doors. Everyone's attention moved to the doors as I pulled my gun. I had it pointed at Tony for five seconds before he noticed it. His eyes moved to the barrel and grew wide. The only word he could find came out in a childish tone.

"Boss."

Paolo and Joey looked away from the door. Both saw the gun in my hand immediately.

"God damn it, Tony."

"Shut up, Paolo," I said. "The gunfire is slowing down,

so we're going to have company soon. We need to get out of here. Is there a way out of here besides the front and the kitchen?"

"I don't run from no one. Especially those fucking commies."

"You can stay," I said. "But I want out, and if killing you gets me there I'll do it."

Tony and Joey brought their guns up. Yelling, "Boss, get down!" was all that stopped me from shooting them. The gunfire from Tony and Joey pushed three men back through the doorway, shattering the glass that led to the coat-check room. The men were clad in black, their pale white skin accentuated by the colour they wore. They took cover from the gunfire in the coat-check area, but the darkness inside the room made it impossible to tell where.

No one moved. Muffled by the walls, a gunshot broke the silence; two more followed seconds later. There was a big gun outside.

I moved right, walking backward, keeping my eyes on the door, and on Joey, Tony, and Paolo, who had overturned two tables for cover. When I got to the wall, I followed it to the far corner of the restaurant. I couldn't stay there exposed in the room for all to see. "Joey, Tony," I said. "I'm going to work my way behind you. The Russians are in a nasty choke point in there. They can't move out of it and into here without getting mowed down, even if you only have two guns. You start shooting at me, you'll lose focus, and the choke point. I'm moving behind you from your left."

"You stay put," one of them said.

"I'm not staying here. If this place is going to turn into the Alamo, it can do it without me."

I started moving down the wall toward Paolo, Joey, and Tony. To their credit Paolo's boys didn't look scared. They had a look of determination on their faces. Paolo just looked angry.

Joey and Tony kept their guns aimed at the door, but they stole looks at me out of the corners of their eyes. They were tense — waiting for an order to come. In a moment, I would be right behind them, and I knew they didn't want a gun behind them too.

I spoke to the two men, trying to sound as calm as possible. "Now, boys, I'm going to pass behind you. It would be smarter for you to keep your eyes on that door." As I spoke I noticed that my arm was getting tired from holding the gun up. "Paolo," I said. "Tell them to let me by. You know it's a smart play."

After a pause Paolo spoke. "You two watch that door. If anything moves, you light it up."

"Thank you, Paolo," I said. Meaning it.

"Fuck you. We're not done. Not by a mile." The angrier he got the less philosophical he became; he spoke more like the thug he was destined to be, and less like the educated gangster he played at being.

I kept my gun trained on the door. I was a prime target alone on the wall without cover. I crouched low, trying to move knee to knee, but no one shot at me from the door. I didn't stop to wonder why it was so quiet behind the doors. I thought instead about the big gun outside. The front of the building was surrounded, and it wouldn't be long before the Russians tried to move through the doors into the dining room again. The Russians would kill me, and so would Paolo if he managed to get out of this alive. The back door was my only option. The fact that no one had come through the kitchen meant that the Russians were concentrating on the front door. They probably thought they could blitz through the restaurant like they did at 22 Hess, but Paolo's set-up was stronger than they expected. The Russians would regroup in the entryway, then hit the dining room hard. I had a small window of opportunity to get out alive.

"Paolo. What's out back?"

He didn't look over at me to answer; he kept his eyes on the door. "What do you think? You know the place. The alley is out back."

"I know about the alley," I said. "Tell me the layout. Everything you can remember."

"Why? You afraid you're gonna get lost running away?" He stopped then and considered his words and mine for a few seconds. "I heard those shots. You think someone's out front, huh?"

"Someone with a big gun. If I leave, I'll take him with me."

Paolo laughed at the idea and told me what I needed to know. "The door is heavy—all the doors here are. The locks are solid and expensive. Believe me. The door, it opens out."

"Describe the alley," I said. "The length and the width."

"It's brick on both sides; maybe ten feet wide. The whole alley is about a hundred feet long. There ain't a back way out—it's bricked off to the right. At the other end there's a side street that exits out to the main roads."

"That's not everything," I said. "Where does the trash go?"

"There's a Dumpster," Paolo said in a sort of "oh yeah" tone.

"Where is the Dumpster? Left or right?" I waited for the answer; it was fifty-fifty. Life or death.

"It's on the left."

The left, that one direction was my only hope. It was the fifty I wanted. I could work my way out of the alley using the Dumpster as cover. It wasn't ideal but it was better than the alternative.

I moved past Paolo's gunmen to the kitchen door. It was maroon, the colour of the walls, and it swung silently back and forth. Beside it was a row of five light switches set in a dingy brass plate. I eyed the coat-check room one last time before I moved through the door.

The kitchen was small and silver. The counters were clean, and the air was warm with dishwasher steam; the room was ready for the restaurant staff to start work in a few hours. The refrigerators hummed low, creating a background soundtrack.

The back door was just as it was described: heavy black metal with large, expensive locks. I took one final look around before I slowly started turning the deadbolts one after another. Each click got me closer and closer to outside. Each click brought more anticipation. On the final click, I stepped back from the door and took two deep breaths. I eased the door open a crack. Outside, in the crack of space that opened, I saw only darkness. I thought back and remembered the sun on my shoulders as I came in. I pushed the door open another two inches and still saw no light. The electric illumination of the kitchen lights revealed a dull, rust-speckled green outside the door. I tried to push the door open further but it wouldn't budge. It was the Dumpster; it had been moved right up to the door. I put the gun under the armpit of my bad arm and tried to shoulder the door open but the Dumpster wouldn't move. I gave up on the door and picked up my gun again. There was no one outside anymore. We were all locked in. It was then that I heard the shots.

There were three in all, and all of them came from a big, big gun. I remembered the echoed shots I had heard from outside and knew that everyone was inside the building now, and they were not going to stay in the coat-check area long.

I looked around the kitchen for another way out but I was stuck. There were no windows, and no other doors. I would have to go back the way I came. I moved to the swinging door. There had been no noise after the last three shots I heard. I doubted anyone could take Paolo, Tony, and Joey with three shots, but I had been wrong before.

The men in the coatroom had seen me cross the room. They knew where I was and they weren't going to let me live. I had to get out of the building, through Paolo and the Russians. I turned off all of the lights, making the kitchen black except for the light leaking in through the spaces in the door.

"Paolo," I yelled through the kitchen door. "Call for backup."

I could hear hushed mumbling, but nothing I could make sense of until someone yelled, "There he is, Tony.

There, shoot him!" Three shots sounded, the first two close together, the last a second behind. One loud shot echoed back, and there was silence again. I waited three seconds then moved my arm out to the grimy light switch beside the kitchen door. I clicked every switch down with the flat of my palm. The room went dark instantaneously. The kitchen and the dining room were both black.

I slipped out the swinging door into the dining room. I kept low, stepped out beside the door using my shoulder to ease it quietly closed behind me. Once it was closed, I put my back against the wall just below the light switches. I couldn't turn them on again with my battered arm; it wouldn't extend anywhere near shoulder height, and if I used the other arm I wouldn't be able to shoot. I took a few breaths and began to slide my back up the wall. I felt the switches touch my back and I flattened closer to the wall. I waited for what felt like minutes until I heard the sound of footsteps on the stairs. One man can move silently, but more than one usually makes enough noise to be heard — especially in the dark. Five switches shifted up with a click under my back, and the lights immediately resumed their electric glow. Paolo was on the floor, shot in the stomach. The amount of blood told me that the bullet had not grazed him, but Paolo was alive with a gun in one hand and a cell phone in the other. Tony and Joey were dead. Their guns lay between them on the floor. At the top of the stairs stood Ivan and his huge gun. Behind him were three men dressed in black holding compact automatic weapons.

Ivan had his gun pointed down at Paolo's wounded body. His eyes and those of the men he was with were on me and the gun I was pointing at them.

"Feels like we've been here before, Ivan. You think you're going to do better the second time around?"

Ivan turned his head to me; his shoulders stayed square to Paolo. "We are here to win the game," he said.

"So this is checkmate. You take the king, and the board is yours?"

"The board belongs to us already. We are just making it permanent."

"The fuck you are, you commie bastards!" Paolo was alive on the floor, and he was making sure everyone knew it.

"Paolo," I said. "Did you make the call like I told you?"

"I'm gonna fucking piss on your graves, you motherless fucks."

"Paolo," I snapped. "Did you make the call?"

He didn't answer for a second that lasted minutes. "Yeah," he said. "I made the call. I couldn't say much, but I got the message across."

I couldn't be sure, because I wasn't looking in his direction, but it sounded like Paolo was smiling. "This looks like a stalemate, Ivan. There aren't any moves left. A new game is going to start soon."

Ivan said nothing to me. He spoke out to his men — in Russian.

"Don't do that," I said. "Keep it English."

Ivan didn't listen. He fired off more Russian in his thick, deep voice.

"Don't do that, Ivan." My voice was cold and serious.

Ivan stopped speaking, but it didn't sound abrupt. It sounded more like the end of a sentence — the end of a complete thought. He had issued a command to three men with guns, and I had no idea what he had said.

I couldn't read Ivan, so I focused on the three behind him, and the light switches against my back. One of the three was sweating heavily and looking at me out of the corner of his eye. He noticed my face and his eyes locked onto me as my mouth pulled tight into a grin. His eyes widened, and he looked to the other Russians. I dug my back into the light switches and shot the sweatiest gunman in the neck. Ivan's gun roared to life as I dragged my back across the switches. The room went dark for half a second, then Paolo fired his gun. The other two unnamed Russians returned fire at Paolo, then at the spot where I had been standing only seconds before. The bullets missed me, ripping into the wall at chest height. I was on the floor, sideways on my good shoulder, using the floor to steady my arm. The Russian henchmen were betrayed by their muzzle flashes. I saw their faces in the strobe light of automatic gunfire. I aimed at the man on the right and pulled the trigger. I quickly adjusted and shot left, where the second flashes had been moments before. I rolled forward from the wall toward the tables. I grunted as I hit my shoulder, but I kept moving. Automatic gunfire bit into the wall from across the room. I could only see under the tables so I had no idea where the shooter was. More shots rang out from my left. Paolo fired four bullets in quick succession, but their thunder was deafened by the metallic click of an empty gun that followed. The shots created two things in the darkness, a scream ahead of me, and a glimpse of a pair of shoes four feet in front of Paolo. I shot from the floor six times above where I had seen the shoes in the muzzle flash.

CHAPTER FOURTEEN

The dark reeked of cordite, and my ears rang a far-off, high-pitched note. I managed to stand using the barrel of my gun to prop me up. I walked sideways until my crippled arm hit the wall. I hissed a sharp intake of breath, and then moved backward along the wall until I was massaged by five little plastic fingers. I used my shoulder to edge the switches up one by one. The first three lit up the rear of the restaurant; the final two lit above me and Paolo.

He was lying on the floor, leaking blood but still breathing. Ivan sat less than ten feet away. I had hit him in the shoulder and chest. The other four shots must have gone wild in the dark. In his hand, limp at his side, he still held his huge gun — another Colt Python. Paolo's eyes went wide when he saw Ivan sitting up with his gun still in his hand.

"Wilson, he's still got a gun. Wilson? Shoot him! Wilson, shoot!"

His screaming seemed to drive Ivan on. The Russian was working at raising his gun. It moved inches off the ground, then nosedived. It rose again, a few inches higher, using the bounce off the ground for momentum.

"Wilson." Paolo was pleading. "*Figlio,* please…shoot him."

Ivan's gun was four inches off the floor, and shaking as I moved toward Paolo. I had to laugh. "King of the jungle."

I looked at Ivan working so hard to get his gun six more inches into the air. I looked at him and said something I knew he would never understand. "You're dinosaurs, both of you. Too busy to notice the meteor."

Ivan might have been puzzled, but it was only for a second. The bullet made everything clear. Paolo grunted his appreciation and slumped to the floor. "Good job, *figlio.* Now pass me the phone."

I looked at Paolo and felt my finger hot on the trigger. I thought about killing him and ending my problems. But then I'd still have to deal with the Russians, and the rest of Paolo's crew once Julian told them I was finally open season.

"Are you and me even? For the disks, for Julian, for Tommy, for everything?"

Paolo eyed the gun in my hand and nodded. "Yes, yes, all is forgiven, *figlio.* Now give me the phone." The look in my eyes told him he would have to do better. "Fuck, after what happened today, I'm going to have more work than ever for you."

I looked around at the carnage in the restaurant. My eyes took in all of the bodies on the floor, and all the holes in the walls. I finally rested my gaze on Ivan, who was no less terrifying in death. His gun remained in his hand as though his body was still fighting even after it was left without a soul. I thought about how many times I had shot the huge man in the last few days and almost laughed. This was what Paolo offered. What his work would bring.

"I don't want more work. I know what you are, and I know what you think of me. I'm going to disappear. Don't look for me. Stay in your jungle and deal with the Russians."

I eased my finger off the trigger and walked away from Paolo. Behind me I heard a whimper from the top of the food chain, then a sob as he reached for his phone.

GRINDER

CHAPTER ONE

I saw him before he even thought I might be the one he was looking for. In one moment all the months of work, honest work, that I thought had worn down what I was, proved worthless. I saw him, out of place on the wharf. His clothing was too metrosexual to be local, and too dance club to be tourist. The jeans were expensive and artificially worn in around the thighs and crotch. His shirt was not cotton, but rather some kind of stretchy blend that stood out unnaturally in the sunlight. The worst was the shoes, their leather shiny and the tips pointed. I knew he was an outsider, and part of me, the part I tried to bury, knew exactly where he was from.

I saw him, but he couldn't see me — not yet. The ocean had changed me enough. I was leaner, harder, and my skin was the colour of worn leather. My hair was long under my hat and my beard was far past the scratchy stage. My clothes were old and worn. I made sure I looked like everyone else who lived on the island before I left the house each day. As I walked around the boat getting ready to offload the day's haul, I watched the out-of-place man. He didn't see me yet, but he would. I was two thousand kilometres from home and too jaded to believe in coincidences. He wasn't here by accident. He knew I was here, and my fisherman's camou-flage wouldn't make me invisible forever. I had to make him see me and make him move on me here. If he had known where I lived, he would have been waiting for me there. He was at the wharf looking to set up a tail. I was still one step ahead. That picture brought him here — that damn picture. I had to make sure here was where he stayed.

CHAPTER TWO

I left Hamilton in stages. The first stage was getting out of the standoff in Paolo Donati's restaurant. Paolo, my former employer, had sent men to bring me to him. I had railroaded the soldiers he sent into letting me drive myself. I was persuasive with them, and I had help—help that spit lead hundreds of metres per second. The restaurant I drove to was Paolo's office. All the city's underworld business ran through the building like blood through a hard corrupted heart. Paolo wanted to see me one last time before he killed me. Paolo had sent me on a job. I stole evidence for him that would wipe the competing mob, the Russians, off the map in Hamilton. What Paolo never told me was that it was also my job to lead the Russians away from him. Paolo wanted them to chase me while he put the final nails in their coffins. It would have worked too. Next to no one knew I worked for Paolo. No one outside of a handful of people knew I even existed. I was an apparition in the city—someone who did jobs quietly. Jobs a man like Paolo would want to distance himself from. I had been used by Paolo, but instead of laying down to die

I went on the offensive and stayed alive. I crossed Paolo for the second time — the last time. The restaurant turned into a slaughterhouse. The Russians figured out that I worked for Paolo and they brazenly attacked the restaurant in broad daylight. A death squad showed up to hit Paolo and me at once, but nothing ever goes according to plan in this city. The Russians couldn't finish the job. Paolo and I survived although we were both a few ounces of lead heavier.

After leaving Paolo and the Russians on the floor of his restaurant, I drove myself to a veterinarian in the sticks. The vet was a large animal doctor who lost her family and then hit the bottle. She was unlicensed, but her work was still good and she would do it quietly for cash. I was sure that no one from Paolo's crew or the Russian mob could have heard of her.

I made it to her house and parked out back. I staggered to her door with a brick of cash in my right hand, and used the solid rectangle of money to hammer on the door. I waited in the dim light for a minute until a porch bulb spontaneously combusted into light above my head. The bright light and blood loss made me dizzy; the glow also called out to every insect on the ten-acre property. Mosquitoes and horseflies circled my body on their way to the bulb, causing me to stumble as I swatted the insects buzzing in my ears with the only arm I could use. I swatted at the flies like King Kong swatted at airplanes. My attacks were less balanced than the huge ape's, and I had to give up and use my good arm to balance myself. I pushed the brick of cash the door frame with my right hand and braced myself for another insect barrage.

The door was flung open and, in shadows behind the porch light, a woman stood holding a large plastic cup in her hands.

"Hep you?" The "L" in "help" was slurred out by whatever she was drinking from the cup.

"I need medical attention."

"You're not a...not a horse. Heh. Do you know that? You're not a horse."

I risked losing my balance again and held the brick of cash out. "I know I'm not a horse, but technically you're not a vet. I know you work freelance...and I know your fee."

She stared at the money and licked her lips. "How much is it?"

"Ten," I said. "You get another five when I walk out of here."

"Who told you 'bout me?" she asked.

"Some Irish guys told me you were good and private."

"Ten now. Five later?"

"Five when I walk out of here," I corrected.

"How do I know you'll pay?" she asked, not drunk enough to miss that part of the deal.

"You don't, but the ten up front should be enough to get me a tab."

She thought about it for a minute. "What's your name?"

"Call me Mr. Ed."

She laughed her way into a coughing fit, wiped her chin on the neck of her shirt, and then led me into the house. I spent a week and a half in my drunken doctor's care until I was able to leave upright and mobile. The bullet in the back of my arm was out, and the painkillers she gave me worked fine. I paid her as promised and drove back into the city. I had to tie up some loose ends before I left for good.

I didn't have a life on the grid. Nothing was in my name directly — everything was layered. The layers kept me apart from everyone and everything. I spent my youth training and learning to live a life of discipline and paranoia. If I was going to get killed, it was never going to be because someone tracked me down through the system. The only point of contact between me and the circles I moved in was the office. The office was clean save a few items that were important but disposable. There were guns that needed to be lost in a place no one would ever find them. The guns weren't traceable to me, but they had a history that could be tied to the fingerprints that were all over the room. The office also had money hidden inside which, in my current situation, had to also be considered disposable. I wasn't going back to the office — not ever — but I needed it cleaned out.

I pulled the car up to a curb outside a row of mailboxes at a plaza on Main Street. The street ran through Hamilton into the smaller suburbs of Dundas and Stoney Creek. The plaza in Dundas was busy from nine in the morning to ten at night with people shopping, eating, bowling, or getting haircuts. I got out of the car and did a little of everything, to blend in and watch for a tail. I picked up a few items and walked with my bags into the post office. I produced a key from my key ring and opened box 113. The box looked as empty as usual, but it didn't matter. I reached my hand in and pulled at another box inside. The second container was painted the same colour as the brown interior of the mailbox and had a finger hole drilled into it so that it could be slid out. I had to lean back hard to move the tiny box with my one good arm. All at once my weight dislodged the powerful magnets I put inside. I excused myself to the woman I stepped back into, and put the box into my shopping bag. The box was still as heavy as I had left it — a fact that brought a grin to my face.

I performed the same routine at seven other plazas outside Hamilton. Each of the mailboxes contained a similar hidden box, and each was untouched since I had left it. Each box contained a brick of cash composed of the same large-denomination bills. In total, I collected two hundred thousand, twenty-five from each box.

My next stop was an Internet café. It was a busy shop bustling with Asian exchange students and employees from the tattoo parlour and coffee shop located on either side of the café. I logged into a local bank account I set up in a name that had nothing to do with me, and checked the balance. I had six thousand forty-three dollars and change. I closed the screen and opened up a search engine. I used the computer to find the phone numbers of the utility companies I paid monthly bills to for the house and office. On paper, the house belonged to a name my uncle created in the seventies. My uncle was a ghost in the system and his death went unnoticed by the law. I inherited the house when I burned his body and I kept the alias alive on paper. I never used the house unless I had to so the bills were never high, but they would pile up if I were gone a long time. I took one of the pens left behind at the work station, wrote the numbers I found on the Internet on a piece of paper, and logged off the computer. I paid five dollars for my time and left the café in search of a phone. I found it down the street in Jackson Square Mall. The mall had once, decades ago, been the city's premier shopping destination, but years of urban decay left it hollow and lifeless. The mall lost its trendy stores in exchange for dollar shops and discount clothing warehouses. Most of the people left after everyone of means followed the trendy stores uptown. The remaining shoppers were bored transients with no way to follow anyone anywhere.

I found a row of scarred vandalized pay phones outside a hotel that exited into the mall. I tried two phones only to find them gum-filled or mysteriously wet. The third was intact and produced a faint dial tone. I pulled the phone numbers I brought, and the pen I stole, and called each utility twice, logging the balance owed first on the house then on the office. Once I recorded each debt, I made my way back to the Internet café.

My unit was still empty so I logged on to it once again. I paid all of my bills, home and office, from two separate accounts. Once I had paid everything that was owing, I tucked the paper away and left the pen where I had found it.

I drove to the house not bothering to wind through any special routes. I was surprised at my direct approach, even more at my internal logic, which made me believe no one could have possibly been on my tail yet. I didn't feel like myself anymore. I was losing the connection to the paranoia that ran my life. It wasn't filtering my every move now; it felt more like a tiresome habit I was happy to be rid of rather than a means of keeping me alive.

I pulled into the driveway and sat behind the wheel. I

hated the house. I had lived there with my uncle until it became mine following his death. My long stay started as a visit, waiting for my parents to return from a "business trip." They never came back, and as a result I was passed on to the only family I had — my uncle. He wasn't mean, he was just distant. He made me go to school, do my homework, and read. The reading wasn't solely for me; it was to give us things to talk about. The reading led to talking and the talking led to my real education. I learned how to read between the lines of books and then between the lines of conversations. Once I learned how to dissect what people said, it didn't take long for me to find out that my parents were thieves. They took jobs that were high risk and high cash. The jobs allowed them to give me a normal life in a house with friends and a school. Once I learned about them, it was an easy jump to become involved with my uncle and his "work." He was like my parents in that he wasn't honest, but unlike them in that he lived a life detached from everything — no kids, no friends, no connections to the world to speak of. It was how he survived intact long after my parents died.

I told my uncle I wanted to do what my parents did, and eventually he introduced me to the life. It wasn't my parents' life exactly — it was his. He taught me to be like him, and like Alice down the rabbit hole, I was whisked off the grid.

CHAPTER THREE

I cleaned out the house in twenty minutes. I took the address book, money from the floorboards, and an old .38 to carry with the Glock I had on me. I unplugged everything and made a plan to mail post-dated cheques to the landscaper who cut the lawn in the summer and shovelled the driveway in the winter. He would also pick up any flyers left on the property. The rest of the junk mail would fall through the large slot in the door, leaving no evidence that the house was empty.

Before leaving the city, I stopped at a pay phone two blocks from Sully's Tavern. I called the bar and got an answer on the third ring.

"Sully's," Steve's low, calm voice answered.

"How would you like to earn ten grand with a handkerchief?"

"I was worried. I thought you went down after that business with the restaurant."

"You, worried?"

"You looked like shit the last time I saw you."

I must have been circling the drain because Steve never said he worried; he usually said nothing at all. Before I could say anything else, he spoke again. "What's this about ten thousand dollars?"

"I need you to get into the office and wipe it down top to bottom. There's forty grand in the baseboard behind my desk and a CD taped to the underside of the window ledge. Grab both when you leave, and ten of the forty is yours."

"You leaving?"

I ignored the question. "That business at the restaurant. Was it on the news?"

"Nah, just gossip."

"My name get thrown around?"

"Nah, but who else is going to start trouble there?" Steve chuckled over the background of clinking glasses and bar conversation.

"I'm leaving for a while. I just need to make sure there are no loose ends at the office."

"Why don't you burn it down?"

It was my turn to chuckle. I was amazed at how easily Steve's mind gravitated towards violence, as though it were the most logical answer and therefore the first suggestion. "There are already enough people involved. Fires bring firemen and cops; I just need to get rid of the prints and the money."

"Guns?"

"They're in a compartment in the closet; they're as safe as they'll ever be, but they need to be wiped." There was no immediate reply; I listened to the sounds of the bar for half a minute. "Steve?"

"I'll do it for free."

"Steve!" I protested.

"I'll do it for free."

I finished talking to Steve and told him I would leave the key in the change return of the phone I was on. I thanked my friend and hung up. By the time he got to the key, I would be in the car and out of the city.

I drove eight hours to Montreal. I found a cheap motel that took cash and slept without worry for the night. I woke at eight and used a washcloth to clean everything around the bandages. The pain in my left arm was unbelievable, but the pills the vet gave me would wear it down. I found the nearest post office and mailed twelve cheques and a note to the landscaper who took care of the house. The note told him I would be away on business often over the coming year. I made sure he understood that I would be coming back home every now and again to make sure that the landscaper would not think he could get away with neglecting the lawn. I also asked him to dispose of any flyers left on the driveway or grass. I wanted no sign that the house was unoccupied. After that, I ate a huge breakfast at a French-Canadian chain that was much like Denny's except for the fact that it offered baked beans with every meal.

Full and dulled from the painkillers, I drove twelve more hours to the only other place I had ever been — Prince Edward Island.

Mom and Dad took me to the island as a boy, and together we did everything that the small island offered. It was more than a vacation; it was my only solid memory of family. I could still close my eyes and smell the water, feel the breeze, and hear the sound of the red singing sand squeaking under my feet.

My return was greeted by a monument to technological advancement. Instead of a ferry crossing, there loomed a huge bridge joining the gap between New Brunswick and Prince Edward Island. A small turn-off advertised the old ferry, but I chose the new bridge instead. I wanted to get to the island as fast as possible. The bandages on my arm were starting to feel moist under my shirt. I needed to find a place to stay so I could rest and heal.

The bridge led to Charlottetown — the capital city, as large as a small Ontario town. The roads introducing me to the island province were different than those before the bridge — their asphalt was tinged pink from the red island dirt used to build them. I pushed myself to drive the thirty minutes from the bridge to the city centre. I had no patience left in me to wait for sleep. As soon as traffic began to bunch at stoplights, I pulled into the first lobster-themed motel I saw. I paid for a week upfront in cash and walked straight towards the adjoining restaurant.

I was greeted inside the restaurant by the smell of frying seafood. The bubbling sound of the fryers muffled the eating noises of the four solitary patrons. I was too tired to attempt eating anything that would require two hands, so I ordered a bowl of fish chowder and an order of fish and chips. The chowder came fast and it was hot and creamy. I had to search for the advertised pieces of crab and lobster until I finally found a piece of each on the bottom of the bowl. The fish and chips arrived minutes later in a red plastic basket. The oily fish and fries lay atop a piece of waxed paper printed to look like old newsprint. The fish was good; it settled deep in my stomach and made me immediately bone weary. I dropped a twenty down and left the restaurant without waiting for the almost nine dollars in change I would have gotten back.

I went to my room without my bags and went to sleep on the bed. I woke fourteen hours later and spent the following week in a painkiller haze. After the seven days at the motel, I felt good enough to travel away from the city deeper into the heart of the island. An hour out of Charlottetown, I stopped at an Atlantic Superstore to look at the community bulletin board, and found a house for rent minutes away from the ocean. Nellie, the old woman renting the house, was pleasant and inquisitive. She gave me directions to the house and met me there in her apron. I put her in her sixties, but her hair still had much of its youthful red. Her face was worn but tight; she was a woman who would age well until she finally could no longer age at all. Nellie fought the urge to ask questions about my long stay for fifteen whole seconds. I told her that I just had to get away from the city, and she instantly understood me as though I had just spoken some immutable truth. She told me five minutes worth of big-city horror stories that I was sure she had never learned first hand before we agreed on the evils of big cities and a price for the house. I paid her up front for four months, in cash, and she left me alone in the house holding the keys.

I hadn't lied to Nellie. I did have to get away from the city. I had made enemies of both sides of the underworld — Italian and Russian — making my presence dangerous on a good day. Add to that the condition of my mangled left arm, and I wouldn't last a day in Hamilton. I needed to start over where no one could find me. I needed to rehab my body. Most of all I needed to find a new way of life; something different from my parents' way, and most important different from my uncle's way. I needed to find a life all my own and shape it myself.

I spent days walking the long road in front of the house to the local beaches and wharves. Each day I tried to swing my left arm more and more to bring back its range of motion. After a month of walking, I could swing my arm to shoulder height making my walks awkward to look at. Once I looked sufficiently stupid swinging my arms, I switched to running in the forests that surrounded the house. I used my arms to pull myself over fallen tress and up hills. I lost my grip often and fell at least ten times a day at first, but after another month I could run for hours unimpeded.

My left arm began feeling normal, but different angles brought with them immense pain. On one of my trips into town for food, I found a gym overtop of a local hockey arena. I ran in the mornings, using the forest to bring my arm back, and used the gym in the evenings. Slowly, I began to be able to move dumbbells off my chest. It took two more months before I felt in shape. I was better, but I wasn't what I was. I knew I didn't have to be like I was anymore, but I couldn't let the wound be what changed me. The wound was like the city holding on to me — letting me know I couldn't escape. I had to get its hand off me. I doubled the workouts and used the stairs at the house to do angled one-arm push-ups. At first, the strain on my joints caused me to scream, but I built up from less than one to sets of ten. By the summer, when my seventh month at the house ended, I could do fifteen one-arm push-ups reversed on the stairs with my feet elevated above me. I pounded out rep after rep, hardly feeling the strain on my joints. It was about this time that I went stir crazy.

The small town offered little in the way of entertainment. There was a grocery store and drug store that combined also covered the town's book, hardware, and appliance needs, and a theatre that played movies already released on DVD. The only real excitement was the fishing. I loved to watch the fishermen bring in their hauls at the end of the day.

I watched in awe as boat after boat pulled in with bluefin tuna that weighed hundreds of pounds. The biggest fish were dragged in behind the boats — the carcasses staying fresh in the briny water that had given them life minutes before. The fishermen took turns raising the giant fish onto the docks. Tour groups stood with the hanging catch for photo opportunities — the captains smiling biggest of all. They got the profit of the catch while the charter passengers got the cheap photo and the priceless story to go along with it.

Once the photos were taken, the largest tuna were taken apart on the dock with a chainsaw. In the same spot in which they had just been immortalized on film forever, they were dissected for the value of their parts and put on ice. The large tuna were soon riding the ocean once more, only it was in the belly of a boat bound for Japan.

I watched the haul every day I could before making the long walk back to the house in the woods. On my way home one night, I decided I would book a charter of my own.

On a cold Wednesday morning, I headed out fishing with a man named Jeff. His boat *Wendy* was worth hundreds of thousands of dollars making me think the giant fish must be worth their weight in cash.

"Good money in this?" I asked as we plowed through the water.

"Charters? Oh, sure, couple a fellas out on the water makes me a good bit for sure," he said.

"Not the charters, the fishing. The boat doesn't look cheap."

"Fishing is a funny thing. When it's good it pays the bills and more for sure, but when it's bad you can't even put fish on the table." He laughed at his own joke for a second before going on. "Chartering is like the middle. It gives me some cash on a slow day, and if we catch something I get that too."

"Win, win," I said. Jeff smiled at me and looked out at the vast expanse of water ahead. The blowing sea air was clean; nothing polluted it with exhaust or pollen. I breathed deep as though for the first time and smiled. It wasn't the cold grin I learned from my uncle that usually came before violence — it was a genuine smile. I was happy on the water.

Once we came to a stop in the water, Jeff pulled a fish from a tub at the back of the boat; it wriggled alive in his hands.

"If this is your idea of fishing, I want my money back."

"Get lost, boy. This is the bait. The fish love 'em. But first..." He put the fish down on a work table and pulled a knife from a magnetic strip that held it above the work surface. He cut the fish into chunks and threw the pieces into a stained bucket. He repeated the process, pulling more fish from the tub to chunk them on the table.

"Why not just do this ahead of time."

"You gotta do it this way. The tuna like it fresh, and if the bait is too cold they'll spit it out before the hook gets in."

"They can spit?" I said. My tone gave away the fact that I thought I was being fed a script meant to entice the tourists.

Jeff stopped his bloody work and looked me in the eye. He pointed at me with the knife, and his words had no humour in them. "You got to get your head around what you're dealing with here. These aren't goldfish you're hunting. These are monsters. Dangerous monsters who know what they like, and aren't afraid to tell you different."

I nodded at the knife and realized Jeff didn't work from a script. "How do you know there are tuna here?" I asked.

"I work this water every day. I know where the monsters are, but you can check the fish finder if you don't believe me, city boy."

I followed his directions up the stairs to the fish finder beside the wheel of the boat. The screen showed a scattering of yellow dots; below the yellow spatter were two large red dots. "What am I looking at?" I yelled back to Jeff.

"The yellow dots are a school of mackerel. Those fishes are running for their lives down there for sure."

I walked back down the stairs to find Jeff looking over the side of the boat at the dark water. "Are the red dots tuna then?"

He smiled at me and put one gloved finger to his nose, closing a nostril. He pushed air hard through his nose, shooting snot over the side. "Those red dots, city boy, are giant bluefin tuna. Not your canned tuna. Big fuckin' monsters for those Japanese fellows to have with rice and sake. Godzillas with gills, for sure."

"How big?"

"Anywhere between two hundred and a thousand pounds. I told you it's no goldfish; it's a bull. It runs fast and it doesn't get tired. This thing will fight you like nothing else."

"How do we catch it?"

"You stand over there and you hold that rod tight. You paid for the experience so you can go mano-a-fisho for a little while. You can let it beat your ass until you're ready to hand it over."

I put a hand on the pole and watched the water lap the boat while Jeff threw bait over the side. The chunks sank fast, leaving no trace they ever existed until Jeff threw more on top of them.

"I want the fish to swim figure eights around the boat. If he's into the bait he'll stick around for more."

On the third toss, I saw a dark shape streak by the boat under the splash of the raw fish. Jeff saw the streak and laughed under his breath. He baited the large metal hook with something white before spearing a large chunk of bait.

"What is the white stuff?"

"Styrofoam, city boy; it came with the new TV. The hook is heavy. The foam gives it a bit of lift so it won't sink before Godzilla gets a chance to pass it by. Secure the pole, city boy."

I grabbed the pole, anchored in the metal holster, with two hands while Jeff threw the baited hook over. Even though the pole was propped up by the holster, I could still feel its heavy weight; it was nothing like the fibreglass rods I used as a kid. I breathed deep and cleared my mind while I waited for the giant below to grab the loaded bait. Jeff and I sat quiet in the boat. No more questions or sarcastic remarks passed between us. I stared at the line, happy for the calm minutes on the ocean. As if the giant below sensed my happiness, the line began to run out, yard after yard, away from the *Wendy*.

"He can run fast and deep for almost three hundred yards. Problem is he swims with his mouth closed. Eventually he's gonna have to slow down to open his mouth and breathe."

The line ran from the pole as though I had shot something into the water, the reel releasing its heavy line as though there were no drag at all. After a long minute, the rapidly fleeing line began to slow, and that's when the real fight began. I stood, heaving against the rod, for what felt like hours. I followed every instruction the suddenly serious captain gave me. Jeff never asked me to turn over the pole; he just guided me in killing the giant.

After an hour of endless fighting, I began to see the head of my foe. My left arm burned with the effort of fighting the bluefin, but I never let go. I was up against my first real test and I was not going to blink. Little by little I began to see more of the head of my enemy; it was heavy and fierce, its eyes alive with fear and the marine equivalent of adrenaline.

As I dragged the fish closer and closer to the boat, Jeff stopped watching me with his hawk eyes and turned to retrieve a huge pole off the a rack at from the stern. The pole was old and worn and had a large black hook on the end. The tool didn't match the many technological advancements on the boat — it was a relic from harder times. It was a grim instrument, one I later learned to call a gaff, and it made the tuna's tremendous opposition all at once understandable.

"Bring it closer," he yelled.

I manoeuvred the tuna beside the boat, and Jeff bent over the side and swung the hook into the flesh behind the head of the bluefin tuna. With my help, he dragged the fish into the boat. It hit the deck with a thud and helplessly slapped its tail against the deck as though it were only airborne and not helplessly dying. I felt a pang of empathy for the fish. I knew what it was to be beaten to the point of death.

If Jeff caught my expression he didn't show it; he just looked over the fish and then at his watch. "We got time to get this back in before it starts to spoil. If we stay out I have to bleed it and pack it with ice. That would take about as long as it would take us to just cruise into the dock."

"How big is it?" I asked.

"'Bout three hundred pounds, city boy."

"How long would it take for one of the real big fish?"

"That's five or six hours of hard work, but it's easier at the end. We don't bring them into the boat when they're that big. We secure them by the tail and tow 'em in to be lifted out with a small crane."

"So you get all the cash for this catch plus what I paid?"

Jeff smiled at me. "Sometimes it pays to be an island fisherman, eh, city boy? But it ain't all easy. No, I gotta haul it in, get it ready with the saw, and then clean up the boat. No, the job ain't all roses, that's for sure."

"Sounds like you need help."

"Had a college kid, but he quit on me. Thought the hours were too long. Ha, I told him you want to make a living on the boat you gotta be out before the sun and you only stop when it's long gone. There's lots of island kids looking for work. I'll take another on before long and work him till he decides he's meant for other things. Kids today don't want to work all day fighting the fish; it's easier to go work at Subway. There the only fish you fight are already at the bottom of a bucket."

I thought about it for a minute — the minute was fifty-nine more seconds than I needed. In the last four hours, I hadn't thought about home or my arm once. "I want to work for you, Jeff," I said.

"Why's a city boy want to get his hands dirty for peanuts? 'Cause make no mistake, that's what I pay. I don't share the profits."

I used the same excuse I'd given Nellie. "I need to get away from the city."

Jeff smiled again. My answer seemed to be some secret code that everyone on the island silently understood. "Well," he said, gesturing at the expanse of ocean, "ya won't get much farther away than this."

CHAPTER FOUR

I spent the rest of the season searching for giants with my captain. I was paid a low hourly wage, and I was treated better—he didn't talk to me like I was an idiot more than three times an hour. I learned the ins and outs of fishing off the coast and in the deep ocean. Because I wasn't paying anymore, I was no longer the one holding the rod. Jeff fought the monsters while I followed orders. Between bouts of frantic reeling, he explained how to sense when to pull and when to let the fish run. The only job left for me was gaffing. Once the fish was close enough to see the panic in its lidless eyes, it was my job to bury the hook behind its thrashing head. The trick was timing the strike so that the gaff sunk deep into shoulder of the fish. The shoulder was dense enough to support the weight of the fish as it was pulled from the water and it was far away from the prime meat. After a few weeks at sea, I could bury the hook deep in the fish without a moment's hesitation. It was like stabbing a person up close. All at once, the panicked eyes went even wilder until they dulled as the fish resigned itself to its fate. If the fish was big enough, I was demoted to harpooner. I would spear the fish, to bring it closer to death and even closer to the gaff. When the true monsters were circling the drain, we hooked them with wire and dragged their carcasses back to port. The part of me that felt remorse for the first fish I saw dragged into the boat vanished after my second trip out. Part of me, a part I tried to pretend was gone, enjoyed the thrill of the fight. It wasn't the cruelty that brought me back day after day. It was the skill of the hunt and the artistry of the perfect blow with the gaff. Fishing felt like reflex. I used the old muscles I had developed working with my uncle and for Paolo Donati. As much as I thought I wanted a new life, there were some things I couldn't unlearn, even out on the ocean away from all the city lights and smells.

At the end of the fishing season, Jeff went on EI, even though he had earned almost six figures from the tuna and charters. I spent the winter in the house…working out and having a nightly meal with my captain and his wife Wendy. Each night, I was invited back into Jeff's home and treated as though I were a member of the family rather than an employee. My awkwardness and lack of social skills wore off fast in the loving home. I learned to enjoy dinner, and began to look forward to it. Soon I found myself keeping tabs on interesting things to bring up over dinner. The dinners expanded to weekends. I watched movies with Jeff and spent time admiring his hunting rifles while I was told stories about the ones that got away. Through all the stories and firearm showcasing, I played ignorant pretending to be in awe of the dangerous weapons.

I loved my new friends. A fact which made it hard to hide what I was. We spoke mainly about fishing and life on the island. When I was put on the spot about my life before the island, I stuck to generic comments and terms like "rat race," which got me appreciative nods. So long as I spoke of the city in clichés, I was safe from further probing — even safer from losing my new friends. My old life was something few would be able to understand, and a good man like Jeff would never allow me to be near his wife and business if he knew what I was. I understood this — he had priorities and they were sacred to him. I was still searching for my own new priorities, and for a while I thought the search was narrowing as I began to truly become a part of other people's lives again for the first time since my parents died. I laughed and smiled more often; I even forgot to check over my shoulder once in a while. The island had healed my body, but it had trouble healing the rest of me.

The winter ended, and we went back on the boat. I was strong and healthy, but tired. I was sleeping less and less with each night on the island. My first nights in my new home had been long and restful, but each passing day took with it precious minutes. I collapsed into an ever shortening dreamless sleep each night waking before the sun in the loud silence of the house.

Together Jeff and I fished and worked charter groups of die-hard anglers out for a new challenge and loud drunken businessmen taking days away from the difficult island golf courses. After each day of fishing, Jeff would take the charter off the boat with the catch and set up for a photo. The people who had chartered the boat crowded together to get in the shot while I stayed clear. Jeff had stopped trying to include me, deciding it was a fight he would never win; he left me to clean the boat while he schmoozed the clients for the last few minutes. I stayed clear of the crowds and their cameras despite the fact that I hadn't been anywhere close to trouble for almost two years. Part of me couldn't let go of all of the years of training beaten into me by my uncle. While I stopped looking over my shoulder all of the time, I couldn't let myself be captured on film for anyone to see. I was happy to clean the blood off the boat and prepare for the following day. Life went like this for months until the day I slipped up and was caught off guard.

Four politicians down from Ottawa caught an eight-hundred-pound bluefin at the tail end of a slow day. I was cleaning up the boat while they took their picture and quietly conversed around the hanging fish when one of the men grabbed his chest and uttered that he was having chest pains. His friends searched his pockets for his pills, but they were in his bag — left behind on the boat with me. Jeff yelled for me to bring down the bag and I did it without thinking. I ran as my right hand searched the bag for the pills. I had them in my hand as I reached the crowd of people around the man, who was lying on the dock. I didn't check to see what kind of safety top was on the pill bottle; I just dug a nail into the plastic and sent a geyser of white pills flying over the dock. I dug one of the remaining pills out of the container and tried to shove it down the man's throat, but he was too far gone. He died on the dock, below the massive fish he helped pull in. Camera flashes pelted the body from nosy tourists who took shots of the scene before I could move out of the way. One of the shots, one with a profile of my face as I bent down to help the dying man, got national coverage in the papers. The man who died was a politician who was pro big business and against protecting Canada's national resources. Headlines like "Nature Fights Back" led the picture out to the rest of the country. I saw the photo the next day after Jeff slapped the newspaper on the back of my head.

"Ya managed to get your ugly face into the paper. Well, half of it anyway, didn't ya, city boy? Yer just lucky my face was in it to balance it out. Yer mug would scare off the tourists."

I ignored the comment as I looked at my face created out of thousands of meticulously placed ink dots. My face had been sent out across the country for everyone to see. It was that front page postcard that brought the man to the wharf; he was there because of the picture. He was there for me.

Few people came to the wharf alone, and no one did it dressed like he was going to a club. The outsider was not dressed to fish or tour — he had no camera, fishing pole, or binoculars. He didn't even seem to be interested in the large fish being cut to pieces by the chainsaw. He just stood at the edge of the pier watching people get into their cars. I pulled my hat down low and bent over pretending to work around the boat. I thought I had an agreement with my old boss, Paolo Donati, and his criminal army. After I helped Paolo survive his very own Russian revolution, he said we were even. The man on the wharf said different.

I closed my eyes and thought about the photo. I stared at it when I first saw it — enraged at my stupidity. I got too comfortable and I paid for it. The picture had my face in it and the boat's name was in the caption. Soon the guy with the pointy shoes would get tired of waiting and watching the wrong people walk by. He would get impatient and decide to walk around the ships looking for the boat named "Wendy." It was close to the end of the day, the perfect time for someone looking to go unnoticed to walk down to the boats. People were coming and going all over the pier; no one would pay much attention to an out-of-place man looking at the ships

I moved to the other side of the boat and took a seat. If I finished the nightly cleanup, there would be no reason for me to stay on board. I wanted to be the only one around when Pointy Shoes came looking for me. I wanted him to be out of his element when he made his play, so I had to wait and make sure Jeff couldn't see me taking it easy while he schmoozed on the dock with the day's charter.

I got up twenty minutes later after feeling the boat slightly shift with the addition of my captain's weight. I scanned the wharf, noticing how empty it had become. There were a few fisherman left hosing off their boats and loading their trucks, and one other man still watching the parking lot.

"Shit, city boy. You're not done yet? I'll help ya get finished, 'cause at this pace you'll be here all night."

"Sorry, Jeff. I just got to thinking and it slowed me down. You don't need to stick around. I'll finish up here. You get home to Wendy; she's probably craving something."

"Don't ya know, that is for sure. Her and that baby have me going everywhere for food. The only thing she doesn't crave is tuna. At least I could bring that home with me. Last night I had to go into Charlottetown for Taco Bell. I wasn't in bed until one." He sighed and looked around at the mess on the boat. "Make sure to lock her up when you're done, city boy."

"Tell Wendy I said hey."

"Tell her yourself at dinner. After you're done here."

The rest of his goodbyes trailed off as he walked away from the boat. I watched him go, making sure to stand straight up on the side of the boat so I could be seen from the parking lot. I watched Jeff pass Pointy Shoes; they nodded a greeting to one another as Jeff walked over to his car. Pointy Shoes pulled a piece of paper from his pocket and unfolded it. I guessed it was the newspaper photo. He glanced at the paper, then turned to look at Jeff again. While his back was to me, I took off my hat. When his head turned back, I made an elaborate production of stretching and wiping my forehead. I didn't look in the direction of Pointy Shoes, but I was sure he was looking at me. I walked to the ladder on the side of the boat while, in my peripheral vision, I watched my audience consult his piece of paper once again. He was comparing me to the paper. I made my way down the ladder to the dock. Once I had two feet on the wood planks, I kneeled at the ropes holding the boat to the dock. I untied one of the knots and began retying it slowly. With my right hand, I unsheathed the knife I kept at the small of my back. The knife was a worn fishing knife that I used everyday; it was battered, but razor sharp. Jeff always made fun of the way I carried my knife, but I could never force myself to wear it out in the open or leave it in a pocket where it was hard to pull free. A concealed weapon always felt more natural.

I put the knife on the dock beside my foot, so that it was hidden from anyone approaching. I flipped one loose end of the rope over one side of the knot then the other, pretending to be unsure about the right way to finish. I didn't have to pretend long before I heard the squeak of old worn wood planks groaning under human weight. Pointy Shoes was walking towards me. Being on my knees made me an obvious target. Every schoolyard bully loved to shove a kid when he was down on a knee tying his shoe. Pointy Shoes was just a bigger schoolyard bully — one with a paycheque.

I looked in his direction as he approached, smiled, and said, "Evening." Looking at him to say hello let me see that his hands were empty. A fact that made me happy.

He didn't smile back; he just stopped eight feet away and spread his feet apart. I didn't want to act first because there was still a small chance that this guy was a tourist or maybe just a reporter doing a follow-up story. "You want to book a charter, you'll have to talk to the boss. I can give you his number if you want, or you can come back tomorrow."

I got no response at first from the man with the pointy shoes. I looked into his eyes and I knew there was no way he was a tourist or even a reporter. His greeting relieved all lingering doubts about what he really was.

"Hey, Wilson."

I remained on my knees as our eyes locked. My face didn't register surprise, instead it pulled into an expression I thought I had forgotten. My face made an ugly grin, my uncle's grin. It was a look that I learned the hard way. Whenever I thought I knew the score, I would see the look on my uncle's face and know I was wrong. The look tormented me, but I was lucky—everyone else who saw it usually wound up dead. I spent years learning my uncle's craft, years surviving his tutelage, until the same grin became my property. Pointy Shoes saw it and it told him something he didn't like. It said I wasn't afraid. It said I wasn't even surprised. It said I knew something he didn't. My grin said all of this in a fraction of a second.

Pointy Shoes was good; he didn't waste time looking confused. He instead reached behind his back under the stretchy fabric of his synthetic shirt. His reaction didn't faze me; I was good too, better than this guy, even after two years of rusting. My right hand found the knife by my foot, and I lobbed it in the direction of Pointy Shoes. The throw was slow and sloppy not because I was rusty, but rather because I wanted Pointy Shoes to use both of his hands. He gave up on whatever was behind his back and decided to try to catch the slowly spinning knife moving towards his chest.

Instinct is a funny thing; every person will always opt to save himself over almost any other choice. It takes years of training and experience to be able to fight the primal urge for self-preservation. Pointy Shoes chose personal safety over inflicting harm on me. He didn't catch the knife; he only managed to knock it out of the air. Pointy Shoes let out a sigh of relief just before my fist crushed his collar bone like a beer can. The blow knocked the air out of him, pushing with it any means of screaming. To his credit, Pointy Shoes stayed standing; he just crumpled inward like he was a balloon losing air. My heavy work boot smashed his instep knocking him off balance and into my hands. The fishing and rehabilitation had turned my grip into something close to a vise. His greasy hair had nowhere to go in my hands but down, dragging his face to my rising knee. Pointy Shoes fell to the old salt-soaked boards as though he were poured from a cup. His body just splashed unconscious at my feet. The few leftover fishermen were too far away to see what had just happened in four seconds beside the *Wendy*, and the sound couldn't have carried over the roar of motors and lapping water.

I bent down and loosened the rest of the ropes holding the boat to the dock. Once the boat was free, I pulled Pointy Shoes into a fireman's carry. I laughed to myself when I realized that holding a full-grown man on my shoulders and climbing a ladder onto a boat were close to effortless. I had healed in time.

I put Pointy Shoes in the bow and went to the wheel to fire up the diesel engine. The engine roared to life and let off a cloud of smoke that I secretly inhaled every day as though it were the scent of a rare rose. The exhaust gave me something that the clean sea air never could. As time went on the smell of man-made pollution was something I craved, something I welcomed like a secret devil.

The rumbling of the engine pushed the boat through the cloud of smoke and away from the wharf. The motion of the boat caused Pointy Shoes to stir. I aimed the boat straight out to sea and walked out to meet my new friend.

Before saying hello again, I took a nickel-plated .32 Smith & Wesson revolver from Pointy Shoes's waistband along with a wallet, keys, and a cell phone from his pockets.

Pointy Shoes had a name: Johnny Romeo. The name told me everything. Someone had reached out to me. Someone who should have known better.

Johnny was too out of it to cause trouble, so I went back to the wheel and guided us through the rapidly dimming light to a spot on the water where I could barely make out the lights from the dock. I yelled to Johnny as soon as I cut the engine. "What does Paolo want? Payback?"

Johnny groaned in response. He had managed to pull himself up to a sitting position against the side of the boat. His synthetic shirt had a sharp angular bulge near his neck. The unnatural distension was surrounded by a growing wetness. Johnny had a compound fracture and probably a concussion from my knee. I picked up a bucket and got water from the bait tank. The fish inside swam happily when they realized I only wanted some of their real estate.

The salt water hit him, soaking his shirt and sending pain through the wound; he sobered instantly.

"What does Paolo want, Johnny?"

"He...he wants to see you."

I was surprised at the answer, but I didn't dwell on it. "Why did he send you and your gun? Was that supposed to lead the way?"

"Fuck, I can't move my arm. Fuck, it hurts. I think I'm gonna be sick."

I hit him with another bucket of fish water just to keep him in the here and now.

"Jesus, he...he just wanted me to find you and make sure you went to see him."

"He here now? On the island?"

"He's back in Hamilton at the restaurant." Johnny barely got his words out before he was sick all over himself.

"How were you going to make me go to him? Were you going to threaten me? Or were you going to force me with your shiny gun?"

Johnny looked away from me and the mess on his synthetic shirt. I read the body language and knew that he had already made a play. "What did you do, Johnny?"

He didn't answer me. He looked into my eyes and I saw that he was an errand boy. He was a hard young man who got cocky, wanted to impress his boss, and had ended up neck deep in trouble.

"You have to go meet the boss."

"Or what, Johnny? What did you do?"

"Heh, I found you yesterday and before I came down to the wharf I had tea with the nice lady who you rent from. Me and her talked all about you. Her mysterious stranger, she calls you. Can you believe that shit? The mysterious stranger who always says hello and pays his rent on time." He burped up some vomit after his last revelation.

"Where is she?"

"Don't worry about her, you got bigger problems. You need to get home."

"Where is she?"

"Fuck you."

I turned and walked back to the wheel. The diesel engine sputtered back to life, violently sending fumes in waves out over the water. I breathed the smoke in deep and felt it burn my nose as I exhaled. Each second I smelled the exhaust pulled away months of the atrophy that had set in from safe living and honest work. Almost at once, fishing with Jeff seemed years ago. I turned the boat around towards the docks and set the throttle to a slow chug. Johnny had managed to get to his feet, but the effort along with the compound fracture caused him to vomit and retch over the side. I retrieved the heavy black gaff Jeff and I used to hook the giant bluefin. The gaff was four feet long and heavy. Its hook was dulled with age, but it would still be sharp enough. The tool hung low in my hands as I walked back to Johnny who was still bent over the side of the boat.

Johnny had just finished another retch and shudder into the dark water. He turned his head in time to see me coming with the gaff in my hands. He tried to turn his body, but my left hand found the back of his neck. My hand held him in place, his chest forced against the railing. I hooked the gaff into his stomach and pulled hard towards me with my right hand. The hook moved through the synthetic shirt like it wasn't there and buried itself in Johnny's guts.

Johnny let out a scream on the desolate water, but the only person who could hear it didn't care. My left hand let go of Johnny's neck and found a metal-studded belt under his ruined shirt; I used it to propel Johnny over the side of the boat into the water. All of the noises Johnny made were eaten by the merciless ocean. I gripped the railing hard with one hand and held tight to the gaff towing Johnny's body through the water. I clenched my jaw shut and held tight as the veins in my forearm began to stand out. Johnny was dragged through the wake of the boat backwards by the gaff. The speed of the water and the weight of his body made sure that the hook wouldn't dislodge. I braced myself and held the gaff at an angle that allowed Johnny's head to stay above the water so he wouldn't die on me right away. His flailing arms and legs created a lot of drag, making his body feel as though it weighed a ton.

After a minute, I pulled Johnny up into the boat by the gaff. He coughed up sea water from his lungs and communicated his agony is low groans. He lay face down on the deck of the *Wendy*, impaled on the gaff. The hook was buried deep in his belly, making the wooden handle stand straight up in the air like a fence post. Johnny lay still while I caught my breath, watching the lights of the docks off in the distance. We were moving so slowly that it seemed the lights were no closer than when I had turned the boat around.

"See, Johnny, this is how we bring the big tuna in once we catch them. We drag them behind the boat until all of the fight in them is gone. Thing is, fish like the water so they can hold on for a long while even on the end of a hook. How long you think you can stay alive in the water on the end of a big hook? Think you're tougher than a fish?"

Johnny had no response for me. His back rose and fell as he took in shallow breaths letting me know he was still alive. "I want to know what you did to the old lady, Johnny. You keep me in the dark much longer and I'll show you how much a fish has to put up with. I'll drag you the rest of the way back so I can get a hold of the chainsaw they use on the dock. You saw them do that today, didn't you? It'll be much easier with you. I promise."

Johnny's eyes fluttered and opened; his lips began to form a word over and over again. I put my hands on the gaff and pulled, lifting Johnny off the deck of the boat. If you ignored the hook in his belly, it would have looked as though he were levitating in a magic show.

"Trunk." Johnny's lips finally found a voice two feet in the air.

"She's in the trunk, Johnny?"

"Trunk. No more. Trunk." His voice was quiet and gravelly, but understandable.

The magic show continued as I pulled Johnny higher off the deck. I muscled him over the side as he continued to groan his new mantra, "No more. Trunk. No more." His body splashed on the water and disappeared as the waves erased his existence. His hands stayed visible above the water in the boat lights, groping for something to hold on to — something that wasn't there. I breathed hard from the exertion and wiped my face with the arm of my shirt. It was then that I noticed my face. For a second time, my face had stretched into that grin I had shelved so long ago after leaving the city. It wasn't a sadist's smile; I took no pleasure in what I had done to Johnny. It was the smile of someone welcoming back an old friend. I knew then that Johnny was wrong — there was going to be more. Much more.

CHAPTER FIVE

I used the bucket to wash the blood off the deck. After three buckets of water, no one would ever know about what took place on *Wendy* after her captain went home for the night. I pushed the engine of the clean ship harder and drove the boat fast through the waves, feeling each impact like a punch. I made it back to the dock in under ten minutes. I collected Johnny's belongings, tucking his gun into the waistband under the front of my shirt — the back already taken by my knife. I pocketed his phone and wallet, but kept the car keys in hand. I left the boat keys in the ignition for Jeff to find and tied off on the dock before making my way to the parking lot.

There were only two cars left in the parking lot — mine and a black Lexus. I used Johnny's key fob to pop the trunk as I approached. Inside, I saw the body of my landlady bound with duct tape. Nellie lay still in the trunk, but her rapidly blinking eyes told me she was alive. Her eyes registered fear when they adjusted to the new light from the parking lot and saw me standing over her, and panic when she saw me pull my knife. I cut the tape on her hands and feet leaving her to handle the strip on her mouth.

"Mr. Wilson! There was a man. He grabbed me and tied me up. He said he was looking for you."

I admired the steel in the old girl. She didn't cry. She kept her wits about her despite just being let out of a trunk.

"That man, he…"

"He's gone," I said.

"You mean you…you…"

"I mean he's gone. Now let's get you home."

I drove, and except for her directions, there was silence in the car. When I pulled into her driveway, I spoke up, putting an end to the quiet. "I'm sorry for what happened," I said.

"Why did he do that to me?"

"He needed me to do something. He took you to make sure I would do it."

"He was just so rough."

"He wouldn't have hurt you," I lied.

She paused and considered my lie before asking a question in a low voice. "What did he want?"

"It doesn't matter now," I said, ending that line of questioning. The answer seemed to satisfy her, and she opened the car door with a shaky hand.

"Goodbye, Mr. Wilson."

I said goodbye, then drove to the rental house. Speed limits on the rural island roads were eighty kilometres an hour; I pushed the car to one forty. I needed to clear out before Nellie decided to call the cops about tonight's activities. I figured I had half an hour until the shock wore off, and five minutes after that until her sense of civic duty kicked in. The house had been mine for close to two years, but no one would be able to tell by looking at it. In the kitchen sink were the spoon, fork, and pot that I used for every meal. There were a few books and magazines in the small living room and a gym bag on the floor of the bedroom I slept in. I picked up the books as I walked through the living room and dropped them in the gym bag. Then I lifted the mattress and collected the even stacks of bills that were distributed across the expanse of the box spring.

I had spent little of the money on the island. The cash paid for food, rent, and incidentals, and could not be traced to me. I had worked hard to keep myself off the grid of the small town. There were only three people on the island who knew where to find me, until today. Now, Paolo knew where I lived making the house, and the island, as safe as a burning building. Worse, Jeff's wife, his business, everything he had was at risk too. They would become chess pieces in a madman's game if I didn't knock over the board. I loaded the bag with the rest of my belongings and stopped to use the bathroom. I scanned the house over one last time as I moved towards the door. In the kitchen, I pulled the house keys from my key ring and left them on the counter before walking out of the house for the last time.

In an hour I was at the bridge, in line to get off the island. The bridge was a provincially funded con. It had cost nothing to enter the province from New Brunswick, and $27.50 to leave. There was no way out that didn't involve a wallet. The government was still the best thief I knew. The visit from Johnny and getting swindled by the province ruined my second experience with the bridge.

I drove the Trans-Canada Highway through New Brunswick at 130 kilometres an hour. I wanted to drive straight through to Hamilton, but I knew the day's work combined with the evening's action would anesthetize me before I got out of the province. I had put two more hours between me and the bridge when Johnny's cell phone started to ring. I had left the phone and wallet out on the passenger seat, so I barely had to take my eyes off the road while I picked the phone up and debated answering the call. Paolo sent Johnny to me, and if Johnny didn't answer his phone it wouldn't take Paolo long to piece together what had gone down.

I opened the phone and answered, "Yeah?"

"Is everything set up?" It was Paolo's voice riding the digital signal from Hamilton to me in the car. "You hear me, Johnny? Did you do what I told you to do?"

"I told you not to come looking for me, Paolo."

There was a ten-second pause before Paolo's voice crossed the country into my ear. "*Figlio,* I need to see you. I need your help."

"I can't help you, Paolo. You said it yourself—I'm a crow. I turned on my own, remember."

Just days before I drove to the island, I had been working for Paolo Donati—the man who ruled the Italian mob in Hamilton. I wasn't Italian, just some kind of mutt with ancestors all over parts of Europe. This made me automatically distrusted by every one of Paolo's crews. The distrust was intensified by my total lack of an identity. No one knew me so no one could vouch for me. I grew up invisible and worked with other invisible pros on all kinds of jobs. My only tie to anyone had been through blood. My uncle and I worked together; he provided the jobs through the contacts he had. Our last job was for Paolo, personally, off the books. My uncle ended up dead and I ended up unemployed. I was invisible, with no connections to any world, legal or otherwise. Paolo knew this and decided that he would use me personally for jobs he needed to distance himself from. I worked against Paolo's enemies whether they were Russians, the cops, or even his own people. No one who saw me would think I worked for a man like Paolo — a fact that made me even more useful. Over the years, I earned Paolo's trust, and eventually the hatred of everyone in his organization. Those who knew I existed saw me as an insult to everything their organization stood for. I wasn't family so I should never have been involved with jobs that should have been left to important made men. But Paolo was different from his underlings. He was unconventional as a leader, and as a result, he was more successful than any of his predecessors. He was educated and loved to muse about the nature of animals. He compared those around him to the beasts of the jungle, showing everyone how short the trip was from jungle to pavement. Better than his knowledge of animals and human nature was Paolo's understanding of the underworld he ruled. He knew how to use the mob and its rules, and more important, he knew how, and when, to circumvent them. He kept me in the fold, under wraps from his subordinates, because I did things that helped him maintain his position as king of the jungle. He believed he had me under control because I was alone and without support. He had no idea that I lived the way I had been trained. I was disconnected and solitary by choice because it made me untouchable. I was invulnerable so long as I controlled every situation by anticipating everyone's next moves. I stayed one step ahead of everyone, and survived in the most inhospitable environment. Everything I did was calculated and covert until my friendship with Steve challenged that.

Without any conscious effort, I had formed a bond with a local bar owner and his wife. Steve and Sandra were my friends — the only human contact I had. One of Paolo's men, Tommy Talarese, tried to destroy their lives, and in doing so set in motion a chain of events that rocked the underbelly of the city. Tommy Talarese wanted to show his kid how to collect protection like a man, after Steve had thrown Tommy's son out into the street. Tommy kidnapped Steve's wife, unleashing the bar owner like a wiry hurricane on the neighbourhood. Steve and I worked our way up the chain of local muscle to Tommy's front door. Many died getting Sandra back, including Tommy and his entire family.

I took the news to Paolo, attempting to spin the situation. Paolo, upon hearing the news, was already thinking of how to use the events to his advantage. That showed why Paolo held such a grip on the city: he would use anything to his advantage, even the death of one of his lieutenants. I convinced him of what he already decided for himself — that Tommy's death was best pinned on the city's other underworld organization, the Russians, rather than on a bartender. Paolo listened to me and did what he would have done anyway. He used Tommy's death to unite his crews to one purpose. Paolo struck out at the Russians, who were trying to take over everything Paolo had established. Paolo fired me and filed away what I did for later retribution. He told me I was a crow because they eat their own kind to protect themselves.

Less than a month later, Paolo brought me back into his employ. My second career with Paolo involved me only with his number two, Julian. I worked jobs that were more hush-hush than before and asked no questions. One of the jobs was stealing a bag from some computer nerds. The bag turned out to be full of Russian property. The Russians came after me, and I had no escape or backup from Paolo. Paolo was going to use what I stole to crush the Russians and he was going to let them kill me before he did it. The Russians were going to act as Paolo's payback for what I did to Tommy. Paolo was also using me to create confusion for the Russians, who had no idea who I worked for and no way to find out after I was dead. Once I figured out that Paolo hung me out to dry, I stole the bag back for the Russians, and they moved on the Italians first. The whole ordeal ended in blood with me in the middle. I saved Paolo's life, and told him I was out. He honoured the deal for almost two years.

"*Figlio,* forget what I said. You and me are square. I need you for a job. The kind of thing you used to do. Please, it has to be you. I'll pay you whatever you ask, just meet with me."

This was a new side of the man who had plotted to kill me. He seemed sincere in his desire to peacefully meet. He called me *figlio,* "son," trying to rebuild our bond over the phone like a horrible telephone commercial. "If you need to see me so bad, why didn't you come yourself?"

"This is a delicate situation. Leaving would attract too much suspicion," he said.

"Sending Johnny attracted suspicion," I said. My voice was cold and flat, betraying nothing.

"Why? What did he do? Where is he? I told him how I wanted this done. Put him on."

"Johnny crossed the line and he paid for it. You crossed the line too. I told you we were done. All you did today was force me to move."

There was a heavy sigh that must have come from deep down inside Paolo fifteen hundred kilometres away. "I was wrong about what I said about you. You're not a crow. You're a lioness. You know what lionesses do, *figlio*? They protect their cubs. I sent Johnny to ask nicely, and what do you do? You overreact like a hungry cat."

"The fancy punk kidnapped an old lady before he even met me. He wasn't here to talk."

Paolo laughed in my ear. "Ah, you see, I'm right. You are a lioness. You protected your own from the jackals, didn't you? Johnny was overeager, probably angry. He knows what you did to Julian — everyone does."

I crippled Julian before I left the city. He was Paolo's number two and a hero to all of the up-and-comers. He was a vicious dinosaur who made his bones crushing other people's. "Julian and I were bound to collide one day. People aren't mad we fought, just that I won."

"They aren't mad, *figlio*; they hate you for it."

"And you want me to come back to that because you

think I'm some lion?"

"Not a lion, *figlio*, a lioness — the mother. This has nothing to do with you being less than a man. No, it's because you left two of your cubs back in my jungle. Those cubs are still here nestled in their bar. I keep them safe for you. Now I need you to do something for *my* cubs. I need to see you."

"Give me a number," I said. He did, and I spoke up. "I'll tell you where and when." I closed the phone before he could argue.

I made it across the border into Quebec just as my eyelids started to get heavy. I found a motel off the highway and paid cash for what was left of the night.

I hit the mattress and all of the trouble I had sleeping over the past months didn't touch me in the lumpy bed. I slept and dreamed for the first time in ages. I dreamed of a city awash in violence and shadows. I dreamed of it and smiled.

CHAPTER SIX

The motel alarm clock woke me before the sun and told me my eyes had been closed for four hours. The sleep felt longer; it felt like the kind of sleep you wake from to find the day half over. I showered and changed my clothes. I dug lightweight olive pants with deep pockets and a grey T-shirt from my bag. I also pulled out a thin blue shirt to go over my T-shirt. The shirt was not necessary in the early September heat, but it buttoned down the front and hung loose, making it perfect for concealing a stolen gun. I left the keys on the night table and was on the road before the water I had splashed on my face dried in my hair.

The road through Quebec was straight for hundreds of kilometres. I drove beside Johnny's powered-down cell phone thinking about home. PEI had always been the island. The rental house was just that, a house. Neither could take the place of where I had grown up invisible to everyone.

Hours after I left the motel, I found myself fighting my way through Montreal traffic. The barrage of cars felt like a scene from *Star Wars*—the one where the kid makes a run at the death star through a sky full of spaceships and laser beams. Vehicles came at me from all angles, most a high-speed blur. I was grateful when a break in the tension came in the form of a small traffic jam. As I sat in the still car, watching six construction workers watch two others work, I decided to power up the phone. It chimed to life and showed it still had half of the battery left. I dialled the number Paolo left me and was left speechless when he himself answered. Any other time I dealt with him, I had to work my way through layers of intermediaries before I could even leave a message.

"You around tomorrow?" I asked, looking at the time on the dashboard clock in the early afternoon sunlight.

"I got some things to do, but I can move them around."

"You want to see me then I name the time and the place."

"And the time is tomorrow. So where is the place, *figlio?*"

I hung up the phone without answering and powered it down. I thought back to all of the dinner-table conversations I had with my uncle. He taught me to read between the lines of books, to use the language to decode what was underneath. It wasn't long before I could do it with people. Using what they said and sometimes what they didn't to decipher what was going on under the surface. Paolo answered the phone himself and he was willing to meet whenever I wanted; he was even willing to adjust his schedule to accommodate me. This was unlike any interaction we ever had before. Paolo was the top of the food chain; he had people answering his calls so he didn't have to get his hands dirty dealing with the mundane. His people understood what he wanted and showed their capability, and worthiness of advancement, by handling the small day-to-day matters. No one was managing me. I got through on what sounded like a personal cell phone — something I never knew Paolo had. The more telling part of the call was his willingness to meet me. Out of principle, Paolo never accommodated anyone. He loved to think of himself as the king of the jungle; he saw himself elevated above all others. He would never obey someone else's schedule; it didn't fit with the personality of a methodical sociopathic kingpin. If Paolo was out to kill me, he never would have changed his methods; he would have seen that as beneath him. He wouldn't try to fool me in order to kill me; he would have kept things as they were and sent men to make it happen, more men after that if necessary. Paolo was into something deep, something big enough to change him, something he needed to see me about. He needed to influence a situation without being directly involved. Using someone who crossed him and left the city two years ago would do just that.

By four p.m., I was entering the outskirts of Toronto. I avoided the 407 highway and its camera tolls even though the road was newer and empty. I was leaving nothing to chance coming home. I was in the city by 5:30 and at a Mediterranean restaurant on Upper James Street by quarter to six. I chose to stop on the Hamilton mountain because most of the action in the city took place downtown away from the bright lights of chain stores and their younger clientele. The restaurant had a sign up that read "New Management." I figured it must have once been a lousy dive and someone must have still believed it could make a comeback. I could tell that the owner and I were the only ones who thought so when I walked through the smoke-grey glass doors into the vacant dining room.

The restaurant smelled wonderful, and I wondered what gruesome hidden secrets caused the management turnover. I took a seat in front of the dark-tinted glass so that I could see outside without being observed from the parking lot. I ordered gyros and ate them with water. The owner was pleasant and chatty, but both qualities faded as I ate in silence. The place stayed empty for the twenty minutes I ate; there were no other staff — just the owner and me. He was a short Arab man with a stubbly shaved head whose body shook from time to time with uncontrollable spasms. With each episode, he seemed to grit his teeth in an attempt to will himself to regain stillness. He was washing a plate behind the counter when I yelled out to him.

"Slow night?"

"No sir, it's off to a very good start."

I figured I was the beginning of a dinner rush in his mind. "How many do you get for dinner?"

There was a spasm then an answer. "Very many, sir."

It was clear the owner was an optimistic, glass-is-half-full sort of guy. "How many people are working with you tonight?" Optimistic owner or not, on his budget he had to be a realist.

He paused and looked away from me then down at the plate he was washing. His answer was sad, "Just me, sir."

I didn't feel bad for cracking his optimism; what he told me was good. "What's your name, pal?"

"I am Yousif, sir."

"Yousif, I think I'm going to get someone else to come down and sample some of your wonderful gyros," I said as I powered up Johnny's phone.

Yousif's optimism seemed to return; he spasmed then smiled. "Very good, sir," he said.

CHAPTER SEVEN

"**M**eet me on the mountain in twenty minutes."

"You said tomorrow."

"And you said your schedule was busy. You want to see me, get up to the Mandarin on Upper James. Wait outside the doors with your phone on. I'll call you when I get there."

Paolo started to reply, but it was no use. I closed the phone and powered it down. I looked out the grey windows at the Mandarin restaurant twenty-five metres across the parking lot. It was a Chinese buffet juggernaut that filled up nightly and probably managed to have a chokehold on Yousif's business. The old owner probably took his lumps from the buffet place and sold the failing business to a naïve person who thought there were many people out there who would choose straight Mediterranean cuisine over a buffet that covered each continent. Yousif was wrong, and he probably had many nights alone in his money pit to mull over his mistake. From where I sat in the empty dining room, I could watch Paolo arrive and decide whether or not I actually wanted to meet him. I ordered a lentil soup and another water, and watched the crowds of hungry families pass me by on their way to the Mandarin.

It took longer than twenty minutes for Paolo to show up; it was more like thirty. He walked briskly up to the entrance and stood there scanning the parking lot and the inside of the restaurant through the glass. He wore black leather loafers — the kind that had tassels instead of laces. His pleated grey slacks hung at the appropriate length over the shoes, and his black golf shirt was tucked into his pants. From my vantage point I couldn't see a little Polo emblem, but I bet it was there. He wore no hat, allowing me to see that it was him from any part of the parking lot. His hair was a little bit thinner and a bit more grey. The only real difference was his posture; his shoulders were up as though tension had wound them tight. As he turned to scan the crowds of people entering and waiting inside, his whole body moved rather than just his head. Something was wrong with the old man. Something was pulling every muscle and tendon tight from the inside out.

I powered up the phone as I finished my last mouthful of soup. I ordered a plate of gyros for Paolo, sending Yousif out of the dining room to the kitchen. The phone chirped its ring in my ear, and I watched Paolo grope at his pockets through the shaded window.

"Yeah?" he said.

"Walk down along the side of the Mandarin. Turn the corner and open the gate. Inside there's a Dumpster. Walk in and close the door behind you."

"You want me to meet you in a Dumpster?"

"Not in, Paolo, beside. Leave the phone on while you walk."

"You're pushing it, *figlio*. I have my limits, and you are on the edge."

"Keep walking," I said as I watched Paolo walk away from the restaurant. I listened to him grumble on the phone as his body disappeared. Soon I heard the creak of a wooden door behind Paolo's complaining. I waited.

"You motherfucker. Where are you, you shit? You think this is funny? You —"

"Shut up and stand there. I'm watching you right now. I want to know who else is too."

"I came alone. Don't you get it? I'm alone. I just want to talk to you."

"Johnny didn't just want to talk," I said between sips from the glass of water on the table. That gave Paolo pause. "I told that kid exactly what I wanted him to do. I had no idea he would be so... overzealous."

"You send shit help and look where it gets you."

"I told you —"

"Shut up and wait there. If someone like Johnny couldn't follow your instructions there are probably others who won't too."

"That is the last time you talk to me with that disrespect. I will walk out of here and make it so you beg to see me. I'll carve an invitation into the ass of that bartender's wife. You got that? Now where the fuck are you?"

I had pushed it with Paolo, and it had shown me nothing. He didn't give up any more information. All I did was piss him off. "Give me a minute. Once I'm sure you're clean

I'll pick you up."

"Once you know I'm clean?"

"It's Dumpster humour, Paolo."

"You motherfucker —"

I put the phone down and watched the lot while Paolo swore. He had been out of sight for two minutes, and no one had followed after him. No one would give him that much rope if they were tailing him. They would want to know what Paolo Donati was doing beside a Dumpster.

I picked the phone up again. Paolo was no longer yelling. I could only hear his heavy seething breaths. "Walk back out front and go into the Mediterranean restaurant on your right."

"You said you were picking me up. I'm not jumping through any more hoops. If you're not there, I will find a place I know you'll run to."

I didn't answer him because through the window I saw him walk back into view still yelling into his phone. I closed Johnny's phone and watched Paolo's eyes open wider in disbelief. He stopped walking and stared at the phone then at the restaurant. I waved to him from behind the glass. He glowered at me — the type of glare that had gotten other people killed. Paolo marched through the doors and sat down in front of me with his back to the glass.

"You got some nerve making me stand next to —" He was interrupted by a plate of gyros being placed in front of him. "What the fuck is this?" he asked in a tone that seemed to force a tremor through Yousif's body.

"G-g-gyros sir. Your dining companion ordered them for you, sir."

"It's cool, Yousif. He just gets grumpy when he's hungry. Don't ya, Dad?"

Paolo grumbled a response and forced a smile at our waiter. Yousif winked at me, his optimism returned. "You won't be hungry for long, sir. Enjoy."

We both watched him walk to the kitchen. It was the brisk walk of a busy man. I turned back to Paolo, who was busy himself staring at his plate.

"Try it, it's good."

Paolo sniffed the steamy food and pushed the plate away. He stared at me, and I stared back. Neither of our eyes moved, but under the table my right hand tightened around Johnny's gun in my waistband. Paolo spoke before I decided to shoot him.

"You look like shit. You know that? You smell too."

I felt my face; my beard was long and my hair was scraggly. When I pulled my hand away I saw the dirt caked under the fingernails of my tanned hand. I didn't look like I belonged in the city, but just a day ago I had fit right in on the island. I didn't say a word—I just stared into Paolo's dark, mirthless eyes.

"You know why you never went anywhere with me?"

"I'm not a people person."

"You're not family, Wilson. Family is what's important. What we do is with family, for family. You, you were good, better than most, but you weren't family, so where could it lead?"

"Did it ever occur to you that it led me where I wanted it too? It lead me to a paycheque."

"Bullshit, *figlio*. You like to fancy yourself the invisible man, and it's true you were hard to find, but you always turned up. You worked for me because you needed something, something concrete. You needed a family and we...we wouldn't let you in. So what did you do? You sold us out for a bartender."

I hated sitting across from a man who was trying to read me as though I were an animal on display. "That was always your problem, Paolo. You thought you were so fucking high and mighty that everyone wanted in with you. But you're half right, I did work for you because you were exactly what I needed. You and your organization had plenty of money, work, and paranoia. I worked for you for so long *because* I could never get close. Your whole set-up was perfect because I was an outsider to everyone and everything. I survived longer than most of your men and I made a hell of a lot more money because I played it my way, not yours or your family's. I never sold you out for the bartender because there was nothing to sell. I was never with you."

Paolo laughed at me then looked away. "Maybe I'm wrong, *figlio*. Maybe I can't see people like I thought, but that doesn't change what's important."

"And that's family," I said.

"Yeah," he said, still looking away. "Family."

"What do you want, Paolo?"

He sighed and then he told me.

CHAPTER EIGHT

"**M**y nephews are missing."

"Which ones?" I asked.

"Armando and Nicola."

"Army and Nicky?" I said. The tone made it sound like I wasn't surprised.

"What?" Paolo asked. I said nothing, so he yelled louder. "What?"

I sighed. "Those two are idiots, Paolo. You know that. Everyone tries to cover up what they do so it doesn't get back to you, but you know about them. They walk around town like big-time gangsters throwing your name and your weight around. I bet they're real scary at that private school they go to."

"You don't think I know what they do? You think I don't fucking know?" His last words ended with his fist pounding the table. "I know what they are like out there, but they are family, and now they're gone."

"What happened?" I asked.

"Week ago, their mother called me and said they didn't

come home to the house. I said they probably were out with some girls, but they still didn't come back the next day. Their phones were off, their friends hadn't seen them. They were gone. The day after that, we found out Armando's car got towed. No one was in it."

"Where was it?"

"Outside a club in Burlington," he said.

Burlington was a city outside Hamilton. The people were richer and the air was cleaner. "You call the cops?"

"The cops got half the resources I got, and no one who knows the boys will talk to the law. The boys are gone."

"So why call me? I don't even know them."

Paolo looked me in the eye. "Someone took my nephews. Someone made them disappear. Someone…"

As he trailed off, I understood. "You think one of your guys did it," I said.

He looked away and nodded.

"Why would anyone who worked for you make a move on the boys? It doesn't hurt you or your power base."

Paolo looked back at me and then at the table. "Lately Armando and Nicola have been using the computer. They put themselves on the Internet on this YouTube. They said some things and some names, and it all got put on the Internet."

I whistled low and found Paolo's eyes. Naming names could get you killed, even if you were the boss's nephews.

"Do you not like your food, sir?" Yousif was back.

"Not now," I said.

"Sir, we have many other dishes I can —"

I cut him off. "Not now, Yousif."

He looked at me, his optimism cracked again. He spasmed, straightened, and then made a slow walk back to the kitchen.

Paolo was still looking at me. "It sounds like they dug their own graves," I said. "If they put names next to events."

"I know," he said quietly. "But they were family." His words hung in the air between us. They could have ignited the cold plate of food in front of him with their anger.

"You want me to find out who did it?"

"I want to know."

"You know what Army and Nicky did. They crossed a line. You can't start accusing your own people over two rats even if they have your DNA. If you knew who it was, no one would question your revenge, but to blindly go after everyone? No one will support that. And if I go around looking into it, everyone is going to know who put me up to it. This is going to dangle me in front of the city and hang you out to dry."

"I want to know." His voice was loud. Yousif dropped a plate in back, probably terrified of the outburst.

I stared into Paolo's fiery eyes. What he wanted would get me killed, and once people figured out Paolo was using me to look into his own people, he would be finished too. Paolo said family was the most important thing, but if he did this, he would betray his second family. Nothing could save him after that. Every ambitious gangster would pull a piece away from him until there was nothing left.

We shared the silence until Paolo could take no more. "I want you to find out who did this, and then I want you to give them to me."

"No," I said. "It's not a smart play."

Before I could say any more Paolo was talking. "I'm not asking, I'm telling you. You're going to do it, or I'm going to finish things with the bartender. You and him killed Tommy and his family for what? His slut wife? If you're not in with me, *figlio*, then I'll do it alone, but before I go down, I'll make things right with the bartender by first making things right with his missus. Once I use her up, I'll put that Irish dog down in the street. Then I'll find the fuck responsible for my nephews myself."

My hand pulsated on the gun under the table. I thought about killing Paolo in the restaurant, killing him and leaving, but he would have insurance.

As if reading my thoughts, he spoke. "I got people watching them now. I can do it from beyond the grave if I have to."

Paolo had me and he knew it. My only connection to the city could still hurt me no matter how far I ran. I rubbed my jaw, forcing the muscles to relax and my teeth to stop grinding. "Who did Army and Nicky name?" I asked.

"Bombedieri, Perino, and Rosa."

"What did they say?"

"You can see for yourself," he said, and reached into his pants.

I tensed and he said, "Easy, *figlio*."

He produced a piece of paper folded over twice. He left it beside the cold plate and stood up. "Call me when you have a name. And I don't want none of this to lead back to me. I go down, I'm taking mister and missus Irish with me, and those two have a lot farther to fall than I do."

He waved goodbye to Yousif, who moved out from the kitchen to hold the door for him. "Nice place you got here," Paolo said.

"Thank you, sir," Yousif said timidly.

"You should think about serving some pasta, not this foreign shit. Even the Chinese place over there has pasta; it's covered in their shit sauces, but it's pasta. That's probably why they're so busy all the time."

"Thank you, sir. Have a good night." It was as rude as Yousif could let himself be.

Paolo left with a smile. I watched him go, noticing his shoulders were a bit less tense.

CHAPTER NINE

I unfolded the paper Paolo had left me. Handwritten in thick black script were three lists under three headings: Bombedieri, Perino, and Rosa. Each list had addresses, names, and descriptions like "#2" written beside the names. I assumed the addresses Paolo gave me were work and not home. I checked the paper over twice, front and back, finding only one address for each name. Paolo certainly had access to that kind of information, but having someone dig it up would surely lead to questions later. At the bottom of the paper was a website URL for a specific page on YouTube. This must have been where all of the trouble started.

The Internet was not something I had used often, but as the world changed around me and threatened to leave me behind, I versed myself in its basic functions. I knew there were people who could swim through the electrical currents of the World Wide Web like a shark, seizing any information that was appropriately juicy. The rapidly advancing technological age created more and more people like that every day, and that would make it harder for me to remain anonymous forever; it would be impossible if, like Army and Nicky, I posted my face and opinions online. The Internet was like a gun. Any random thoughts or comments shot out from a computer keyboard in the form of a binary bullet could not be retrieved. It existed in some form in the ether, and there was no chance of erasing its existence or denying it had happened. I wondered about the bullet Army and Nicky fired on YouTube, and what kind of damage it had caused.

I folded the paper up and put it into my pocket. I paid the tab and waited patiently for Yousif to come out and hold the door for me. As he approached, I saw that his jaw was set. My guest had been rude to him a few minutes ago, and he was finding it hard to remain a good host.

"Goodbye, sir," he said in a polite, curt way.

"Good luck with the dinner rush tonight, Yousif."

All at once, his pleasant demeanour broke through. "It will be very busy, sir. Very busy indeed."

The door swung awkwardly closed behind me as Yousif had another tremor. His arm tightened on the door, and it stopped moving before it formed a seal. I heard him sigh with relief as the spell ended. As I entered the parking lot, I could hear him continue talking to himself. "Very busy soon. No rest tonight."

He was right, I wouldn't rest tonight — not ever, I feared.

It had been almost two years since I had been in the city. It was possible that the last few Internet cafés I had used were still in business, but it was more likely that they were gone. Most small businesses in the downtown core quickly went the way of the dodo. None of them survived long in the infertile concrete. The city reached out and drained the businesses dry with stagnation, or it started to work on the employees, killing their bodies with pollution or their minds with constant vandalism and robbery. The old places didn't matter. I didn't want to set foot in the downtown core before I had to. Every street corner had eyes, eyes looking to pass on information for a score.

I pulled the car onto Upper James and drove north, admiring the economic prosperity the Hamilton mountain enjoyed. Everything was different a few hundred metres in the air. The cars were sleeker and quieter, and the stores were bright and busy. As I drove closer and closer to the core, the stores got smaller and smaller, as though they were tightening in preparation for the city's assault.

Eventually, as I neared the escarpment access, I found a used computer store that had spawned from a decades old two-storey house. I parked the car on a side street and made my way around front to the door. The original front door had been replaced by a glass door encased in a heavy mesh with thick reinforced bars. The door had "Cam's Computer Den" stencilled at eye level. I pushed it open and immediately felt the heat of multiple computer hard drives and the warm bodies of several cats. The warm stale air rushed at the door like a genie escaping from a bottle.

A voice came out from behind a counter piled up with old computer keyboards and monitors. "Hep you?"

"What?" I said as I approached the counter.

"Ken I hep you?"

I saw a man hunched over a desk; he wore a headband that held a magnifying lens in front of his face. The desk light in front of him beamed an impossibly bright light down on the soldering iron in his right hand. He was a heavy man in the way that refrigerators were heavy. The back of his neck had a roll of fat that bulged out as though it were going to burst. His plaid shirt was a vast tight expanse over his back, stretching the pattern into something that resembled a magic eye poster. He sat on a stool with his legs spread wide apart. I imagined his almost-splits was only possible because it was necessary — he had to have a place for his stomach to rest while he was off his feet. His garbled speech was because of a piece of metal he was holding between his pursed lips.

"I need to use the Internet," I said.

The man barely turned. "Don't do dat here, I dust fix compuders."

"You have to have Internet access here. I just need it for a few minutes."

"Go find an Internet café."

"Twenty bucks for five minutes."

He turned all the way around so I could see his face. His goatee pushed itself out of the heavy fat folds in his face. One of his eyes was huge in the magnifying lens. He pulled the piece of metal out of his mouth with a fat hand, its skin straining like a full water balloon.

"You think I'm fucking stupid?"

I stared at him, unmoved by his question.

"I'm not leaving you alone with my equipment so I can be on the hook for whatever shit you wanna download."

"Listen —"

"No, you listen. Take your money and go look at your sick shit somewhere else."

I had had enough of the fat man. It may have been sitting with Paolo and taking his threats, or the stunt Johnny pulled on the island. Whatever it was, I was tired of assholes. I walked around the counter towards the fat man and his headband. As I got closer, his magnified eye twitched faster and faster. Finally, he put his hand up to his face and lifted the monacle. His fat hand obscured his vision for a second, hiding my rising palm. I gripped his nose and squeezed. Immediately his eyes watered and his huge paws enveloped mine. The fact that he worked with his hands all day made his grip on my hand like a bear trap. I didn't mind losing my hold on his nose; I let go so I could get my left hand on his Adam's apple.

My fingers dug deep into his fleshy neck, finding the small cartilage box in his throat. His voice involuntarily squeaked, and his huge hands rushed to mine again. His grip was powerful, but mine was better, and this time I had no interest in letting go. All the time spent on the fishing boat made my grip like a pit bull's jaws. The fat man's hands slid came away empty as he pawed at his neck. His hands continued to work at my fist, but they slackened when I applied pressure. The fragile cartilage in his neck bent under the strain, and his throat closed, sending the fat man to his knees. The immense pain was nothing compared to the lack of oxygen. His enormous body required a vast amount of air to stay vertical; I imagined it was supplied in huge gasping breaths twenty-four hours a day. Cutting off the air was a vicious shock to his already weak system.

As his face reddened, I leaned in close. "I'm no pervert, I just need to use the Internet for five minutes. You can stay in the room with me if you don't believe me."

I let go of his throat and listened to his breathing start again. It sounded like a steam engine starting to move. "Forty," he said between gasps.

"What?"

"Forty for the Internet. You said twenty. I want forty. Forty gets you the Internet, and I won't call the cops about the choking thing."

"I could just finish the job and shove a buffalo wing down your throat. The cops would buy that."

"Then you wouldn't have the password for the Internet. You'd have to go somewhere else. Be a pain in the ass killing me and then having to drive around town to find an Internet connection and a buffalo wing to bring back here. All that work for forty bucks." He seemed to smile under his hands, which were rubbing his nose and throat simultaneously.

I pulled out two twenties and put them on the counter. "Show me the computer."

CHAPTER TEN

The fat man told me his name was Louis while he pulled off the headband and unplugged the soldering iron. He said he'd always been into computers and after his parents died he just moved up from the basement into the rest of the house. The shop sprung out of the constant piles of circuitry he accumulated around the house. He locked the front door and flipped off the open sign then led me into the back room to a desktop computer.

Louis brought the computer out of sleep mode with a fat finger. He opened an icon and entered a password I noted to be a random sequence of letters and numbers. He was right, if I had choked him out, the computer would have been useless. Once Internet Explorer was working, Louis took a step back and opened his hands in a gesture that said, "It's all yours."

I stood in front of the computer and called up the site Paolo had scribbled on the piece of paper he gave me. A black box appeared on the screen with a play button in the centre. I clicked the button and watched the file load, and do something it called buffering, in a matter of seconds. Beside the loading screen, I saw thumbnails of other posts by the boys — there were at least fifteen. Fifteen times at least, Army and Nicky had put themselves out on the Internet and let their mouths run.

"Fast connection," I said.

"Oh yeah. Once you go high speed, there's no going back. I can download a song in thirty seconds —" The computer interrupted him as it began to play the file. "Who are they?"

Two teenagers appeared on the screen in the little play window. Army and Nicky were brothers who were only a year apart, but they could have passed as twins. Both boys had tall over-gelled hair that stood in shiny triangular peaks. Their white teeth gleamed in their almost identical acne-speckled faces. Both boys got their father's pointy nose and their mother's full lips. The boys were pretty, not handsome.

All of their prettiness ended when their mouths opened. They spoke in loud profane street language that all at once sounded inauthentic. It sounded as though they were mimicking the way they thought a real hip-hop gangster might speak.

"Holla at your boyz! The Donati crew is back on the air," Army said. "We still be bringing the thug to the world and ain't nobody going to stop us, ya heard."

"Nobody gonna stand in the way a tha' Donati crew, we gotz mad guerrilla tactics, yo." Nicky brandished a gun, which came into view when he added his two cents.

Army went on, "We got the roots everywhere — in the

Hammer, even in the U fucking S. We the princes of the city. All of it gonna be ours. It's ours by blood. We own this rock."

"I'm gonna get me a blinged-out crown," Nicky chimed in while mimicking putting a crown on his head.

"Those goombahs won't be able to hold on ta what is rightfully ours. Fuckin' Bombedieri thinks he's big shit running numbers. Oh the 'Bomb' is the man all right…with his calculator. Dom the Bomb is a real Texas Instrument kind of gangster. He's got a long way to go before he gets respect." Army made a gun with his index finger and thumb and shot the camera when he mentioned respect.

Nicky spoke up again, building on Army's revelation about Bombedieri. "Shit, Perino thinks he's big time 'cause he pimps shit out of that store of his."

Both boys stopped and did a silent sign of the cross, their faces suddenly angelic, before they started laughing.

Nicky continued, "He hasn't pulled a trigger on a gat since he killed Carerra four years ago. He thinks he's gold 'cause he shot that fucker into his soup. But gold gets tarnished, yo."

"Bitch," Army yelled.

"Bi-atch," Nicky confirmed.

"Rosa is tough," Army said. "I hear that boy pulled the trigger nine times last year."

"I hear that boy pulled a lot of triggers last year…with his teeth." Nicky delivered the joke with all the glee of a child telling his first knock-knock joke, and then both boys laughed at their apparent outing of Rosa while making dick-sucking gestures with their hands and cheeks.

"It's our time," Army said. "It's time the Donati crew showed the Hammer how real thugs do."

Nicky pulled off his shirt to expose a tattoo across his chest. It read "gangster" in big black Gothic letters. "We ain't into playing, we into being. 'Cause that's how we roll."

Both boys high-fived. "It's our time," Army said again and then he reached forward off the screen. Suddenly, booming rap music pounded out of the computer speakers. The music was too distorted with bass to be understandable. After a minute of music and on-screen posturing by the boys, the screen went black. The site offered the option to view the other postings by the boys. I scrolled down the screen instead of opening more of the videos. There were comments from viewers all the way down the screen. Most thought the boys were a joke; many were scathing in their hatred of Army and Nicky.

"What a bunch of douche bags," Louis said. I nodded in silent agreement. "I mean…they're white kids. They look like such posers. No one could take that crap seriously."

This time I didn't nod. Louis was wrong; someone took these boys real serious. These two morons crossed a line. Crossed it so far that even genetics couldn't save them. They didn't just slip up and say the wrong thing at the wrong time; they broadcast names, crimes, and gossip for the world to hear. And here I was having to put it all on the line to find these two jokes.

"Why did you pay forty bucks for this?" Louis asked.

"I had to see it before I started," I said as I clicked the tools folder and erased the browser history.

"Started what?"

I didn't answer Louis's question, I just got up and walked to the door.

"Do you know those kids?" Louis asked.

I didn't answer as I opened the door. I didn't know those kids, and after seeing the video I was pretty sure no one who did would ever be able to recognize them again.

CHAPTER ELEVEN

In the car, I sat with the air conditioning on while I fiddled with the radio and used my thumb to loosen the muscles in my jaw. The rough massage gave me a break from the constant grinding of teeth I had since I met with Paolo. I passed stations pumping out unfamiliar music by even more unfamiliar groups. Music had become even more artificial since I dropped off the radar. I spent too much time on the boat listening to the rhythmic beat of a fish finder, out of range of anything that could transmit the changing popular culture. I turned off the radio, realizing it was keeping me in place when I should have been moving.

I pulled the car back into traffic and drove the Hamilton mountain. I found Stonechurch Road, which ran the length of the city, and settled into its stop-and-go rhythm. While I sat at a light, I powered up Johnny's phone and called Paolo. He picked up without saying a word.

"Can you talk?" I asked.

"Not now."

"I'll call back in ten minutes," I said. I heard an animal

grunt before the line disconnected. Paolo was angry that I gave him an order. He was even angrier that he couldn't do a thing about it. Once Paolo was off the line, I dialled another number from memory; it was a number I knew would still work.

"Sully's Tavern," Steve's voice said after two rings.

"Do you ever take the night off?" I asked.

The reply came immediately. "Some of us can't pick up and leave at a moment's notice."

"How you doing, Steve?"

"Good." His surprise was over, and he was back to his usual short responses. "You in town?"

"Yeah."

"I have your money and those tools you told me about. I took it all after Sandra and I cleaned the place up."

"You took Sandra to clean up the office?" I asked.

"I told her where I was going, and she said she wanted to come."

I marvelled at Steve and his relationship with Sandra. I spent every waking moment trying to stay off the grid, trying to keep every interaction transient, and here was my only friend, a person connected at the hip to his wife. He told her everything and didn't even think about a need for secrets. For a quiet second on the phone, alone in my car, I envied his attachment like a paraplegic envied a sprinter.

"Any problems?"

"Nah, wife thinks you need help decorating though. You working?"

"That's why I called."

"Where?" Steve was ready to meet me, to do whatever.

In his mind he could never repay the debt he thought he owed me.

"It's not like that. I got found, and someone we know pulled me back here for a job."

"How did you get pulled?" It sounded as though Steve was suddenly speaking through clenched teeth. Steve knew what I was like; he knew there was very little that could force me to do anything. He knew he and Sandra were about the only leverage someone could use on me. He was starting to see red, and I had to derail him before he put down the phone. Steve had the capabilities of a dirty bomb. He could absolutely destroy everything around him, but worse than that, the carnage left from his explosion would be felt for years to come.

"Steve," I said to no response. "Steve…Christ, Steve, listen to me. I'll tell you how I got pulled back, but you have to hear me out. Are you listening? You can take care of this but you have to hear me out."

"Tell me."

Steve's quick response fazed me for a second. He was listening more than I thought. Maybe things had changed since I had been gone.

"I thought you would have been out in the street by now."

"Things change," he said, reading my mind.

"So you'll cool it and let things play out my way?"

"Things haven't changed that much. Tell me."

"A guy came to see me; he told me to come home. After a long talk, I found out why."

"Tell me straight — no one is listening."

"You don't know that," I said, thinking of Paolo.

"I do, Wilson. Now tell me straight."

I figured I owed Steve the truth. "Paolo found me," I said.

"You were fishing on film."

I pulled over to a chorus of honking horns and punched the dashboard. "That fucking picture," I said.

"Ben saw it. He loves fishing and he showed me the fish when he saw it on the front page. Big guy didn't even know who the politician was. I saw the fish and I saw you. The beard looks good."

Ben was a giant of a man who grew up on a farm in rural Ontario. He still clung to his roots, often wearing overalls to tend bar. Steve hired him after Sandra was kidnapped. Ben's job was to keep her safe when Steve stepped out. Ben was capable; I had seen him break up brawls alone. The brawlers weren't punks either — they were hard men. Ben blasted through them with giant fists like Thor with two flesh-and-bone hammers.

"Paolo saw the picture and sent a guy out to see me."

"He dead?" Steve asked.

I didn't answer the question. "I got in touch with Paolo, and he told me he needed me for a job."

"Doing what?"

"Job doesn't matter. What's important is he said he had a man watching you."

"Yeah?" Steve's answers were getting shorter. Soon it would be grunts then blood.

"Whoever it is, he's watching you to make sure I play ball."

"When?"

"Over the next day or two."

"No. When can I deal with this?"

I smiled. "You have changed. Two years ago you would have your hair up, and you'd have been in the street already."

"I am in the street — phone's portable."

"Don't do anything yet. I can fix it."

"When?"

"Give me a day, two max. Find whoever's watching and keep tabs on him. Wait for my call before you do anything. I can fix this, and then he'll be gone and everything will be cool."

"I think I already found him," Steve said.

I pressed the phone harder into my ear out of fear that Steve could instantly make the situation infinitely worse. "Will you wait for my call?"

I heard traffic digitized through the phone lines. Then Steve sighed and answered. "Two days. Any more, and I can't promise anything."

"This guy can't get beaten to death on the street; that will just bring more heat. If he goes, it's got to be quiet, like he didn't exist. Once I handle my end, no one can know what your stalker was up to. That means no one can find him."

"Call me when I can move."

I said goodbye and hung up the phone. I nosed the car into traffic again, hearing fewer horns than when I pulled over, and moved back towards Upper James and the Mediterranean restaurant I was at an hour before. Traffic had come to life since I had been online. The roads were clogged like the tunnels in an ant farm. It was like the mountain was channelling downtown just for me. I looked around at the frustrated commuters and smiled. I enjoyed the feeling of being back in the city. With each breath, I felt like I was uploading what I was, one file at a time. I felt more like myself than I had in a long time. The only problem was the scraggly reflection in the rearview. I didn't look like me — which wasn't a bad thing — but I didn't look like anyone else from around here either — which certainly was. I would stand out in a crowd to almost anyone, and I wasn't about to go up against just anyone; I was going to tamper with the lives of dangerous men. Dangerous men who would notice an unkempt loner in their periphery.

At the third red light, I rolled down the window so I could smell the black diesel leaving the bus in front of me. I lost myself in the smell of the city in some sort of grey-concrete zen daze. The fumes mingled with the roar of the bus engine, dulling the cell phone chirp from the seat beside me. I got my head in the window and opened the phone on its third ring.

"You want me to call you back, stay off the line," Paolo said.

"I saw the video," I said.

"Something, ain't it? Stupid kids are like parrots repeating everything they hear." Paolo never stopped comparing people to animals. He loved to show everyone how low they were on the food chain compared to him.

"Parrots are smart, though, aren't they?"

"Being capable of speech doesn't make anything smart. Let's see a parrot make me an omelette. That would be one smart fucking bird."

Traffic picked up and I stayed right, riding the slow lane back to the plaza. "The video, they mention three names," I said.

"*Figlio,* I gave you all the information you need. Did those two years make you soft? You never needed me to hold your hand before."

"I never had to wipe your nose before," I said, and instinctively moved the phone away from my ear to avoid what was to come.

"You little fuck!" Paolo screamed. "You think because I asked you for help you're worth all this trouble? I let you go as long as I did because you were on the back burner. You never got out, you never left; I just put you on pause. If you want, I can finish this myself, but if I do then I don't need you. And if I don't need you, what the fuck do I need the bartender for? Not to mention those nice people who own the boat you were working on."

I knew the threats would come and I still walked into it. I cursed myself for being so hotheaded. Deep down, though, I wasn't mad at Paolo, or my temper. I was scared that I wasn't what I had been anymore after being away for so long. If I couldn't do what needed to be done, it wouldn't be Paolo who killed my friends, it would be me.

I could still hear Paolo seething on the phone. I decided to ignore the outburst. "I never needed you to hold my hand before because I knew all of the players on the board. I don't know these names that well."

"You only fuck over people you know? That why you screwed me over for the bartender?" Paolo was still acting petulant after two years.

"Who are they to you? Are they important?"

"After you whacked the Commie bees' nest, they swarmed all over us. They knew our people and our business. They had been planning to take us out for a long time, and someone had fed them current information. A lot of people died or just disappeared. Those Russian fucks tried to take all the leaders away so the family would just fall apart. I had to promote prematurely to fix all of the holes. Bombedieri, Perino, and Rosa got an early leg up, but they were eager and they were workers. We hit that bees' nest back hard. Bees calm down around smoke, so we lit a whole lot of fucking fires."

"How important are they to you?"

"They're family, but they're not *family*. They got to move up pretty high pretty quick and so they never spent the years making connections or learning how to act. They're a rough crew — not at all like their predecessors, but they earn in spades. They're big players, but they got no real support. They could be gone tomorrow and no one would cry about it. They made enemies out of a lot of the people they left behind when they became management. People who were none too cheery about their sudden advancement. No one comes right out and says it, but I heard whispers."

"From Army and Nicky?" I interrupted.

"I never talked business with them because they were never going to take over."

"Anyone tell them that?"

Paolo was silent for a moment, then he spoke quietly. "They were never in this life. They went to private school, for Christ's sake."

"So did you."

"These kids ain't me. They don't have the instinct. Even back then, in those schools, I had it — everyone knew. My nephews never even showed interest in this life. They liked the money and the respect, but any sign of trouble and they'd cry to their mother. I never told them no 'cause everyone knew they were never going to go to work."

"Everyone but them," I said, more to myself than to Paolo. "You saw that tattoo, heard that music. They thought they were in the life already. They acted like they had a crew and they were the up-and-comers."

"Stupid parrots," he said.

"What I want to know is, who is the most likely to move on your family?"

"None of them. They're made. They know the rules."

Rules. There was a time when I tried to speak to Paolo about rules. "You told me there were no rules, only the law of the jungle."

"There are rules if I say so."

"Fine," I said. "Who's got the most balls, and the most pride?"

Paolo thought about it for a second. "Bombedieri," he said.

"Army and Nicky said he was just a numbers guy."

"And I told you they were never involved in the day-to-day business. That shit they said on the Internet was garbage. You don't get to *just* be a numbers guy — we aren't the Ontario gaming commission. Dom Bombedieri spent a lot of time getting everyone in the neighbourhood on side with how he runs things. Everybody: the police, the

Russians, even those Chink gangs stay clear of his rackets. But there was a time they didn't, and he made sure everyone knew where he stood about that by making a lot of people lay down, *capisce?* That's how he got the name 'Dom the Bomb.' My nephews would have had no idea about what he was into, or what he did to get into it."

"So he's not the pushover Army and Nicky said he was."

Paolo laughed. "I don't promote pushovers. Bombedieri's as bad as they come — more so now that he works quiet. He's like a pike. You ever see one of those? Ugly fish — all scale and bone. But it comes up under bugs on the surface and takes them without warning. That's what Dom the Bomb is like now that he's in charge. No one sees him coming."

I wondered if Army and Nicky saw him coming when they disappeared. If it was him at all. "The address you gave me for him. What is it?"

"His uncle Guy runs a cleaning-supply store. Dom uses part of it as his office. He's got his own entrance out back and he and his crew run their business out of it. He is in charge of everything west of James Street."

"Big chunk," I interrupted.

"I told you, I don't promote pushovers. He took over that part of town when Lolli and Porco disappeared. It was a lot of territory to take over, especially with those Ivans hitting made men, but Dom made it work. He runs that part of town for me, and he does it real well now that he's learned a thing or two."

"Who's his number two?"

"*Figlio,* I gave you a list. The list had all the information you need. I didn't bring you home so we could play phone tag like a couple a fruits. Use the list and get the fucking job done."

"One last thing. Tell me about his number two."

Paolo sighed. "It's a kid named Denis. Denis is Dom's cousin on his father's side. All I know is Dom vouches for him. I don't micromanage everyone's operations. As long as the money comes in, I don't give a shit who's on staff. Dom vouches for him, and that is enough because if something gets fucked it's Dom who will be responsible."

"He at the store a lot?"

Paolo began to get annoyed. "Yeah, a lot. His father owns it. He's always there. He makes sure his old man never has to get involved with Dom's business."

"How old —"

"No more questions *figlio*, not a one. You get out to these men and you start finding things out. Don't call me again unless you have good news for me. I'm not playing twenty questions while you waste my time. Got it? If I have to I'll give you some incentive to work harder, but I don't think the bartender would like that."

"I just don't want to be in the dark again. You did that to me before."

Paolo's voice became low and he spoke slowly, enunciating each word carefully so that there was no way I would misconstrue the threat. "I am almost sorry I brought you into this at all. When I am totally sorry, I will make sure that you feel worse."

I hung up the phone without saying goodbye. I didn't worry about Paolo's threats. He never threatened me before;

he never had to. With Paolo, you always had one bite at the apple before he forced it down your throat. The constant threats meant Paolo was in a bad situation. I had to make sure I knew everything I could, so I didn't go down with Paolo like some kind of kamikaze.

I parked the car back in the restaurant parking lot and looked around at the other stores in the plaza. I saw the Mandarin looming huge from the concrete taking up five storefronts. Beside it was a shoe store, then a chain dis-count-clothing store, a religious paraphernalia shop, and a menswear chain. Mark's Work Wearhouse sold clothing for construction workers and professionals alike. I got out of the car and walked straight through the crowded lot full of hungry buffet seekers to the automatic doors of Mark's Work Wearhouse. I breezed through the entrance past the registers to the menswear section.

I found several different types of pants hanging on dis-play racks. I passed the denim and lighter-colour pants until I stopped in front of a dark brown pair of cotton pants. The material was durable and advertised as wrinkle-resistant. I flipped through the rack and pulled my size to hold them up in the light so I could examine the pants front and back.

"They got secret pockets too," a woman's voice said. An older woman with short blond hair and an athletic build approached me from behind a rack of clothes. "Sewn into the leg are concealed pockets. You can carry all kinds of things in the pants and no one would ever know. My hus-band carries his BlackBerry and one of them multi-tools; you know the kind, with the pliers and all those gadgets. People are always so surprised when he gets them out because you honestly can't tell where he gets them from."

"Perfect," I said. "I need a T-shirt to go with the pants and something heavier to wear if it gets cold."

"No problem," the saleswoman said. She walked two aisles over and pulled out a black T-shirt with a little pocket on the front. "You look like a large."

While I felt the shirt's cotton material, the woman found a black lightweight jacket made of a water resistant material. "You can wear this zipped or unzipped depending on how cold it gets."

"They're both great," I said. "All I need is boots."

She looked down at my old boots, stained by fish and boat grease. "You sure do. Those need to go wherever it is boots go to die. You want something similar?"

I stared at my boots, realizing that I hadn't noticed how gross they were. I looked up and nodded.

"I know how it is when you love a pair of shoes, believe me. I still have shoes I wore in high school. Can you believe that? High school. They're too small now. Funny how shoes get smaller. But I could never part with them — sentimental reasons, you know. I'll find you a nice pair of boots so you won't feel too great a loss. Follow me."

Not more than a minute later, I had a dark pair of steel-toed boots that looked a lot like the boots on my feet must have once. I took all my things to the register and paid cash for everything. As I shovelled the change into my pocket, I asked where the nearest drugstore was. The teenage cashier told me that there was one of the chain drugstores on the other side of the plaza.

I stowed my new clothes in the trunk of the car and

walked around the plaza past a video store and used-record shop to the Shoppers Drug Mart. The store was located in an adjacent plaza that had spawned off the one I was in like a tumour. The plaza had a retail chain drugstore, supermarket, and pet store, as well as an unemployment office and a gym. No one who used the unemployment office could afford the goods offered by the big-box stores in the plaza. The prices were only deals to the middle class. Everyone else had to trudge farther into the city to find deals on items that the bigger chain stores had already rejected.

The Shoppers Drug Mart had the same smell in every store. The perfumes and colognes mingled with the antiseptic smell of the pharmacy to create a scent that could be found nowhere in nature. The chain store had almost anything anyone could ever want. Eventually, I thought, every store could be a Shoppers Drug Mart.

I immediately found the men's aisle and picked up a razor and an electric hair clipper. As I searched for the rest of the toiletries I would need, I found the stationery aisle. At the end of the row beside the different notepads was a digital recorder. It had a back-to-school sale sticker on it, and I figured it was something university students would use to record their professors. The item was in a locked display case, and it took me five minutes to flag down an employee to get it out. Ten minutes after that, I was back at the car loading more bags into the trunk.

I wasn't hungry so soon after eating with Paolo, but I would be in a few hours. I decided to stock up on some food to eat later. I had already exposed myself several times buying clothes and toiletries in busy stores. I hated being in the open around so many people, but it was something that had to be done. I knew that I would be unrecognizable to most of the people I encountered once I shed my clothes and beard, but I still wasn't happy. It was a long shot that someone would recognize me at this plaza after almost two years away, but I was having no luck with long shots. I had already gotten my face in every major publication in the country, which was something I thought impossible until it happened. I had interacted with enough new faces already, so I decided to make my way back to the Mediterranean restaurant. I found Yousif waiting just inside the doors — alone.

"Hello again, sir. Are you hungry again? Well, you came just in time. Very soon we will be busy."

"I need some takeout. Something that will keep for a few hours. Can you get something together?"

"What would you like, sir?"

"You decide what's best. You're the restauranteur."

After a twitch that was part pride and part surprise, Yousif was off to the kitchen. He was so excited that he didn't say another word. Two sales in one day must have been a record.

I walked around the empty restaurant looking at each of the immaculate tables in the dining room. I mentally went over what I had bought. I had clothes, stuff to clean myself up with, and a gun. I ran my hands over my hair and was thankful I bought the clippers. My hands moved down my neck to my lower back, and I stretched, feeling the muscles loosen slightly. My hands felt the hard sheath of my fishing knife. I smiled to myself and added the knife to my checklist.

The knife and the gun would get me by, but eventually I

would run through the six remaining shots in the revolver. I needed a tool to make conversations easier, something less loud and bloody. It was hard to get someone to talk after you shot them, and a knife was only as good as your resolve to use it, and once you cut someone they weren't quiet — even the hard ones screamed. I wanted a sap, but finding a sap would force me to mingle with more people. The kind of people who lived in the core of the city. Those type of people would be more in my element, and they had memories like elephants. There would be a good chance I would be recognized even with the fisherman's disguise I wore. The food came and interrupted my train of thought.

"I gave you a wonderful selection of tapas and —"

"I trust you, Yousif; it smells great. Thank you for taking the time to make this up for me. I know you are busy getting ready for the dinner rush. What do I owe you?"

Yousif beamed with pride and looked around his empty restaurant, mentally going over all the chores to complete before no one showed up. "No charge, sir."

"How much, Yousif?"

"You have been good to me today. I only ask that you return with a guest for a full meal, and that the guest not be the man you brought earlier."

I laughed and said goodbye to Yousif, promising to return for a proper dinner. I was amazed at how easy it was to make a friend. I realized it happened because I put myself out there. I made myself noticeable — something I spent a lifetime trying to avoid. I swore inwardly at myself and wondered if I had lost a step. I wondered if I would survive the next few days so out of practice. My frustration was interrupted by a small dog, which found its way under my foot. The dog yelped, then growled.

"Watch where you're going," an old woman said. Her hair was puffed with extra aerosol hairspray, making it almost transparent. Her scalp showed through the hair like a glossy, veined egg. The dog made me think of different canines I had come in contact with over the years. One mean dog in particular split his time guarding a bookie and gnawing on a heavy rubber bone. I remembered the bone in particular because as a teenager I picked it up to play a game of tug with the dog. The animal stared at me, shocked, before latching on to my sleeve. I screamed and dropped the bone, trying to escape a game of tug I then wanted no part of. The bookie screamed too, and told the dog to let me go, but nothing happened. I watched helplessly as the dog's eyes met mine for a split second before disappearing in a blur. The shake of its powerful head almost pulled my arm out of the socket. The dog paused and growled, preparing for another shake. As the attack started, another movement caught my eye. The heavy chew toy hit the dog behind the ear, as he closed his eyes and wrenched at my arm. The blow was so fast nothing in the room had time to prepare a reaction. The dog fell sideways as though it were suddenly struck by lightning, and my arm came free.

"Keep your dog under control, or I'm gonna think you have no discipline. I don't work with people who got no discipline." My uncle's voice registered no shock at what had just happened. The only giveaway that he was agitated at all was the veins bulging from his forehead.

"Sure, sure, Rick. The dog just wanted to play. Got

carried away is all. We can still do business. You're okay, eh, kid," the bookie said as he came around the desk and put a leash on the unconscious dog. "Come on, ya worthless fleabag, get out back." The limp dog was dragged by the leash out the back door.

While the bookie was out of sight, my uncle leaned into me. "The dog was just trying to keep what was his. Remember that. If an inbred mutt will go that far for a piece of rubber, imagine what someone will do to you for money. There's always dogs looking to take a bite."

I nodded my head and rubbed my shoulder, but I never looked up. I stared at the chew toy still on the floor, glossy with drool.

I took the food with me on a stroll around the sidewalk of the plaza. Within minutes, I was in front of the giant pet store. The store advertised huge deals to customers with one of the pet store cards, and other monumental deals to those without. I walked inside and ambled around the empty aisles past the fish tanks and birdseed until I came to the dog accessories aisle. I didn't think dog accessories warranted a whole aisle, but I was wrong. There were dozens of bones among the hundreds of toys made by just as many manufacturers.

I walked the aisle twice before stopping at a heavy rubber bone meant for big dogs like pit bulls and mastiffs. I bent the heavy bone in its cardboard packaging, noting its give. The bone would work perfect. Swinging it back would bend the rubber slightly, forcing it to snap forward, adding momentum, when it was swung in the other direction. It was a good, hard sap.

I paid for the bone and took it and the food to the car. I

edged out into traffic and drove Upper James once again. It took three minutes for me to find an airport motel. It was a place in between cheap and expensive, offering rides to the nearby Hamilton International Airport and convenient entertainment at the next-door Hooters and Italian restaurant.

CHAPTER TWELVE

I paid for a room with cash, leaving a small deposit I was prepared to never see again. I brought all of my bags into the room and spread the contents on the bed. I opened the food and ate a piece of oily grilled bread while I decided what to do first.

By the time I finished the bread, I was stripped and ready to plug the clippers in. I stood over the sink in the cramped bathroom with the clippers set to the second-lowest setting. Each pass over my head sent hair into the sink in greasy clumps. The dead hair smelled of the boats and fish. The odour was deep in the hair and would never have washed out; it was as much a part of the hair as the colour.

It took ten minutes to cut my hair. Once I was sure I had gotten every spot, I set the clippers down a notch and began trimming my beard. The dark coarse hairs fell like dandelion spores into the sink. I trimmed everything down and began shaving the shortened facial hair into a presentable beard. It wouldn't stand out in the city anymore, but it would obscure a face some people might remember. With my appearance acceptable, I got in the shower.

I unwrapped the motel soap and used half the bar to get the last summer's worth of work on the boat off of me. Each swirl down the drain brought a bit more of me back. I was less the fisherman and more the invisible man with each passing minute under the water.

I quickly towelled off and, without dressing, ate the rest of Yousif's food on the bed. Beads of water dampened the comforter, but I didn't pay the dampness any mind. After my dinner, I threw everything on the bed onto the floor — except the revolver. I propped my head up on the pillows and used my left hand to control the television remote. I watched television in the dark, catching up on reruns and flicking by newer shows I had never heard of. I fell asleep alone in the dark, one hand on the remote, the other reflexively curled around the revolver.

I woke the next afternoon and put on the new clothes. The pants and shirts had fold lines in them, but I was sure they would fade away. I didn't feel bad about the twelve hours' sleep I had; the past few days wound me tight, and the next few would not be any easier.

I retrieved the belt from my old pants and put it on, making sure the knife was concealed behind my back under my shirt. I tried to put the gun into my waistband, but it was too noticeable under the knife, and too bulky under the front of my T-shirt. I had almost given up on carrying the gun on me at all when I remembered the hidden pockets in the pants. The gun fit tight into a concealed thigh pocket. It wasn't good for a quick draw, but it was much better than leaving the gun in the car.

I picked up the toiletries, clippers, old clothes, and garbage and put them all into a pillowcase. I figured the pillowcase was more than a fair trade for my deposit. I had to take everything with me. The takeout containers would lead to Yousif and then to a description of me and Paolo.

I left the room key on the dresser and made it to my car without being noticed. I drove into the next parking lot I saw and emptied the pillowcase into three separate Dumpsters. I had to individually force each item under the padlocked chains holding the lids closed. Once everything was gone, I got back in the car and drove towards the mountain access. Upper James led down the mountain, becoming James Street when it left the rocky incline. The road was just as worn and craggy as I remembered and it bounced me around inside the car. I caught sight of my reflection and noticed the change in my appearance. My face was more different, and more the same, than it had been in a long while. A fact that made me smile.

I found the cleaning-supply store that Dom Bombedieri ran his crew out of and spent the next few minutes circling the neighbourhood. There were kids outside hanging out even though it was 1:30 p.m. on a school day. None of the kids was doing anything wrong; they just hung around or played keep-away with basketballs. None of the kids eyed me twice as I circled, so I wrote them off as lookouts. I pulled to the curb two storefronts away from the cleaning-supply store and opened the glovebox. I pulled out the cell phone, mini recorder, and dog bone, then shifted in my seat to load the phone and recorder into a pants pocket concealed near my calf. After that, I reached into the back seat and picked up the jacket.

I got out of the car and put the coat on, leaving it unzipped. The bone fit into a pocket on the side of the jacket, leaving five or six inches hanging out. I didn't care because it didn't appear threatening or stand out. If asked why I was in the neighbourhood, I could say I was looking for a lost dog. The bone would as good as prove what I said to anyone. Everything in place, I locked the car and walked past the store.

The sign just read cleaning supply, and the window displayed several steam cleaners and large floor waxers. There was only one man inside; he was seated behind the counter watching a small TV. I continued down the street before circling the block to get back to the store.

The door had no chime, so Uncle Guy didn't look up from the television until I was a few feet away. I had already figured out he was alone in the showroom and spotted the only exit, a closed door ten feet away from Guy behind the counter, when my presence was acknowledged. He snorted loudly and swallowed whatever he moved in his throat before he stood. He was a fat man with huge features. His large nose and heavy cheeks were peppered with blackheads. They were so large I thought I could work them out with needle-nose pliers. He wore a golf shirt with maroon pants that were hiked up high on his waist, making his torso look short and wide. The golf shirt must have once been washed with the pants because it was dyed an uneven light pink. Guy wore it without an undershirt, and the tight top showed every roll, nipple, and imperfection. He looked at me through dirty greasy glasses and spoke. His breath was stale from smoking.

"I'm losing a fucking bundle on AC Milan here."

I didn't respond so he continued — beginning with another snort. "What can I get for you?"

I looked around the store, making a big production of it so Guy's eyes followed my gaze. "What have you got that takes out blood?"

Guy snapped his eyes back to mine and looked at me, suddenly unsure. "What do you need to take blood out of?"

"Dom told me you're the man to see about cleaning a place right. If you know what I mean." My voice didn't come out weak or wobbly like a liar's; it came out smooth — a conspirator's voice with just the right amount of malice.

Guy leaned back in close — smiling now. "What the fuck did you get into, hunh? What's the blood on? Wood? Carpet? Concrete?"

I looked down at the dingy brown-carpeted floor. "Carpet," I said. "Old worn-in carpet."

"If the carpet's old, you'll have to do the whole floor or else someone will know the one spot was cleaned. How long has the stain been on the floor?"

"Not long," I said. "Not long at all."

Guy paused for a wet snort. "I got a couple a steam cleaners that will take anything out as long as it's fresh. The size you need depends on the size of the stain. How much blood is there?"

"There's gonna be a lot of blood, Guy," I said as the side of my mouth started to move. The grin formed on my face and it did to Guy what it used to do to me when I saw it on my uncle's face. He was unsettled, unsure of what to make of it. It occupied him while my right hand pulled out the rubber bone.

"Gonna? What the fuck you mean gonna? How much blood is there, stunad?"

I didn't answer. I was too busy swinging the bone up from my hip. I swung it like an overhead tennis serve. The bone arced back as I made a split-second pause in midair, and then shot forward with my arm's change in direction. The hard rubber pounded into the fat face, popping the swollen nose like a water balloon. Blood went all over the thin pink shirt and counter. Guy put two bloated hands up to his face. The fingers, thick like rolls of toonies, tried to hold back the sudden gush of blood.

I took a handful of the greasy, thinning hair on the top of his head and pounded the hands with the bone. I beat them away from his face and began swinging at his short, fat, tyrannosaurus arms. Guy's limbs began to writhe over his head, simultaneously trying to protect his head and avoid the blows. I had to climb over the counter to keep a hold on him. I kept swinging, moving up the flailing arms back to his head. His arms soon became too beaten to cover up his head, and there was nothing to protect the dog toy from cleaving skin away from the browbone. The strikes beat him down to the floor behind the counter.

Guy bled into the carpet and began to sob. The sound was like a child crying in the night. They were heavy sobs accompanied by heavy snorts. The sobbing meant I did my job right. He was hurt, bad but not out, or worse, dead. I didn't waste time checking on him; he was a man who had covered up countless beatings and worse. Why did he deserve better than he gave to his customers?

"Help! He's having a heart attack! Someone call an ambulance!" I didn't know if Guy's son Denis was in the store or not, but if he was I had to get him out and keep him off balance. Paolo said Denis never left his dad alone, and I had to rely on Paolo's intel. Sure enough, the door behind the counter opened and a man emerged from the back room. The man was a younger replica of Guy. He was not as fat, not as greasy, but equally ugly.

"What happened?" he yelled as he approached.

I put panic in my voice. "He grabbed his chest and collapsed!"

Denis reached his father. "His face! What happened to his…" Staring at his battered father, Denis never saw the bone coming; it hit him in the temple and shut him down.

I patted Denis down and freed a gun from a holster at his back. I also pulled out his wallet and cell phone. I stuffed the wallet and phone into my already full pockets and tucked the gun into the front of my pants.

I left father and son on the floor together while I locked the front door. I pulled the blinds down over the windows, dimming the room. I freed Denis's gun from my waistband and thumbed back the hammer as I moved behind the counter and checked Guy and Denis. Guy still sobbed and gurgled on the floor. His beaten arms tried to rise off the floor to his face but repeatedly failed. Denis was still out, his temple darkening from the impact of the sap.

I moved through the doorway into the next room; it was lit by too many fluorescent lights, and the aggressive glare hurt my eyes. The room had huge crates and boxes along the wall connected to the storefront. The crates and boxes were labelled with different brand names that I'd heard of before. The boxes looked heavy and likely dampened all sound coming in and out of the room. Denis probably had no idea anyone was out front with his father until he heard me yell. The rest of the room didn't belong at all. There was a flat-screen TV with surround sound set up around two huge leather couches. Behind the couches sat a large desk with a computer terminal. The TV was tuned to the same soccer game as the TV behind the counter. A darkened bathroom was through a doorway beside the desk. A quick check showed me that the bathroom got none of the expensive upgrades that the other room got. It was white, or it once had been. There was piss on the floor, and the seat was up. I backed out of the empty bathroom, careful not to touch anything.

All in all the back room was small, but it looked like what it was — a comfy clubhouse for thugs. I turned off the television and walked back out front into the dimmed sales area. Both father and son were still down on the floor together. I walked past them to the first vacuum I saw — a huge industrial model. I pulled the power cord out of a large retractable spool on the back. The cord came out and retracted with a loud snap when I let it go. I tucked Denis's gun back in my pants, freed my knife, and unwound the cord until there was none left. I cut the power cord into three-foot sections and threw them over my shoulder. When I finished I had six sections in all.

I righted Guy's chair and yanked Denis up to his feet. He surprised me, surging up with the momentum of my pull.

He rammed me hard into the counter and tried to drive me over it. I lowered my body and forced him back. I didn't bother pushing his shoulders. I put two hands on his face and shoved — making sure to dig my thumbs into his eyes. His head lurched away, but his arms kept pushing against my body. I drove forward harder with my thumbs and felt his arms start to slacken. His hands stopped trying to shove me over the counter and began to pull at my thumbs. His rage and anger about what I did to his father made his bulky body impossible to hold. He shook his head free from my grip, moving it back and forth like a dog shaking a rat. With my hands loose, he stepped back, maximizing the four feet of space between us.

His eyes looked red and livid, and his wild right hook proved what they were telling me. Denis was fighting for his life, but his sloppy style and heavy breathing let me know he had lost his head and was just running on rage. I wasn't like him. My chest rose and fell evenly; the surprise of his playing possum had long worn off. I stepped into his wild hook, making the fist no real threat at all. The hook turned into a grab once it couldn't hurt me with bone-on-bone blunt force. Denis pulled my body closer, forcing me into a headlock. He was surprisingly strong for someone who looked so out of shape. My neck compressed under his damp armpit. The pressure wasn't immediately threatening because my right hand guarded my throat, but the choke would eventually slow me down. My fist punched repeatedly back and forth like a piston, battering Denis's ribs, but the folds of flesh and his loss of sanity made everything I did ineffective. He cranked harder on my neck and rested more of his weight on my frame. He was screaming in my ear as he tried to wrestle me down like a steer.

The pressure, combined with the hot, smelly air under Denis's arm, began to make it hard to breathe. I gave up punching and grabbed a fistful of his right pant leg. Holding his leg in place, I moved my right hand away from protecting my neck. The pressure surged higher without my arm pushing against the choke, and my vision began to dim around the edges as the air was forced out of my throat. With the last seconds of consciousness I had left, I pulled Denis's gun from my waistband. In one motion, I cocked the hammer back and put the barrel of the small revolver against his shin bone, right between knee and ankle. I pulled the trigger and felt the smelly vise release my neck. Denis was still screaming, but the pitch was higher now that he was on the floor with his shin bone splintered.

The sound of Denis's screams gave his father strength, and Guy surged off his back onto his hands and knees. Before he could get any higher I cut him off, pistol-whipping him on the top of his head. The greasy hair on his scalp offered no protection, and his body slammed to the floor.

Denis still screamed while he clawed at his leg. He tried to cradle his leg, but each time he attempted to touch his shin his hands flinched away as though he was touching fire. I walked past him and righted the chair. I looked at it for a few seconds and realized two things: the chair would no longer help me do what I needed to do, and I had to shut Denis up. In this neighbourhood most people would ignore screaming, especially those who knew what really went on in the back room of the store. But if I let Denis do enough yelling, eventually someone would call for help, either from the cops or from the boss, Dom the Bomb. I picked up one of the pieces of extension cord and walked back to Denis. I flipped him over and looped the cord around his face like he was a horse. I put my foot in the centre of his back and pulled with two hands. The cord fought against his strained lips and teeth until it gave up a little slack as it slid into his mouth. I choked up on the cord and held it in my left hand as I pulled Denis's left arm behind his back. I stepped on the wrist with my heavy boot and heard him whimper a little louder against his gag. With the one hand immobilized, I turned back to his bit and tied it off behind his head. Once it was tied, he could no longer scream — he was only able to grunt through his bit as I finished tying him up.

I kept my foot on his left arm and pulled his right hard behind his back. I put a knee on his spine, brought Denis's hands together, and tied them with extension cord, feeling no remorse for his predicament. His feet followed without a fight. Any movement of his feet would have meant excruciating pain for his damaged shin. Once he was restrained, I flipped him over and looked at the gunshot wound. Blood leaked through the hole the bullet made, and the fabric of his pants tented on jagged shards of bone that were pushing out from around the wound. I took another piece of cord and tied a tourniquet around Denis's leg four inches below the knee. The knot was tight, and within a minute the blood loss was already tapering off. I used the rest of the cords to tie up Guy; his battered, unconscious body offered no resistance.

The situation was a disgrace. I spent years meticulously

planning jobs to go off without a hitch, and here I was knee-deep in a father-son massacre. What I had done inside the cleaning-supply store was everything I wasn't; it was crude, blunt, and out of control. I was being used and it was only the beginning. I let the anger wash over me for ten seconds before forcing it back down. I had to force my teeth to unclench when I noticed the grinding was an audible sound inside my head. Inside I knew that the state of Denis and his father was not because of me. I had no real intel on either man or their boss. All I had was some names on a slip of paper. Paper provided by a man who was teetering on the edge. Paolo forced me to move on two men I had never seen at a pace he knew to be reckless. He was not the calculating man I had known anymore; he was a grief-stricken uncle and a vindictive mob boss. Both sides of his personality were pushing me hard to find out who took Army and Nicky. When I did, I wasn't sure who would be taking revenge. As bad as the situation was, it would only get worse unless I became the one controlling the chaos. I had to make sure this clusterfuck never came back to bite me or Paolo, because if it did, it would bite Steve and Sandra too.

With his father still out, Denis had nowhere to look except up from the floor at me. I pulled the recorder from my pocket and turned it on.

His sweaty, pale-white head began to shake back and forth. "No," was the message I got.

"I'm going to take off the gag and we're going to talk," I said.

His head shook harder, pleading with me to leave the

gag on. He grunted at me and bucked on the floor. His teeth gnashed at the cord in his mouth as though he was trying to hold it in place. I used two hands to roll him onto his front. Denis squirmed harder, trying to move farther away from the counter — farther away from me. I grabbed the cord tied around his head and pulled his skull from the floor with it. His body arced up in an armless upward-facing dog while I slid the knife in sideways between the cord and his hair. The knife was razor sharp, but I still had to saw at the cord for a couple of seconds to get it off. The sudden release and lack of hands sent his head straight to the floor. His skull impacted like a melon falling in the produce aisle. The sound was flesh, bone, and teeth breaking and bruising.

Denis moaned into the floor until I rolled him again.

"No!" His word came as a loud mumble. He was not afraid of me. He was afraid of his boss. Paolo said Bombedieri was still working — just under the radar. Whatever he did, it scared Denis more than being tied up with a hole in his leg. He wouldn't talk into the tape recorder. He wouldn't unless I became the scariest thing in his universe.

"We need to talk," I said.

He shook his head hard, almost banging both sides of his face on the floor with the frantic side-to-side motion.

"Denis, talk to me and I leave. Don't, and I stay here with you and Dad. I don't like soccer, Denis, so I'll have nothing to do here but work on you. I just want you to tell me a few things so I can leave."

He stopped shaking his head and looked me in the eyes. "No," he said.

I stared back at him and said nothing. I grinned at his smashed face. He looked at my face and he found in it something unsettling because he stopped staring at me and began to strain his neck in the direction of his father, looking for help that would never come.

I stepped past the bodies into the sales area. I walked past the different floor cleaners until I came to a display of bleach, the bottles stacked in a pyramid on the floor. I hefted one of the bottles off the top of the pyramid and checked the label. It was concentrated bleach. I turned the bottle further and looked at the warning label. Words like "severe" and "damage" popped out at me. The label also warned of sensitization if the bleach hit damaged or broken skin.

I carried two bottles behind the counter and set them on the countertop. Denis had shimmied himself past his father to the doorway leading to the back office. I grabbed him by the leg and dragged him back beside his father. I put one heavy boot on his ankle and stood on it with my full weight. For a second I felt his bones move and crack; it was like standing on thin ice. He screamed even after the cracking stopped. I contemplated gagging him again, but the screams stopped when I began unscrewing the bleach bottle.

"No, no, what are you going to do?"

I didn't answer. I pulled the safety seal and hefted the bottle up with my left arm. My work in the city had once left the arm useless, but I had worked to make it strong again. The months of work it took were hell, and once I finally became whole again I got dragged back to the city so the whole process could start over again. Denis wasn't responsible for that, but he was part of the machine that was. He could point me in the direction of the people who set the wheels in motion. A fact that made it easy to tilt the bottle.

The milky liquid fell from the mouth of the bottle to the ruined pant leg. At once, the cotton fabric of the pants began changing colour, becoming lighter and whiter with each splash. The liquid soaked the pants and flooded in the hole left by the bullet. Denis's legs shook hard trying to move away, but his ankle was pinned under me. His restraints made any momentum he could have gained impossible. All he could do was scream as a half bottle of bleach hit his legs as though it were some sort of chemical waterfall.

His screams woke his father, and the old man looked on in horror while he struggled against his restraints. Denis's eyes were wide in his ugly face. The bleach burned the skin, but worse than that, it made the wound more sensitive. The bottle had not lied about sensitization — every nerve ending in the wound was on fire because of the bleach.

I put the bottle down and looked at the newly pale pant leg I had created. Denis was all screamed out; his mouth just silently opened and closed. His face had gone more pale, and his bloodshot eyes bulged out, unblinking. I was now the terrible centre of his universe. Bombedieri no longer existed. I was all he could see.

I picked the bottle up again with my left hand and the recorder with my right. I tilted the bottle halfway and felt the liquid settle at the edge of the mouth.

"Tell me about what Bombedieri is into, Denis."

"Oh, God. Oh, God."

There was still some residual fear of Bombedieri in Denis's mind. I let a little more liquid hit his leg to wipe it away.

Denis screamed before he started talking in fast, rambling sentences. "He runs the neighbourhood. He controls everything: drugs, gambling, girls. He even pays off the cops."

"More," I said. "What has he done recently?"

"He killed those bikers. He shot them. Him, and Tony, and Phil, and me. We shot those guys in their car and left them there in the field. No one knows it was us, but we did it."

I didn't know anything about bikers, but the information was important. Information could be used more places than MasterCard. It also proved that Denis was involved with everything his boss did. Denis didn't sit on his hands in the back room all day, he was a player. If Bombedieri was involved with Army and Nicky, Denis would know.

"What about kidnapping?" I said.

"What? No. We don't do that. There's no money in it. Oh God, my leg is on fire. It's burning."

I splashed more bleach on the leg, and Denis screamed through every octave. I shut the recorder off and asked my last question.

"Bombedieri take Armando and Nicola? Is he working an angle?"

The pain moved to the back of Denis's mind for a second as he looked up at me. He realized he had no idea who I was or why I was there. He probably thought I worked for the bikers he crossed until I asked about Army and Nicky.

I splashed more bleach and asked again. "Did your boss do something to Armando and Nicola?"

"No! Jesus, no! He hated those two, but when we told him we wanted to hit them for all that shit they pulled he said no. He said we couldn't do it now. That it would fuck up our operations in the neighbourhood. He said they were off limits."

"You sure?" I said as another splash hit the pale pant leg.

"We didn't touch them, I swear. We were too busy with the bikers to deal with those fucks. Please, no more. Please. Please!"

I cued up the tape and played it back. As the tape played, I stopped being the centre of Denis's universe. I was slowly eclipsed by Bombedieri. "You're going to run," I said. "I'm gonna pass this tape on, and you don't want to be here for the fallout. You and your dad need to get out of here and never look back. You gave up your boss, and there's no way he'll let you off for that. Especially after the bikers get their copy."

"I'm dead, then," he said, exhausted.

"Your life here is over, but you're not dead. Not yet anyway. You two need to go, and go far."

I wiped the bottle with my sleeve and left out the front door. Denis didn't move as I walked away from him. He just lay silent on the floor, letting shock set in, temporarily taking him away from his death sentence.

CHAPTER THIRTEEN

I used my elbow to open the door as I left the cleaning-supply store. Once I was outside, I casually stopped to look at the hours of operation. I pulled my sleeve over my hand and wiped the door handle as I leaned in to see the hours posted on the glass. I nodded my head as though the opening and closing times pleased me, then walked away from the store to my car.

Denis had to run. He and his father had to clean up the mess I left and get as far away from the city as they could. The tape I had on Denis was more deadly than a cruise missile. If the tape got out, which he believed it would, there would be nowhere safe in the city for him. I counted on his fear, on the utter terror Bombedieri put in him, to send him running.

I walked up the street to the car, watching every window and alley. I had seen no one watch me go in, but I knew that fact didn't cover me going out. As I moved up the street, I passed a kid sitting cross-legged on the pavement playing a guitar. His black leather case was closed beside him, and

I had to step over the neck of it as I walked past him on the sidewalk. The kid didn't look up at me while he played; he kept his red head down. He didn't even pick up the pace of the song to earn a donation for his effort and skill. He just played his song, oblivious to the world.

I saw my car up ahead, and on the trunk sat two men in their early twenties. Instinctively my hand began to swing closer to the front of my pants as I walked. I still had Denis's stubby revolver tucked in my waistband. The two men, if you could even call them that yet, were in faded ripped jeans and old unlaced high-tops. They were at an age where they weren't children anymore, but at the same time they could never be considered men. The only word that came to mind was "punks." One was blond, and his hair stuck out from under a sideways baseball cap. The hair was meticulously placed so that it shaggily hung over one eye. The other had long, greasy black hair that made it hard to see most of his face. His long beard covered everything below his nose so the only bit of skin I saw was a small patch of forehead. Both of the men looked pale and strung out. Their knees bounced on the bumper to an irresistible, soundless, chemical-induced beat. The dark-haired one shoved the blond with a heavily tattooed elbow as I got closer. Both looked at me. My mind raced as my eyes met the two pupils I could see peeking through the mess of hair on each punk's face. There was no way these two were after me. They were white punk-rocker kids — about the farthest thing from Paolo and his organization — and yet there they were, waiting on my car.

I stopped three cars away, my hand near my belt, and

looked at the two punks on my trunk. Before I spoke, something pulled at my mind. The guitar player had his guitar case closed. He wasn't there for money, so he had to be there for something else. The guitar was no longer being strummed — I couldn't hear it — but I could hear singing. I recognized the words as being from an old Ramones song.

"Beat on the brat. Beat on the brat. Beat on the brat with a baseball bat. Oh, yeah…"

As the song behind me grew closer, I watched the two punks on my trunk tense their shoulders and squint their eyes as though they were about to be hit with a snowball. Just before the second "oh, yeah" of the chorus I tried to roll forward. My head and shoulders started the roll, but the baseball bat that smacked across my lower back ended my attempt.

I fell to my knees and fought to pull air back into my body as the two skinny kids jumped off my car using the bumper as a springboard. I watched the two pairs of feet approaching as I listened to the singing continue behind me. The guy had moved ahead in the song and was laughing as he sang, "What can you do-oo." The singing was terrible, but it bought me the seconds I needed. I got a quarter of a shallow breath and rolled off my hands and knees onto my back. My right hand groped for the pistol and yanked it free from my waistband. I had the gun out and moving to the centre mass of the red-headed punk standing over me, but the ball bat to the back did the trick. I was slow on the draw, and the kid above me had time to swing the bat low, connecting with the snub-nosed revolver in my hand. The gun went off when the bat connected with it, but the shot went wide.

"Holy shit! He's got a gun," one of the voices behind me said. The voice was not full of fear; it was equal parts laughter and excitement. "Give Dirty Harry an encore."

Another swing didn't come. The punk with the bat had stopped his attack. His face was down, and he was checking to see if he was shot. I knew there was no way I could pull the other gun from the tight pocket on my thigh without getting brained by the bat, so I kicked out instead. The toe of my heavy boot found the soft spot between the redhead's legs. He cringed and then crumpled in on himself, collapsing to the pavement.

I got to my feet just as two sets of hands began laying into me. The punches were wild and everywhere at once.

"Come on, Dirty Harry, make my fucking day," one voice said as a fist hooked into my ribs.

A kick to the side of my leg wobbled me, and I heard, "Oh ho, that was lucky. I was lucky that time, Harry. How lucky you feel now?"

It was as if I was being swarmed by bees with knockout power. I covered my head and tried to weather the storm, but a punch to my exposed and injured back changed that. The blow to my back straightened my body as though an electric current was shot through it. The two punks behind me saw me straighten, and they began to focus on the back of my head. I bent forward and kicked out behind me like a barnyard mule. My foot found something solid, and I heard a grunt. I staggered forward, still covering my head, trying to get away from the three attackers.

A hand grabbed my ankle, and I looked down to see

the red-headed singer holding on to me with two hands. I kicked out with my right foot, and my boot split his eyebrow open. The blow was enough for me to get my feet free. I kept staggering forward until I was shoved face first into a parked car. The punk with the hat and the bangs had done the shoving; he was still untouched and ready to go. I pushed off the car and flung myself backwards into the punk's body. Once our bodies connected, I leaned forward and then slammed the back of my head into his face. The impact had me seeing stars, but I was free to run again. I looped around the car and began stumbling up the street towards my car, using the other parked cars on the street as a buffer to separate me from the three punks. I fumbled for my keys and managed to get them out five feet from the bumper.

"Batter up, motherfucker."

I heard the words in conjunction with the feeling of the bat. The impact hit me in the back again with such force it made my teeth rattle. I bounced to my knees, not even feeling the pavement. The car keys fell from my fingers, and I pitched forward. I saw the pavement accelerate towards my face then lurch to a stop and reverse away from me. Three sets of hands stood me up and began beating me. Fists pummelled my face and guts all at once.

"Get his ass into the van."

"Ah, come on, Mickey. My fucking stomach hurts from that asshole's foot. Let's use his car. We were gonna jack it anyway. This way we don't have to come back for it. Harry here won't mind. His feet are burning up anyway from all that kicking. Ain't that right, Harry? You got a real *hot*

GRINDER 307

foot." With the last two words, the kid with the beard, that I had kicked, stamped down hard on my foot with his heel. The boot absorbed the impact, and I didn't feel a thing. I screamed out anyway to avoid a second blow somewhere softer. The impact of the foot stomp on the steel toe must have hurt the punk with the beard. His worn-out Converse high-tops would offer no protection against that kind of activity. He took my scream for gospel as he shifted his weight from one foot to the other. There was no way he was going to try for another stomp.

Mickey, the redhead the punk with the beard was talking to, pressed a hand to his damaged eyebrow. Out of the corner of my eye, I got a good look at him. He was tall, six feet five at least, with red hair — real red, not dyed. His arms were large but not muscular. He was probably stronger than most people simply because of his unnatural size. He had thick leather bracelets on his wrists and a pair of dead eyes that gave his face a sort of zombified look. He seemed to manage talking without moving his lips. He sighed. "Fine, fine, whatever. Let's just get this fish back to the whale. You two put him in and drive him back in his piece of crap. I'll get my guitar and follow you back in the van."

"Righteous, let's get some fucking drive-through on the way back. I'm jonesing for a Frostee."

"Gonzo, you are taking him straight back. We can't fuck this up. You heard what the whale said."

"Ah, come on, Mickey. Me and Ralphy just want a snack. Look at Ralphy's mug, that asshole cracked the side of his face. He probably needs to get his head in a cast. He needs something cold, something soothing, something chocolate."

Ralphy stopped adjusting his sideways hat and tried to speak. He failed on his first attempt and brought his hand to his face in pain. Through the hand cupping his face, he finally got out, "Yeah, dold."

"Plus I don't want to eat that shit the whale puts out. I hate that Italian shit. I want a burger with extra cheese."

Ralphy nodded and forced a "mm-hm" through his hand.

Mickey shoved Gonzo and Ralphy hard, and they almost dropped me. "Get him back to Domenica's. Then we can eat. Got it?" He poked Gonzo hard in the sternum with the top of the bat for emphasis. Blood trickled down his face from the wound I gave him with my boot. Mickey felt the blood and swiped it away with the edge of his hand.

"All right, all right, shit. Just wanted to eat is all. You're so fucking critical. Fucking guy from Oasis was like that, and look where they are now."

This seemed to really piss Mickey off. "Oasis is a shit Manchester band. Up on stage singing about champagne supernovas and shit. They champagne super suck. Now get his ass in the car before I make *you* ride in the trunk."

Mickey's anger spurred everyone into motion. I was thrown backwards against the bumper and the rear of the car rammed into my lower back. The blow crumpled me to the ground, pushing the small specks of gravel on the pavement into my knees. Mickey's tall frame loomed in front of me, and I swung for it. The punch got no help from my back, making it less than a weak swat. The other two laughed at my offence, and each took a handful of shirt and collar. One of their shaky hands lost its grip on my coat, so my ear was used to pull me off the ground.

"Hey Mickey, Harry here kicked me and he messed up Ralphy's face. We should get a chance to get him ready for his ride."

My eyelids fluttered as Gonzo launched his fist into my head. He put his weight into it, and both of us went down. With double vision, I didn't know which of the six men around me to grab on to. Twice I got it wrong before my hands found the one that had hit me.

"Get the fuck off me, Harry!" Gonzo shrugged my weak grip off and got back to his feet.

Ralphy stood over me with his identical twin. He cradled his cheek and grunted twice through his pursed lips at the tall redhead. The redhead seemed to understand the grunts and replied, "Yeah, fine, but make it quick."

Ralphy began to stomp me in unison with his twin. I tried to block out one, then the other, until I figured out which one was really Ralphy. The stomps weren't that hard, but they were fast and rhythmic.

Gonzo was bent over the side mirror adjusting his hair and beard. He stopped twirling his greasy hair to laugh. "He's playing your tune, Mickey."

Mickey looked at me hard and then began bopping his head to the tune of the feet bouncing off my ribs. He began to sing along with the beat; the song was near the end of the chorus. "Beat on the brat with a baseball bat. Oh, yeah. Oh, yeah." There was a pause and then two more stomps: "Oh, oh."

Mickey looked around the street and stopped thinking the beating was so funny. "All right, all right, get him in the car. The whale wants him alive and like ten minutes ago."

Once again I was in my car, but this time I landed on the fabric floor of the trunk on top of the spare. The shocks bounced with my weight, and the lid closed before I could even turn over.

As soon as the lid closed, I began to feel my body. Nothing was broken; the kids had cracked a rib at worst. Ralphy had sacrificed power to show off his musical talent on my midsection. Two teeth were missing from the side of my mouth where Gonzo had hit me, and one of my eyes was swollen, but it didn't matter — I couldn't see in the dark anyway. I knew the double vision would pass quickly, probably before the trunk lid opened. I was beaten up, but my head was clearing. The three punks had not frisked me after they saw the gun. I was alive in the trunk, and still armed.

It was hard to breathe with my rib cage resting on the spare tire. I adjusted my body in the cramped space until I found the least uncomfortable position. The fact that I wasn't frisked meant the three punks had probably never done this type of thing before. Another clue was their urge to stop for drive-through with a live body in the trunk.

Once I figured out that my back wasn't going to get any looser in the quarters I was in, I worked the nickel-plated revolver I took off Johnny back on the island out of the concealed thigh pocket of my pants. I got the gun free as the car roared to life and jerked away from the curb, causing my back to spasm again. I bit my lip to stifle the scream and thumbed back the hammer on the revolver. I stayed in my cell, in the trunk of the car, sore, angry, and holding a dead man's gun.

CHAPTER FOURTEEN

The ride in my own trunk was rough and bumpy. I could have pulled the glowing knobs that released the back seats and gotten out, but then I would have had to kill Ralphy and Gonzo. I fought down the urge for revenge. It was tough to do — like swallowing a jawbreaker — but it had to be done if I was going to learn who wanted me delivered to them.

I felt a heat in my face that I knew was not a result of the beating I had taken. What I had known deep down was just proven to me. I was out of shape. Not physically. I wasn't hard anymore. Too much time away without the constant buzz of danger and paranoia had let a mental atrophy sink in. There were parts of me that had not seen use in two years. I had controlled the situation with Denis and his father, but I hadn't trusted my gut on the sidewalk. There was a time when on impulse alone I would have taken apart the singer on the street and disappeared before anyone knew what was happening. But I ignored the itch in my brain and walked past the punk. I ignored his panhandling in the wrong kind of neighbourhood, and his closed guitar case. I had gotten lazy, and it had cost me. I was riding in my own trunk to my execution.

Everything that had happened was my own fault. I had ignored every lesson my uncle had ever taught me. I had not planned what would happen inside the cleaning-supply store before I walked through. I just moved on two dangerous men because I was pushed hard by Paolo. I should have slowed things down and made a move when I knew everything would be covered. I could have walked into an empty store, or worse, an early meeting. I realized that being pushed was no excuse for what I had done in the cleaning-supply store. Being locked in my own trunk had a way of forcing me to reflect. The trunk was a cramped, smelly wake-up call. I remembered what I already knew. I had to make everything work for me; I had to be the one pushing the action, or I would constantly be on defence. No matter how good someone's defence was, they always get scored on, and this kind of game was sudden death.

I figured that whoever pulled me off the street had to be involved with Paolo in some way. How else could they know where to pick me up? What I couldn't figure was: who would use three greasy kids as heavies? They didn't look Italian, and they didn't sound Russian. Someone hired these three and they knew doing so would cover their tracks. I was only sure of one thing — they came at me outside the cleaning-supply store. That meant they weren't with Bombedieri; his men would have moved on me inside. Denis was right: Bombedieri had nothing to do with Army and Nicky disappearing.

Once my breathing had slowed and my heart rate was down, I opened my eyes and looked at the blackness inside the trunk. There was nothing useful to pick up — the car was cleaned the day I took up fishing. All I had was the gun, knife, and electronics. The bone sap was still in my pocket, but it would be useless when I didn't have the element of surprise.

I shifted around in the trunk and pulled the sap, phone, and recorder out of my pockets. Whatever I was going into, I didn't want to give up a safe phone and the only information I had gathered. I pulled up the covering on the floor of the trunk and put everything underneath, in the back corner. It felt lumpy when the cloth cover was put back on, but it would be a good enough hiding spot.

I was double-checking my work when my body was thrown forward. We had stopped. The engine stayed on, and the trunk lid stayed closed. After a minute, the car inched forward, only to stop again. After another minute and another lurch, I heard Gonzo yelling up front. His words were muffled, and I couldn't make out who he was speaking to until I heard another voice up front make a whiny grunt. Gonzo yelled louder than before, and I caught the words, "Oh, oh, and two Frostees too! I need two chocolate Frostees!"

We were in the drive-through. Gonzo and Ralphy had a body in the trunk of a stolen car and they were stopping for burgers. I had to bite my tongue to keep from screaming out in anger. Three complete idiots had taken me off the street. The humiliation hurt worse than the beating did. My self-pity was interrupted by more voices from the front seat and more lurching. I listened to the incoherent exchanges until the car peeled away and I was thrown to the back of the trunk. The car went through a series of tight turns until it settled into a long acceleration. We were back on the road, and the smell of greasy food was wafting through the seats into the trunk.

The smell of the food made my stomach turn and made it hard to keep my mind on the blow to my ego. The part of my mind that was beyond such trivial matters became louder and took over. I decided I would let the kidnapping play out until I had no other choice. If they tried to search me, I would have to make it tough in order to conceal the revolver in my waistband — no small feat when I was out-numbered three to one.

I closed my eyes again, ignored the nauseating smells, and resumed my deep breaths. I let the harsh rocking of the car sway my limp body rather than thrash it around. I opened my eyes periodically, looking at the glowing seat release knobs. They looked like PacMan. I stared at the plastic and thought of my uncle. He taught me to play the video game and to stay one step ahead of the ghosts, to play their game better than they ever could. I remembered the feeling of control I had when I could finally manipulate the ghosts, when I could lead them instead of just run from them. Being in the trunk made me mad, being in the city made me furious. My jaw had been tense for two days as I dealt with the problems of the past, problems I thought were dead. In the trunk, over the noise of the city, I heard my uncle laugh. His words hit me then, and I remembered what I had buried in my mind while I worked the ocean.

"Don't get mad. It's a weakness someone will exploit. You need to be able to think without connection to your emotions." It was advice I learned in a coffee shop over an out-of-date video game. But I learned to live the advice, and I stayed out of trunks. My uncle would only give me change if I played the game his way — the right way. And now, stuck in a trunk, I realized I had stopped playing his way. I wanted more quarters so I could get out of the trunk. I wanted to play another round because all at once I remembered everything. I realized that my jaw had loosened on its own for the first time in two days. It loosened because I was grinning in the dark. The grin was something that years on the boat couldn't touch or wear down. It came from deep inside and it was part of me, a part I couldn't deny or dull no matter how much I thought I could, a part that breathed air for the first time in years in the stale, cramped confines of the trunk.

I swayed in the trunk for five more minutes until we jammed to another stop and the car became silent. We were there. I closed my eyes and covered my face, making myself look weak and hurt. I stayed there for two minutes, until I heard a conversation through the metal lid.

"I can't believe you never tried to make your own Frostees, Ralphy boy. Everyone has tried that shit."

"Dou did?" Ralphy's mouth was messed up from my head.

"Of course, bro. Chocolate, ice cream, and milk. I even threw in Nestlé's Quik to make it extra chocolatey."

"And dow das it?"

"I used too much milk. The blender exploded all over

the kitchen. My mom was super pissed."

"Dour mom had do dlean it?"

"Man, I was so high I just fell asleep at the table. I was gonna do it, but I just dozed off for a second."

"No wonber we could never practice at dour place."

The trunk opened, shining light through the spaces of my bent elbows over my head.

"Wake up, you fucker. This Frostee is killing Ralphy's mouth 'cause of you."

I groaned, and they both swore before stepping back to set their Frostees down. "Seriously, everything he says is all fucking garbled. He sounds like he has marbles in his mouth."

"I dan't even daste it. My deeth durt doo much."

"See? What the fuck was that. 'Dan't even daste.' If he was our lead, I would have fucking left your ass in the street. Fuck the whale and what he wants; he's not more important than the sound. Count your blessings, Harry."

They each reached in and together pulled me out of the trunk hard, straight onto the pavement. I stayed limp, making it more of a chore. They muscled me vertical, each of them using an arm to hold me up. Once I was standing, they both bent at the waist to pick up their Frostees. It would have been easy to kill them both while they concentrated on their dessert. Ten minutes ago, I would have. But it was a new game, so I just let them fuck around. Another set of hands slapped me on the back of the head — Mickey was back. I groaned louder in response.

"I told you not to stop for fucking food."

"Come on, Mick. We worked up an appetite with Harry

here. We had the munchies."

"Deah, de munchies."

"Hurry up and get his ass inside."

Mickey walked ahead, not bothering to help his two partners. Ralphy and Gonzo had to pull my limp body behind Mickey while they tried to eat the last of their food. I dragged one boot along the ground and let out low groans every ten seconds. The groans were met with laughter or a "Shut the fuck up, Harry." Every now and again, I rolled my head and took in my surroundings. I was in a poorly paved parking lot outside a squat building. There were several cars near the rear of the lot, old models, all rusted and dented. I was dragged to the back of the building to a door guarded by two large Dumpsters. The back door had no handle, no peephole: it was faceless. One of the Dumpsters had the word *Domenica's* stencilled on the side. I had no time to try to decipher the word. The smell of rotting food wafting from the two Dumpsters filled my nose and told me all I needed to know.

Nothing on the list Paolo had given me included anything about a restaurant or the name Domenica's. Bombedieri, Perino, and Rosa were not in the food business, according to the information I was given. Someone outside of the people I was dealing with knew I was back.

Mickey banged on the door with his palm when we caught up to him. He didn't offer to relieve Ralphy and Gonzo of my weight, even though they were obviously struggling. The sound of the knock echoed in the parking lot. We waited for a minute until a dishwasher in a soaked, filthy white apron opened the door. Immediately steam and loud techno music hit me; it was like a pipe had burst at a busy nightclub. The dishwasher said nothing to the three men. He just ran outside to hold the door. He averted his gaze as I passed by, refusing to acknowledge the hostage he had no intention of helping.

I was muscled through the door by the two weakening punks. My dragging foot caught on the step into the building and tore the leather on the toe of the boot. The damage was worth the "oof" that came from Ralphy's and Gonzo's lips as they almost fell. They swore and dragged me on, too tired to hit me anymore. The kitchen was busy with people in white coats chopping and dicing vegetables. Like the dishwasher, none of the kitchen staff looked my way. Beyond a swinging door that served as an entrance to the kitchen was a dance floor. It was dark and buffed to a high gloss. In front of the dance floor was a stage piled with heavy amplifiers and other equipment. I groaned and looked over my shoulder to the rear of the restaurant. Behind me, through an empty doorway, were tables in a darkened dining area. Domenica's was more than a restaurant — it was some kind of club. I was dragged to the centre of the dance floor and held in place by my captors.

"Leave him there. Let him go. Take your hands off him," a voice behind me said.

I knew right away who the voice belonged to. I knew of only one person who repeated himself that much. The three punks called him the whale, but I knew whose place I was in. Domenica's was Julian's club.

I didn't hear his footsteps. He glided into view from behind me, a mammoth tripod. Julian walked with help from a cane. I knew that the cane was my fault. I had hit Julian with a stolen truck two years ago in an attempt to stay alive. I had gone through Julian, Paolo's number two, to get back the information I had stolen from the Russians. I had hit him the hardest way I knew how and I hadn't killed him; I just slowed him down — permanently.

Gonzo spoke up. "Boss, he's pretty fucked up. We did a number on him outside Bombedieri's. If we let him go, he ain't gonna be standing. You want us to put him in a chair?"

Julian stood in front of me and my two young punk crutches. "Let him go. Take your hands off him. Turn him loose."

Ralphy and Gonzo looked at each other then at the giant tripod in front of them. I felt them shrug and then chuckle. At the same time, they unhooked their arms from mine and stepped away. I didn't fall. Instead, I stood up straight and looked Julian in the eye.

"Quite the number. Real professional work," Julian said, looking at me but speaking to the two who had just been carrying me.

"He was out. He didn't make a peep the whole ride. Not even at the drive-thr —" Gonzo stopped himself.

"Boss, we did it just like you said." Mickey took over and began speaking for the group when he saw things getting away from Gonzo.

"Go do your sound check. Set up. Get ready for tonight," Julian said to Mickey in a quiet, stern voice.

Mickey understood the threat underneath Julian's tone and pulled Gonzo and Ralphy away to the stage. They may have called him the whale on the street, but the three punks knew what Julian was and wouldn't dare oppose him in his presence.

"Let's go," Mickey said.

Once I was able to stop faking injury, I did my best to take in everything around me. Julian was ninety-nine percent of my surroundings. His bulk and rage filled the room like a silent gas ready to ignite the air. He periodically leaned on the cane for support as though his massive body might teeter over at any moment. The black suit he wore was heavy, and it hid his physique. The size was still there, imposing and terrible, but I couldn't tell how much of the size under his coat was still muscle. His hair had a bit more grey to it, and it was heavily gelled, giving it the appearance of constant wetness. There was also a smell emanating from his huge frame. It was cologne and sweat. There was so much body to cover that the cologne could not hope to cancel out the body odour; it could only tinge the smell of sweat. The nights of hot kitchens and dance floors did not agree with Julian. His suit held on to the smell, and it had probably become unnoticeable to Julian. The smell probably remained unknown to him because everyone around him would be too terrified to mention it.

Without a doubt, Julian was still a force, but he was no longer the immovable object he once had been. He instead seemed to be an irresistible force driving those around him, but who was it he kept around him?

"What's with the greasy kids, Julian?" I asked.

Julian looked at me without saying a word. I watched as veins on his forehead woke and began to pulse at the surface of his skin. "The kids," he finally said. "The kids, they do jobs for me. Things I can't do for myself. They're my hands. You should understand that. You were someone's hand once. Someone who did jobs for someone else."

I understood what Julian had inside his restaurant. He had his own version of what Paolo had. Julian had organized three outsiders to do his work for him. Three strung-out punks who were loyal, vicious, and, most important, deniable. No one would expect that the three punks worked for Julian. Even if they admitted that they did, no one would take their word for it. Julian had his own restaurant and his own agents. He was like a photocopy of Paolo. Everything was similar, but just a little less perfect than the original.

"I'm no one's hand anymore, Julian."

"Bullshit!" he roared. "What the fuck are you doing here if you're not someone's hand?" He seethed in front of me; his massive chest forcing the fabric of his suit farther and farther off his chest. "Maybe you're just his dog, then. His pet. An animal. Dogs come when you call and they love you more when you're mean to them because they got it in their head that it's always their fault. That your problem, Wilson? You his old dog hanging around for a kick, a punch, a beating?"

Static from the amplifiers interrupted Julian's rant.

"Goddamn it!" Julian bellowed over the noise.

"Sorry, boss," Mickey yelled back.

Gonzo yelled to Ralphy, "Harry's name is Wilson. That's even dumber than Harry." Ralphy laughed and then held his cheek, suddenly in pain.

"Fucking pieces of shit. They aren't good for much, but they got me you, didn't they? Outside of Bombedieri's. Why did Paolo bring you back from that tiny island to go there?"

My eyebrow raised a centimetre.

"What? You thought no one would find out? That old man has everyone watching what he does. Everyone is waiting for him to slip up just a little more. He can't handle the Russians. He can't even keep his family in line. But you know that, don't you?"

I said nothing. Julian was prepared to talk, and I wanted to hear every word he had to say.

"That old man is falling apart. There's no one left to hold him up. His little *figlio* ran away, and all at once he was blind."

"What about you?" I asked.

"Oh, you know about me. I was better than you ever were. But after your little stunt, I was useless. The old man thought there was no way I could keep him safe with one hand on a fucking stick all the time. I'm lame, a cripple, a fucking gimp. I got set up with a place to retire. A gift for all my years of faithful service."

"Seems like a nice place," I said.

"It's a fucking dive. All I get is dirty kids who are into loud music. No matter how hard I try to get people in to eat, I end up with a full dance floor of dirty kids and an empty dining room. This place is like a curse. I renovate it, rename it, change the menu, but no one will come in unless there's loud shitty music. This is my reward, my legacy, a building full of shit. Shitty people and shitty music."

As if on cue, static electricity erupted again from the amplifiers. Julian turned and yelled, "I swear to God, Mickey!"

"Sorry, boss."

"How did you know I was back?" I said.

Julian laughed and at once, he seemed to forget about the cane and amplifiers. "The guy Paolo sent after you, Johnny, he's my guy. My *paisano*. Most of Paolo's guys are after what he let you get away with. He can lock me away in this hole like a fucking family embarrassment, but there are others who remember me. Johnny told me he was going out east to find you. Johnny said Paolo was sending him because he was loyal. You see? That old man doesn't even know his own people now. But Johnny did his job. He found you and brought you back."

"No," I said.

"No?"

"I found him. Then I came back."

Julian's eyes narrowed, and I could see we were almost through talking.

"Check, check," Mickey said into the mic.

Julian's cheek twitched.

"Check, check, one, two," Mickey said again. Gonzo hit the drums in a loud semi-rhythmic beat.

Julian's eyes fluttered.

An electric guitar came to life, and Julian exploded. He turned to the stage and screamed, "Shut that stupid shit up, you worthless fucks! Turn it off!"

At once, the three stopped what they were doing. Their hands froze, and their jaws went slack. Julian stopped yelling and said, "What?"

"This," I said.

CHAPTER FIFTEEN

The barrel of Johnny's revolver, the revolver I had brought back across the country, was out of my pants and pressed firmly into Julian's neck. Two inches of the barrel disappeared into neck fat, showing me how far Julian had fallen from what he used to be.

Julian roared at the band, "You didn't frisk him?"

Mickey spoke into the mic. "We took his gun from him on the street. Then we knocked him around. He was out cold on the pavement. We didn't want anyone to see us so we just put him in the trunk. He was out cold, so we thought it was safe."

"Boss, he never made a peep at the drive-through. He was out," Gonzo piped in.

Mickey shot Gonzo a look that shut him up. They both turned their heads to look at their boss. Julian's shoulders heaved up and down as though he were growing in size.

"Enough," I said. "How did you know where to pick me up?"

Julian didn't turn to look at me; he glowered at the

band while he answered my question. "What? You think I wouldn't know why he brought you back? What you were here to do? I knew exactly what that old man would do. I always know what he'll do."

"Did you know he'd put you out to pasture here?" I asked. I took his silence for a no. "Who took Armando and Nicola?"

"I don't know. I'm not in the loop anymore. No one runs things by me and no one officially tells me anything. I got contacts who remember the favours I did for them, so I hear some things, but those new guys Paolo brought up when he put me away on the shelf — them I got nothing to do with."

"So you think it was someone in Paolo's circle?"

"I don't know. I do know that no one would have dared try anything like this when I was around. No one. They knew who to fear. Now, no one has history. No one fears. No one respects. No one knows what family is about. They're all out to make money."

"Army and Nicky weren't involved in the business. Paolo said so."

Julian chuckled. The movement of his massive frame caused him to wobble on his cane. "You can't make money if you can't maintain your reputation. Those two assholes said some dangerous things. Someone would have to respond."

"Why? Those kids are connected."

"Are you stupid? You got rocks in your head? Did you learn nothing in all the years you spent with us? It's like I just told you — no one's connected anymore. Paolo has to promote new guys all the time. Family's not important anymore. How could it be, when people are getting replaced every day? Money and power are the new family. There are a lot of people who wouldn't blink at killing two loudmouth kids — no matter who their uncle was. Nothing holds these young killers in line anymore. They're like wild animals."

I eased the gun out of Julian's neck, and his tensed shoulders relaxed. He just finished a sigh of relief when my leg kicked his feet out from under him. Julian tried to stabilize himself, but his cane was no help to his heavy body already on its way to the floor. He hit the glossy dance floor with an impact that I could feel through the soles of my boots. Julian didn't waste any time on the ground; he rolled onto his back and began to sit up, using his hands for support.

"Why did you come after me again?"

Julian looked angry and unafraid from his spot on the floor. "You look at me and you gotta ask why? I owe you. I did this for payback. Revenge. Vendetta. You left me a gimp. You cost me everything. I'd give anything to do the same to you, to take away from you everything you have and leave you broken, so that everyone knows I'm more than some crippled owner of some dive. I'm not this, I was never supposed to be this. You should be this."

Out of the corner of my eye, I saw Gonzo moving behind his drum kit. Ralphy was moving his eyebrows up and down, trying to instruct his friend in some sort of idiot code. Mickey stood still, guitar in hand, towering over the microphone stand in front of him. His shark eyes, sunken in his pale face, were watching me. His face was blank, as though he was watching television, a rerun he had seen before that could now barely hold his interest. I moved the gun away from Julian's chest towards the amplifier to the right of Gonzo. I pulled the trigger and heard the boom followed by the screech of the damaged amplifier. Gonzo and Ralphy jumped; Mickey didn't even twitch.

Ralphy fumbled with the amp cord, finally managing to pull it free to end the deafening squeal. With the cord loose in his hands, he began to giggle. Gonzo joined in. The insane laughter must have been infectious because Mickey's deadpan face began to twitch into what he must have thought was a version of laughter.

I watched them laugh. They looked like hyenas holding musical instruments. I tilted my head, never taking my eyes off the animals on stage, to look at Julian. He was biting his lower lip as he looked away from the stage at something only he could see. I bent at the knees and picked up the cane that had fallen from Julian's hands when I knocked him over. Gonzo and Ralphy still howled while Mickey contributed a bit of shoulder shaking to his smirk.

I held the cane in my hand and was surprised by its weight. The cane was a solid piece of wood with a polished sphere of metal at the top. I knew the cane was custom made for Julian because few people would have the sheer strength to use something so heavy as a walking aid. I looked at the band members, who were still lost in their hysterics, and let the gun hang loose at my side. I stared at Mickey and watched him laugh his creepy laugh. I felt my lips pull, and I matched his smirk with my own grin. His shoulders stopped shaking as hard, and his smile dimmed a fraction, changing his expression into something more confused than entertained. I flipped the cane over with a toss and lifted it above my head. I let it pause in midair before I sent it hurtling down onto Julian's ankle.

"Jesus!" was all Julian could scream before the cane hit the ankle again. Each time I brought the cane down on Julian's ankle, Mickey's smile moved down another millimetre. The cane bounced off the bones in Julian's leg at first. Each impact propelled the metal sphere back up into the air like a happy child on a trampoline. But each blow generated less and less spring as the skin bruised and the bones began to shatter. I hit Julian's ankle long after he passed out. I crushed the bone and kept going. Gonzo and Ralphy caught on to what I was doing and they stopped laughing, only to start up again while watching me work. I stopped when Mickey was done smirking.

"You want to sing me your song again?"

Mickey didn't answer.

"No? No tune to sing? You see this right here," I said, pointing to Julian's soft unconscious frame. "This happened before. You could call it my greatest hits. I bump into you three again, it won't be like it was on the street. There won't be a song. You won't see me coming — you'll feel it."

Mickey still didn't move. His mouth hung slightly open, and his shark eyes stared back at me unblinking. I dropped the cane with a clatter and brought the pistol straight up at Gonzo. The revolver's humourless black eye stared at the laughing kid, unimpressed. Gonzo stared into the barrel and stifled his giggles. He looked into the gun's one eye and then into both of mine. He whistled the tune from *The Good, The Bad, and The Ugly* and then began laughing again. I walked to the stage stairs, keeping the gun's eye on

Gonzo. Mickey watched me approaching without saying a word. Ralphy had gotten another case of the giggles and said, "Oooh, scary," through his swollen mouth.

I stopped three feet from Gonzo and said, "Give me the keys."

Gonzo patted his pockets and shrugged his shoulders. "Sorry, man, they must be in my other pants." He and Ralphy began laughing at his joke. These punks were something new. No real crew would use such violent, immature addicts. Whatever they spent their free time pushing into their blood had changed them. They didn't look at the world like everyone else. They were manic, psychotic snowflakes. They had just witnessed their boss getting beaten and had wound up with a gun pointed at them and they couldn't stop themselves from giggling. It wasn't nervous laughter, either; it was the laughter of things in the dark. It was the laughter of predators. They were too young and stupid to understand that there are things that even predators have to learn to fear.

"Check again."

He patted his pockets and lifted his arms in an "I don't know" gesture. I sighed and looked away. Gonzo turned to Ralphy and began to laugh again. "My other pants. I don't even own these — they're yours. Remember? I lost mine after that show."

Ralphy laughed a bit too hard; his hand flew to the cheek I dented with my head.

"Hot foot," I said, remembering how funny they thought it was outside my trunk. Gonzo looked back, still laughing, but now half puzzled about my words. I let him think about it for a second, and then I pulled the trigger.

The revolver sent a piece of lead straight through the old Converse All-Star Gonzo was wearing. The shock and pain cut through all of the chemical giddiness. "What the fuck, man? What is your problem?"

Ralphy stood up behind his drum kit, but I waved him down with the gun. Out of the corner of my eye, I saw that Mickey had not moved an inch.

"The keys," I said.

"Fuck! They're in the car. I left them in the ignition."

I walked away from the three kids and Julian's unconscious body. Everything hurt, but Julian would be worse. I was alive and back in control. If I could have, I would have laughed like Ralphy and Gonzo.

CHAPTER SIXTEEN

The keys were in the car as promised. I took the Volvo out of the restaurant parking lot without stopping to retrieve the electronics I hid in the trunk. I left the restaurant and watched each street sign fly past the windshield as I tried to get an idea of where I was. At an intersection, I saw that I was on Duke Street. A sight that made a bell ring in my head. I pulled out the sheet of paper that contained Paolo's information and looked at the addresses. Luca Perino worked out of a place on James Street — which was less than a minute away. I couldn't believe it. I was right where I needed to be.

Paolo's info put Luca Perino inside Ave Maria — a little shop that sold Catholic religious items. A huge portion of the city was Italian Catholic, and religious stores were a common sight throughout Hamilton. The colossal statue of the Virgin Mary I saw in the window of Ave Maria as I drove by told me the shop blended in just fine in the city. The shop would repel most people. Almost everyone preferred stores that catered to their vices rather than their spirituality. Those that did venture in off the concrete would either know about the shop's dual identity and not mind — seeing it as commonplace in the community — or the customers would be so pious they would not even think to notice the blasphemy taking place behind the counter.

I drove slow in the right lane eyeing the rows of cars on both sides of the street. I was looking for one vehicle in particular, according to Paolo's intel — a white Cadillac Escalade. The Escalade had been a mob staple since its inception. It was a sort of moving billboard broadcasting the fruits of criminal success to the community. A white Escalade was a bit different than the standard mob black, but I figured an up-and-comer would want to be part of the trend and at the same time identify himself as special.

The car wasn't on either side of the busy street, so I used Main Street to circle around to Hughson, which ran behind the shop. I drove slowly up the less busy street and stopped in the parking lot behind Ave Maria. There was no Escalade, only a rusted Dodge Shadow parked in an employees-only space along the side of the building. There were two other employee spots vacant, something that didn't sit well with me. A shop this small and this specific would never have more than one employee working at a time, two tops. Of the prospective employees, there was no way that they all were drivers. Stores like this would not offer enough cash to pay for a car, and the deeply religious women who typically worked behind the counter were usually unmarried or widowed, making them lower-income wage earners and thus frequent bus passengers. One of the two vacant parking spaces was much bigger than the other. The hand-painted lines were a bit wavy, but they were clearly designed to contain two cars of different sizes. No one painted parking spots behind stores like this — it was too much trouble. Someone had gone a long way to ensure that a really big car got a permanent spot. I was sure I could figure out what kind of car fit inside the painted lines.

I reversed the Volvo and backed into a spot that offered a view of the parking lot from a safe distance. No one in the parking lot I was watching would be able to see me inside the dark interior of the car. From Ave Maria, the Volvo would look like just another car taking up a free space on a side road. I unfolded the paper Paolo had given me and took the time to really look at the information on Luca Perino. Perino was in charge of his little world around James Street. His number two was a man named Marco Monaco. The paper gave me the address of the shop, physical descriptions of everyone involved with the business, and a phone number. With the car stopped and no one in sight, I decided to call the number and see what happened.

I eased myself out of the car, being careful not to twist my ribs more than I had to. I opened the trunk and pulled back the fabric covering on the floor. Underneath a spot of blood left by my face while I travelled in the dark was everything I left. I took everything in the trunk and got back into the front seat. I powered up Johnny's phone and dialled the number.

"Ave Maria," a pleasant female voice answered. She sounded older than her twenties but younger than her fifties. Beneath her words rose the sounds of hymns from a sound system in the store.

I decided to take a shot at it. "Ah, yes, hello. My name is John Clark, and I work for the city of Hamilton."

"How can I help you, Mr. Clark?"

"Well, you see, this is one of the rare calls I make that I enjoy. One of the calls I make where I can actually help you. You see, the city reassessed your area last year, and somehow in the shuffle we neglected to adjust your property taxes. As a result, we owe you some money."

"Well, that is a first. The city paying money to the people instead of the other way round." Her voice sounded very chipper. She was genuinely happy about my lie.

"I need to come in and have some papers signed before I can make out the cheque. Let me check my computer...I would need the signature of a Mr. Monaco. I have him listed here as the owner."

"Mr. Monaco's not the owner, Mr. Per —" She trailed off into a quiet murmur as her mind caught up with her mouth.

"Hello? Miss?" I sighed, knowing she was still on the line. "Darn phone. Hey, Jerry, my line went dead again. Can I use your —"

"No, it didn't. I'm here. I'm sorry, I just got confused. You're right, Marco is the owner."

"Is that Mr. Monaco?"

"Yes, he is." Her voice was chipper again. She had decided that although Luca Perino was in charge, his name was probably off the official books. After all, he was a big wheel in the mob. The woman on the other end of the phone wasn't one of those ignorant religious patrons of the store — she knew the score.

"Is he there now? I would love to get this taken care of right away."

"I'm sorry, he's not usually in until six o'clock."

The dashboard clock read 4:00. Julian had held me up, but not enough.

"I will have someone walk over the papers then. I'm off at five," I said.

"I'll let him know you're coming. He'll be so pleased. It's not every day that someone gets money back from the city."

"No, it's not," I agreed. "Thank you so much for your help."

"God bless you, Mr. Clark," the woman said, and then she hung up.

I closed the phone and shifted to put it away in my pocket. As I arched my ass off the seat to get at my pockets, I felt nothing but a searing pain through my torso. Every part of me burned, and although I was sure there were no broken bones, the pain made me question the health of my organs. I got the phone in my pocket without screaming. I kept my body off the seat so that I could stash the digital recorder in my pants too.

Once I was back in the seat with a new coat of cold sweat on my brow, I leaned over to the glove box and pulled out the cord that came with the digital recorder. I spent a minute testing the cord in each hole in the device before finally managing to fit the cord into its corresponding hole. I had at least two hours before Marco Monaco, Luca Perino's number two, would pull into his small parking space. There was no way I was going to spend two hours with my rapidly cramping body inside my car. I needed to move and loosen up. I got out of the car, taking everything except the rubber bone with me. I checked the parking sign on Hughson, making sure the car wouldn't be towed or ticketed where it was, and walked away.

I walked down Hughson until I hit King Street. King was second only to Main in its possession of legitimate businesses. The stores that lined the roadway were, for the most part, legitimate, successful retailers. The places that worked under the radar and off the books were all on the veins that led into the major arteries of commerce like Main and King. I walked the street in between the numerous bodies of pierced kids and unwashed adults. I passed a strip club and several pizza places, while I scanned the street for an Internet café. I found one on a side street just off King. I walked into the deserted café and paid up front for thirty minutes.

I opened the web browser and pulled up a free e-mail account I kept. I plugged the digital recorder into the computer and listened to the chime of hardware recognition. I clicked the Attach icon and pulled the file off the digital recorder. Once the transfer was complete, I addressed the e-mail to myself and sent it off. The e-mail was in my inbox by the time I had the recorder back in my pocket. I cleared the web browser three times and shut the computer down before I got up to leave.

I walked out of the café without another word to the employee behind the counter and followed my nose onto King Street towards a pizza place I passed on my way to the Internet café.

The pizza place sign just read "pizza" in big, bold, neon

letters. The walls of the tiny restaurant had a repeating phone number stencilled all over them with the words "Two for One" added in anywhere they would fit. There was a counter directly open to the street that everyone had to wait in front of for their food. I didn't like being exposed to the entire street, but rusting in the car like the tin man was not an option. I waited patiently and used the constant flow of young women in slutty clothing as an excuse to scan the crowds around me. I was not a man hunting the mob; I was a hungry pervert, like the rest of the men in line.

I ordered two slices of pepperoni pizza and a Coke and waited under a minute for the lukewarm Italian food to get to my hands. I took the food with me across the street to Gore Park.

Gore Park is a small patch of grass in the heart of the city core. It could be walked around in under three minutes, but no one ever did it. The park was like a safari of human suffering. Homeless kids, derelicts, and people on the verge of becoming either were in constant supply. No one stared into the park when they were at the red light on King Street — it just seemed like an invitation for disaster. Seeing everyone look away from the park made it almost magnetic to me. It was a rare find in the city. A place where a person could be invisible while being completely visible.

I walked past the homeless until I found a vacant rock. The pizza bag offered little resistance as I tore through the grease-soaked paper. The right side of my face, on the other hand, put up the fight of its life. I had lost teeth from the side of my jaw, making chewing difficult. I spent half an hour using my tongue to mash the pizza against the left side of my mouth before I swallowed. The Coke's acidity burned the empty sockets in my jaw, so I didn't drink often.

I ate to the point of physical exhaustion. The food felt good in my stomach and it was quickly taking the edge off the pain I felt. I tore the last of the food into bits and fed it a piece at a time to the gulls that had slowly been surrounding me while I ate. The gulls made me think of the island. They made me remember what it was like away from the city. The island wanted me back, but nothing could pull me away. Paolo had anchored me here, tied me to the city I tried to leave behind. I looked at my hand as I threw the last piece of pizza to the birds. My hands were no longer good for tying off knots and setting lures. I was back to what I had been. My hands were gnarled mitts again — useful for beating and stealing. Each uncomfortable breath made the island seem more like a fantasy and the city a painful reality. Suddenly, the greasy pizza felt like a stone in my stomach, and all I wanted was to be moving.

By the time I slid back behind the wheel, it was 5:15 p.m. I looked through the windshield and noticed that the little space was full. A black, two-door Mercedes was in the lot beside the beat-up Dodge Shadow. Marco was early for work.

I didn't want to go in and repeat what had happened at the cleaning-supply store. There wouldn't be any bleach here, and I wasn't interested in beating up a female employee of a religious store unless I had to. I knew I wasn't going to heaven, but I wasn't so far gone that I was going to start doing the devil any favours. I needed to get Marco out of the store without raising suspicions, so that I could deal with him alone.

My body stayed still in the car as my mind raced over the possible ways to handle the situation I was in. I no longer felt pushed to act right away. I didn't feel apprehension or anger. I searched my mind for the feelings, but they weren't there anymore. The sickness from the pizza had evaporated, and I was left in the car. I was focused without connection. I was my uncle's nephew again.

After two minutes of thought, I arched off the seat and endured the pain of retrieving my cell phone. I dialled Paolo, who answered on the fourth ring.

"I need something," I said before he could even finish his greeting of, "What?"

"I told you not to call unless you had good news. I told you I would get you some incentive if you needed it. Is that why you're calling? To test me? I can make a call right —"

"It wasn't Bombedieri," I said.

"How do you know?"

"I asked the right people the right questions the hard way."

"And you think they'd tell you anything? You have gone soft."

"I asked real hard. I know I'm right, and you know it too."

"How do I know?" he asked.

"You brought me back into this because you know what I am. I'm a grinder, I'll find out everything. Bombedieri is only concerned with his turf and bikers."

"What did you do? This can't come back on me." Paolo sounded mildly panicked. He instantly knew I had done what I said because I mentioned the bikers. Bombedieri's move against the bikers must have been a real hush-hush job.

"It won't. Now, I've given you your good news. It's your turn to give me something."

"Give you — give you — You work for me, remember?"

"I'm out of the loop, and things are going to have to start moving faster."

"Why?"

"Never mind why. It's nothing," I lied — deciding to leave Paolo in the dark about Julian's misfit crew. Julian would send them after me again. He'd have to; his pride would accept nothing less than me dead in a painful way. He had known I would go after Bombedieri; he would figure out Perino, too, once he was conscious and lucid again. I had to settle up before he was back on me. Knowing I had dealt with Julian and that he was already informed about why I was in the city would put Paolo into damage control. He would have to erase all evidence of everything he had me do. That would include erasing me. He would correct his mistake by killing me, and he'd use Steve and Sandra as bait to get the job done.

"*Figlio*, don't you lie to me. What happened?"

"Everything is working like clockwork. I just don't want anyone to have the chance to start talking to one another and compare notes. Time has a way of ruining things."

Paolo seemed to buy my story. "What do you want?"

"I need you to call Luca's number two."

"Marco? Why?"

"Tell him something happened at Bombedieri's and you

need eyes and ears at his place. Tell him you can't get a hold of Perino, and you need someone you trust over there to investigate."

"Then I'm involved. I told you I can't be involved. What the hell is wrong with you, *figlio?*"

"Nothing you say will hurt you. You're the top guy in the city. You have eyes everywhere, so you easily found out something was wrong at Bombedieri's. You don't know all the details and you need to find out. All true so far."

"Stunad! When you grab him, he'll figure it out. You're not thinking."

"He won't tell anyone anything. In ten minutes you'll call his cell phone again, and he won't answer. Then you send someone else in his place. Marco will get there eventually, but he'll never mention a word about why he was late — not even when you punish him for slacking off."

"Punish him? Why would I want to —"

"If anyone didn't do what you said right away, what would you normally do?"

Paolo was silent on the phone. His silence was like the sound of a basketball swish. I had scored a point on the old man. I was thinking ahead of him.

"You just do what you would do to any disrespectful hood. Even when you come down on him like a head-on collision, he won't say a word."

"Why not?"

"I'll make sure it's in his best interest to not say a thing." I hung up the phone, forcing Paolo to act, because there was no other alternative on the table. He wanted to know who was behind Army and Nicky's disappearance and he had no one else he could use to find out. Paolo had to work with me until he got what he wanted.

Minutes later, the back door opened, and Marco Monaco ran out with his keys in his hands. He was going so fast that he almost missed me leaning on the wall beside the back door. He ran two steps ahead of me before he looked over his shoulder to confirm what he must have thought he saw. He had a hard time seeing me behind the rubber bone swinging at his face.

CHAPTER SEVENTEEN

arced the bone high over my head and brought it down like a volleyball spike. Monaco, a small man with ratlike features, didn't make a sound in the split second it took him to notice the bad situation he was in. His mouth formed a small O just as the blow connected above his ear. Then his eyes crossed and closed. His knees went next — all at once.

The keys Marco was carrying were on the pavement beside his body. I bent at the knees, to save my back, and picked up the keys and Marco's wrists. I dragged Marco to the passenger side of his car and opened the door. I bent and lifted the little man's unconscious frame into the car, but it was next to impossible with the shape my back was in. I left the gangster on the ground while I went around to the other side of the Mercedes. I lay across the seats and used my upper body to pull Marco's torso into the car. When he was half inside, I got out, went around to the passenger door, and bent to lift his feet in. For a second I thought I wouldn't be able to straighten, but I managed to climb my way to a vertical position using the car as support. With

Marco's feet inside the car, I quickly pulled his laces from his leather shoes. I knotted both laces together and used them to tie Marco's wrists behind his back. The rope was thin, but it looped the bony wrists enough times to make a solid binding.

Once Marco's wrists were tied, I got in the front seat beside him. I freed the gun from the holster on his hip and glanced at the Glock 9mm before putting it under my thigh on the seat. The Glock was something I knew. It wasn't flashy and it wasn't the most powerful handgun out there; it was just accurate, reliable, and dangerous.

I started the car and clicked the cigarette lighter down. I leaned in the seat and breathed deep. I tried to relax my back with each breath, but it was slow going. The metallic click of the lighter brought me back to the here and now.

Riding out another spasm, I looked over at the man beside me. His skin was tinged olive and his hair grew straight up from his scalp in a finger-in-the-light-socket sort of way. I looked from the welt on his temple to the acne scars on his face. This little man was part of the puzzle. He was either innocent or guilty, but either way he knew something that I needed to find out, and I was going to grind it out of him.

I clicked the lighter down again and reached over to Marco. I grabbed his bony nose between my thumb and forefinger like grandfathers do when they say, "Got your nose." In my case, I actually tried to rip it off by twisting it and pulling it away from his face.

Marco came to just after I heard a wet snap.

"Oh my God! My nose! Stop it! Stop it!"

I stopped and watched as Marco tried to cup his nose only to realize that his hands were not responding. He leaned forward, head against the dash, and strained against the bonds. I pulled the lighter and pushed it behind Marco's ear. The circle of metal burned through the hair growing on the side of his neck and sent his body reeling back off the dashboard.

"What the fuck was that? What did you just do?"

He finally looked at me, and then at his gun. He stopped talking when he saw his Glock pointed at him. His ratty buck teeth bit his lower lip, and his eyes watered. "Wh — what do you want?"

I clicked the lighter back in its space. "Marco, you need to fill in the blanks for me."

"Blanks? What blanks?" He was already calm. The blow to the head and the burn already seemed distant as he clearly spoke to me.

"I want to know about Armando and Nicola."

Marco looked at me for a few seconds, then he smiled. "That's why Paolo called me. I thought it was weird that he called me to check on Bombedieri. I said to myself he's probably got dozens of people he could send, but he tells me to go. Why me? But who says no to the boss's boss? Man, I shoulda known. So, how'd you figure out it was Luca P. who did it?"

I didn't let the surprise I felt show on my face. "Everybody talks," I said. "I just found the right people."

"You're lying."

"Why do you say that?"

"Because people don't talk about this. Luca P. did it, but

he didn't talk about it to anybody. He doesn't even know that I know."

"If people don't talk, then how did you find out?"

Marco let out a sigh and looked around.

"No one's coming," I said. "If they do, I'll just drive us away, so spill it. All of it."

When he said nothing I pulled the lighter again and showed it to his eye — up close.

"All right, all right, shit. I was just thinking, but I'm done. Okay? I'm gonna tell you everything, okay? So knock it off with the lighter."

I sheathed the lighter. "Why so co-operative? Shouldn't you put up a fight?"

"That's what I was thinking about. Way I see it, Luca did something on his own — without me. I'd stick with him on that if it was a job. I ain't no rat, but what he was into... He killed Paolo Donati's family. That's a death sentence. I'm not dying for something I had no part in."

"How do you know it was Perino who took the boys?"

"I saw them the night they disappeared."

"With Perino?"

"No, I saw them here. Luca gave me and the other boys the day off. That never happens. But hey, who says no to a day off? I slept in and spent the day playing soccer. At dinner, my mother tells me she lost her rosary."

"You live with your mother?"

Marco looked annoyed. "Don't judge me. Just listen. She lost her rosary and she tells me she needs a new one so she can pray to the Virgin for my Nona, who's in the hospital. So we get into this big fight 'cause I tell her I'll get her one tomorrow when I go to work, but she says, 'What if Nona dies tonight?' So I finally cave in and I go down to the store to get a rosary. I got a key and I know the security code. It's no big deal. But when I pull in, I see the parking lot is full. Luca's car is there with two others. The BMW that was there was Army and Nicky's."

"How do you know?"

"They had a personalized licence plate on the car so everyone knew who owned it. No one else is riding around with DONATI on their bumper."

"Who owned the other car?" I asked.

"I don't know. It was a big van, blue, and the bumper was rusty. I knew what those kids said about the boss online. Add that to my day off and there was no way I was going in there. I got the hell away."

"What about the rosary?"

"I got a friend to loan me his mother's."

"You ever ask Perino about what you saw?"

"I know what I saw. What good would asking about it be?"

I nodded my head as I pulled the tape recorder out of the cupholder and turned it off.

"Oh shit. You were taping me? You were taping me. I told you everything. You don't need a tape. Come on, you don't need that. I'm dead if that gets out."

He stared at the electronic device as though it were a black widow spider. The recorder was much deadlier than any arachnid. There was no anti-venom that could save Marco from the tape; it was a death sentence pure and simple. The rat-faced gangster watched me put the recorder in my pocket. He knew his only chance of survival hinged on what I did with it.

"Where were you going just now?" I asked.

"I was told to go check on Bombedieri. That's where I was going."

I pulled the knife from behind my back and watched Marco's eyes open wide. I used the barrel of his Glock to force his head against the dash while I cut the shoelaces and put away my knife. When he sat up, I patted the pocket holding the tape recorder.

"In about two minutes, people are going to hear what you told me. Understand?"

He nodded.

"If you were lying, you just did it to the wrong people. If you were telling the truth, you might have just earned yourself a promotion."

Marco actually smiled at me, letting me know he told the truth.

"Get yourself to Bombedieri's and do whatever you were told to do."

"I can go?"

"In a minute. Get out of the car."

I took the keys out of the ignition and got out while Marco stared at me with a puzzled look on his face. When his door finally opened, I closed mine and walked around to the back of the car. Marco closed his door with his foot while he rubbed his wrists. "Fucking shoelaces hurt, man," he said as he came to meet me behind the car. He shut his mouth when he saw the gun in my left hand, away from the street, pointed at his belly.

I threw him the keys. "Open your trunk," I said.

"Why?"

"I'm going to give you your gun back. Then you're going to get moving. The gun is going in the trunk. You can get it out when you're gone." I turned the gun around and held the barrel in my right hand.

He nodded, accepting what I said.

"You're really just gonna let me go?"

"Marco, you're set to inherit this whole place. The boss needs to keep the system working. He needs someone who knows the ins and outs. You and me are done. You got a job to do now, and so do I. By tomorrow your paycheque will be much better; so will your parking spot."

He popped the trunk with the key fob and lifted the lid straight up with his right arm. He turned his head to me and laughed, still holding the lid. "I hate this fucking spot. I had to get this car 'cause it was one of the only ones that would fit. If that ain't bad enough, I gotta put up with the boys always asking me if my girlfriend loaned me her car for work."

I looked inside the trunk and was happy with what I saw. "You won't have to worry anymore, Marco." He started to laugh until my left hand grabbed a handful of his shirt. I swung the Glock by the barrel and the butt hit Marco in the centre of forehead like a hammer. He stiffened and began to fall back like a hewn tree. My handful of shirt guided his falling body into the trunk. The open cavity sucked him in head first.

CHAPTER EIGHTEEN

"**Y**ou won't be taking over, Marco. You're just at the start of a long night. Some people are going to want to talk to you, so you just need to sit tight." If Marco heard me, his limp body didn't show it. I pulled his keys off the pavement and fished the wallet and cell phone he was carrying out of his coat. My pockets were full enough, so I threw the phone and wallet in the back seat. Marco didn't move while I opened and shut the door. He didn't even stir when I pulled his hands out of the trunk. I laid his wrists across the edge of the trunk twice, the second time pulling more of Marco out of the trunk so that his weight wouldn't drag his hands back into the trunk again. Once the small hands were resting on the lip of the trunk, I checked the parking lot. No one had come out since I put Marco inside his own car. No one was watching, so no one saw me slam the lid down on the small, limp wrists protruding from the trunk. No one saw me hammer the screaming gangster back into the trunk it erupted from, either.

Marco was alive but broken in his trunk. His right

wrist, still visible on top of his again unconscious body, was dented. The bone ruptured the skin in a sharp point showing signs of a compound fracture. His chest rose and fell evenly as I leaned in and used my fishing knife to cut the glowing plastic seat release cord at the back of the trunk. The shoelaces would not have held anyone in the trunk for long. Two broken wrists and no seat release would hold him there until someone decided to let him out.

I closed the lid and moved Marco's car out of the small spot into the larger one. There was three feet of space on either side of the car. The little Mercedes would almost be able to open both of its doors all the way without touching another car. The white Escalade would not be able to boast the same feat. It would also not be able to fit into Marco's little space.

I left the two-door in the parking lot and got behind the wheel of my car. I turned the key and backed up twenty metres to a new parking spot concealed by shadows. It was invisible from Ave Maria, but it would allow me to see the Escalade pull in from either direction.

I waited, watching the back door of the store. I wondered when the woman behind the counter, who drove the Dodge Shadow, would leave, and if she would hear Marco alive in his trunk when she left. As the hours clicked by, it was a question that came to be all I could think about. I was debating going back to the Mercedes to help Marco sleep again, or sleep deeper, when the whole idea stopped mattering. A white Escalade took up my entire rearview. The driver's side mirror that showed objects larger than they appeared made the huge Cadillac look like a rolling iceberg.

The car drove past me over the curb aiming directly at the huge spot now fifty percent full of Mercedes. The Escalade was so large that it hid both parking spots in front of it. I couldn't see through tinted glass, but I knew who was inside the behemoth.

The white door opened at the same time as my own. The doors closed in stereo as well. I was jogging towards the tall, thin, olive-skinned man as he shook his head and rifled through a pocket in his coat. As I closed the distance between us, I estimated Luca Perino's height at six and a half feet. He wasn't big — just tall and thin, the kind of thin that mothers everywhere tried to kill with food. His bony shoulders his tented jacket as though the hanger was still inside the fine tailored suit, and his short hair did little to conceal the jutting bones of his skull. His metabolism had probably outrun many plates of food when he was a child.

When I was less than twenty-five feet away, I stopped running and hit the panic button on Marco's key fob. The Mercedes went haywire, and Luca Perino took his phone away from his ear. He walked around his huge suv to the Mercedes as I clicked the panic button on and off. I could see him five feet from the car as I got closer to the lot. My approach was concealed from view by the huge car, but that wouldn't last. Perino would see me coming unless I gave him something to look at. I popped the trunk using the keys and watched Perino walk slowly towards it. I rounded the bumper of the suv trailing in Perino's wake to see him bending at the waist to closer examine the contents of the trunk. There was a moment of realization about what was in the trunk, and then the tall man was accelerating to his full height with the phone in his hand meeting his ear at six and a half feet.

"Don't do that," I said, pointing Marco's Glock at the narrow chest of Luca Perino. He had a perfectly trimmed mustache and a vertical strip of hair below his lip. His face had small eyes and a small nose that made him appear childlike. His giant bony fingers, holding the phone next to his ear, ruined the facade. They looked like aquatic predators — all bone and tendon.

"Put the phone down in the trunk."

Luca Perino did not move; instead he spoke. "I remember you. You used to work around here. You didn't have the beard, but the rest of you looks the same." He pointed at me with a sinewy finger. "You look like shit. Little Marco do all that to you?"

I felt my back repaying me for the jog. I extended the gun towards Luca's centre using a hand on the SUV to hold me up. "Put the phone down in the trunk."

Luca held his ground, and his phone. "A lot has changed in the last few years. I've changed. I'm not some nobody thug anymore. I run this neighbourhood for a big name. Maybe you didn't know that. Maybe you should reconsider what you are doing."

He looked confident in front of my gun, towering over the body in the trunk.

"Say the name," I said.

"Who?"

"The big name. Say it."

Luca looked a little unsure.

"Say it," I said.

Luca didn't say a word.

"You don't know me," I said. "The fact that you saw me around doesn't mean anything. Things haven't changed that much from where I stand. The city is still run by one man, and I still have to do what he says. Just like it was before, I'm chained to the old man. He's still the same, and I'm back to being what I was. You, you're new but you're not different. I met people like you before. You're taller, but you're the same."

"Tell me what I am, tough guy."

"You're a big shot running your own turf. You've been doing it a little while now and you're starting to believe the hype. You think you're a big-time player and you're being held back by people with less vision than you. So you, like most before you, did something stupid because you thought it would work out. But it didn't. Just like before, he sent me to find someone like you, and here we are."

"You are really fucking far gone. I have no idea what you are talking about. None."

"Say his name," I said, and I took my hand off the bumper. I stepped towards the tall man towering over the trunk like a scarecrow. His bony hands still clutched his cell phone, but his fingers were whiter.

"Donati," he said.

"Now tell me what you think that old man is going to say when he finds out you took his nephews. Do you think all of those changes you went through will save you? Or will it be just like old times?"

Luca Perino didn't get a chance to answer. A vehicle coming towards the parking lot interrupted us. Headlights shone through the dim evening murk just before the sound of music over a harsh engine caught up with them.

CHAPTER NINETEEN

"**P**hone in the trunk now," I said as I covered the rest of the space between Luca Perino and me. His huge hands groped for the Glock as it got closer, but they retracted when my steel toe bit into his long shin bone.

The gun was in his ear as I pulled the cell phone free from his tight grip. I threw the phone into the trunk and shut the lid as music grew louder over the roar of the approaching engine. Through the tinted panes of the Escalade, still diagonal in the lot behind the parking spaces, I could make out a pair of headlights. The car stopped, and doors opened and slammed.

The engine stayed on and music poured out of the vehicle. I saw a break in the light streaming through the dark car glass — someone had walked in front of the headlights. I grabbed Luca by the belt, pushing the gun harder into his ear. I dragged him back between the Mercedes and the Dodge Shadow. When my back touched the brick of the building, I used my foot on the back of Luca's knee to put him quietly down on the pavement.

From in between the cars, I could see two bodies at the back door of Ave Maria. In the dim light, I could see that one of the men was tall like Luca, but this one was more solid. Beside him was a smaller figure in a hat that was turned sideways on his head. I could tell without getting any closer that it was Mickey and Ralphy. The two at the door probably meant that Gonzo was the one keeping the music on in the car. He wouldn't be much good for walking in the shape I left his foot in. His presence in the car and the headlights illuminating the lot kept us pinned down.

The car still belted out music while Mickey and Ralphy banged on the back door. They didn't pound on it with any urgency. Ralphy hit the door rhythmically using both hands and the toe of his shoe. Mickey nodded his head with the beat and then murmured something to Ralphy. He started the beat again with greater intensity, and Mickey bopped his head along with the faster modified drumbeat. The punks hit the door with familiarity — it wasn't the knock of a first-timer. Something was off, those doped-up leg breakers should have been scared shitless to hit a mob door like that, but the two of them showed no hesitation or second thoughts.

The door never opened. I figured the woman inside, behind the counter, knew to stay away from the back door and the type of customers who would use it. Her job was the front door of the front, and judging by the closed back door, she stuck to it.

"Why are Julian's guys here at your door?" I said in Luca's ear. He didn't answer, he just shook his head back and forth letting me know he wasn't going to say a word. It wasn't much of a head shake. The gun in his ear made part of the motion impossible.

"Why are they here?"

He just shook his head harder. I didn't need him to answer. Julian's guys were here because they were after me. They were here just like they were at Bombedieri's. But something nagged at me. At Bombedieri's they were waiting outside. Here, they were at the door, knocking to get in. Who would let those two into a back room that served as a criminal front? Mickey and Ralphy were street level; there was no way they should be high enough on the food chain to get into a neighbourhood boss's backroom office. They would be met on the street by someone under the boss to keep everything separate.

Whatever their reason for being at the door, the whole situation was turning to shit around me. Julian was pushing to kill me and he seemed to know everywhere I would be before I did. Julian was two for two in interference, and I couldn't keep surviving our encounters if my hands were tied. I had the info Paolo asked for. I had Marco on tape explaining that Luca was behind what happened to Army and Nicky. It was half of what Paolo wanted; the other half was deniability. Paolo didn't want anyone to know that he was looking into his own people. He especially didn't want anyone to know he was using me to do it. To keep Paolo in the shadows, and get me out of the line of fire, I had to make it out of the parking lot alive.

With that thought, any instinct to hold off, to try to keep Luca Perino breathing, went out the window. My hands were free of red tape — I was disconnected again, and it felt good. Luca couldn't see me grin behind his back. My face didn't change at all when I pulled the Glock from his ear and buried it in his back — right behind his heart. I pulled the trigger and I was moving before his body hit the pavement.

The music from the car on the other side of the Escalade obscured the shot, but it wasn't loud enough. The shot was sure to bring Mickey and Ralphy over to investigate.

I flattened myself on the pavement and slid under Luca's Escalade. The darkness under the suv was total, and my shadow disappeared once I was underneath. I held the Glock in my right hand and the Mercedes keys in my left.

I watched from my stomach as two sets of feet walked towards the Escalade. No feet emerged from the vehicle on the street. The music didn't slow down or quiet — it just pumped out a loud, constant drone. It probably made the gunshot non-existent inside the vehicle.

I opened the trunk with the fob when the two sets of shoes got within feet of the Mercedes. I took deep breaths and visualized what I had to do while I waited for their discovery.

Ralphy saw it first. "Holy dhit, Mick! Deck it out, dere's a dody in the dunk. Dhit, man, dere's one over dere too. It's ducking Luca P., man."

As soon as I heard the recognition, I hit the panic button. The feet beside the suv jumped and moved around in circles as Mickey and Ralphy looked in every direction. I slid out on the other side of the Escalade and ran at the headlights in front of me. The Glock in my hand fired three times, in a quick burst, at the windshield. In half a second, I put a bullet in the centre of the driver's, middle, and passenger's side of what I finally saw as not a car, but a large blue van.

I thought for a second that I was shot while I was in motion towards the van, but each step dulled the pain into decreasing stabs of agony. There was no bullet hole — it was my back reminding me of the beating the three punks in the parking lot had laid on me. The reminder made pulling the trigger easy.

No one returned fire from the van as I crossed the headlights to the driver's side. The bright beams left my vision scarred by a constantly returning bright blotch every time I blinked. Underneath the blotch and over the sight of the Glock, I saw Gonzo slumped against the passenger-side door. I got into the van and had it in reverse by the time Mickey and Ralphy ran out from behind the Escalade. I tried to crouch down while I drove, but my ribs and back made it impossible. I had to lay sideways, my head in the lap of the bleeding Gonzo, as I drove away.

Bullets punched the side of the van as I blindly spun the wheel, shifted into drive, and slammed the accelerator to the floor. Once the metal-on-metal thuds stopped, I pulled myself up, keeping my eye on Gonzo's chest wound and the gun he dropped to the floor below him.

"You had me fooled, Gonzo," I said. "That fat bastard made me think he was out, and that you and your friends were the only help he could find. Nah, he used you because no one would ever see you coming. Especially not Army and Nicky."

Gonzo let out a low laugh over the sucking sound from his chest wound. He laughed low and hysterically until he died. Two minutes later, I was outside Domenica's.

CHAPTER TWENTY

Julian had never been out. He might not have been Paolo's right hand anymore, but he was still in it up to his ears. Julian was behind everything that had brought me back. Inside Domenica's, on one good foot, was the one person with the answers. He was the owner of the unknown van that Marco saw at Ave Maria. The old me, now behind the wheel of the van, wanted to visit with Julian, and there was nothing to stop me from doing it anymore. I had let him live because there would be more questions if he were dead. Alive, there was a chance he might have talked about Paolo using me, but he'd have proof of nothing, and no one to pin it on, because I planned to be gone by the time he could get anyone to listen to what he had to say. Now he was involved, and it was my job to find out what he knew. For a second, behind the wheel, I was happy to be employed again.

I wiped the steering wheel and door handle with my sleeve and left the van around the side of the restaurant under a burned-out street light. The darkness and the locked van doors would ensure that no one would find

Gonzo for a while. The restaurant parking lot was empty except for two cars — a black BMW and a grey Audi. Julian was involved in very dangerous business; he needed to keep everything quiet if he wanted to pull off whatever he had planned for Paolo. After what had happened earlier, he must have given the kitchen staff the night off, so they couldn't witness what was to come. He sent the house band for me, and he must have been waiting for them to come back with my body. Whoever was with him had to be involved with what happened to Army and Nicky. It was too late in the game to be bringing in new people. The reason I had been dragged back to the city was inside the building in front of me.

The front of the restaurant was dark. There were only a few lights on in the back of the building, and they gave off a faint glow under the awning above the front doors. The street light in front was bright enough for people to see the closed sign. I tried the front door, ready to break it open if I had to. The door surprised me by moving inward when I put a little weight against it.

Walking into Domenica's was different the second time around. This time I was able to use the front door and do it with my head up and eyes open. Inside the door, I was met by a small desk. I flipped through the book on top and saw that it belonged to the hostess. Each page was dated and contained a list of times for reservations. No one had ever made any advance plans to eat in the restaurant. The book told me that Julian was right: he had no business at the restaurant — at least not the kind he wanted. The restaurant branched out behind the desk. The dining room was dark, but I could make out tables and chairs set up all over the square room. Behind the tables and chairs was a swinging door and a counter that allowed food to be passed from the kitchen into the dining room. The light at the back of the restaurant was coming from the hallway behind that door. The stage and bar were through an archway to the right. The whole section was dark but I silently checked it anyway. Systematically, I moved around all of Domenica's front rooms. No one was waiting for me in the shadows.

Access to the kitchen was possible through two doors, one just off the dance floor, the other in the dining room. The swinging door between the kitchen and the dining room was identical to the door near the stage I had come through earlier when I was dragged from the car by Julian's punks. I inched the swinging door open, careful not to make any noise, and stepped into the kitchen. The only light in the kitchen came from a long hallway on the left reaching back into the rear of the building. Only half of the fluorescent lights in the hallway were lit. The appliances around me used the dim hall light to cast toothy shadows on the floor. I moved from one dark place to another, looking for any sign of the people who drove the two cars outside. Five metres down the hall that led to what must have been another back door was a single flimsy door, which spilled a brighter light out from underneath.

The door read MANAGER and inside two voices could be heard. I stood to the side of the door and listened. I could hear random words that were louder than others, like, "hospital" and "no," but nothing else was clear.

Before moving any farther, I pulled the digital recorder

from my pocket. I turned the device on and slid it into my back pocket where the microphone could still pick up sound.

Once it was firmly in my pocket, I stopped wasting time. Mickey and Ralphy would be coming back as fast as their feet could carry them. I went through the door foot first to find Julian behind a desk with a foot up. An old man was wrapping the foot until the Glock in my hand spoke its loud, single-syllable language to him.

"Jesus," Julian shouted. He stretched to see the old man's body fall to the floor. The movement caused the chair to tip, and he had to wave his hands frantically to get the necessary momentum to stay off the floor.

"Put your hands on the desk, Julian."

He stared at me until he decided to do what I had said.

"Okay. Yeah. I'm doing it."

"You lied to me, Julian. You said you were out of everything, and here I find out you still have your fingers in the pie."

"I didn't lie to anybody. I'm here in fucking Siberia where Paolo left me. This middle-of-nowhere club."

"You might be in the middle of nowhere, but you were still working an angle with Luca Perino. You and him were behind what happened to Army and Nicky. Your boys used their van when they went to see Luca and Paolo's nephews at Ave Maria."

I moved closer to the half-bandaged purple foot on the desk. Julian saw me looking at the foot. "You admiring your handiwork? What you did. Crippling me twice. You fucking hit me with a car, and what does that bastard do? He lets you walk. He lets you go and retires me. You worked for him for what? Years? I put in decades, and what does that old man give me for my loyalty? This shithole!"

"You didn't retire," I reminded him.

"'Cause he said so. No, I didn't. I'm not some old horse you just put out to pasture when he goes lame. I'm better than some stupid animal. Everybody knew that — except for Paolo. People remembered me. They respected what I did. They knew what I earned, and it wasn't this. People knew what happened to me wasn't right. I didn't put my time in so some outsider could take me out. Paolo made some enemies that day."

"So why not go after him? Why Army and Nicky?"

Julian stared at his dead foot. "He made enemies, but they weren't going to go up against their boss. No one would stand for that. Paolo had to fall. He had to hang himself. Take himself out. Fall from grace. Then he could die."

Julian's words rattled in my brain, and all at once I saw his angle. "You knew what he would do if you killed Army and Nicky?"

Despite the pain in his foot, Julian nodded and laughed.

"You got Luca Perino to help you make a play on the boys knowing Paolo would go after his lieutenants under the table."

"After he retired me, he had no help left. No one he could trust."

"You didn't know he'd get me," I said.

"If it wasn't you, it would have been somebody else. That old man would go after his own people in a heartbeat. I mean, look how he treated me just for getting hurt. Imagine what he'd do to someone he thought deserved it. Someone who went after his nephews. His *family*." He spat when he said "family." "See how he treats family? The hypocrite. Everyone saw where Paolo's loyalties lay when he screwed me. They saw what happened to me. Everyone saw!"

"So you got in Luca Perino's ear," I said, imagining the events taking place in my mind.

"I showed him the writing on the wall. He knew what was coming. It was only a matter of time till he had a shitty club of his own."

"He didn't see all of it. You were going to use him to kill Paolo, weren't you?" Julian said nothing so I kept going. "You convinced him to kill Paolo's family with you, and when Paolo went crazy you would convince Perino the time was right to take out the boss too."

Julian stared at me hard, letting me know I was on track.

"I bet you still have contacts with the rest of the big players in other cities. You'd tell them that Paolo had gone off the deep end. He went after his own guys and started an internal war. Then you'd tell them that you could clean everything up and get things back to the way things should be. The other families would just want business as usual, and you figured they'd use you because you were a name they could trust. A name that earned more than it got. You were going to parlay that grip on a cane into a grip on the city."

Julian still said nothing. His hands stayed in his lap, and his destroyed foot stayed on the desk. I looked down at the man on the floor and then back to Julian. His eyes were on the Glock pointed at him. He wanted to get up and take it, but he knew his body wouldn't let him. He stared at the gun until he saw my left hand pull the tape recorder from my pocket. I clicked it off and held it in my hand.

"You took a big chance with all of this."

Julian looked at the recorder as he spoke. "I spent my life putting Paolo up. Me. My muscles, my sweat, my blood is what let that old man sit in his comfy restaurant and spout off about fucking animals all day. It was no chance that I took. It was an experiment, survival of the meanest. Heh, Paolo loves experiments, and this one was right up his alley. I wanted to see if that old man could keep order in his own house. If he could, then I belong where I am. But if he couldn't take care of his own, then his seat belongs to me because I put him there."

Julian's experiment went just like he thought it would. Paolo turned on his own people without a second thought. Just like he turned on Julian. Just like he would turn on me.

"You know Army and Nicky have family in Buffalo. Big shots."

"Yeah, I know. Pop Guillermo, their cousin, is over there. So what. How's he helping me. What's he done for me?"

"I'm saying this tape gets loose, Paolo won't matter. If he doesn't get you, someone else will."

"There's always someone," he said.

"Luca Perino is dead," I said as I put the recorder away in my pocket.

Julian looked up at me, confused; he didn't understand what I was saying. I didn't try to explain myself. Instead, I pulled out the phone and dialled the number I had called more than once over the past few days. Paolo answered on the second ring. After he spoke I said, "I know what happened. Everything."

"Where are you?"

"Place called Domenica's. You know it?"

"'Course I know it. I gave it to Julian. Why are you there?"

"I have everything wrapped up here. You need to come here and finish this. This can only end with you." I hung up the phone before he could reply.

Julian stared at me. His jaw worked back and forth, grinding his teeth down. I put the cell phone in my back pocket and pulled out the revolver I took off Johnny, the pointy-shoed messenger, endless days ago. I put the Glock under my armpit and wiped the revolver clean with my shirt. I put Johnny's gun, still loaded, on the corner of the big desk and waited for Julian to look away from it to me.

"This is your chance to have one less someone. But if you come after me in any way," I said, patting the recorder in my pocket, "this will make sure I don't come back for you alone."

I backed out the door, watching Julian watch the gun. As I moved into the dining room, I could hear Julian grunting as he tried to get at the gun. After a minute of what must have been agony, the noise stopped — Julian had something more deadly than a working foot. I let Julian live because there was too much about him that I didn't know. How many more people like Luca Perino was he involved with? How many other people knew I was back in the city? If others like Julian knew I was involved with Paolo and the attacks on two of his lieutenants, I would never be safe.

Worse, Steve and Sandra would never be out of danger. People would use them to get at me. People with less restraint than Paolo. Keeping Julian alive, but on a leash, was the best way to survive. Julian's sins against two made kids gave me what I needed to cage the hobbled beast. He would not come after me like Paolo did. What I had on Julian would also keep Steve safe. He would no longer be a bargaining chip. Julian was my way out.

I went through the archway to the stage and moved into the deepest shadow I could find. In the dark, I waited. Minutes slowly turned on the clock mounted on the wall above the doorway. After the minute hand had worked its way halfway around the clock face, Paolo walked in — alone.

"Figlio?" Paolo whispered as he walked into the dining room. He never looked my way; he was focused on the kitchen, and the bright light spilling out of the office door I left open at the end of the dim hall. I watched him disappear into the kitchen and then move out of sight. I left the shadows and walked to the door. A single shot rang out in Domenica's as I left.

Outside, I dialled the phone and got an answer on the second ring.

"Sully's Tavern."

"It's finished," I said.

"No, it's not. He's still out there in his car."

"He needs to disappear without a trace. No one can see him go. Can you do that?"

Steve didn't answer or hang up. The hard plastic phone just landed on the bar. Once again he was loose. I hoped it would be the last time.

I ended the call and walked away from Domenica's towards Ave Maria and the car I left behind. The car would still be there. It was too far away for anyone to notice it. There would not be cops around it, either, because the woman at Ave Maria knew what kind of men she worked for; she wouldn't call in any suspicious gunshots. As I walked, I took apart the phone and lost it piece by piece. The gun went next. All that was left was me, but I couldn't lose myself in the city so easily.

CHAPTER ONE

The beeping woke me up. It was a steady drone, pounding out beat after beat. It was my heart I heard being digitally reproduced for an audience. The machine beside the bed was monitoring its uniform spasms. I lay with my eyes closed, ignoring the beeps, focusing on the other sound that erupted intermittently. I waited for what felt like ten minutes until the eruption happened again. A wet phlegmy cough started low in someone's gut and fought gravity all the way up. In the midst of the coughing fit, I opened my eyes and looked around the room. A second later, I closed them and tried to recreate the scene in my mind while the coughing subsided. The room was white, as were the machine and the bed rails. Handcuffs joined my wrist to the bed. The chair by the door was overflowing with a lot of bad suit. The fabric was worn and out of style. Every pocket on the jacket brimmed with papers and the tops of pens. There was also an angular bulge on the right side of the coat, visible under the thinning material. The suit and the gun bulge had cop written all over it.

Almost 4,000 beeps later, the cop got up from the chair. He had to take a few seconds to get his wind back from the exercise.

"Don't go anywhere," he chuckled.

The door creaked twice, open then closed, and my eyes opened. I was in a windowless box of a room. Fluorescent lighting showed every imperfection on the walls and the floor. Every scuff and scratch stood out and showed the age of the hospital room. I breathed deep and felt the air rush into my nostrils. The antiseptic scent made me nauseous. The sudden pang of discomfort tuned me in to every other pain I was feeling. A wash of anguish rolled over me. My head ached and my ribs hurt. I tried to reach up to my face, but the shackles held me solid. The chains slammed against the bed frame with a loud metal-on-plastic crack. The sound was an explosion in the small white room. I lay back and closed my eyes — expecting company, but no one came in.

I opened my eyes again and stared at the ceiling thinking back to the last thing I could remember. I had been forced to work a job for a mob boss. I had told Paolo Donati that I was done being his problem solver, but no one quit on Paolo. He used my friends to force me into finding who had kidnapped his nephews. I became a fixer again and found out that Paolo's nephews were kidnapped as part of a coup. His former right hand, Julian, wanted the brass ring and thought going after the boss's nephews would unhinge Paolo enough to knock him off his throne. The two mob heavies were on a collision course with me in the middle. I did the only thing that would keep me above ground.

I led Paolo into his enemies' web and let nature take its course — after I got Julian admitting on tape that he killed the two kids. The info was enough to keep Julian away from me forever: the kids had powerful relatives in the States who would be honour bound to settle up with Julian if they found out what he did. I remembered walking away from Domenica's, Julian's restaurant, a free man. Then I remembered leaving the pavement. Everything after that was blank.

I took the alone time in the hospital room to research. There was nothing nearby that I could get my hands on, nothing to use against the cuffs holding me down. Everything I could touch was flimsy and soft. I kept looking for an option until I heard the doorknob twist. The door swung in, and the wheezing cop wedged himself back into his chair. I fake slept to the tune of beeping and coughing with crinkling plastic on drums. The cop ate at a rapid pace, pausing only to unwrap the snack on deck. It was as though he thought someone might burst through the door and take the food right out of his mouth. After about a minute, my nose picked up the scent of stale cigarettes. The cop was a smoker and enough of an addict to leave his post to sneak a smoke break. I tried to run through scenarios in which I could get my hands on the cop and out of the cuffs, but my arms had barely enough slack to reach the thin mattress. My lack of options took my hands out of my equations. My feet were free, but there was no guarantee that I could kick the cop in a way that would still leave me access to his keys or his gun. I couldn't lift his piece or pick his pockets with my toes anyway, so I let the idea drift out of my mind.

I had to play the waiting game until a new opportunity presented itself.

I lay chained to the bed for two days feigning unconsciousness. Every time the fat cop took off to sneak a cigarette, I stretched out as best I could and looked for anything I overlooked before that would help me escape. I was always disappointed.

On the third day, I was counting the perforations in the ceiling tiles with my eyes when the door opened earlier than I expected it to. I usually had a few minutes and a few hundred beeps before I had to begin faking sleep again. I quickly adapted to the schedule change and resumed my conscious coma, listening for the cop's breathing. What I got was something entirely different. Rubber-soled shoes squeaked as someone approached the bed. It wasn't the doctors or nurses — their footwear didn't make a sound. The fat cop had worn-in dress shoes that slipped on the glossy floor. I had heard him stumble and break his fall on expensive medical equipment several times. This was someone new.

The fluorescent light dimmed outside my eyelids as the person who was now standing over me took a huge deep breath and slowly let it out. This was not like the fat cop's breathing — this person was in shape. The breath lasted over thirty seconds. I took a slow breath of my own to slow my own heart. I didn't want the monitor giving anything away. Just as I finished exhaling, a heavy hand closed over my nose and mouth. The hand pressed down and the bed groaned in response. The machine beside the bed monitoring my heart picked up speed, but my body stayed slack.

The beeping quickened its pace, becoming more and more of a solid sound as another hand tore the monitor pad from my chest. The machine registered a flatline. It was going on too long. I could no longer afford to play dead. My mouth opened and found part of the hand over my lips. I bit down hard and tasted blood.

"Shit!"

The hand moved away as the door flung open. The fat cop rushed in, at his snail's pace, ahead of a nurse and a doctor.

"Morrison!" the fat cop said.

"Don't worry, Miller. Our patient woke up. It's a miracle." The man who had been suffocating me was pressing his thumb over where I had bit. His face was to the door, giving me only a look at his suit; it was tight, but not like the fat cop's. The material was taut across muscular shoulders and arms.

"But the nurse's station got an alert that his heart stopped. Whatever was monitoring his vitals said he was dying."

"When you left for your little break, our patient must have removed the sensor. The alert wouldn't have happened if you managed to stay at your post."

"Sir, I…"

"Shut the fuck up, Miller. Get everyone out of here. I'll deal with you later."

"Now hold on a minute, I have to check on my patient."

"Later, Doc, later. Right now he has to check in with me. When I got what I want from him, you can have him."

"I am his physician, and while he is in this hospital he is

under my care. Hospital protocol demands I check on him after an alert," the doctor protested. He had a hard time realizing that he was outranked on his own turf.

"Miller, get them out of here now!"

The fat cop turned and spread his arms. The pudgy net swept up the nurse and the doctor, both of whom obviously wanted no contact with the sweat-stained blazer, and forced them out of the room. The man over me slammed the door behind them before crossing the floor and unplugging the heart monitor. He dragged the fat cop's chair to the bed and sat down. He didn't say anything right away. He was too busy pressing an old tissue from his pocket onto the bite on his hand.

"You broke the skin."

"You tried to kill me."

"Nah, it was reverse CPR. It always works on fake coma victims."

"What if the coma was real?"

"Reverse CPR's got only one side effect I know of."

"Where am I?"

"Hospital."

"Who am I?"

"Cut the shit."

"Who am I?"

"I said, cut the shit." The cop stood, and I got my first good look at him. He was tall, maybe six-three, and muscular, not bodybuilder muscle but wrestler muscle. His body conveyed a sort of all-over strength. Not the kind that came from lifting a dumbbell over and over again, but rather the power that evolved out of years of driving people off their feet and then grinding them into the ground. His skin was dark, not black, more of a deep tan. It wasn't the olive complexion of the Mediterranean I was used to; the features were more foreign, the nose wide and flat and the forehead large. I had not seen this look before. The dark hair on his head was trimmed short. It was strong healthy hair; the kind that held its shape without gel. This cop was a tough bastard. It radiated off him. I could sense it like dogs sense other dangerous canines. He leaned in over me and outstretched his hand again.

"I know who I am. I want to know who *you* think I am," I said. My words stopped the hand from covering my mouth again.

"You're a guy who's in a world of shit. Way I see it, I don't know your name, but I know you're a killer. We found you in the road in front of that wop front, Domenica's. You had a gun on you, a knife, and a dog bone. There was something that looked like a tape recorder, but it got mashed to bits when the car hit you. Funny part is, the restaurant was closed. There were three cars out front: one registered to the owner of the place, the second to a very bad man — one outside my department and paygrade. The owners of the first two cars weren't around, but the owner of the third vehicle, a van, was there. He was dead in the passenger seat. Caucasian, long hair, beard, name Gary Ford. Most people called him Gonzo though. Seems Gonzo was at the hospital earlier for a *fall*."

"Must have been some fall to have killed him."

"Nah, he walked out of the hospital with a clean bill of health. Well, he didn't walk so much as limp. The emerg

Doc said the wound looked like a gunshot through the foot. Bullet went right through, so there was nothing to recover, but the impact drove some of his old canvas Chuck Taylor Converse into his foot. Into the...metatarsal bones, the doctor called them. Gonzo swore up and down that he stepped on a pickaxe in his garage when he fell down some stairs. Good story, except a pickaxe won't send pieces of canvas into bones in the middle of your foot. The Doc called it in, but the greasy punk took off. He ended up dead in the van before we could bring him in. Dead from two more bullets. That brings me to you."

"You think whoever tried to kill me with the car shot this Gonzo guy too?"

"No, I don't think that. A drunk driver hit you. You shot Gonzo with the gun you were carrying. Ballistics will prove it, once I run the gun."

"Tell me," I said.

"Tell you what?"

"I've been here a long time. Why haven't you run the gun yet?"

"Heh, you're not as dumb as I thought."

Neither are you, I thought. This cop had me dead to rights whether he knew the whole story or not. The gun they had on me would tie me to Gonzo all right. It would also tie me to a gunfight and two bodies outside of Ave Maria, a local religious store and mob front. The fact that the gun had not yet been run through the system meant that the cop standing over me wanted something.

"Tell me," I said.

"You're not a suspect yet, just a person of interest. One

word from me and the prints I took off you get attached to a murder charge. You're a person of interest *only*, for now, because you and me got similar interests."

I shifted around in the bed trying to get comfortable. When I found a spot that didn't feel like I was on a hot spike, I spoke again. "What interests are those?"

"You want to stay out of jail and I want you to stay out too."

"We do see eye to eye about that, but you can't always get what you want."

"That's a good song. Back on the island we got that record."

"What island?"

"New Zealand."

That explained the features I couldn't place.

"So did we send some fat, pale cop there, and we got you in exchange?"

"Nah, mate, I'm local. Have been for years and years."

I shifted on the bed again.

"You can't always get what you want," he sang. "But if you try some time, you get what you need. Song's true, and you're going to have to figure that out."

"So what do I have to do to get what I need?"

"Nothing too taxing. I just want a bigger fish."

"And you think I can get you one?"

"Figure you can. Found you in front of a mob den with two abandoned cars belonging to some underworld heavy hitters. I think you know some things about some people that I don't know...yet."

"You think that talking to you will improve my

prognosis? I'm already on a list somewhere if what you say is true. Someone will want payback, and it won't be hard to get at me when I'm chained up like King Kong."

"Good film. I even liked the remake. But that might just be me rooting for a hometown face. You ever see his *Lord of the Rings*?"

I shook my head.

"Blow your fucking socks off, ya know what I mean? That was epic, just epic. Not like you, you're not epic. You're not even on anyone's radar. No one even knows you're here outside of Miller and me."

"The nurses," I said.

"We fed them a lie about you being a cop killer."

"Explains the violence and why they let it happen," I said, nodding.

"Some in the west just don't appreciate Maori medicine. To them you're just passing through. You're not even worth their time, and they won't miss you when you're gone. There's no one to miss anyway: you're not even in the system yet, and as far as the Italians know, the drunk driver outside Domenica's hit a bum, not far off on that one, eh? But you're on my shit list, and you'll be there until you give me something better to spend my time on. If you don't come up with a name for me, I'll hunt you down with a blue army behind me, and I'll make sure the Italians aren't far behind. Your best bet is to help me out and then get the hell out of town, mate."

"You're some cop, Serpico."

"I'm local, but I still got some of the old island ways inside me." He accelerated fast to his feet and hit his chest with a closed fist. The sound echoed off the tight walls. His face became wildly expressive as his tongue shot out to his chin and his fist rose in the air. It was something that could have looked ridiculous, but this imposing man had the eyes of a believer. His display of the old ways was an eye opener. This man wasn't soft, he had a fire inside that hardened him. This ritual showed me what he was underneath the suit and cop shield. I understood the cop, but I wouldn't let him know.

"That dance mean it's going to rain?"

"That is no dance. It is part of the peruperu. It brings the god of war. It's the old, old ways."

"You think what I can tell you will lead you to war?"

"I don't want you to talk to me. I said I want you to get me a fish, not draw me a map to the fucking watering hole."

"How can I get you anything from here?"

"You got a few days to figure out how you can get me what I need. After that, I just process you and take what I can get with the prints on the gun. I don't care how you do it, just try not to break any more laws getting me what I want. I'd hate to have to arrest you again. You'd hate that too, that Maori medicine is a bitch the second time around."

The big cop got up and reached inside his jacket. His hand came out with a white business card. He handed it to me and then bent to plug the heart monitor back in. The machine said its thank you in steady electronic beats.

"Call the number on the back when you get me my fish. Wait too long, and the picture we took of you while you were out will start making the rounds at roll call; your prints will go into the machine too."

I didn't watch the cop leave. I studied what he had handed me instead. Detective Sergeant Huata Morrison's card had two numbers on it — business and cell. It was a generic cheap business card, thin and plain. The only exception was the handcuff key taped to the back.

CHAPTER TWO

I pulled the key off the back of the card and fit it into the cuffs with my right hand. I managed to find a position where I could use my thumb and index finger to turn the key. I felt the mechanism start to slowly turn and the cuffs begin to release. I opened the cuffs slowly, one size at a time until I could slip my hands from the metal rings with little friction. I couldn't walk out right away — there were too many people around, not to mention the fact that all I had to wear was the thin, assless hospital gown I had on. If I could get clothes, I could get to the car. The Volvo I rode into town on should still be parked close to Ave Maria. Its years of wear and tear would make it virtually unnoticeable in the urban jungle. It was like a boxy European mechanical tiger hiding in the long concrete grass. No one saw it coming and no one saw it go. Under the hood, the car was all after-market improvements. It would give any souped-up sports car on the road a run for its money. The car was more than a conveyance; it was a temporary bank too. In a compartment inside the trunk, under the spare, lay a few hundred thousand in cash in a fireproof box. Paolo Donati had put me in a dangerous spot a few years back. I left the city in a hurry with enough travelling money to last me years. Paolo found me in two, and I brought the balance back across the country with me, just in case I had to buy my freedom or the bullets I would need to take it. I never planned to be in town for more than a few days, so I never set up a safe place to stash the cash. I had to be prepared to leave without more than a second's notice, and I couldn't afford to leave my money behind. My need outweighed the danger of leaving all of my eggs in one basket.

If the car was still there, the spare key would be with it. I would have money and transportation. With that, I could get everything else.

The artificial light in the room gave me no sense of what time it was. The fluorescent bulbs hummed constantly, letting anyone who opened the door see me without getting too close. It could have easily been seven in the morning or seven at night. I would have to wait for visiting hours to end and the night shift to begin before I could move. The only distinction between day and night came from the interruptions caused by shift change. I always had a sense that the night shift started when there was a long lull between suspicious nurses looking in on me. The night shift was run at its own pace. Nurses came more infrequently and did their best to let the patients sleep; they tried even harder to ignore me. It would be the best time for me to slip out.

I didn't think my guard would be with me in the room anymore. He was waiting for me to wake up so that I could be interrogated. Now that I was conscious, and my interrogation had been completed by the big cop Morrison, I figured the plan would be to leave me to heal before I was fed to the system.

I closed my eyes and relaxed. I was sore everywhere, but I could still move. Some of the bumps I took before the accident seemed not to hurt as much as I remembered. I checked every body part with a movement starting from the top. My scan halted when I moved my hips and felt discomfort from the catheter. The tube hurt, and I knew it would have to come out. I slid my right hand free under the sheet and felt around my dick. There was nothing permanent holding the tube in place; that meant there was something anchoring it inside my bladder. I would have to dismantle the urinary device, but that would have to wait until I was ready to check out.

My mind raced. I had let Paolo Donati control me, and it had cost me. I was in the city because he forced me, to come home, and I spent every moment of my return playing keep up. I had to juggle Paolo, his threats, his job, and his timetable in order to survive. I had managed to hand Paolo over to Julian to end the juggling, but I had still wound up behind the eight ball. A drunk driver was an 80 km/h monkey wrench. Everything I worked for, the life under the radar and off the grid, compromised because of some asshole overdoing it during happy hour. I let myself give in and feel all the rage inside. My fists clenched, and I felt my nails pierce the skin of my palms. After ten long seconds, I let everything go and started planning.

When the day shift ended, I would move. I didn't know my way around, but I had no time to reconnoitre. I had to play everything by ear. I went over everything I knew about hospitals in my head. There were both elevators and stairs on each floor. Each ward was usually broken down into patient rooms, offices, supply cupboards, and a central desk for admitting patients and keeping track of the streams of information passing from machines, to doctors, to nurses, and finally back to machines again. To get out to the elevators or stairs, I would at least have to pass the nurses at the front desk. Any movement would be trouble; the staff had been informed that I was a suspect in a murder, and that fat cop had camped out in the room with me for days. The staff would be on edge about my presence, more so now that it was common knowledge that I was conscious. Hospital security would not be far away from my door; I was probably a stop on some guard's nightly rounds. I lay in the bed and thought about my options until my eyes caught sight of something on the ceiling — a smoke detector burrowed into the faded ceiling panels above me. Smoke detectors were in every room, and they connected to a loud alarm. I imagined that hospital protocol would demand an evacuation if a fire threatened the patients. Alarms brought chaos, chaos brought confusion, and confusion brought a smile to my face.

With a plan formed in my mind, I relaxed a little more. I spent the rest of the day in and out of sleep. When I was out of dream land, I occupied myself by bopping my head to the beat of the heart monitor or holding my breath to see how fast I could make it go.

My games were interrupted by a doctor and nurse who entered together.

"What time is it?" I asked.

The doctor looked put out. "A little after five, almost dinner. Now that you're awake, you can eat tonight. Er, well," he stuttered, looking at my chains, "someone from security can aid you in your eating."

"Any chance you can get these off?"

Zero hesitation came with the answer. "No."

"Fine. What hospital am I in?"

"St. Joseph's, Mr....ah, I don't have a name for you. It would seem that you were brought in without any identification. What is your name?"

"James. James Moriarty." The name wasn't mine. But it served the man who evaded Sherlock Holmes well. Someone would find humour in the name eventually. It wouldn't be funny at first, but once I got loose and disappeared someone would chuckle under their breath about it.

"Well, Mr. Moriarty, is there any chance that you know your health card number?"

"Not off the top of my head."

"Social Insurance number then?"

"Starts with a five. Second number is a four. Does that help?"

"No. Well, you look fit, I'll see about food being sent round. Need to keep your strength up for the trial."

The nurse let the doctor out of the room first. As he passed, she paused to sneak a look in my direction. I winked, and she jumped as though she had been Tasered in the ass.

The door closed, and I was left alone with the beeps. Hours passed, and food never arrived. I wasn't surprised.

Labelled as a cop killer, I was sure to be on everyone's shit list. If food did show up, I wouldn't eat it. I would fake stomach troubles to avoid the real ones that would surely come later from eating a tampered dinner. The noise in the hall got quieter and quieter as visiting hours waned. Eventually, it took minutes for me to hear any sound at all. A nurse poked her head in and looked me over from the door while I pretended to sleep. She left the room without turning off the lights. It was like that every night. I was constantly on display under the never-ending fluorescent glare of the lights so that none of the nurses would have to step into the room to get a look at me pretending to sleep.

I used the catheter, gritting my teeth the whole time at the plastic handcuff that locked my dick to the bed. I had to wait a bit longer.

My wait was interrupted by a nurse tumbling into the room ass first. She hit the ground and shuffled backwards across the floor to the wall as the man who pushed her entered. Behind the man was a young woman.

"Fuck your visiting hours. We are not here to visit. We are here to make things even."

I knew the face. The Russian accent spun the Rolodex in my mind to the name that matched the mug — Igor. I had shot Igor in the shoulder a few years back when he had tried to kill me in my office. Igor and another henchman had shown up to find out what I knew about the robbery of some Russian property, and he ended up on the wrong side of a bullet. Igor failed his boss and named names to me. I let him and his partner live to save me the trouble of disposing of their bodies. For betraying his boss, I figured he'd have to hide out for the rest of what should have been his short life.

"What? You don't remember me, mystery man?"

"I remember you, Igor. I thought you'd have been smart enough to hitch a ride out of town on the Siberian Express."

"Leave? Why would I be leaving? You killed Mikhail. That was a big favour. No one knew who he sent out to see you, so I was in the clear. And because you killed Gregor too, I was the only one who knew what had happened."

"So it was me who killed your partner?" Igor was lying—running some kind of game. I killed Mikhail, but Gregor walked out of my office with Igor.

He turned to the dirty-blond-haired woman behind him. He laughed in her direction, and she replied in kind.

"You see, baby? He is a worthless liar, a dog. He kills Gregor, and he can't even man up to it. Not even at the end."

The dirty-blond was five-ten and dressed in the finest clothes the girls' department could offer. Everything was too tight. Underneath her open jacket I could see her breasts spilling over the bra cups. The jeans had a big "I" belt buckle above the zipper. The buckle was studded with glittering crystals and was ornamental only. The jeans cut into her flesh and made the flab on her stomach spill over the material. The belt buckle was Igor's way of branding the girl. He showed the world she was his with his very own tacky mark.

"Introduce us, Igor."

He chuckled. "This is Tatiana. Tatiana, this is a dead man."

Tatiana smiled at me, then winked at Igor.

"How'd you find me, Igor? You're a low-level fish, and I'm not even sure you know my name."

The fish comment pissed him off. "I am no fish, and your name is not important. One of my own little fish told me about some murders outside of a club we know. I came to see who was involved, because perhaps the people I work for could benefit from such information. Information pays highly, but it turns out that it is me who will be benefiting and you who will be paying. Your name is not important to me because you will be dead and forgotten in a few moments."

"See, you *are* low level fresh off the dock fish. The scared nurse on the ground has more intel than you."

Igor reached into his right jacket pocket and freed a snub-nosed revolver. The draw was fast because the front sight on the gun had been filed down. Igor had never graduated to a holster. He was still carrying guns in his pockets like a fourteen-year-old on his first stick-up. Despite the fact that he had found me, Igor was still unprofessional.

"What is his name?" he said, pointing the gun at the nurse on the floor.

"James...James Moriarty."

"See? A gun is like information ATM. It gets me everything I need. We are all friends now. *Da*?" He smiled a crooked smile at me. The smile was the work of shitty Russian dentistry. When he laughed, I caught a glimpse of shiny stainless steel teeth glinting from the back of his mouth.

"How'd you find me, Igor?"

"When you left, you killed important men in our organization. Positions had to be filled. Sergei Vidal recognized my useful skills, and I was promoted. I now do what Mikhail did."

I was amazed at how different mobs from different cultures managed to operate synchronously. The Italians under Paolo Donati made similar promotions when the Russians had decimated their ranks. It was the premature elevation of the new generation that led to his nephews being kidnapped and eventually his death. It looked like the Russians promoted the same breed of youngster when they faced similar losses. Mikhail had run a neighbourhood until we crossed paths. Sergei Vidal, the highest ranking Russian crime boss in the city, cut me a deal after I killed Mikhail. He promised me that we would be square if I got him back some disks I stole. I got most of the disks back, keeping only one for personal insurance. Sergei and I were in a stalemate last I checked. Igor's visit said different.

"So you came here thinking you could sell some information to Sergei? Some promotion you got — you're nothing like Mikhail; he was management, you're just an errand boy. Do you think Sergei would still let you be his bitch if he knew how badly you screwed up the first time you came after me?"

"There you go lying again." Igor aimed the pistol at my head from five feet away from the bed. If I slipped out of the loosened cuffs, I'd still be too far away to stop him from killing me. "You see, Tatiana? He lies right until the very end."

"Just pull the trigger, baby. I want to see you kill him."

"Tatiana, you ever see him with his shirt off?" I asked.

She didn't answer. She instead looked to Igor with confusion on her face. I could tell she wanted to know what I meant, but Igor was running the show, so she looked to him.

"Go wait in the car!"

"But you said I could watch. You promised, baby."

Igor slapped her with the back of his empty left hand. She grunted with the impact, but she didn't cry out.

"I knew you would chicken out. You always chicken out. You are like a little…"

Igor punched Tatiana in the stomach and she crumpled to the floor. She was allowed less than a second to rest before he pulled her up by her hair. "You shut up and get out! I don't explain myself to you, whore. Do as I say and get in the car. Do not let anyone see you, understand?"

Tatiana had nothing else to say; she just nodded, turned around, her head hung low, and walked towards the door. She looked over her shoulder at Igor and caught sight of the nurse on the floor.

"What are you looking at?"

The nurse started to stammer out a response, but Tatiana's shoe cut her off. The nurse back crawled into the corner of the room as she tried to avoid the kicks. Isolated, with no where else to go, she covered her head and cried. Tatiana kicked the nurse until Igor pulled her away and shoved her towards the door.

"I told you to get the fuck out of here."

Tatiana took one last look at the nurse's body — the woman was still sitting up but no longer conscious — and went out into the darkened hallway.

"You two have a real future, Igor."

"Shut up."

"Hard to call me a liar when I know about the bullet hole I put in your left shoulder."

"Shut up, you motherfucker! No more talk."

"If you kill me, Igor, my deal with Sergei is done."

He paused and squinted at me, over the barrel of the gun, confused by my words.

"Deal?"

"Sergei and I are square. You not knowing that means you aren't high enough on the totem pole to be pulling any triggers. You know that though, don't you? Makes me wonder why you're ready to shoot me in the middle of a hospital without permission from your boss."

"Revenge. You cost me everything."

"Sounds to me like I gave you everything. I let you live and I killed your boss. If you took over for Mikhail, you run a neighbourhood now. You're something of a player because of me."

"All that means nothing without closure. Everything I earned, and I earned it, means nothing without getting the closure I need. I can't do my job right, I can't earn, I can't even fuck! What you did to me ruined me, and I can't get past it. I need other people to do everything for me. Do you know how hard it is to come up with reasons why you can't work? It's exhausting. I'm always…" he motioned his hands up and down until he found the word, "juggling reasons and excuses. I need to get out of the cycle, but I won't be able to get my head right until I get back what you took from me."

Igor took a breath and wiped tears from his face. He dried his hand on his pants, then took a two-handed grip on the butt of the gun. He closed one eye and levelled the barrel with my forehead. The gun trembled a little at first, then more and more. He was working up his nerve, and he would get there unless I pushed him off course. Igor used the term "closure"; the word sounded strange coming from the gangster's mouth. He said the word slowly as though it were a serious matter. I focused on the term and used it to try to pull Igor off track.

"Killing me like this is not going to give you closure. What are you proving by just pulling the trigger while I'm chained down? You did none of the heavy lifting. Someone else did everything for you again, and you're just going to take the credit. No wonder you can't get it up; you can't even hold a gun straight."

"Shut up."

"You think Tatiana is downstairs checking out the real men?"

"Shut up."

"Men who can do their jobs. Men who fuck their women instead of beat them. Men who don't cry themselves to sleep at night."

"Shut up!"

"You don't like what I'm saying? Then prove you're better. Prove it, you limp dick." Under the covers my hands slid out from the cuffs. "Don't just pull some trigger and let the bullet do the work like everyone else does. Do something for yourself."

The trembling hands got worse, and the barrel shook away from its path to my forehead. Instead of a bullet exploding towards me, the squat revolver accelerated towards my face. Igor swung his arm up, as he advanced on me, preparing to pistol whip me.

"Shut up! Shut up!"

My hand met the Russian's wrist as it came down at my skull. My other hand grabbed the barrel of the gun and forced it up to the ceiling. I kept pushing the gun forward towards his wrist until it broke free of his grip. Igor, wild with rage, drove his head forward into my nose. I turned my head enough to take the blow on the side of my forehead. The head butt caused me to lose my grip on the gun, and it fell to the sheets. Igor's hands found my throat, and he bore down on me.

"Shut up! Shut up!"

His eyes were wild, and he was foaming at the corners of his mouth. I had coaxed him to move on me, and I was paying the price. The choke was strong, but I had been in worse scrapes with better men. I didn't waste time searching for the gun or working on the fingers of the hands on my windpipe. My left hand took a handful of hair, and my right formed an index finger fishhook. I gouged into Igor's mouth, hooking the soft flesh surrounding his bared teeth, and ripped away. His cheek tore, and Igor wailed. The sudden pain cut through the temporary insanity and broke the chokehold. Igor recoiled in pain, grabbing at his face as he lost his balance on the bed. He rolled to the floor while I sat up and grabbed the gun. The fat black revolver was ugly-beautiful, and it fit my hand like a glove on a cold winter day. I put my feet on the ground for the first time in days and felt the cold touch of the floor tiles. Air flowed up into the gown, and I felt my skin tighten. Igor still pawed at his cheek, trying to hold the newly separated flesh together while he screamed. His screams were dampened by his hands over his mouth, and the sounds came out as muffled grunts. Blood was streaming down Igor's wrists and dripping through his cupped hands onto the floor. I took a fistful of Igor's hair and pulled his head forward so that the blood stayed off his clothes. He yelped a little louder in pain for a second, then the butt of the revolver put him to sleep.

CHAPTER THREE

When the adrenaline receded I became suddenly aware of the pull from under my gown. The catheter line was taut, and the pain radiated into my core. I had no idea how the plastic line was forced into me, and I learned the hard way, after one painful pull, that there was some sort of anchor inside my bladder holding the tube inside me. However the tube was locked in place, the bag couldn't come with me. I pawed Igor's pockets looking for a knife but found only car keys. I used the sharpest key to saw at the tube just above the bag. It took thirty seconds for the dull key to wear down the medical plastic. I threw the bag in a medical waste disposal box and gave removing the tube one last try. The catheter retracted with my pull, and I grunted as each centimetre of the tube came free. When the catheter was all of the way out, I saw that the anchor that once held it in place was now a flaccid balloon tinted pink with a sheen of blood and urine.

Free from the catheter, I wasted no time stripping Igor. Within minutes, I was wearing his fashionable jeans and leather jacket. I also felt the bulge of his wad of cash in the pants and the weight of his revolver under my new belt.

Igor was unconscious in my gown. I bent at the waist and picked him up. It wasn't pretty; I kept the Russian face down, using his waist and a handful of hair to lift him, to avoid any more blood on the clothes. I flopped his slackened body on the bed and roughly turned him over. I closed the cuffs around his wrists until I felt bone stop the mechanism. Killing Igor would bring too much heat down from both the cops and the Russians. Hurting him would have to do. The beating wasn't severe enough to do him any serious harm; the further damage to his psyche was another story altogether.

I checked the nurse's pulse and found her to still be soundly out. I left her where she was and creaked the door open. The halls were dark and empty save the sound of two women talking somewhere down the corridor. I tilted my head out, but I couldn't see the owners of the two voices. I looked back at the nurse on the floor behind me and watched her stillness. It wouldn't last forever. If she made enough noise coming to, or anyone peeked in and saw her — the hospital would be in lockdown fast.

"Fuck," I said under my breath. I pulled the gun from under the coat and gripped the barrel. I walked over to the nurse and looked at her closely. She was beaten up, but she would live. I dragged her body behind the other side of the bed so that no one would prematurely rouse her from her concussed dreams either.

I turned off the lights in the room, eased the door open again, and saw that the hall was still clear. I walked down the corridor, away from the voices, and took the first stair-well I saw. I took the stairs down to the main floor and found another set of stairs leading to the parking garage. All at once the steps were concrete and coated in chewed gum and grime. The light fixtures followed suit and became suddenly more sparse and cheap, offering light only on each landing. I took the first exit into the parking garage. The lot reeked of urine and mildew, and I breathed deep, enjoying the scent of the city. Even in someone else's clothes and wanted by both sides of the law, I couldn't shake the nos-talgic smell of the city. Fuck freshly baked bread, it had nothing on the city air.

I walked through the rows of cars, down the ramps, to the exit. There were no security guards, only an electric arm to guard against anyone trying to sneak out without paying for parking. I didn't even break pace, just ducked under the arm and strode to the crosswalk. St. Joseph's was just out-side downtown and close to everything. It was a short walk down St. Joseph's Drive to James Street. The road was busy with young people making their way into the downtown core for fun on Hess Street or in the dozens of pubs located on every other block.

The streetlights were on, and I was sure that the stars were out above the layer of constant pollution in the sky. I put a kilometre of distance between the hospital and myself before stopping on the curb. I waited two minutes for a cab to come down the mountain access, past the hospital, on its way to drunken downtown fares. I stepped out in front of the cab and got in the back while the cabby got over his shock.

"You can't jump in front of cars like that! You'll get hit!"

"Take me to the north end of Wentworth."

"Seriously, what the fuck were you thinking?"

"Drive to Wentworth, or I step out in front of another cab."

"Fine, asshole. Whatever."

As we drove, the cab driver ran through the list of pedestrian-initiated accidents he had seen. I didn't participate in the conversation. Once I saw that his dashboard clock read 11:38, I just kept my eyes peeled for an open store and for Ave Maria. As we clocked down Wentworth, I saw empty storefront after storefront. I almost missed Ave Maria; its old dark brick camouflage blended into the city too well. I let two streets go by before telling the cabby to turn off the road onto a quiet side street. We made two right turns before making our way behind Ave Maria. I watched the alleys and side streets as the cab got closer to the Volvo. One hundred metres away from the car, backed into an alley, I saw it. There was a dark sedan parked in the shadows. A small orange glow pierced through the dark and gave away someone sitting inside. I knew someone would be watching the alley. Before my hospital stay, I had killed two people there and maimed another. Someone would have noticed my work, and they would have eventually picked up on the Volvo collecting dust just down the street. I was sure it had been searched, but that didn't bother me; the money was well hidden. No one doing a fast street search would find it unless they knew exactly where to look. There was a chance the car would be conveniently "stolen," but if that happened, no one would be able to get a look at the owner.

Whoever was watching the car was looking for some face time — probably the bloody kind. The watcher in the car was a low-level grunt, either cop or robber. Whoever they were, they would need to be dealt with if I was going to get back what was mine. And I was going to get what was mine.

"I need to get to a Shoppers Drug Mart. One of those huge twenty-four-hour stores. You know where one is?"

"As long as you promise not to get hit by a car in the parking lot."

"I promise, Mom."

"Mom! Listen. I'm just trying to do my civic duty. I see too much stupid crap night after night to stay quiet. But you, you don't care. So do what you want. Lay in the street if you feel like it. I don't care anymore."

"The street would be quieter."

"All right, pal. I get it. You don't want an earful from me on your dollar. Just make sure you don't end up getting a bumperful, okay?"

"You wouldn't have hit me," I said.

"What makes you so sure?"

"I've already gotten my surprises for the day. Three in a row, God ain't that funny."

The cab driver made a confused grunt, then shut up and drove in silence. The Shoppers was on Main. It was one of the old-school stores that used to be a Big V before it was bought out. I paid the cab driver to wait out front while I went inside. The $400 I took off Igor would pay for everything I would need.

The store was a ghost town. The cashier, a fat woman with short blond hair and several moles, said, "Hello," without looking up from her magazine, and I grunted a matching response in the direction of the greeting. I walked through the aisles, skimming through all of the logically assorted items until I found what I was looking for in the small home improvement section. I picked up a roll of duct tape and an exacto-knife. A gas can also caught my eye, and I put it under my arm. A few aisles away, I found a thin baby blanket, a duffel bag, and a black baseball cap.

I paid in cash for everything I picked up and added a Nestea from the refrigerator beside the register, a package of mixed nuts, and a Three Musketeers to my purchase.

Back in the cab, I put on the hat and loaded the duffel bag while we drove back to James Street. When we pulled to a stop across the street from where I was first picked up, I paid the cab driver.

"Now you watch out for pedestrians."

"Me? Me? It is you who should be watching out. You walked in front of me right over there. Remember? I almost…"

I shut the door and walked back to the hospital. Instead of going to the parking garage I came out of, I walked to the front of the hospital. The lot was half full of cars despite the late hour. The cars were empty, and I saw no sign of anyone leaving the building as I approached. The half-empty lot meant that no one had found Igor or the nurse yet. There was an attendant in a booth collecting tickets, but no other security backed the lone worker up. The lot had no outdoor cameras mounted to protect the cars either. The hospital must have thought that the presence of a human being would cancel out the temptation of a new BMW alone out in the open. Whoever was in the booth was old hat at the job. I could see him leaning back in a chair with a newspaper spread in front of his face. The attendant never noticed me walking across the lot into the decorative foliage on the other side of the concrete. I took a spot between two large evergreen trees and ate the mixed nuts and candy bar. I didn't take a sip of the iced tea; I left the glass bottle of Nestea at my feet.

I waited and ate until sirens began approaching from all directions. The parking lot attendant saw the rapid approach and raised the wooden bar for the cops. Five squad cars raced into the lot and took the handicap spaces. I picked around for cashews while the five cars shed their uniformed occupants. Eight cops in all ran into the hospital. The door was held open for them by an out-of-shape security guard who knew that the police presence meant it was time for him to get off his ass. He held the door and looked official until the men passed, then he just looked put out. I had finished the cashews and moved on to Brazil nuts when another car showed up. The car was not a squad car, it was a police sedan. It had no markings to establish its credentials, only the generic Ford features that let everyone know what kind of car it really was. As the car passed me, I saw the safety barrier for transporting suspects. I also noticed that Detective Sergeant Huata Morrison was driving. He paused in front of the entrance and put the car in park, but a security guard opened the door, pointed at the no stopping signs, and waved him away. Morrison put the Ford into gear and drove into the lot to find a spot.

I left my spot among the trees and walked onto the lot.

From his booth the attendant couldn't see me moving out of my spot in the shadows. His back was to me, and his eyes were on something in his hands. He was probably on a cell phone — texting someone about the action.

Morrison found a spot in the middle of the lot and pulled in headfirst so that the car faced the hospital entrance. I was ten metres away when he opened the door. I sped up my pace and closed the gap as he put one foot on the pavement. Morrison put down his other foot and got out of the car dragging his suit jacket along with him. His back was to me as he put the jacket on. His broad shoulders made it difficult, and he had to raise one arm high in the air to slide the jacket over his shoulders. His stance was wide, and just as his suit jacket slid on, my foot connected with his groin. Morrison had no time to scream because my arm was around his windpipe before he hit the ground. My right hand found my biceps, and my left hand went behind the big man's head. The rear naked choke was textbook; the kick to the balls left the cop defenceless, and it let me get in tight. His powerful frame surged against the choke for a few seconds, but the hold won quickly. Some people can fight a sloppy choke for as long as they can hold their breath, but a good choke doesn't attack the airway. The flesh and bone vise around Morrison's neck cut off circulation, not oxygen, and no one can hold out against a loss of blood to the brain for more than a few seconds. I kept the choke on for another fifteen seconds before letting it go in favour of a grip under the sagged shoulders of the big cop. I backed into the car first and pulled Morrison into the driver's seat.

It took under two minutes to tape Morrison into the car.

He was straight up in the seat, duct taped to the headrest. The tape covered his forehead and eyebrows; another section of tape secured his throat to the seat as well. Both of the cop's hands were attached to the steering wheel at ten and two. I turned out all of Morrison's pockets and put his phone, wallet, and gun on the dashboard in front of me; then I drank the Nestea and checked the lot. No one else had shown up, and no one had left the hospital. The lot was quiet; the only interruption came from the cell phone. Morrison's phone was on vibrate, and it marched across the dashboard like an angry bee buzzing in an out-of-control fit. The phone call was expected; I figured the first response cops were waiting for Morrison to show up and take control of the situation. He was late to the party, and someone wanted to know why. I took one last swig of iced tea and dumped the rest into Morrison's lap. He came to slowly at first, then all at once. His eyes went wild, and he strained against the tape. I let him pull and yell for a minute, then I let him feel his gun against his neck.

"You! What the fuck are you doing? I'll get you for this. I'm gonna lock you up and fucking eat the key. Hey, what are you doing?"

I put two pieces of tape over his mouth and nose and watched him struggle. He pulled so hard at his bonds that the steering wheel started to creak.

I pulled the tape off with one quick motion and heard a huge gasp of air.

"That Maori medicine is no fun, eh, Detective Sergeant?"

"I'm a cop," was all he could get out.

"And here I thought you were a fisherman looking for

the big catch. Or was that all bullshit? You just let me think I was supposed to be working for you while you tipped off your boss. Way I figure it, you were the only one who knew who I was. You don't even really know that, but you got ideas about me that aren't far off. So you tip off the Russians, and you earn yourself a bonus giving me up."

"I don't know what you're talking about."

"The only thing I can't figure is why you left me a hand-cuff key. Have the Russians got something on you? You're into them for some big numbers, and you thought I might kill whoever is holding your bill and end your troubles?"

"No idea, mate. I have no idea what you are going on about. What Russians? I got called back here because they found you gone and a nurse dead in your room."

"Dead? How?"

"Someone cut her throat."

"Hard for me to do in a gown."

"Heh, you seem to be managing," he said.

"If you didn't tip the Russians, who did?"

"I don't know."

"Who knew I wasn't a cop killer like you said?"

"No one outside of me and Miller."

"That fat cop?"

"Yeah, but he's straight."

"Well, two people knew I was there, and you said it wasn't you who gave me up. It's got to be him; probably made the call on one of his smoke breaks."

Morrison said nothing. If he was telling the truth, and my gut told me he was, then it was Miller who was crooked. The fat cop made more sense; no one would give me a way out of the cuffs if I was worth more dead than alive. Miller must be the one on the take. Once he was off guarding my unconscious body, he told the Russians about me, hoping I was someone recognizable, to make a little extra. He figured since they found me outside Domenica's, and his boss was having me guarded, I must be worth something. So Miller reached out to Igor. He had to work directly for Igor in one form or another because anyone else would have sent the information up the chain to Sergei Vidal. Had Sergei found out, I would have been safe. The head of the Russian mob and I still had an understanding. I had enough evidence on him to send him away for life. I figured our deal was still in place because if Sergei wanted to end it he would never have sent Igor to punch my ticket. Sergei would have dispatched someone closer to the top with orders to kill me. I'd gone up against Sergei's best before — they would have done better than Igor.

Morrison was quiet and motionless in the seat beside me.

"You still want your fish?"

"You're the fish now. You have to pay for that nurse."

"Use your head, Morrison. I didn't kill anyone. I got a visit from a Russian, someone who knew me and wanted to settle up old debts. He tried to kill me, but I talked him out of it — with my hands. When I left, he was on the bed, and the nurse was very much alive. If you check the bed, there will be blood from the Russian to back up my story."

"Bullshit."

"You know it sounds right. Why else would I be here now?"

"So what do you want?"

"Same deal. I get your fish, you forget about me."

"Which fish?"

"That's up to me, but I can tell you they'll be cold water fish from up near the Black Sea."

Morrison tried to nod his head in agreement, but he stopped when he realized he couldn't move. "It will have to be one big fish to square everything."

"Let me worry about that. I just need some information from you."

"What?"

"Where do the Russians go these days? The only place I knew was the Kremlin, but it's probably gone."

"Yeah, someone shot that place up a few years back; killed a bigwig." A thought came to Morrison; I watched it form in a series of facial twitches. "That was you. That's why the Russians showed up tonight. Word on the street was that was some kind of internal cleaning thing."

I ignored him. He had a real cop's mind. He listened, and he remembered. I had to make sure I gave away nothing because even taped to the seat this cop was dangerous. I repeated myself, "Where do the Russians meet these days? Where do all the big names end up at the end of a long, hard day of crime?"

Morrison thought about it. "There are three places," he said. "There's a hall on Sanford, a restaurant on St. Claire, and a bar on Sherman where it meets Barton."

"All the big names congregate in these places?"

"Congregate? Look at you. Mate, you are one educated thug. I don't think I've heard that word since Sunday school.

No, wait — that was congregation. Mean the same thing, ya reckon?"

The cop was still filing away everything I said, stringing clues together into a noose. I grinned in approval towards the window so he wouldn't see. The silence hung in the air until he answered my question.

"If we lose any of the major players, or we need to pick up a tail, it's where we start looking."

"Keep your phone on, I've got your number," I said as I got out of the car.

"Hey! Hey, let me loose before you rack off. Hey!"

I walked back to the evergreens, away from the screams of Detective Sergeant Huata Morrison. I walked straight through the sparsely planted trees and out the other side. I jogged down James Street, away from the hospital, and into the first bar I saw. The dingy clock on the wall read 12:58. I ordered a Diet Coke and called a cab.

By the time the ice in my Diet Coke had melted, the cab had shown up, and I was off. I had the cabbie take me to a gas station that sold cell phones. The drive took us all the way into Westdale, a ritzy suburb of Hamilton that had old money and the university.

I filled the gas can I'd bought earlier and went inside to buy a lighter and a prepaid cell phone. The Asian man and woman behind the counter gladly accepted my money and slowly made change while their black cat walked across my path over the top of the gum display. By the time the change was in my palm, the cat was at my feet — rubbing its back against my leg. I pushed the cat away with Igor's shoe. The cat rolled to its feet and rose — tensed. Its back was high, and each hair bristled in anticipation of a fight. Teeth were showing, and a guttural hissing climbed up out of the cat's mouth.

The lady behind the counter looked upset. "You no like cat?"

"No, I don't like the cat."

"Why not? You think cat got bad luck?"

"I don't know if a cat crossing my path is bad luck, but fuck him if he wants to try and rub it against my leg."

"Hunh?"

"He wants to ruin my day, he's gotta work for it like everyone else."

No one wished me a good night when I left.

CHAPTER FOUR

Back in the cab, I set up the phone and called the operator to test the signal. The electronic voice of the operator let me know everything worked. I powered down the phone and watched Westdale slip away. The rich houses and profitable small businesses slowly turned to rotted buildings and vacant storefronts. I had dreams that went like that. Everything good flying away like shrapnel while I watched from inside a cage. My parents went first, then my uncle. The only thing left was me. Dreams like that pushed me to make sure that there was nothing left to lose.

I succeeded for a time; nothing touched me. But over time, my guard wore down, and Steve and Sandra, a local bartender and his wife, became my friends. A few years back, one of Paolo's men, Tommy Talarese, tried to destroy their lives, and as a result he set in motion a chain of events that rocked the underbelly of the city. Tommy Talarese wanted to show his kid how to collect protection like a man after Steve had thrown the kid out into the street. They kidnapped Steve's wife, unleashing the bar owner like a wiry hurricane on the neighbourhood. Steve and I worked our way up the chain of local muscle to Tommy's front door. Many died getting Sandra back. I put everything on the line for them that night and made enemies with the Italians.

Steve and Sandra were two people, like my parents, who wouldn't give in. Two people who lived life on their own terms, who refused to let anyone, even mobsters, control their lives. I envied their freedom, their connection, and I made sure they kept it. By protecting their connection, it became my own. They were my weakness, and Paolo Donati exploited it. The old Italian boss used them to get me under his thumb again. I had gotten out and started a life away from what I had been — until a man came calling with a message. Paolo could touch me no matter how far I ran, and he could touch Steve and Sandra too. I was forced to come back to work a job for Paolo. Someone had kidnapped his nephews, and he feared it was someone on the inside. Paolo needed me, an outsider, to look into his own men. I found out who killed his nephews and arranged a meeting with Paolo. With Paolo gone, I wouldn't make the same mistake. I would leave Steve and Sandra out of this — I had learned that being my friend had worse odds than terminal cancer.

After fifteen minutes of driving, the cab neared Ave Maria and my car. We passed the front of the store, and I told the cab driver to pull over. It was two in the morning, and the street was empty. I got out with my things and walked to the driver side window to pay.

"Thirty even, pal."

I showed him the gun I took off Igor. "I got a .38. Can

IN PLAIN SIGHT 417

"Holy shit! Don't kill me."

Igor's ugly revolver coaxed the cab driver out of the car. He was a squat man, five-five at the most. He wore old pleated pants and an old, out-of-style checked shirt. The pants were held up by suspenders, but they weren't the ugliest part of the outfit. On top of his head, the cab driver wore a Blue Jays cap. The front was white foam, and the back was a blue mesh. The foam-fronted hat was barely pulled down, making it look like it was ready to float away. I guessed he wore it to make him look taller — all it did was make his head look misshapen.

"Open the gas cover."

The driver leaned back in the open door and pulled at a lever. There was a metallic click behind me as the small plate unlocked and popped open. The driver stood up slowly and put his hands in the air voluntarily.

"This is like the third fuckin' time this year. Holy shit, I'm tired of people robbing me. Fuckin' knives and the *'gimme the money.'*" He mimed an impression of a stick-up and then put his hands back up. "I'm fucking tired of this shit."

"Shut up and sit on the curb."

"Do this, do that. Yes, sir, I'll do whatever you want 'cause you're the big man with the gun."

"Sit down before I put a bullet in your ass."

He sat, and I pulled the baby blanket out of the duffel bag. I soaked it with gas from the gas can until the fabric was sopping wet. I put the can down and ripped the aerial off the roof. I used the metal rod to jam the cheap wet fabric down into the gas tank. I pushed a wad in, cleared out the antenna, and then pushed another mass of blanket in again. I repeated the process until two-thirds of the blanket was gone. I left the antenna in the tank with the blanket and got behind the wheel.

"Sure, just take the car. It's not like it's my life or anything. It's just a hobby. I work double shifts until five in the morning to cut the stress."

I pulled away from the curb watching the rear-view. The cab driver got off the curb and fished through his pockets looking for a phone. I grinned because I saw the phone on the seat beside me. He was having no luck tonight either; it felt good to meet another member of the bad luck club. I drove the car down the first right and hooked onto the road that ran behind Ave Maria. I took the lighter from my pocket and held it in my fist. I forced myself to calm down and drive slowly down the road. In the alley ahead was the same dark car I passed before. This time there was no giveaway that there were any occupants inside. I drove past the alley to the Volvo and dropped the duffel bag out the window. As the bag hit the pavement, I hit the brakes, shoved the gear shifter in reverse, and forced the pedal into the floor. The car screeched back to the mouth of the alley hiding the dark car. I got out of the passenger side of the cab and flicked the lighter alive. The feeble flame shuddered as I walked before maturing into a blaze when it touched the blanket. I ran to the Volvo as I heard a car door open.

I made it to the duffel bag when the explosion sent me sailing to the pavement. I regained my footing and hustled to the car. My hand went under the wheel well and pulled free the spare key. I opened the door and threw the duffel bag across the seat hard enough to bounce it off the opposite door. The engine turned over without any coaxing, and the car roared to life. The Volvo was a different breed of animal when compared to other cars on the road. The engine was a transplant; something customized to sprint. The V8 400 horsepower engine sped me away from downtown and the mess I made, leaving only rubber behind on the pavement.

I had no idea who was watching the car. If it was the cops, the plates and the car description were whizzing past me in the air to every squad car in Hamilton. I had to get somewhere safe; somewhere I could be local while at the same time out of sight like a rabbit in a magician's hat. I hooked the car onto King Street and ran two lights. I rolled past Dundurn and floored the Volvo onto the highway putting distance between myself and the city at 140 km/h. In under a minute, I took the exit to the suburb of Ancaster and used the empty streets to drive back towards the edge of the city. I stopped on a side street before turning onto Highway Two and checked the car for bugs. I didn't want someone tracking me with a laptop to pick me up as soon as I stopped driving. When I was satisfied the car was clean, I got on the road again. I rolled down Highway Two eyeing the view off the side of the escarpment. The city of Hamilton looked full of promise from above. You couldn't see anyone hitting his wife, shooting up smack, or trying to kill a person in a hospital bed. The city from this height was a mirage.

At the bottom of the hill, I turned into the parking lot of a fleabag motel. The Escarpment was in an odd pocket of the city. There were expensive high-rises a stone's throw away in one direction and cheap apartments rented to immigrants in the other. The motel was in the middle, and its clientele leaned towards the low renters. The Escarpment Motel offered hourly rates and parking in the rear — everything I needed to stay under the radar.

I parked the car and walked into the office. A young kid sat behind the counter watching an old horror movie.

"What'cha need?"

"Room," I said.

"How long?"

"Week."

The amount of time made the kid's eyebrows raise, but his pupils never left the screen.

"Week'll cost ya two hundred bucks," the kid said as he slammed his palm around the desk beside him. His eyes were glued to the movie, and he wasn't going to miss anything. His hand stopped on a rectangular piece of paper, and his fingers traced its perimeter before picking it up. "Fill this out."

I paid with ten bills and scratched a name on the registration card. He absentmindedly handed me a key with a twelve etched on the back.

"Can I borrow a screwdriver? My luggage locked up on me, and I need to get into it so I can change."

The kid sighed and got out of his chair. He backed away from the desk and bent at the knees in a way that allowed him to keep his eyes on the television. After a minute, he found the toolbox. It took one more minute for his unguided hands to zero in on the screwdriver.

"Here," he said, throwing the screwdriver in my

direction. It was a good throw considering he wasn't looking. "It's a multi-tool, so it's got everything."

"Thanks."

"Just bring it back when you're done, or I'll add it to
your bill."

"Any more on the bill and you'll have to add a star to
the motel."

The jab went over the kid's head, but he didn't seem
bothered. He sat down and resumed his movie-watching
trance.

I went out to the Volvo and drove it several doors down
from the room. If anyone came looking for the car, I didn't
want them using it as an arrow pointing directly to me. I
used the cheap multi-tool screwdriver to take the plates off
the Volvo. I took the two plates with me to the next parking
lot. The apartment building next door was upscale enough
to have tenants with cars, but still too shitty to provide a
safe underground parking garage. I walked through the
lot until I found an old car with two flat tires. No one had
moved the car in months. I used the multi-tool to replace
the car's plates with the Volvo's. I took the boosted plates
back to the motel and completed the switch unnoticed
before walking the screwdriver back.

"Thanks."

"Man, when you go back to your room, turn on channel
149. Romero is such a genius. Just look at those zombies go."

On the TV screen, two lumbering monsters chased a
woman around a cage. Bloodthirsty spectators screamed
bets and waved money in their fists. It was some sort of
post-apocalyptic gladiator game. The girl on screen did

anything but kick the shit out of her slowly approaching attackers. The game in the cage was almost at an end, when out of nowhere, except to anyone watching, a handsome man shot his way on screen and killed the two zombies. He took the girl out of the cage and backed off the angry spectators with a hard stare.

I left before I got roped into a review of the talents of George A. Romero. The carnage on the screen reminded me of something else, not a movie; I thought about the nurse who had been murdered on the floor of the hospital room. Someone had put her down after she was already out. Igor was the obvious doer, but he was chained down. That left the girlfriend. Igor sent her away, but it was probable that she was the one who came back and got Igor loose. Once he was free, either one could have dealt with the nurse. I've known enough blood-thirsty women in my life to know Tatiana was as much a suspect as her man. I let myself into the motel room and sat on the bed. Igor was damaged because I had beaten him before, and the embarrassment destroyed his ego. I had broken something in him that was always destined to give way. He blamed me for his weakness, but he was already weak when he first came at me years ago in my office. I showed him what he really was when I put him under the gun. He saw his reflection for the first time in the shine of a bullet, and what he saw didn't measure up. Plenty of people figured out they weren't cut out for the life on the same day they learned that they were just man enough to fill a grave.

In the hospital room, he lied about me killing his partner to Tatiana. The lie was as good as a confession — he was the one who had killed his partner. Igor must have done it because his partner was one of the few witnesses alive who knew he failed to do his job. He killed his partner and in that instant put on a disguise. He thought everyone bought whatever manufactured confidence he wore like too much cheap cologne. He was living a lie, and I was the only one left who knew what the lie truly was. He came to kill me so that he could fully become his false self. It was more than revenge for Igor; killing me was survival.

Whatever fragile mental case Igor was didn't matter. He found me. He was connected and just powerful enough to be a problem. Worse still was the cop. The dead nurse would put enough pressure on him to renege on our deal. I had to steel his nerve if I wanted to stay out of jail.

I stripped off Igor's clothes and lay above the covers, lights off, with Igor's gun in my hands. I slept easily because I knew what I was. I didn't lie, to myself like Igor did. I knew my nature, and I wasn't ashamed. I also knew what had to be done when the sun rose.

The next morning, my body woke itself up. I turned my head and saw the clock read 12:23. The dim room was smelly. The smell had always been there, but I was too charged up on adrenaline the night before to notice. I was also aware of my body. Morrison had told me I'd been hit by a drunk driver. Laying in a hospital bed, it didn't feel so bad, but after a night of moving I felt different. My ribs and forearms were sore, but my hip was agony. I was sure that the car had hit me there. I stood and stumbled to the washroom. I grunted and felt my dick pay me back for my medical malpractice with the catheter. It took a few seconds for the blood flowing out of me to fade into pink urine. I looked away from the mess in the bowl to the tiny square mirror hanging over the toilet. A week's worth of growth had been added to the beard I had before the accident. My hair had been clipped so short two weeks ago that the small bit of growth was unnoticeable.

I stumbled back to the bedroom, the only room, and pushed the bed up onto its side. I used the tiny bit of space on the floor to stretch. I spent an hour on the floor, stopping only when I could stand up straight without wincing, then I went back to the bathroom and washed in the cramped shower stall.

There were no towels, so I dried using the bed sheet and then put Igor's clothes back on. I walked out with the empty duffel bag and opened the trunk. Under the carpet, below the spare, was the compartment full of cash. I had not bothered to move it away from the car before because I was always just a surprise away from bolting. The money had to stay close. Now, with the car no longer anonymous, it wasn't safe to leave the money inside. I loaded the bag with the cash and walked out to a bus stop. I waited fifteen minutes inside the graffiti-tinted bus shelter for the right bus to pull to a stop. I got on and noticed that my clothes were wrinkled and stained enough to match every other jobless passenger who was riding the bus with me at 2:30 in the afternoon on a weekday.

I rode the bus up the escarpment and into the suburb of Ancaster until I saw a gym roll past the window. I got off at the next stop and walked back to the gym. The hours posted on the outside window began early and ended late. The gym was open every day at 5:30 a.m. and closed every night at midnight. Through the glass, I could see that the equipment was old, and there were few patrons inside. The time of day didn't matter; good gyms were always busy. This particular establishment was old, and they seemed to have problems keeping up with the new chains that offered a constantly changing line-up of fad activities like hip-hop Pilates. I took one last look inside before I walked back to the bus stop to wait for another ride.

At 3:30, another bus picked me up and took me to a busy commercial development on the edge of Ancaster. The strip, just off Golf Links Road, contained a store to cater to almost every human need. Within two hours, I had picked up clothes, food, toiletries, a towel, a folding knife, and a combination padlock.

I took the bus back to the gym. Phoenix Fitness was still open and still not very busy. This time I left the windows alone and walked straight inside. A kid in his twenties manned the counter, talking on the phone and drinking a health juice drink from a straw. I looked at him, and he glanced at me before waving me through and turning his back to continue his conversation.

"I got to work tonight too, yo. No, not here, at West 49. I couldn't get out of it. We'll go out after, man. I'm gonna get fuckin' tanked. I don't give a shit if I have to work tomorrow — I'll just power through. I've been hung over here before. Hell, I'm a bit hung over now. Yeah, yeah, right."

I stared at the kid's back and watched him talk. He

was fit, with the kind of bulk that came from heavy daily workouts. His hair was short and styled stiff with gel, and his head bobbed with each agreement he made out loud into the phone. There was a pause in the conversation as the kid took another sip from his drink. He put the cup down beside him and laughed at a joke I couldn't hear. I was tired, not from lack of sleep or injury, just tired of assholes throwing their weight around. The jock behind the counter was just another jerk-off who thought he could push me around. I was tired of being pushed by cops and crooks and now by over-developed minimum wagers. I picked up the cup, feeling the weight of the remaining fluid inside. I stood with the drink in my hand for thirty seconds until the desire for liquid arose in the kid again. His hand began groping around the counter for the container while he spoke into the receiver. I set the drink down on the edge of the counter so that part of the cup was off the side. The phone conversation became shorter and shorter as the kid focused more and more on the missing container. After three failed gropes towards the spot the drink used to be, he turned around to see it in front of me. He stared at the drink, confused at its location, then at me to see if it was a joke. I didn't smile.

"I'll call you back," he said to whoever was on the other end of the connection.

He reached for his drink, and I shook his hand. The kid was startled by the gesture, but he recovered and pumped my hand hard with a testosterone-filled challenge. I let him squeeze with little resistance. I could have turned the hand-shake into something mangling, but I didn't want this kid to remember much about me.

The kid, happy with his winning grip on my loose hand, let go and gave me his best tough guy greeting. It was full of artificial street and imaginary persecution. "Wha'choo need?"

"I need a month pass. What will that cost me?"

"Cost you fifty bucks."

I peeled off a fifty and put it on the counter. He reached for the money, but my hand never moved — it stayed on top of the bill.

"This fifty get me a locker?"

"Yeah, but no spa or tanning. That stuff is extra."

I chuckled at the idea of using a spa or tanning bed. "I'll get by," I said.

The kid reached for his drink, and I met his hand with the money. He couldn't hide his disappointment as he took the money instead of his drink. I put the duffel bag on the counter in front of the drink and asked if I had to fill out a form.

"It'll be faster if I do it." Thirst had made the kid efficient. "What's your name?"

"James Moriarty," I said, expecting the question.

"Spell it."

I did. I pulled an address and phone number out of the air and listened to the kid pound the keyboard in front of him. The card printed, and the kid laminated it, stealing glances at me and the bag guarding his drink the whole time. When the card was finished, I took my bag off the counter and walked to the change room. I heard him reach for the cup and then swear as it fell to the floor. There was a splat and then more swearing as I pushed open the locker room door.

I found my locker and set my bags down on the small ledge below that was supposed to act as a bench. There was only one other person in the change room — an old man, totally nude. He slowly took a shaving kit and towel out of a locker and walked by me to the showers. He never glanced at me or attempted to hide his nakedness. He was too old to be ashamed and too tired to try to suck anything in. I waited for the shower door to close before dumping out one of the shopping bags onto the ledge. I transferred the cash from the duffel to the empty shopping bag. I set the stuffed plastic bag inside my locker and sealed the door with the brand new lock I picked up earlier. As soon as the lock clicked shut, I spun the dial through the first two numbers of the three-number code so that I could open the lock fast when I came back. I refilled the duffel bag with the things I sprawled across the ledge and walked out to the workout floor. I strolled through the gym to the back exit that was propped open to pull in cool air from outside. I left through the back door, my money safe inside a makeshift safe deposit box. The kid at the front counter would be too busy to notice that I never walked out the front door. He would just assume it happened while he was cleaning the mess from his drink. I learned that trick a decade ago as a way to swipe things from department stores. The classics never went out of style.

CHAPTER FIVE

The bus ride back to the motel was uneventful. No one looked at me twice. I got off at the stop near the motel and walked slowly past the office. The door was open, but the guy from before wasn't there anymore. Instead, a short red-headed woman was behind the desk, television off, head down, working. I watched her stamp two pieces of paper before filing them and starting again. It was a good sign. Had anyone been around asking about me and pressing her for information, she'd have been on the lookout. Her busyness signalled everything was still kosher. The car was where I'd left it, as were the curtains. No one had done any obvious searching. I walked past the door and stopped in between my room and the next. I put my back against the wall and my hand inside my coat on top of Igor's revolver. My left hand found the key fob in my pocket and double clicked. The Volvo obediently beeped twice, calling out to the device in my hand. I watched the window, but the curtains stayed closed. I pivoted and watched the curtains in the neighbouring room, but the curtains there mimicked my own. Anyone who could have found my room would have known about the car. They would have moved on me when they heard the car out of fear of losing the advantage of surprise. Satisfied, I drew the gun, opened the door, and slipped into the darkness of the room. It took only twenty-five seconds for me to make sure the two rooms were clear.

I checked the time and got into the bathroom. I used the small mirror and sink to shave my beard to alter the appearance Igor and Morrison had seen. I put on the new clothes I had bought — dark khakis and a black T-shirt. The cooling October air would let me get away with a sweat-shirt, but I went instead for a black lightweight waterproof jacket with several deep pockets. The jacket blended with the pants and concealed Igor's revolver. The Glock police pistol that I'd taken off Morrison tucked into the back of my pants, and the folding knife went into my pants pocket.

Dressed and shaved, I went out to the Volvo, got behind the wheel, and dialled Morrison. He answered after one ring. "Morrison."

"You must be out of the car."

"You son of a bitch. I'm a cop, and you pull that shit. You're done. You forgot what I got on you? When I'm done, everyone will have seen your face. It's gonna be front page, mate. You're gonna have nowhere to hide."

"You run the prints?"

"Not yet, but I'm going to. It's at the top of my to-do list right after arresting you."

"I thought you wanted a fish."

"Fuck you and your fish. You're big enough now that you killed that nurse."

"That was on you. You leaked info, and it got her killed."

"No, mate, that's not how anyone will see it. It's all about spin, and I'm gonna spin you into the ground."

"I'm sorry you feel that way."

"I bet you are."

"I'm sorry because I already got what you wanted."

"What?"

"I got your fish, and it's better than a nurse killer."

"Who is it?"

"Doesn't matter now. We're through."

"Now don't be hasty, mate. Maybe we can work something out, provided you give me something big."

"What? You'll just let me slide — I don't buy it."

"Where you're sitting right now, you've got no choice. You can be on the news tonight for sure, or maybe not at all. You serve me up something nice that I can use, and I'll be good to you. You try and dance with me again, and no amount of medicine will bring you back."

"Ten-thirty, be ready. I'll tell you where to meet me." I hung up the phone before Morrison could protest. He already had enough on me to make me an inmate for life, and showing him up in his own car hurt his pride. But angry as the cop was, he was greedy. When he found me, he knew I was into something he couldn't put his finger on. His gut told him enough about me to push him into springing me from the hospital. He was willing to go outside the law to get someone better than me. That kind of ambition was stronger than heroin; it would call to him louder than his bruised ego. It would also make him dangerous. He had no loyalty to me; I could only count on the knowledge that Morrison was only out to build himself up by taking someone else down. I had to push him off centre to get things where I needed them to be. I pulled the car out of the lot and headed to Sherman Avenue.

Morrison had said that the bar on Sherman was a popular mob hangout. I chose the bar because it would attract the kind of people I was looking for more than the restaurant or hall he told me about ever would. I eased the Volvo through traffic until I found Barton and Sherman and the Hammer and Sickle. The bar was a single building set back from the street with a stairwell leading down to a front entrance. At street level, there were window seats behind tinted glass. There were no neon pub signs, which were so common to the bars of Hamilton, and no patio. The bar was not looking for the patronage of the locals; it catered to a specific audience who wanted nothing to do with the trendy bar scene.

I checked the mirror. No one was behind me. I slowed the car to a stop in the middle of the street and looked through the tinted bar windows. The window seats were empty, and a blond woman was wiping a table down. It was only 7:30 — still too early for the bar to be busy. There would probably be after-work drinkers inside stationed at regular seats getting a buzz to fight the tension headache brought on by sitting behind a desk all day. The people I was looking for would not be stopping by for a drink after work. By my watch, the people I wanted wouldn't start work for another few hours.

Headlights caught my eye in the rear-view, and I accelerated away from the restaurant. I turned at the corner and

stopped to check out the rear lot. Of the four private parking spaces out back, three were filled with black Mercedes.
The back also had a Dumpster and a rear exit door. I drove
into the vacant spot and got out. The Dumpster smell hit me
as soon as I touched the pavement, a sign the bar was active
and not just a front. I checked the cars first; the three hoods
were cool to the touch. I scanned the lot for anything I
might have missed and got back behind the wheel. I looped
the building twice more searching the area for anything
that might become a problem. There were no loitering men
or suspicious vehicles anywhere within two blocks — until
my car parked across the street from the front door.

It took just over three hours for me to spot what I had
been waiting for. One man, in his late fifties, flanked by four
younger men approaching the bar. No one spoke as they
entered. They weren't friends — they were employer and
employees. The old man was wearing a dark grey suit under
an unbuttoned trench coat. His associates all wore black
leather jackets. The styles varied, but they were all part of
the standard bodyguard uniform. The men all had short
haircuts and hard faces. None of them wore jeans. I figured
the pleated dress pants were a sign that the bodyguards
often had to follow the old man into nicer places than the
Hammer and Sickle, and they knew enough to blend in.
They didn't know enough to wear shoes that were made for
work though. Their shoes were shiny leather, stylish; none
appeared to have a strong toe or tread. Professionals never
compromised functionality for appearance. They worried
about the job first and how they looked second. Only lack-
eys cared if their shoes matched the occasion. One of the

underlings held the door while another scanned the outside of the restaurant. I had my hand on the key in the ignition ready to move if I was made, but the scan passed over the car once, then twice.

The fact that none of the men noticed a car parked across the street as a threat confirmed what the shoes told me. The rabble moved into the restaurant, in a sloppy huddle, keeping the old man in the centre until the door was cleared.

The location, the clothes, and the poorly practised movements confirmed that the old man was a heavy in the Russian mob. He wasn't top shelf; the security was too sloppy, but he could have been a numbers man, an under-boss, or even a visiting associate from back home. I had never seen him in dealings I had with the Russians.

I started the car and drove around back of the restaurant to the still vacant space beside the Mercedes. I parked and put the keys in the front pocket of my jacket. I took off the seat belt and shifted so that I could get at the knife in my front pocket. The folding knife was a middle-of-the-market product with a four-inch blade and a sturdy locking mechanism. The handle was plastic with a raised grip that would resist prints. The blade would stay sharp for as long as I would need it, then it would sink in a sewer as deep as I needed it to.

I opened the knife and got out into the autumn air. I reversed the knife in my fist so that it could only be seen from behind me and used my free hand to ease the Volvo door shut. No one was walking by on the street as I moved to the side of the nearest German import. I hammered the knife into the rear tire, just above the rim, then moved to the other side and did the same before starting on the second and third cars. The slow leaks eased the cars gradually to the pavement; the movement was too subtle to set the car alarms off. I jogged around the building as the last of the air hissed from the tires. I opened the front door using my sleeve over my hand. My shoulder shoved the inner door open without suspicion. Without slowing down, I walked into the bar towards the tables.

Despite the city's smoking ban, the air was acrid with the scent of unfiltered European cigarettes. The clientele had shifted away from after-work drinkers to a more upscale type of clientele: the kind of upscale that still lived in the wrong part of downtown. The kind of people who could not get used to the quiet of the suburbs. The kind of people who drank hard alcohol in mob bars, dressed to the nines late on a Wednesday. At every table I passed, fair-skinned men and women with light hair were seated. Each face possessed the sharp features of Russia and the cold eyes of a hard people. The women were dressed stylishly, too stylishly for the bar — too stylishly for the city, and they were all far younger than the men they accompanied. Each young woman leaned into conversations with devotion, expressing interest in subtle nods and not-so-subtle displays of cleavage. The men all had the same dangerous expressions and the scars to verify them. The fancy rings and jewellery on hands, wrists, and ears fooled no one. They weren't bankers or lawyers — they were hoods who made good in the city.

Few faces turned from their dates to watch me walking by. My clothes were dull and nondescript, and they pulled no one's eyes to me. Anyone who did happen to look my way saw that I carried my own dangerous expression. There was no point trying to camouflage myself inside the Hammer and Sickle — the men inside could smell their own, and trying to mask what I was would only make me more conspicuous. To them I was just another grinder — they just had no idea who I grinded for.

I found the entrance to the kitchen behind the bar. One segment of the counter was raised to allow rear access, and the blond waitresses covering the tables used the space to move freely back and forth. My eyes glanced from the bar to the biggest group of people. My body followed my eyes, and I loped around two tables so that I approached the seated group of men head on. The old man I saw enter was in the centre of a corner booth. He was flanked by his men — well protected from contact with anyone in the bar. Anybody who wanted to speak with the old man would have to work through the layers of muscled insulation. I didn't want to talk with the old man. I let him see me coming. We locked eyes, and he gave me a hard stare. His look dissolved when he saw my face pull into a grin. Confusion cracked his ice-hard stare. Then I drew the police pistol and put a bullet in his chest.

The bodyguards did two things. The men directly to his left and right shielded themselves, while the men farther out lunged for the old man. They tried to climb over the cringing men to plug the red plume pumping out from under the old man's shirt. I pivoted and immersed myself in the pandemonium that had erupted. I had a few seconds to disappear before the bodyguards came to their senses and came after me. I threaded through the crowd and grabbed one of the waitresses. She probably thought me to be just an inconsiderate coward; I was no coward — I was just an inconsiderate man in need of a human shield. The sound of a curse coming from the waitress was deafened by the bark of a gun shot mingling with the cymbal crash of a bottle shattering behind the bar. I bent low and hustled behind the bar. I left the waitress blocking the doorway and ran into the kitchen as more bottles gave up their spirits to the air.

As soon as I rounded the first corner, I straightened and ran to the exit. The door was still closed — all of the kitchen staff stood frozen, staring at the doorway to the bar. I guessed shots weren't unheard of but probably unusual at such an early hour. I shouldered open the door and slid behind the wheel of the unlocked Volvo.

Inside the Volvo, I revved the engine and rolled down the window. I aimed the Glock out the window at the back door, resting my arm on the window sill. It took five seconds for the door to burst open and four bullets to send everyone back inside. I put the Volvo in reverse and screeched onto the street. I hooked backwards onto Sherman, shifting into drive while the car slid across the worn pavement. No shots came from the back of the restaurant, and no cars followed me as I raced away from the Hammer and Sickle.

I pulled into the first Tim Hortons I saw and parked out of sight from the road. I powered up the cell phone and called 911.

"There were shots fired at the Hammer and Sickle on Sherman. A man is dead. Please hurry. Oh, no!" I hung up the phone, powered it down, then walked into the coffee shop. I spent an hour eating muffins and drinking tea before I decided to turn on the phone again. I pulled out Detective Sergeant Huata Morrison's card and dialled his cell number.

"Morrison."

"It's me."

"You're late and I'm busy. But something tells me your tardiness and my working late are related."

"Where are you?"

"You know where I am, you fucker. I'm at the Hammer and Sickle." His voice turned into a harsh whisper for a moment. "A place I told you about. Some mobbed-up loser bit it, and guess what? None of the three employees who were working in the apparently empty bar here saw a thing."

"Sounds like you're in for a long night of detective work."

"Nah, I got a suspect. Just escaped from the hospital. I should be able to tie this up real easy."

"So you don't need any tips?"

"Tips?"

"You know, clues to help you solve the case."

"Nah, I don't need tips. I just need to have a talk with the bartender. Seems like he forgot to tell me about a suspicious customer who came in. Some joker with short hair and a beard."

"Sounds like leading a witness."

"An island boy like me does not know about such things, mate."

"That description won't match the ballistics," I said. My voice stayed monotone while my mouth turned up into a tight grin.

"Ballistics?"

"Yeah, that's my tip. I know that the crime was committed with a Glock police pistol. I even know where the gun can be found. Serial number is still on it too. No fingerprints though."

"You son of a bitch."

"How's your suspect list now?"

"You can't pull that shit on me. I'm a cop!"

"How long will that last when I tip the papers about the gun?"

There was a pause, then a sigh. "What do you want?"

"To stay a person of interest and to keep my prints and picture out of everything."

"That's impossible. There's a dead nurse in your hospital room. You're the prime suspect."

"Fix it," I said.

"I can't."

"You're acting like you have a choice. This is a new game. Now we're fishing in a boat together. You need to do some of that leading with a witness at the hospital."

"Leading to what?"

"Who's to say I wasn't a person of interest to more people than you?"

Morrison caught on. "So you were kidnapped. Probably already dead. Whoever killed that kid in the truck we found you near must have killed you too to keep you from talking."

"I stay dead and invisible, you stay Detective Sergeant."

"So we're partners. You got me and I got you."

"Looks that way."

"Can't be that way forever, mate. Something has to tip the scales eventually."

Morrison was right. No matter how crooked, he was still a cop, and no cop would put up with being pushed — they're too used to being the aggressors. There was no telling the amount of clout he had. He didn't fear bending the law to keep me from being printed or to get me out of the bed, so someone had to be on his side, someone big. Given enough time, he could spin the shooting at the club or fuck the ballistics reports. What I had on him only had a shelf life of a few days; then the scales would start to tilt in his favour again.

"Original deal then," I said. "I'll get you a fish, and you'll forget about me. Otherwise, I just cut bait and settle for taking you down with me."

There was no answer from the phone. I knew the cop was stuck where he didn't want to be. He was working with a crook instead of turning the screws. He was off balance. I had to keep him there because as long as he was uncomfortable, I had room to move.

"Give me a few days and I'll be in touch. I need one thing though," I said.

"What? Haven't I done enough for you?"

"I need info on a name."

The cop's voice became serious. He wanted me to lead him to something bigger. Any name I needed was something he could use to get ahead. I had to be careful about what I asked for — too much information could make me useless.

"What name?"

"Russian guy. I only got a first name: Igor. He's not street level. He's got enough clout to have that fat cop on payroll."

"I told you Miller's no rat. He's been my partner for years. I trust him with my life every day—he's solid."

"Solid like you? The CPR and the business card you gave me didn't seem by the books."

Morrison grumbled before hanging up, and I knew I'd hit a nerve. I swore under my breath into the dead connection. I had misread the cop. All this time I took him to be as bent as the rest of us, but I got it wrong. He was bent, but he didn't see it that way. In his mind, he was out for the greater good. He was a cop, and nothing he did was wrong because he was the law. Letting me out of the hospital was justifiable because it meant something worse would come in. Worse still, if Morrison thought he was a good cop, he would never really let me off—it would conflict with his own fucked-up logic. He would string me along until he achieved whatever goal he thought meted out justice, then he would turn on me. I was on the other side, and to a cop that meant I couldn't get away.

It had been years since I had met anyone who saw the world in sides. Simple logic made for dangerous people; they were easy enough to predict, but they brought chaos down all around them. Morrison had blinders on; he took an oath and wore a badge, and he figured everyone else felt the way he did about being a cop. He couldn't swallow the fact that one of his own people worked off the books for the Russians. He defended Miller twice when the evidence pointed to the contrary. That kind of myopia was like deep-seated racism; the kind that was bred into kids from the moment they took in air. His beliefs wouldn't wash away, and he would always be at their mercy. Morrison was blind and determined. He wouldn't forget about me, and he would trail that fat cop and the Russians along behind him until they could take their own shot. More people were going to get hurt before Morrison was done. I figured it was best that I was the one doing the hurting — I already had a head start.

CHAPTER SIX

The next morning, I went for breakfast at a Greek restaurant near the motel. Greece on King was too nice for the neighbourhood, and I took advantage before management clued in and decided to relocate. I slid into a booth that contained a discarded morning paper and leafed through the news. I was into the front-page story about a shootout at a local bar and the supposed links to the Russian mob, when a young woman approached the table. She was tall, about five-ten, with dark skin and dark hair. She wore little make-up and a black shirt and pants. The woman radiated beauty. I almost had to look away when she smiled and asked me if I was ready to order. I regained my composure, ordered steak and eggs, and got back to reading the paper. I didn't let my eyes wander to her ass as she walked away. I learned to shut out my pants long ago. It was always a fight, but I wouldn't let myself lose focus on a job.

I got to the end of the article, and twelve words floored me. I read them over and over again. The twelve words made me realize that I didn't need any help from Morrison to find Igor. The paper told me everything I needed to know: *The funeral will be at Thomas and Dunne on King and Wellington.* My feelings of stupidity for missing something so obvious were interrupted by the waitress pouring me a glass of ice water.

"You don't look happy," she said.

"I just realized I lost something."

"Not your wallet?" She looked concerned.

"No, not my wallet. The upper hand."

"Which glove is that? Left or right?"

The waitress waited for an answer, but I got back to reading the article — looking for anything I might have missed. The food came five minutes later with a side order of cold shoulder. I ate and thought about what I had said to Morrison. I asked him to find Igor. I gave no description, just the name and position of a man. It was possible that Morrison would be unable to put a face to the name right away. There might have been more than one powerful, mobbed-up Igor in the city, but it wasn't likely, and I knew it. All I could hope for was that the upcoming mob funeral would take precedence over everything else. Cops would be running security and surveillance to make sure they kept everything safe and on film. It would be a dangerous event despite the police presence. The cops would use the guise of security to plant themselves right outside the graveyard, and every Russian with a gun and a scar would be brazenly walking across the grass to the gravesite. Every member of the Russian mob, hopped up on anger and chemicals, would be daring the cops to touch them. Funerals were often places where wanted criminals had no problem showing their faces. The cops never touched them out of fear of the backlash from the rest of the made funeral attendees in front of the greedy camera lenses. I would have to join in the throng of media and police onlookers to find Igor and follow him home. I was on a cramped timetable, Morrison had a lead on me, and I had a lead on Igor. We all couldn't be in the lead forever.

I finished the steak and eggs, paid up, and checked out the waitress one last time. She caught me and flashed a glare that made it easier to look away. I nodded goodbye to the cook and left the restaurant with the newspaper under my arm.

I picked up the car from the motel parking lot and drove into the city, keeping an eye out for the kind of store I needed. The men's shop on Ottawa Street North wasn't a chain but a decades-old independently run business. The sign out front looked as though it had weathered a quarter of a century out on the street. I drove down the street looking for a place to park, only to be sent back the way I came. This part of Hamilton housed fabric and textile wholesalers. The clothing here would be plentiful and cheaper than anywhere else in the city. The tailor would also have put enough time in to have seen everything at least twice.

I finally found a spot in the parking lot of a retirement complex. As I walked to the men's shop up the street, I checked behind me to make sure I was clean. I didn't see a tail behind me, only an army surplus store. Something about the Ottawa Army Surplus registered in my mind. I had heard the name before from people in my line of work. I turned around and walked into the store.

An old bell announced my arrival, but there was no one around to notice. I walked the aisles looking at the peacoats and heavy work boots until I heard the shuffle of old feet. A grizzled man came out of the back room to meet me. He was the age that had no age. He could have been seventy as easily as he could have been ninety. Under a worn blue vest, he wore a faded red plaid flannel shirt and green pants pulled up to just below his nipples. Black suspenders locked the pants in place just in case they tried to make a break for it. The guy was too old to be working. He had to be some kind of serious broke to be behind a counter at his age. I knew I was in the right place; money would get me anything I needed. I just hoped the old man had the kind of anything I wanted.

"Sorry 'bout that, son. I was in the crapper."

"I understand," I said.

"Hell you do, boy! At my age, nature calls all the fucking time. Haven't been fishing with my buddies in years 'cause I have to piss so much. It's not natural."

I said nothing.

"Whachoo need?"

"I'm looking for holsters," I said.

"For what?"

"Two guns. A Glock and a small Smith and Wesson revolver."

"Where you want to carry these guns?"

"I need a shoulder rig for the Smith and Wesson, and a belt holster for the Glock."

"Who told you to come here?"

I didn't know the old man, or how far he crossed into the wrong side of the law, so asking about holsters was a good way to feel him out. His demand of a reference told me that I had asked the right guy. I played along. "Friend of a friend," I said.

The old man grumbled and walked through the doorway to the back room. When he turned, I caught sight of a hard hump under the back of his vest. Below the hump was another bump — one much more deadly.

The old man came back a minute later with several shoulder rigs, a belt holster, and a metal case.

"Most of the shoulder rigs I got are too big for a small S and W. What barrel length are we talking about? Two inches?"

"Yeah."

"That's no good. You need something better?"

Igor's gun wasn't reliable, and I couldn't risk using the Glock again. "What do you have?" I asked.

The old man opened the case and turned it around on the counter so that I could see inside. Three guns were nestled into custom foam pockets. There were two fat black revolvers — a four-inch barrelled model 36 Smith and Wesson .38, and another Smith and Wesson .38, but this was the model 40. The other gun was a cheap Saturday Night Special. The guns were all bigger than Igor's small revolve, but none of them was in any condition that looked reliable.

As if sensing my thought, the old man spoke up. "They'll all fire. Tested them myself."

"What's behind your back?"

The old man frowned and harrumphed to himself. "What's behind my back?" He reached behind himself and strained to twist the gun out from under his vest. His bony, blue-veined hand came back holding a large black shape. The gun was heavy and ugly. There was no mistaking it.

"How much for the belt holster, that black shoulder rig there, and your Colt?"

"The .45 ain't for sale. It's mine. What's in that case there is all I got for you."

"Five hundred for the Colt and the two holsters," I said.

"Five hundred, hah! Thousand." And just like that, the Colt was on the market.

"Seven fifty and you hand it over with a spare magazine and a box of ammunition."

"Eight," he said.

"Done."

"Hee, hee, son, you made a fine purchase. Colt like that got me through Korea alive."

"Let me see it," I said, ignoring the mention of Korea. The old man wanted to sell the gun with a story; I had no time for old gun battles half a world away. I had my own gun battles a few streets over to deal with.

The old man stopped guffawing and got serious again. He slid out the magazine and passed me the gun.

I worked the slide and dry fired the gun. The trigger created an obscene snap like a loud "Fuck you." The gun was well oiled and in good condition.

"Wrap it up," I said.

The old man's humour returned at once, and he hustled behind the counter for a bag. He put the Colt in the shoulder rig and put everything in the bag. I peeled off the money and laid it on the counter. The old man snatched it faster than I would have bet he could move and laughed out loud.

"Pleasure doing business with you, son. And just so you know, the gun will have to be reported stolen. If you get caught with it, I'll call you a thief, and I'll press charges."

"I get caught with the gun no one will notice you. The gun will get swept under whatever rug they hide my body under."

The bell showed me out to the street, and I walked to the tailor. There was no bell to let anyone know I entered the men's shop. The sales floor was one large room lined with suits, shirts, pants, and ties. I walked along the racks inside the warm shop and smelled the pungent aroma of espresso being brewed. I spent a few minutes like that until I heard a man singing. The song wasn't in English — it was sung in a deep, rich Italian. The voice belonged to a man in his fifties with a full head of white hair who walked out from behind a curtain. His skin was olive, and his eyes had the type of puffy bags that sleep could never erase. He was dressed in an expensive black cashmere sweater and a pair of chocolate brown pants. His shoes were a shiny dark leather, and they went long past the toes into a narrow tip.

"*Buongiorno* — How can I help you?"

"I need a suit — light-weight, black, white shirt, and a tie. It will need to be tailored immediately."

My demands didn't faze the man. "*Bene, bene*. This can all be done. What suit you like?"

I found a middle-of-the-road suit and handed it over. He

nodded at the suit and ushered me behind the curtain he came out of to a change room. Inside, I put on the shoulder rig and belt holster while I spoke through the door.

"You see the mob funeral coming up?"

"Russians, *pah*. They act like animals. They don't know how to behave like people. My family came to this country with nothing. My father scrimped and saved until he could buy us a house. Then he brought his sister and her children over and let them live with us. It was cramped, and some nights there was no food for the table, but he never once acted like those animals."

Through the door I replied, "But your people are no strangers to crime."

"You talking about the mafia? Some men went that way, yes, but not my father. Not my family. But even those who did, they never acted like those Russians. There was a code, there was honour. The mafia helped build this city; they helped protect immigrants who would have starved in the street. Immigrants less proud and less fortunate than my father. We are different."

I could have spent the better part of the day showing this man how every mob is the same. There's no honour. There's only a desire for money and power. Every mob kills for it — they bleed to keep it and cut to take it.

I kept my mouth shut and opened the door. I got what I wanted. I understood where the man stood.

"You look good in that suit, but the way it hangs. It's…it's…What is wrong there? Come here."

The man's hand felt the jacket. His touch was gentle as he felt over the fabric. He grunted when he felt the Colt in the shoulder harness.

"What's your name?" I asked.

"It's...my name is...I am Ottavio."

"Ottavio, I have a funeral to attend. The funeral of those Russian animals. I'm working under cover, and I want to blend in, so I need you to get rid of the bulge here, and here," I said pointing to the guns.

"You are police, eh? Oh my God, you had me worried. I thought you were Russian for a moment and you were going to kill me for what I said. Of course I will help you get those animals. Anything for the police. My *zio*, my uncle, was a police inspector back home in Palermo. He made my family very proud."

"So you understand how important it is that the suit fit well and that it conceals everything?"

"Of course, officer, the suit is no problem. It will hide everything." Ottavio winked when he said the word everything; his version of the word seemed more pleasant than mine. "I once tailored for a magician. No one ever saw where he kept his doves. Only I know his tricks, eh?"

The rest of the fitting went quickly. Ottavio made adjustments for an hour while I drank espresso and ate a few biscotti. I left a few hundred lighter, with the suit in a garment bag. I kept the Colt on, under the coat, close to my body.

CHAPTER SEVEN

I wasted a day waiting for the funeral. I spent the entire time in the motel room watching local news, shitty daytime talk shows, and sitcoms. I ate greasy pizza and Diet Coke I bought nearby and waited.

The next day, dressed in my new suit carrying the new Colt and the revolver I took off Igor, I left for Dodsworth and Brown. I left the Glock inside a vent I managed to unscrew in the cramped motel bathroom. I couldn't risk having to fire it; the ballistics would ruin everything I had set up and create a window for Morrison to escape through. He could prove his gun was stolen and put me back on his leash.

The funeral home had a viewing from eleven to two. After that, the body was being laid to rest at a Russian church on Sanford, just down the street from the Russian hall Morrison told me about. St. Peter's Church was a large building housing a huge cemetery for the city's Russian population.

I parked three blocks away from Dodsworth and Brown

and waited. There were other nondescript cars waiting closer to the funeral home, and in them men sat with telephoto lenses pointed in the same direction. As long as I parked behind them, I wasn't in danger of getting on film.

I could barely make out the faces of the people going in and out of the funeral home, but it didn't matter — I was waiting for the drive to the cemetery. I spent three hours waiting. At 2:15, the long procession of high-end European cars began. From my spot, I saw inside each of the cars as they passed me. In the twelfth car, a bright yellow BMW, were Igor and Tatiana. Neither noticed me as they slowly passed. They sat silently in the car, smoking. No other yellow cars passed by with the procession — the rest were modestly coloured expensive vehicles. I waited for the line of cars to end, and for the three unmarked police cars to follow, before I drove to St. Peter's.

At the church, there were no spaces in front of the building at all. I did two drive-by's and saw none of the three unmarked police sedans that followed from the funeral home. I snaked through the nearby side streets for a few minutes until I came across the three cars. All three were abandoned, their engines still ticking. The cops would be trying to set up at the entrance and near the grave site so that they could get clear head shots of everyone coming and going. I drove two streets over and parked in a court that had a footpath leading towards the church. The path was wide enough to drive through, and I parked the car in a spot on the road that would allow me access to both the street and the path. If I had to leave fast, I wanted options. I jogged back to the three unmarked cars two blocks over.

I looked around and saw no one on the streets. My hand went inside my jacket and came out with the folding knife. I put the blade into six passenger side tires. Not even the squirrels turned their heads to look at the quiet hissing I left behind as I walked away.

I headed back to the church and scanned the street corners. I found the first cop two streets up with his lens pointed towards the church entrance. Outside the entrance, eight men and two women stood, all smoking in the sunlight. If they noticed the cop, they never let on. I stayed on the opposite side of the street, away from the lens, as I walked past the church. Around the corner, I spotted Igor's yellow BMW. The car looked to run about sixty grand — forty if you tried to re-sell it yellow. It was a vehicle that screamed, "Look at me! I have money and fine things, but they're useless unless you look at me."

I passed the car and walked down the road. Each driveway had a car or two parked in it. I had to pass four Japanese imports before I found an empty driveway. I followed the brick path to the backyard, where a wooden fence separated it from the church property. Through the slats, I watched the cemetery and a long procession of men and women walking behind a casket. I put my hands on top of the fence and hoisted myself over. No one noticed me landing inside the cemetery grounds — all eyes were on the casket. I quickly made my way to a large tombstone and bent, pretending to clean off the dirt and debris on the stone. There were still two cops somewhere with cameras, and I would be in their sights unless I was careful. The cops wouldn't be allowed inside the church grounds; the funeral was private, and that meant the law too. They would have to find a spot somewhere nearby that offered a good view of the funeral. I scanned the trees on the other side of the cemetery until I saw a beam of light reflect off glass in the foliage. Inside the dense trees one of the cops was getting a great straight shot of the whole guest list.

I kept my head low and walked along the property line away from the funeral. I moved off the lawn and into the trees of the small forest bordering the cemetery, following a path probably formed by the feet of hikers and kids on their way to bush parties. Back in the trees, I made my way around to the spot where I'd seen the glint of the lens. I had to go slowly to avoid making any noise; the ground was littered with beer bottle and pop can landmines. It took five minutes to work my way to the photographer I had noticed. The police paparazzo was in front of an old fire pit standing with a large camera to his face. He didn't know I was behind him until the .45 pressed into his neck.

"Put the camera down," I said.

"I'm a cop, asshole."

"Put it down, now."

"Are you fucking crazy? I'm a cop."

I pushed the .45 hard into his neck, forcing him to bend. Instinctively, both his hands held on to his camera to protect it from falling to the ground. My left arm jerked back, then drove forward into the cop's side. The blow was sudden, and I timed it to the cop's exhale. He had no way to protect himself from the sudden impact. I heard a crack like a pop from a campfire and then a sharp intake of breath before the cop dropped his camera and fell to his knees.

No one in the funeral procession one hundred metres away looked towards us. I pulled the cop's gun and threw it into the forest, then holstered the .45 and freed the cuffs from the cop's belt. The cop offered little resistance while I shackled his hands behind his back. He lay gasping, trying to get his wind back, while I clicked through the stored pictures in the digital camera. There were a couple hundred shots, but I moved through them fast. I saw a shot of a yellow BMW and deleted it. I got rid of another few close-ups of Igor too. The new stitches on his face from where I yanked his cheek open made him easy to spot. When I was through all of the shots, I sat up the cop, who had managed to start breathing normally again.

"What's your name?"

"Broke my ribs, you fucker."

"Cracked maybe, but not broke. Name?"

"Bill."

"All right, Bill. I need to know a few things, then I'm gone. No one will ever have to know about this. You do it fast, and you can get shots of the rest of the funeral."

"I'm gonna find you, and I'm gonna... Hey! What are you doing?"

"Erasing your work. Tough to explain why you came back with nothing to the brass. Might get you bumped off this little task force. Maybe put back in a car on nights."

"Stop, stop." Bill was whining.

"You going to play ball?"

"Fine, fine, what do you want?"

"I'm going to click back through the shots. You tell me who's who. Names, rank, territory, everything."

"I don't know everybody."

I turned the camera and took five rapid shots of the cop cuffed in the dirt.

"Hey, what are you doing? Stop that!"

"I'm gonna hand this off to one of the other cops and let them deal with you. You'll be a real hero."

"Shit, don't do that."

"Then stop jerking me around. You're not working the entrance. You're set up to get shots of the big players. They don't give that job to someone who doesn't know all the faces."

"All right, all right. I'll do it."

I clicked through each frame and listened to Bill tell me who was who. There were a lot of faces, and I asked about each. I didn't care about any of them, but I didn't want Bill to know that. When Bill assigned Sergei's name to a picture of a man at the front of the procession, I listened closely.

"That's the man in charge, Sergei Vidal. He runs the whole Russian mob in Hamilton and Niagara."

"Why Niagara?"

"The casinos and the circus. He uses the Russian circus to get his people into the country. The casinos are the next step; they're already full of crime and money — Sergei used the Russian imports to muscle his way in, then to keep what he took. It only took a few years for the Russians to become major players. The other gangs just couldn't stop them; it's impossible to put fear into the Russians. They've all made their bones under some of the meanest gangsters in the world, and most have done time inside prisons that make puppy mills look like a Hilton. The Russians make a killing off the casinos and use the circus to launder the proceeds. It's a good system. The books are easily fudged, and everyone in the circus is on the payroll, or their family back home is used as blackmail."

"Who guards him?"

"Always five or more men."

"But who guards him? Used to be a big guy, Ivan, but he's gone. Who took his place?"

"Those two on either side of him are his personal security. They're former Russian military. Served in Afghanistan and Chechnya."

"Names?"

"Nikolai and Pietro. Nick and Pete to everyone. I don't know their last names, too many V's and backwards letters. Mean motherfuckers. They killed four Cambodian kids last year when they took a run at Sergei in a nightclub. The kids used machetes and tried to swarm him. They ended up cut to pieces themselves. No witnesses of course, only stories."

We went through thirty more shots until we got to the cars. I asked detailed questions about everyone who seemed important so that Bill would have no insight into what I was really after.

"Where is the third camera?"

"What?"

"I saw one out front, you in the trees, where is number three?"

Bill was over caring about betrayal. "Parking lot," he said.

"Keys are behind your back, Bill, your gun is ten metres that way," I said, pointing in the wrong direction.

Bill began fumbling behind his back while I walked away down the path. He grunted as he lost his balance and rolled over onto his side. I heard him gasp and swear under his breath as his damaged ribs made contact with the ground.

I left the trees and climbed the fence without looking behind me. I came down over the fence without anyone watching from the funeral procession.

"Nice suit."

Shit, I thought. I turned, already shrugging my shoulders, as Morrison's meaty fist collided with my head. I shrugged enough to take most of the blow with my shoulder and trapezius muscles. I brought my hands up, but a second punch never came my way. Morrison closed the distance between us in two steps and took the lapels of my coat in both hands. In a fraction of a second, he pivoted below me and used his hips to get me airborne. I felt his back, like a heavy tree stump, rise, lift me, and throw me. I landed three feet away from the beefy cop. The wind was out of me, but I had been there before. I saw his feet approaching and rolled off my stomach onto my side, my hands already reaching for the foot I knew was coming. Morrison took a big soccer kick at my ribs, but it never connected. My hand blocked the kick, and I rolled away. I put my hands out again, ready to block another kick, but it didn't come. Morrison dove onto my back and looped an arm around my neck. Instinctively, my jaw pressed into my chest, protecting my windpipe from his forearm.

"Back home, I was a national champ in judo, mate." His breath was hot in my ear. "I've twisted bigger and better than you. Only this time, there's no ref to make me let you go."

Most people fight a choke in a blind panic. They strain at the threat — pulling at whatever obstructs the airway. Not me, I learned all about chokes in my teens.

As soon as my uncle took me under his wing, I never had a moment's rest. If my back was to my uncle or my guard was down, he was on me. It didn't matter what the task was; doing dishes, taking out the trash, even brushing my teeth might be met with a barrage of sneak attacks.

One August morning, my uncle came into the kitchen arms full. He was carrying a load of dry cleaning he said was for a job, and he stumbled over a chair I left pulled out. I cringed at my stupidity, knowing I would pay for it, and bent to pick up the clothes. A plastic dry cleaning bag went over my head as I came up with my arms full. I could see the blurred kitchen through the bag as I groped for the counter to hold myself upright. My uncle pulled me to him, with two hands, as the bag fogged with more and more hot air and spit. After thirty seconds, I gave up on the counter and pulled at the hands around my neck. I was exhausted and panting as panic set in. I went to my knees, scratching at the hands, but the clear prison never let up. Blackness took me seconds later.

I woke up on the floor to find the dry cleaning gone. My uncle sat at the table, expressionless in his chair, eating cantaloupe.

"You still ain't ready, boy."

I coughed and sucked air deep into my strained lungs. "Bag was a dirty trick."

"Oh, you think so? You think there's a fucking rule book out there? You think there's a penalty box for people? Forget that shit and tell me what just happened."

"You choked me out," I said.

"Tell me what you did about it."

"I tried to stay on my feet. Then I tried to get your hands off my neck. You were too strong, and I ran out of air."

"Why didn't you tear open the bag?"

I sat there dumbfounded.

"It's a plastic bag. You could have opened it with your finger. Why did you care about the counter or my hands?"

"I...I..."

"CIA uses clear bags. People tear open black ones, but the clear ones — no one touches those. It's psychological, I suppose. You panic and your mind goes into a primal sort of thinking. You can see through the bag, so your brain doesn't register it; it focuses on the hands and body first. That shit doesn't matter though. Dead is dead no matter what your mind-set. You have to think clearest when you're dying. That's when you have to keep your head, or else someone else is going to take it. What good is thinking if you forget it when you need it most? School's out for today. Get to the gym."

I walked out with my head low, the lesson burning in my cheeks. There were other tests after that, but I never lost my head again. I stayed calm when I needed to, and I stayed conscious — most of the time.

Morrison's forearm worked under my jaw. He rotated the bone back and forth using his whole body to pull his limb against my windpipe. I ignored the pain, and the arm, choosing instead to dig a thumb into his eye. He screamed in pain, and the hold loosened a fraction. My other hand found his balls, and I squeezed hard. The choke came loose, and I rolled away. I was on my feet before he was; Morrison wasn't using his hands to stand — they were holding his face and his crotch as he tried to get up. He saw me coming, and he covered up as I had, but I circled around his guard and pounded a kick into the base of his spine. He yelped, and his hands left his front in favour of his back as the impact shot up my leg. I saw his eyes focus through the pain and knew he wasn't done. We both drew on each other at the same time.

"Noise isn't what you want," I said.

"Fuck you. You don't know what I want," Morrison said as he got to his feet one shaky foot at a time. In his fist, he held a snub-nosed revolver.

"Using your drop piece?" I asked.

"Seem to have misplaced my service issue. Where'd you pick up the .45?"

"Yard sale. Why are you here?"

"I'm here to see the players. I love it when shit doesn't go their way. I had to take a personal day just to get here."

"You let them see you?"

"Nah, I'm not suicidal, mate. Rubbing it in is bad business. I'd end up on the business end of a drive-by if I rubbed it in at a funeral."

"So you saw me and … What the fuck happened to your eyebrows?"

"Fucking tape you put on my head took off my eyebrows. I had to fill 'em in with a make-up pencil. It's big laughs at the station."

I chuckled, but the gun never shook. "So you saw me, and you figured it was payback time?"

"That's right, fuckwit."

"You'll just be a dead cop next to a cemetery full of suspects."

"Not if I shoot you first."

"Then you're an off-duty cop using his drop piece on his personal day next to a cemetery full of police cameras and Russian gangsters. How many questions would come out of that?"

Morrison thought about it.

"Climb back over the fence and watch the rest of the show. You can see everything fine from behind the tombstones. You stay here, it's gonna get loud," I said, dusting off my suit with one hand; the other kept the .45 aimed at centre mass.

"We ain't done, mate. We're gonna settle up somewhere private. Just you and me."

"It's hard to look threatening when your eyebrows can't furrow."

He took a step towards me, but I waved him away with the .45. "Go, funeral is about to end, and neither of us wants to be here when that happens."

Morrison slid over the fence quicker and quieter than I thought a man his size ever could, making me think the judo claim was no joke. I'd spent so much time trying to figure out what Morrison wanted from me that I'd underestimated him. He might have been a little crooked, but he was more than a bruiser. He was a good cop. I never saw him watching me in the cemetery. He got through my radar and almost crushed my throat. I had to remember that even off balance Morrison was no slouch. As soon as he disappeared, I jogged out of the yard, crossed the street, and went through two backyards before I set foot on the street. I was far enough down the road to make the church hard to see. But that meant it was hard to see me from the church. I found the court where I had parked my car and slid behind the wheel. I drove over to the street where Igor's yellow BMW was, backed into an empty driveway on the opposite side of the street, and waited.

The cars on the street began moving fifteen minutes after I parked the Volvo. Igor's yellow eyesore stayed put for another twenty minutes. His car was the second to last left on the street when he came sauntering around the corner. Tatiana followed in his wake — stumbling every fourth or fifth step. The way he let her trail behind told me that see-ing her like this wasn't new. She stumbled coming out of another stumble and turned her ankle. Tatiana went side-ways into a bush just as Igor unlocked the car with his key fob. He stamped his foot, marched back to her, and yanked her out of the shrub. He slapped her with his left palm and dragged her by her left bicep to the car. One of her feet kept rolling off its sole and dragging sideways on the pavement as he pulled her. She didn't seem to notice the pain, and Igor didn't notice, or care about, the extra drag. He pushed her against the rear door and held her up against the car with his hip while he opened the passenger side. She laughed and said something to him before he shoved her ass first into the car. He bent and crammed her feet inside before slamming the door. Igor ran a hand through his hair and looked around for witnesses before walking around to the driver side. On the curb, half in the gutter, lay the shoe Tatiana had been dragging sideways on the pavement.

The engine of the yellow car started, and I watched Tatiana's window roll down. Her hand came out holding a cigarette until the car screeched ahead and she had to sacrifice it for a steadying hold on the window sill. I started the Volvo and rolled after the BMW.

Igor drove like an asshole — too fast on residential streets and hooking in and out without signalling on busier roadways. All he achieved was getting to the stoplights faster than anyone else. I stayed far back and let him blaze a trail, knowing there was no way I was going to lose sight of that bright yellow car.

We raced into the core of the city and joined King Street. Igor bobbed and weaved until he screeched his tires onto Bay Street North. The street had cars parked on both sides, leaving only one lane for through traffic. Igor raced down the centre lane, forcing oncoming traffic to swerve into vacant parking spaces for cover from the yellow blur flying at them. Igor put some distance between us while the honking motorists pulled out of their temporary hiding places. I waited for my turn to use the street and then sprinted, pedal to the floor, down the pavement. The Volvo reacted fast, and the power of the engine surprised me. The souped-up machinery under the battered hood came to life like a waking animal — its guttural growl turned into a roar — and went zero to sixty in a few seconds. I caught up to Igor fast, and I had to slam on the brakes to avoid getting too close. He had slowed from his breakneck speed to turn into a driveway. I pulled to the curb twenty metres away and watched Igor once again drag Tatiana. She fell onto the driveway, not being able to keep up with only one high heel on. Igor used her arm and hair to get her vertical and kept his grip to get her the rest of the way into the house. He dragged her inside and slammed the door. I left the curb and turned the corner without looking back at yet another abandoned high heel, this time on the doorstep.

CHAPTER EIGHT

Bayfront Park was across the street from Igor's house. From a parking lot behind a seasonal ice cream shop, I could see his yellow car in the driveway. The ice cream shop had probably closed a few months ago after the kids went back to school. Most of the graffiti on the back of the small shack was new and done in a variety of mediums. Gang signs and love notes were temporarily etched in paint and marker all over the wall. The spot was a good choice because I wouldn't have to worry about a cop checking on the car — joggers used the Bayfront all the time, so there were always a lot of cars parked nearby. It was 4 p.m., and I had no idea how long I was going to have to wait for Igor to come out of his house. I figured I had some time and pulled out of the lot. I drove into the city, found a Middle Eastern restaurant that advertised shwarma, and went inside.

The restaurant was dark, and the walls were without decoration. There were no tables, only booths lined with a dark maroon vinyl. One booth at the back was loaded with kids. A white kid, a black kid, a Filipino, and an Arab sat yelling loud jeers and obscenities to each other across the tight booth.

"I own you in Runescape. I pawn you like a noob every time."

"Sure, sure, George. That's why I sold my points to Matthew for fifty bucks. You suck, George."

I knew they were speaking English, but I had no idea what was being said. I walked past them and smiled at the woman behind the counter. She looked at the kids and rolled her eyes.

"What do you want today?"

"What do you eat?"

"Pardon?"

"What do you eat when you eat here?"

"Oh, I get the shwarma dinner with the garlic and hot sauce."

"Give me two and an iced tea."

The woman got to work filling Styrofoam containers with salad, rice, and chicken. She then topped the meat and rice with two heavy sauces. The kids quieted as two of them broke from the pack and stood in line behind me. They gave me tough stares when I looked in their direction, and I resisted the urge to show them the butt of the .45.

"Do you like Runescape?" the blond kid with braces and a sideways hat asked. He laughed to his friend as soon as he asked the question, thinking he was embarrassing me.

"What do you want?" the girl behind the counter demanded to know from the boy.

"Could I have a can of Mountain Dew?"

"Go sit down and leave my customers alone. I'll bring it

to you when I'm done."

The girl finished my order and took my cash.

"Where's my Mountain Dew?" the blond kid asked again the second the money touched the till.

The girl sighed and turned, leaving the till open, to get a can from the lowest rack of the fridge. She banged her head on the open drawer as she stood, and the boys all laughed at her. She followed me out on her way to the boys' table. I left to the sound of the boys asking her if she liked whatever Runescape was. My .45 stayed in my jacket, and no one watched me leave.

Outside, I put the food on the floor of the back seat, where it would be held in place by the small space on the floor behind the driver's seat. I looked back at the restaurant, through the window at the kids, and ground my teeth. Being forced to work for Morrison made watching the bullies impossible. The big cop was using me just like the kids were using the girl behind the counter. I needed an outlet—something to release the pressure before it came out all on its own. It was then that I noticed the bikes leaning against the wall just below the window. No one else was visible in the lot, so the bikes must have brought the four assholes to the restaurant. They weren't locked up, just left in view from the window. I got in the Volvo, adjusted the mirror, and put the car in reverse. With a sudden bump, the car backed over the curb. There was a metallic crunch and then grinding as the bikes compressed under the old steel bumper of the Volvo. The bumper was worn and dented, so I didn't worry about any new dings standing out. I shifted back into drive and left the lot as the kids from inside ran out to stare at their bikes. I was around the corner too fast for my plates to be seen and lost in traffic before they could call anyone to complain.

I drove back out to Bay Street North and parked behind the ice cream shack again. The yellow BMW was still there. I spent an hour eating and waiting until I had to piss. I dumped what was left of the iced tea and used the bottle. I wasn't leaving again without Igor, so the bottle was the only option.

At 6:30, Igor left the house and started the BMW. Tatiana stayed inside, and her shoe stayed on the porch. Igor tore out of the driveway and headed towards downtown using Barton Street East.

He changed lanes every few seconds and kept the car a few kilometres over eighty the whole way. I pushed through traffic relying on the red lights and the colour of the car to keep him in sight. Ten minutes later, he turned a quick right on Mary Street and parked the car in a lot behind a commercial property. The spot he took was near the rear exits, and it had a sign above it that I couldn't make out from the street. I kept going, then turned onto a side street where Igor wouldn't see me turn around. When I looped back onto Mary Street, Igor was walking to Barton. I crept up the street with my lights off, watching him cross the street and go left at the corner. I gave him a few seconds before I pulled the car to the intersection. I watched until he turned into a doorway of a strip club. The Steel City Lounge was a low-end joint that catered to the off-duty prison guards from the nearby Hamilton Detention Centre. I swung my head right and looked at the detention centre a couple hundred metres down the street and knew it was looking back at me. The building was like a predatory beast always on the prowl. The Barton Jail was a maximum security facility that held the worst and the dumbest. I flipped off the building from the car, checked the rear-view, and reversed back down the street to a curbside parking space.

I pulled the keys from the ignition and followed Igor's trail to the Steel City Lounge. I passed the building, looking inside the open entrance. If there were bouncers frisking anyone, I would have to put the guns back in the car. What I saw made me happy. There was no cover, no dress code, and a sign proclaiming that everyone was welcome.

I walked around the block looking at the side and rear fire exits and at the fence surrounding the parking lot behind the property where Igor had parked. There were several holes in the perimeter of the fence and one portion around back that was almost falling down. It looked as though a car had backed into the fence and no one had bothered to fix it up.

When I came back around, I loosened my tie and walked right inside. I wasn't at all worried about being spotted. I had been invisible for over a decade. As a teen, my first lessons in invisibility started early. Invisibility was a necessity. Until I learned to blend in, I had been barraged with questions about why I was out of school.

At first, I just didn't look people in the eye; it warded some people off, but it didn't make me invisible. The hard men and women my uncle associated with just shoved me and demanded to know why I wasn't where I should have been. It wasn't that they were concerned about my education; they could give a shit about the three R's. They knew that a kid hanging around attracted attention. Someone else would want to know the same thing they did, and if I didn't have an answer, any job I was on would be spoiled like milk left in the sun. At first, I tried to tough my way around my inquisitors, once going so far as to tell a safe man to fuck off when he questioned me. He didn't respond, he just looked at my uncle and then knocked me out — chipping a tooth in the process.

That night, while I sat with a bag of frozen peas on my jaw, my uncle asked about my mouth. I told him it was all right because of the peas, and he assured me that it was as sure as fuck not. He said it was too saucy for such a green kid. I told him about the question and how I thought going on the offensive would make it go away. My uncle laughed. "You can't be mean every time. That will usually just bring on whole other sets of questions. You can't let them see you, boy."

"You mean stay in the car?"

"You can't always stay in the car. You have to be able to walk around in plain sight. What I'm talking about is being invisible in front of everyone's eyes. You have to learn to be a ghost, and not like Casper. I mean fucking gone."

"How?"

"It's all in your head. But you won't believe me until I show you. Get your coat."

We drove to west Hamilton and parked in a lot that housed a variety store, a fish and chips restaurant, and a pool hall. We walked down the steps to the pool hall, and my sinuses were all at once struck with the smell of dirt, smoke, and spilt beer. My uncle took a deep breath and exhaled slowly. He put an arm around me and pointed to a row of pinball machines and video games.

"These here are mob-owned, boy. I once saw a local tough guy put a pool cue through one. Next day, a leg breaker shows up to cart away the machine and to find the guy that broke it."

"What happened to the guy?" I asked.

"Darndest thing, the truck that was hauling the machine away hit him in the street." My uncle laughed as though he had just heard a particularly funny joke instead of a tale of street justice. "Here's ten bucks. Have some fun."

I forgot about being invisible and spent an hour playing Golden Axe. There were three characters to choose from, a big Conan-looking guy all muscle and sword, a beautiful warrior woman with a sword and implants, and a dwarf with a big axe. I chose the dwarf with the axe because hardly anyone ever picked the dwarf. The game had spent years killing the barbarian or the broad, maiming their digital good looks long into the night. In my mind, everyone was scanning for the next buff hero — no one would see the dwarf coming until the big axe spoke up and said hello in its brutal language. Time flew by, and on the hour my uncle put his heavy hand on the back of my neck. His fingers dug hard into muscle and nerves as he spoke in my ear. "Lesson's not over, boy. You've been here an hour, what's the guy behind the counter look like?"

I instinctively tried to turn my head, but the calloused mitt on my neck wouldn't let me.

"Speak up. What's he look like?"

"I don't know."

"Why not?"

"I didn't look at him. I was busy."

"Son of a bitch might as well have been invisible, eh? That's the first trick. When you don't want to be seen, you have to be where the person's interest ain't. The guy behind the counter pulled it off without trying because you're young and stupid, but there's a science to it. You have to notice everything around you. Take in everything that happens and everything that don't. You want to be unseen, you move when other things happen. You pick your spots. You can be nowhere in plain sight as long as you feel what's around you. You move with the room, and it's like you're not even there. Understand?"

I nodded my head as much as the hand on my neck would allow, but my uncle wasn't finished.

"It's different when you're in a room with one or two people. Then you're part of the room because you're a focal point. There's nowhere to hide in the spotlight. You sit quiet in that spotlight long enough people feel like they have to say something to fill the void. And our kind of people don't know anything polite. If you make them wonder, they're gonna dig at you until they find something they understand. Only your words will make you invisible. You got to make people uncomfortable, make them want to look somewhere else. And I'm not talking about the 'Fuck you' shit you tried. When you want to stay invisible, you have to use remarks that put people on the defence. Put something mean and uncomfortable out there, then fade back. People will be glad to ignore you then. But what you put out comes from observation. You have to watch how people talk, how they stand, what they look at. You need to find something that will rattle them in the few moments you have, then you go at it with precision, not brute force. If you put out anything that sounds like a challenge, everyone will get your scent. A challenge is primal. Every animal recognizes it and instinctively pays attention to it. You challenge someone in our world everyone will see you, because they'll be trying to put your lights out. Understand?"

It was a week before someone else on the job asked me why I wasn't in school. I had studied hard, and I was ready. "I thought you said this guy was a pro, Uncle Rick. You sure this is the guy we need to see?"

There was silence in the room until my uncle spoke. "Are you?"

"Yeah, yeah, sure, Rick. I was just making conversation. Let's get down to business."

No one spoke to me again that whole afternoon. No one even looked my way even though I was three feet away from the conversation the entire time. When no one was looking, my uncle rubbed my head. Rare praise from the man who raised me to become a ghost.

That night, my uncle took me to one of the big box electronic stores in Ancaster. On the way in he said, "What you did today was good. Now I want to see if you can move with the room. Each of these minimum wagers inside here works on commission. They're hungrier than sharks and less decent. I'm gonna move around the store for fifteen minutes, and you're gonna come with me. If we get stopped, it won't be because of me. It'll be because you couldn't flow with the environment. Don't screw up, boy. Understand?"

We spent twenty minutes in the store. The last five were spent moving within feet of the bored employees. I moved with my uncle for a while, until he seamlessly shifted behind me and began following me. The automatic doors were the only thing to recognize our departure. There was no head rubbing this time — only a small compliment and a big criticism.

"You might have a knack for this, but you almost screwed up. You looked at the girl in the music section, and she saw you. The employee there picked up on her distraction, and he almost followed it to you. You don't shut off your dick, you don't vanish. Understand?"

I nodded and got in the car.

The Steel City Lounge advertised thirty dancers, but I counted only twenty on rotation for the dinner crowd. The seats in front of the long stage were full of beefy looking men with short haircuts and faded tattoos. Each seemed comfortable with the close proximity of the man beside him, making me think that they were guards from the jail winding down after a long shift. The girls were the opposite of everything they looked at all day, and they watched with a carnivorous interest.

I took a corner seat and scanned the room. Igor wasn't on the bottom floor — he was in the second floor VIP area talking to a topless waitress and playing it cool, judging by the look on his face. Around him were four pale men in dark suits and sunglasses. They spoke to random girls who weren't talking to Igor and kept their eyes on him at all times. Igor said something over the head of the owner of the tits he was looking at, and all the men laughed loudly enough for me to hear them over the music. The attention and fake laughter meant Igor was important to them.

The strip club looked to be Igor's haunt. It was clear he was the man in charge from his free movement in the VIP lounge and the number of cold-looking sycophants he garnered. How much business went down in the club was up in the air. Igor claimed to be doing what a neighbourhood boss named Mikhail did before him. I figured that meant he collected money from all of the blood-stained hands of the mob in the area and passed the dirty currency on to his boss, Sergei Vidal. Igor wasn't enough to get Morrison off me, but he knew who I was, so whatever went down had to include him. I had to find out what Igor was into and how it got back to his boss, because Sergei was no fish — he was a whale, and he'd definitely get me off the hook.

CHAPTER NINE

I sat in the strip club for six hours. I steadily ordered drinks from the waitresses and poured them on the floor a bit at a time. The carpet under my feet was dark and industrial grade; it was probably used to getting wet, and it hid my drinks just fine. I tipped well enough to stay seated but not well enough to get any company. The club was full of plenty of other men looking for an eyeful and more than willing to pay for a handful. The girls almost instinctively avoided me. They knew which men had money to spend like bees knew which flowers had pollen.

Igor was big man on campus in the Steel City Lounge. People showed up with heavy duffel bags over their shoulders and left with them empty under their arms or crumpled in their fists. Whatever was in the bags never came down the stairs — there had to be a safe upstairs in the VIP lounge.

Loud thunderous music pounded out of the speakers and moved my glass across the table a millimetre at a time whenever it was empty. I was seen, but never noticed, not even by the waitress. I was part of her route. She brought me a new drink when she came by like a robot. No one else looked my way — I was in a pocket between the action. On one side, the stage dazzled lonely men with lights and implants. On the other, the bar hummed with customers ordering food and drinks. Igor never looked down unless it was to order one of the stage performers up to his lounge at the end of her set. When the dancers began to leave, and not get replaced by another Stepford whore, I realized how long I had been in the club and the toll the time took on my bladder. I took in the room and waited for my spot. I had to wait for the room to cough so I could move in the space provided by the spasm. I moved when a drunken customer got handsy with a girl and a bouncer had to deal with him. No one's eyes followed me; they were all glued to the beating. I was part of the room, the background no one pays attention to, just like my uncle had taught me to be.

The bathroom was disgusting and empty, but I used it all the same. I took my time drying my hands, timing my exit. I left the bathroom in tune with a loud entrance of another girl from the speakers. I waited outside the bathroom for the peeler to hit the audience with a tease. Within a few seconds, both of her clear heels left the stage as she slid upside down on the pole towards the floor. Men hooted and hollered as I moved under the VIP stairs and out the door.

I pulled the car out front and killed the engine. I let the back window down to avoid clouding the windows and waited for Igor.

One by one, drunks stumbled out empty handed and alone. Igor left, unaccompanied, at 3 a.m. with nothing more than what he showed up with. He got in his car and peeled away.

I didn't follow. Instead, I waited outside. I wanted to see if he left moving the contents of whatever was in those duffel bags to one of his guys. I saw three of the VIPs leave together, but none of them carried a thing. I got out of the car and followed them on foot down the street. Like Igor, they'd parked in the lot behind the strip club. They were loud and boisterous as they walked around the building. They didn't turn their heads once to see me two metres behind them. I let my footsteps fall in the same tempo as theirs, and I slowed my breathing down. I moved closer and put my hand on the butt of the .45. It would have been easy to put a bullet into each of the three men. I was so close I could do it before any of them turned around to see who it was that was killing them. It was clear that Igor didn't work with pros; he had men on staff who were sloppy like he was. They were probably childhood friends or the only people who didn't laugh at him. I stopped following when the three men turned off the sidewalk and stepped into the lot behind the building. I had learned enough about Igor's business and the help for one night.

I got back behind the wheel and watched the rest of the employees leave. No one left with anything larger than a purse. When the windows went dark, I drove out to Igor's house on Bay Street and made sure the yellow car was there — it was. I drove back to the motel for a couple hours of sleep and was back behind the empty ice cream shack at 6 a.m. with a bagel in hand. I ate, drank, and pissed in a bottle in the car until 2:30. Then I followed Igor to a salon to watch him get his hair cut and his nails done. He went from the salon to Limeridge Mall, where he bought shirts and pants at Urban Behaviour while I watched him and pretended to shop at a nearby HMV.

Igor was back home at five. I noticed that someone had picked up Tatiana's shoe while we were gone. I left the car behind the vacant building and jogged across the street. The blinds in the windows were all turned. No one saw me as I ran down the driveway, past the yellow car, to the side of the house. The side of the house was all brick, and there were only two doors to be found. One leading to the garage, the other into the house. Neither door was unlocked, and both seemed to have a handle lock as well as a deadbolt. I moved around the back of the house, where a deck sat below a long row of kitchen windows. There was no way to pass unseen to the other side of the house, so I retraced my steps and crept around the front of the house to the other side.

On the other side, I found a basement window unlocked and screenless. I crouched and examined the dimensions of the window. I figured I could wiggle my way through the small space with little trouble. Around the corner to the backyard, I found myself on the other side of the deck below a kitchen window; it was up, and I could hear voices coming from inside the house.

"How could I take you to the salon? I told you I had a 2:45 appointment. You don't get up till 4:30!" Igor was screaming in heavily accented English.

"You could've woken me up!" Tatiana slurred when she spoke, but she seemed to be holding her own in the loud conversation.

"Do I look like a fucking alarm clock? I am the one who makes the money, I put food on the table, now I am to wake you up too? *Nyet.* Do you clean? *Nyet.* Do you sleep all day and get high? *Da!* That's what you do!"

"Maybe it's because I am bored. You don't take me out. You don't talk to me. If you could get it up, at least you could fuck me."

There were loud stomps building in intensity and force. "What did you just say to me?" Igor demanded to know.

"Igor, I...I...I am sorry, Igor. I didn't mean it. Please don't!"

Sounds of domestic violence trickled down through the window into the backyard.

"I am a man, you treat a man like a king, you junkie! Clean my house and clean yourself up. You talk that way to me because of the shit you put in your arm. You're high already. You're lucky I don't cut it out of you."

It was only 5:00. Tatiana had only been up thirty minutes, by Igor's clock, and she was already in the early stages of being high. It was a regular thing, judging from the similar state she was in at the funeral. Tatiana was sobbing loudly between the slaps and crashes.

"You want to be my wife and you act like this? How can I marry a junkie? You were high at Marko's funeral, for Christ's sake. Everyone saw you. They saw me holding you up. How can I marry you?"

"Who said I want to marry you?" Tatiana's voice was more distant and slurred from the beating and the growing effects of whatever she injected. "At that funeral, I had to get high. I am so sick of listening to the jokes behind my back. They all say them just loud enough for me to hear. All those wives and fucking mistresses laughing at me. They all think you're a fag, you know. You spend all that time at the strip club, and you fuck no one. Imagine if they found out that you don't even touch me. Imagine if they found out you can't even touch me with the help of that Viagra. Maybe you are gay, and I am what they call a beard."

"Shut up, you filthy junkie. Shut up!"

"Homo. Queer. Cocksuc—"

There was a sudden gurgling and then the sound of Igor screaming. Water sloshed inside, and a mist sprayed through the screen on the kitchen window. Igor was drowning Tatiana in the sink. After half a minute, I heard a gasp and a wet cough.

"You watch your mouth. Just watch what you say. I want you clean when I get home. Clean and with dinner in the oven. You know what that is, right? It's where I'll put your head next time you talk to me that way."

There was more coughing and the sound of the front door slamming. I hurried around the side of the house and saw the yellow car reverse onto the road before rocketing out towards the core.

I ran across the street and got in the Volvo. Within a minute, I was at a light, three cars behind the yellow BMW. I was used to Igor's erratic driving, and I let him get ahead knowing I would catch up at the next light. No amount of speed would get anyone through all greens downtown—the timing wasn't there. As I drove, I thought about Igor. Tatiana let slip the fact that he was impotent. That jived with everything Igor had said in the hospital room and everything I had noticed about him. His life was all one big masculine front. The yellow sports car, the aggressive driving, the strip club office he had. Everything was an attempt to convey a message of masculinity. Tatiana said wives and mistresses thought he was gay; that meant Igor's facade wasn't fooling anyone. But he wasn't gay; he wasn't always like he was, he was mind-fucked from being shot in the shoulder and left to die. Being in a gunfight and losing had hurt something inside him, something he believed he needed to kill me in order to get back.

I had met men like Igor before: pros who lost control of a situation and could no longer cope with the job. Soldiers and cops called it post-traumatic stress disorder. Problem was, our job didn't have benefits or a retirement plan, and none of us had a shot at a real job and an ordinary life. Most of the people like Igor either went down on the job, or they did it to themselves. They didn't even need to pull the trigger most times. They just showed the wrong people that they couldn't be trusted, and it would get done for them. No pro was going to let some cracked egg take them down. If they already knew too much about a job, it just made sense to kill them before they compromised the workers or the paycheque. There were no retirement parties or gold watches, just a loud send-off moving at a few hundred metres per second.

Igor went another way. He got some kind of insight into himself and learned about closure. He figured killing me would reboot him. Missing a second chance at murdering me must have pushed him even closer to the edge.

Igor's mental state aside, it was clear that he was an

earner. The bags coming into the strip club were numerous. Enough for Sergei Vidal to keep a squirrely maniac on the payroll. Money trumps crazy every time.

For a few seconds I was a car length behind Igor and saw a phone to his ear. He was still on it when he parked behind the Steel City Lounge. I waited on the side of the road, watching through the chain link fence for him to get off the phone. Seventeen minutes later, Igor hung up and walked to the club. I reversed up the street and found a spot on a side road near where I had parked the day before. I caught up to Igor and joined the ranks of a rowdy softball team, ten feet behind him, who had decided to celebrate a win with beers and g-strings. Igor glanced our way, but he never made me. I was invisible within arm's reach.

I spent seven hours inside the Steel City Lounge. More bags came in, and even more flesh jiggled by. Igor never looked my way, and no one bothered me in my spot. Igor left late and alone again, and his crew left a bit after him carrying nothing.

I didn't follow anyone home. Instead, I drove out towards the Flamboro Downs Racetrack. A few years back, an unlicensed veterinarian patched my arm up after I got tagged by a bullet. She was a down-on-her-luck drunk, and she would do almost anything for money.

The drive took just under an hour. I pulled into her driveway at 3:30 a.m. and pounded on the front door. The knocking woke up several neighbourhood farm dogs, and I heard horses from the barn neigh and snort. I pounded again, thinking I had to rouse Maggie from a drunken sleep. What happened next I wasn't prepared for. A man opened the door.

"Who the fuck are you?"

"I need to see Maggie," I said. I said it with confidence, like I had an appointment. Most people will overlook almost anything if it seems official, even being woken out of bed at three in the morning. This guy wasn't one of those people.

"That's not what I asked you. I asked who you were."

"I have business with Maggie." I stopped trying to sound confident and turned my shoulders. My right hand hung near the .45 holster. There was a chance that Maggie could be patching someone else's bullet wounds. I looked the man up and down and checked the blackness behind him for any movement. The man was shirtless, soft, and wearing only Toronto Maple Leaf boxer shorts. Both of his hands were empty and visible, and he had an erection. I had woken the guy up, and he was no pro. Anyone getting a bullet patched by Maggie would make her open the door while they stood inside with a gun on her. They would get her to send me away. They wouldn't open the door with only their boner pointing at me.

"Charlie?" a woman's voice said from inside, breaking the tension.

"You get back to the bedroom. I'm dealing with this."

"But, Charlie, who is it?"

"You do what I tell you. I have this."

"I need to see Maggie," I said.

"Me?" I heard her say.

"Damn it! I'm calling the police."

Maggie appeared over the man's shoulder, and I could

see things were different. As her eyes widened and remembered me, I saw the lack of broken blood vessels in her face, her healthy hair, and her thinner body. She had cleaned herself up. I ground my teeth realizing she wasn't what I needed her to be anymore.

"Charlie, this is just an old client. He probably needs something for his horse. You put that phone down and go back to bed. I'll be back inside in a sec."

"Banging on the door at this hour, he's lucky I didn't shoot him."

"I know, baby. Go back to bed." She walked outside in her bathrobe and closed the door. "What do you want?" Her tone was cold and flat.

"You look good. Being clean agrees with you," I said.

"What do you want? I don't do what you need anymore."

"Doesn't change a thing," I said.

"It changes everything."

"No, it doesn't. What you did is what you do. That kind of work never goes away. You'll still do it, just maybe not for money." I opened my coat, and she saw the .45.

"Oh, my God."

"He's not here. It's just you, me, and Charlie."

"Charlie," she whispered.

"I need one thing, and I'm gone," I said. "This time I'll stay gone. I understand you've changed, I accept that. But I'm here now, and that is something you have to accept."

"Charlie doesn't know what I did. The things I done."

"Get me what I need and he won't learn it from me."

She sighed, and her shoulders sagged. "What do you want?"

"Ketamine and a syringe," I said.

"You on the stuff? That shit ain't for fooling around with. It's dangerous."

"I need it and I'm gone."

"I don't feel right about this. I'm no drug dealer."

"You were a lot of things. I just need you to be one thing for a few minutes more."

She looked at the house, then at me. "Come on out to the barn," she said.

Maggie threw on some shoes from behind the door, led me out to the barn and into a room filled with stainless steel. She opened a cabinet and gave me a vial along with a syringe in a sterilized paper packet.

"Here, now I'm a drug dealer." She started to cry.

"If I were to inject an animal, where would be the best place to bury the needle?"

"What? An animal?"

"A two-hundred-pound animal that needs to be out cold fast."

I couldn't fool her. "Oh, no. You can't. It's too dangerous. You could kill a person."

"Without this, that will be the only option."

She thought about it. "A quarter of the bottle will put a man down if you get him in the neck."

"How fast?"

"Twenty seconds. He'll be limp, and he'll hallucinate terribly while he's under. Too much and you'll put him in a coma...or worse."

I put the vial and syringe in my pocket. "You look good. I hope it's permanent," I said. "I promise I won't be back."

I left to the sound of Maggie sobbing. I was back at the motel by 4:30 and back at Igor's by 9 a.m.

CHAPTER TEN

It was eight at night when Igor jogged out to his banana
BMW and screeched away from the house. I followed
behind, catching up at the lights. Igor was on his phone
again, and from the nodding and shaking of his head, I
could see that it was an animated conversation.

He parked on a side street and walked into the Steel City
Lounge by 8:15. I gave him room and waited until 9:00 to go
inside. The street clothes I had changed into made me just
another guy looking to blow off steam after work. When I
took my seat, I saw that it would be different tonight. The
VIP lounge was roped off, but there were no girls upstairs.
Two men stood on guard behind the velvet rope, smoking and scanning the crowd. Every twenty minutes, a man
appeared from behind them, said a few words, nodded,
then retreated back where he came from. There was a room
upstairs, and something important was happening inside.
Forty-five minutes later, Igor appeared on the balcony towing a large duffel bag. The bag was much bigger than any
that had come in during the last few days. Judging by the

way Igor rubbed his shoulder when he set it down, it was heavy.

I didn't get up until Igor started lugging the bag down the stairs. I threw down a ten to cover the drink and walked outside. I ran to the Volvo, drove fast around front, and found a spot on the street in front of the strip club where I could watch for Igor. I loaded the syringe while I sat waiting in the car. If he had more than one bodyguard come along with the money, I wouldn't be able to use the ketamine. What I had planned would only work if Igor had no alibi. I had seen grifters do part of it time and time again. The set-up played on human nature and the social instincts grilled into Canadians since birth. The rest would play out on its own.

I swore under my breath when Igor came out flanked by the two men who stood watch upstairs in the VIP lounge. Igor held the bag himself, over his shoulder, and marched under the bulk of the cash in the duffel. I started the car, leaving the lights off, and checked the mirrors. Two guards was bad — it meant there would have to be a change in plans.

I crept up the street behind the three men and let them turn down Mary Street towards the parking lot and Igor's car. The Volvo nosed around the corner, and I saw Igor shoving the bag into the passenger seat of his car. The BMW was cramped when it was just Igor and Tatiana; there was no way the money would ride shotgun while the two men rode in back. Igor slid in after the money and started the car. The bodyguards stayed on the street, and one of them slapped the roof twice. They each took two steps back from the car to give it room to back up. I stopped thinking about how to deal with the bodyguards and quickly accelerated past the men in the street. Igor was taking the money alone to Sergei. It made sense given what I knew about Igor. He tried to prove to the world that he was a man twenty-four seven. That kind of guy would bring the money alone because he would want everyone to see what a success he was. Having bodyguards come too might spread out the accolades. No matter how stupid carrying that much cash alone was, his ego wouldn't let him be rational.

I used two side roads to get on Barton Street ahead of Igor and waited in the jail parking lot to see which way he would go. Thirty seconds went by before Igor pulled around the corner towards me. I put the parking brake on, got out, and began crossing the street. The needle was out in my fist along the side of my leg; my thumb was on the plunger. The yellow BMW tore up the street, and I picked up the pace. It might have been the lack of sleep that made walking into the path of Igor's car so easy; it might just as easily have been the adrenaline high from being on the grind again instead of just rebounding. My face pulled into a familiar grin as I stumbled in front of the car and bent my knees, ready to dive if Igor didn't slow down. Igor saw me in the path of the headlights and hit the brakes. I jumped in the air and let the rapidly slowing car catch me with its hood. My body rolled up to the windshield and raced back down to the pavement.

The door opened, and Igor was out. "What the fuck? Are you crazy? How did you not see me? If you dented the car, I'm going to kill you."

Igor played into the second typical response. When grifters faked being hit, they hoped for the usual Canadian response: a mortified, polite, apologetic driver. Even if it wasn't their fault, most Canadians will think it was and offer to help the victim — even though the real victim is them. Nine times out of ten, drivers will cut cheques to get away without involving the cops. The money keeps them safe from the law and their conscience. But the other type of driver was Igor's type. They could care less about other people. They only cared about themselves and their cars. I didn't care which response I got out of Igor; it wasn't a grift, I didn't want money — I wanted him.

While Igor checked the car over, I clawed at his pants and pulled myself to my knees. I wasn't hurt, but Igor didn't know that. He turned towards me and got even more irate. "Get the fuck off me!" Igor tried to shove me back, but I surged off my knees, coming up under his right arm. My left hand came around his back and took a fistful of his hair while my right hand slammed the syringe into the side of his neck. I forced Igor against the hood as I pushed the plunger down with my thumb and sent half the bottle of ketamine into the Russian's neck. I expected Maggie to recommend the smallest dose possible in an effort to ease her conscience, so I doubled her prescription, figuring half the vial would be enough to do the job but probably not enough to kill him.

When my thumb wouldn't go any further into the syringe, I let go of the needle and wrapped my arm around Igor, pinning his left arm to his body. Igor thrashed and bucked, but the hood of the car held him upright, and my body, pressed against his, gave him no room to move. He was strong at first, but he began to weaken after a few seconds. Within ten seconds, he was drooping in my arms. I dragged him to the passenger side, shoved him in the car, on top of the duffel, and got in behind him. I drove the car off the street into the jail parking lot, watching distant onlookers stare at the car from the rear-view mirror until the wheels hit the jail parking lot. Contact with the jail sent many of the people on their way, as though what had happened had made some sort of sense. A few other stragglers still stared at the parking lot and fished in their pockets for phones. I turned the BMW off and put the keys in Igor's pocket. I got out of the car and reached in for a handful of Igor's hair and shirt. My hands pulled him into the driver's seat and buckled him in. Then I pulled the bag across his lap and onto the pavement. Igor's chest was rising and falling, and his pulse was still easy to find. He whimpered in the chemical daze while I pulled the syringe from his neck and closed the door. The drugs, working their way deeper into Igor's system, turned his muscles to jelly and sent the Russian forward until his head hit the steering wheel.

The duffel was heavy as I carried it to the Volvo. I put it in the passenger seat, disengaged the parking brake, and drove out of the lot, using the second exit, towards the motel. The whole grab took under three minutes. I figured some of the witnesses might call the cops, but there would be nothing left for them but a drunk sleeping it off in his car.

On the way to the motel, I powered up the cell phone and dialled Detective Sergeant Morrison's cell number. "Morrison?"

He picked up on the second ring.

"You find anything on that name I gave you?"

"Igor? There's a few Igors, but I know the one you asked about. Seems to be in charge of drug revenue. He's not dumb though, I can't find a house in his name or any employment records. All I could find out was that he was a fill-in for some mope that got shot in a Russian bar, and since then he's been holding his own."

"Who told you this?"

"Couple a cops. And a few CIs."

"Who's the cop?"

"Fuck you."

"Miller?" I asked. No response came. "How about the CIs? Are they in the mix or just people with ears?"

"They're in the mix enough to be at that funeral you crashed. We ain't finished, you know."

I ignored him. "Did you play up that kidnapping angle that we talked about?"

Morrison sighed. "Yeah."

"So the cops think whoever took me killed the nurse too?"

"Until I can prove different. And I can prove different whenever I want. You know that, right?"

I pressed on. "Why did they take me?"

"We figure you saw too much. So did the nurse. See? What I say goes."

"Who's running the investigation?"

"I am."

"So we're almost done."

"I told you we ain't finished, not by a fucking long shot,

mate."

I ignored him again. "How fast can you get in touch with your CIs?"

"Why?" Morrison dropped the base and anger from his voice. He sensed the promise of a bust.

"Spread the word that Igor took some money that didn't belong to him."

"What money? How much? Where'd it come from?" The questions came hard and fast.

"Just put the word out tonight. You have four hours to do it."

"Why four hours? If you know something about Igor, tell me."

"Morrison, do one other thing."

"Tell me what you know."

"Let slip to Miller that Igor is on the outs and you heard Sergei Vidal is after him personally."

Morrison's anger flared. "You keep trying to put everything on Miller like I'm supposed to believe you over him. He's been with me every step of the way. He's saved my life more than once, and his kids call me uncle. I told you before, Miller is a good cop."

"Then you got nothing to worry about. Just let it slip casually later on tonight. If you do this, you'll get your fish."

"When? Who's the fucking fish?"

I hung up the phone and drove the rest of the way to the motel. Morrison trusted the fat cop. It was more than just the brotherhood of blue banding together against a crook like me, they had history on and off the job. He had blinders on about the idea of Miller double dipping. I just hoped that Morrison's need for a big bust would push him past his myopia enough to leak what I told him to say to Miller. He broke a lot of rules, and put himself on the line, to get me to work with him, so I figured he'd use Miller too if there was no other way. Morrison was greedy, and he'd find a way to rationalize telling Miller what I said to get what he wanted. If he really felt Miller was clean, he would decide there would be no harm in telling him anything because it would go nowhere. But if Morrison did have any doubts about his partner, what I said would push them to the surface. Using Miller kept Morrison off balance and out of focus. I needed to keep pushing him so he stayed off his game.

Back at the motel, I pulled the duffel into the room. The bag was big enough to take up most of the space in front of the tiny bed. I closed the blinds and unzipped the bag. Inside were packets of cash, all denominations separated by bill and bound with paper bands. Igor had been on his way to a big drop. One thing was for sure, the money would be missed.

There was nothing else in the bag with the money. I checked the pockets and the liner to be sure. I had been burned by a hidden GPS in a bag before, and it wouldn't happen again. Satisfied there was no GPS, I put all of the cash back in the bag and zipped it up. This money was going to be chum in the water. This much couldn't go missing without repercussions, and Igor would be on the hook for it alone because he left with it in his tiny yellow sports car. There was no way he could pay it back either — it was too much cash for Igor just to take out of a bank account and replace. The missing money would do two things: it would put Igor at odds with his boss, and it would force him to do something stupid. Igor was an emotional wreck; I figured a failure of this magnitude would push him over the edge. He would have to do something crazy to stay alive, and I was going to be there when he went for it. I needed something big to shake Morrison off me, and Igor would get it for me. I had to use whatever scheme Igor came up with to take him out of the game, because eventually he would pass off blame on me for the money being gone. If Sergei Vidal believed him, it would be a short jump for the synapses in his brain to connect me to the robbery years ago that reignited war between the Russians and the Italians. Then I would be up against the whole Russian mob instead of just one sick head case.

The radio alarm clock bolted to the bedside table told me I had just over three hours until Igor's vitamin K–induced sleep should start to wear off. I put the money in the trunk and drove to the closest drug store. Inside, I bought caffeine pills and Red Bull. I stood in the parking lot chewing the pills and washing them down with swigs of the cola. I had been on too many stakeouts for too many days, and the shitty food and shittier bed were catching up with me. I had to wrap this up soon, or I would slip up.

When my hands began to open and close on their own, I got behind the wheel and rode the caffeine buzz all the way to the Barton Street Jail.

On my first pass, I saw the yellow BMW parked where I left it. It was 11:35 p.m., and traffic on the street was minimal. I slipped into a space across the street and watched the car — nothing moved for six hours. The extra large dose of ketamine did its job better than I expected. Just before six in the morning, the door opened, and Igor fell into the street. He threw up and then pulled himself up off the ground using a tire and the hood for help. When he was vertical, he massaged the side of his neck in between dry heaves. After one particularly nasty bout of vomiting, his head snapped towards the car, and he stumbled to the open door. He looked inside, through the driver seat, to the passenger side, then into the cramped back seats, and finally into the trunk. From inside the Volvo I heard the scream that followed. Igor pulled out his cell phone and thumbed it frantically. He never moved his lips. Instead, he put the phone to his ear and just listened. After thirty seconds, he collapsed against the side of the car as though the phone had just dealt him a nasty physical blow. Someone on the other end of that phone was looking for Igor; worse, they were looking for the money.

CHAPTER ELEVEN

I sat up straighter and got ready to see how the Russian would play this. Igor closed the phone and stumbled behind the wheel. He could go one of two ways: back home, or towards whoever it was he was going to see before I robbed him. The yellow BMW trickled out of the parking lot towards Igor's house.

I let the BMW stay six car lengths ahead of me and watched as it swerved in and out of lanes. Igor usually cut in and out of traffic with razor-sharp precision, but the BMW was not making those expert merges anymore. The car was making lane changes that started too far back and involved Igor riding the medians between two lanes for too long before he finally tugged the wheel enough to get into the next lane. The drugs were still heavily in his system, and they had screwed with Igor's perception and reaction time; they didn't affect his lead foot. Igor ran two red lights and made it home a full minute before I caught up. I left the car behind the ice cream shack and circled around the back of the house to the kitchen window.

I kept low until I was underneath the sill. I stole glances inside, but I couldn't see Igor anywhere. I scanned the yard for any neighbours who would be able to see me from their breakfast table, but the trees covered me. I let my head slowly creep up towards the window so I could take a longer look inside when a window two stories above me shattered. Pieces of glass fell, along with flowers and water from what used to be a full vase, onto the lawn. I hustled to the side of the house and around to the front door while Igor's screams poured out of the now jaggedly open window.

I climbed onto the side of the porch, accessible from the corner of the house, and walked towards the front door, head low, as though I belonged there. The unlocked doorknob noiselessly turned under my palm, and as soon as my body cleared the door, I had the Colt out. The big pistol followed my eyes through the first floor — finding nothing. All the while, I could hear Igor yelling upstairs. I took a spot beside the staircase, impossible to see from upstairs, and listened.

"On the take? On the take! Why would I be on the take? Who is saying such things?"

There was a pause while Igor heard a response in his ear.

"How is it all over the streets?"

Another pause.

"Well, how does some fuck at that shitty bar know anything?"

Pause.

"Where else? At the Strip Club! Holy shit!" Igor's curse was breathless as though the words left his mouth with every bit of air in his lungs. "We have to stop this before it gets to Sergei."

Pause.

"What did he ask you?" Igor was starting to squeal. "Well, what did you tell him?"

Pause.

"What do you mean you said you didn't know where I was?"

Pause.

"I don't care if it was Pietro who was asking. You work for me, no one else! If anyone asks about me, you say I had business to handle, but it is finished tonight. You hear that? Tonight. Everything is back to normal tonight. Put that out to everyone and shut up whoever is doing the talking."

There was a long pause.

"What do you mean there was a cop looking for me too? What cop? Was he a fat pig of a man?"

Pause.

"So who was he? Does anyone know him?"

Pause.

"Who talked to him?"

Pause.

"Did Pietro see the cop?"

There was one last silence before I heard Igor scream "Fuck" so loud that I knew it meant the call was over.

Christ, Morrison was a mover. I had leaked a single first name two days ago, and he was already catching up to me. I saw that his playing loose with the rules in the hospital was, in his mind, a safe bet because he was a born hunter of men, able to turn a name into an address almost overnight. He never had a doubt in his mind that he wouldn't be able to track me down the same way he found Igor. But I wasn't like Igor. He was a mid-level collector with an organization holding him up and watching his back. I was a different breed, a grinder. I survived for decades without a safety net to keep me from falling to my death. I was bred to survive in the dark, and there was no cop who would round me up in a day. But if Morrison proved any more capable than I thought him to be, he would find himself being chased with a worse sentence than jail time not far behind. Morrison wasn't just my problem anymore. Igor had to share the load, but the Russian also had to deal with Pietro. He was one of Sergei Vidal's bodyguards that I saw stored in the memory of the cop's camera. His presence meant a noose was forming around Igor's neck.

"What's wrong, baby? Bad night?" From my spot below, I could hear that Tatiana's accented voice was slow and slurred — she was still high from the night before.

"Shut up, junkie."

"You're the one who's yelling. I'm just trying to open the lines of communication like Doctor Davis said."

"Shut up."

"You strike out at that lame-ass strip club of yours? One of the girls find out that you are dickless? Is that it?" The doctor's lessons were apparently over. Tatiana laughed with the humour and courage that only a needle could supply.

"Everything is falling apart, baby." Igor sounded on the verge of tears.

"Ha. Are you crying, you little bitch? That is such a turn-off, you know? Aw, does Baby Igor need his baby bottle?" Tatiana broke into a case of the giggles that only stopped when Igor spoke again, sounding sad and pathetic.

"Seriously, I need you."

Tatiana did a slurred impression of Igor. "Seriously, I need you." She tried to laugh at him again, but only a gurgle came from her throat.

"Stupid, fucking whore!"

Tatiana's body rolled down the stairs without warning. She landed with her eyes shut. They stayed closed as I backed away into the kitchen. Igor thumped down the stairs and dragged Tatiana's unconscious body into the kitchen. I stood down the hallway, in the mudroom off the garage, watching the carnage.

"I come to you with my needs. I try to be open. I try to communicate. I do everything Dr. Davis said to do, and you laugh at me. Me! Let's see you laugh at this."

Igor turned on the gas burner and shoved Tatiana face first towards the hot element.

"I'll show you how to cook with the stove since all you know how to do is heat up that junk you shove in your arm."

Tatiana screamed and came out of her semi-conscious state. She bounced off the burner and came back at Igor like a feral cat. Her hands clawed at his face, and she screamed guttural obscenities at him. Igor screamed as her nails found his cheeks. He flailed at the girl, then shoved her back into the stove again. Tatiana showed she was as hard as the Soviet hammer on the old flag. She picked up a kettle off the stove top and swung it like a haymaker into the side of Igor's head. The impact of the stainless steel appliance opened the Russian's stitches and sent water onto the floor along with Igor's ass. He turned onto his stomach and tried to get up while Tatiana kicked him.

"No more! No more! I am tired of you whining because the whole world knows you are a pussy. And when you can't get anything done, you realize the world is right, so you come home and beat me. Well, no more. How do you like getting hit, you pussy? You faggot! You motherfucker!"

Igor covered up and staggered to his feet. He silenced Tatiana with a backhand — putting her down hard. He tried to kick her, but he slipped on the water from the kettle and went down beside her.

Tatiana was still yelling. "How many times did I have to make you pull the trigger? How many times did I have to hold your hand so you could do your job? You are not a man. You could not even kill a man chained to a hospital bed. If it weren't for me the police would have found you crying in those handcuffs. You are a fool, a coward, and I hate you."

"Shut up!" Igor screamed. He took two handfuls of Tatiana's hair and used her head to steady himself getting up. She screamed as her head took all of his weight. Igor spread his feet wide and pulled Tatiana up to the stove. He again put her face down on the burner. She screamed and bucked, but Igor never let her go.

"Say something now! Say something! I didn't need you for anything, you junkie whore."

Smoke came up from the burner, and the smell of burnt hair and flesh wafted down the hall. Igor kept holding the girl down even though she had gone into shock and stopped struggling. I didn't move from my spot in the mudroom. Tatiana said it herself; she had to push Igor to pull the trigger. She had to hold his hand. She helped create a monster, and now her creation was returning the favour. She was as ugly as Igor, and, like the rest of us, she deserved worse than she got.

Igor finally let the girl go, and she fell soundlessly to the floor. He picked up the kettle she hit him with and held it over his head with two hands. He let out a scream as he crashed down on Tatiana and beat her to death.

CHAPTER TWELVE

I had Igor cold. He had just murdered an accomplice to countless crimes in the middle of his kitchen. But how easily could Morrison connect Igor to the mob? He said himself that he had little on Igor. There were rumours about his being a drug dealer for the Russians, but no real paper trail existed. Igor wasn't going to be enough for Morrison, not like this. I needed more.

All I had to go on was the missing money. The money would lead me to someone bigger than Igor. When they dealt with him, I would have something to trade Morrison that would connect all of the pieces.

Igor sobbed, bent over the counter. He went on like that for five minutes. When he was finished, he dried his eyes on his sleeve and looked at Tatiana. "Stupid junkie," he said. "Look where your mouth got you."

He walked away from the body, sat at the kitchen table, dialled a number into his cell phone, and waited.

"I need to see you," he said after a minute. "I don't care if it's early, I need to see you."

Pause.

"No, you listen, pig. You're on my payroll. That means you work for me. Now get your fat ass out of bed and get over to my house. We have things to discuss."

Igor hung up the phone and walked away from the table. While he was in sight, I watched him peer over the counter at the body of Tatiana. He shook his head and then went up the stairs. A few minutes later, I heard the sound of running water. I stayed downstairs with Tatiana while Igor showered and cleaned up. I stayed out of the blood and the mess as I worked my way through each drawer in the kitchen. In the back of the drawer beside the fridge, I found instruction manuals and warranties for all of the major appliances. Underneath the manuals in their ripped plastic sheaths, I found a book. The spine was creased, and the pages were dog-eared and heavily highlighted. Igor had worn out his copy of *I'm Okay, You're Okay*. I read the back cover and realized that Igor believed that he had adopted a "position" about himself that determined how he felt about everything. His position was listed as "I'm not okay — you're okay." This kind of position was said, by the back of the book, to contaminate rational capabilities and leave people open to inappropriate emotional reactions. I wondered if trying to kill me in the hospital or killing a girlfriend was something Igor considered to be an inappropriate emotional reaction. The book must have been the gateway to the doctor Tatiana was screaming about. For me, the book was just another window into Igor's broken mind. I wiped the book with my sleeve, put it back, and went on to the next drawer. Inside, I found a spare set of house keys with the second set of dealer keys for the BMW. I pocketed both, went through the rest of the drawers, and got back to the mudroom before Igor came downstairs. He walked right through the mess to make himself breakfast. He was eating toast when there was a knock at the door. I heard Igor get up to open it. Someone was let in, and two men stood in the foyer talking.

"I don't like meeting you like this — it's dangerous."

"Shut up."

"Seriously, I'm not just talking about cops. Word is Sergei is looking for you."

"Where did you hear that?" Igor sounded panicked.

"Cops at the station heard it on the street. What the hell did you do?"

"There was a complication."

"Did that complication scratch up your face like that?"

"No, that was Tatiana."

"Hunh, I always knew that bitch liked it kinky."

"Not anymore."

Igor walked back into the kitchen, sat, and pulled his chair up to the table. There was a long pause while Igor's guest looked at the body. I moved my head out just enough to see what I already knew was there. The man had his ample back to me as he looked in front of the stove. The huge mass of cop was covered in the same worn shitty suit I had seen when I first opened my eyes in the hospital. Detective Miller was Igor's rat in the department.

"What the fuck happened? Did you do this?"

"She did it to herself."

"I can't be a part of this. You fucking murder a chick,

your chick, in your kitchen, then call me over. I'll go down as an accessory."

"You can go down as a crooked cop too. I have tapes and witnesses of you taking my money and getting me around police search and seizures. So you can maybe go down for her, or you can for sure go down because of me."

"Shit. Shit!" Miller said.

"We're both in the shit, but we can get out. I just need cash."

"How much?"

"A lot. I need a load of cash to pay Sergei for the loss and the embarrassment. It's money I do not have."

"So we're fucked."

"No, detective, I just need to know where there is a lot of money so that I can take it."

"You want me to help you steal money?"

"No wonder you are a detective. You are very smart. I wonder if you are smart enough to tell me who it was that was looking for me in my club tonight."

"How the fuck would I know?"

"It was a cop."

"Shit, it must have been Morrison. He came to me the other day and asked me about you. Well, he asked about a man named Igor; he didn't know any specifics, but I figured he meant you."

"And what did you tell him?"

"Nothing. I told him there were a lot of Igors. It's fucking true enough, your mothers weren't that creative back home. I said I'd look into it and get back to him."

"Why is he after me?" Igor asked.

"He wouldn't say."

"So how did he find me then?"

"Fucking guy is a police beast. He finds whatever he's looking for. What's fucked up is why he didn't talk to me about his lead on the strip club."

"Maybe you are not trusted," Igor said.

"Fuck that, Igor. Me and Morrison are tight. He eats at my house twice a week, for Christ's sake."

"Does he know about our deals?"

"Hell no!"

"Then you are not all that tight, *da*?"

"Don't give me that Russian shit. That accent doesn't fool me. You grew up here, Igor. You're about as Russian as that red fucking salad dressing. Let me deal with Morrison. I'll get him off your back while you get the money," Miller said.

"Where will I be getting my money?"

"If you need it fast, then we got to hit the chinks."

"I'm listening."

"I got word the other day that the Fat Cobra Society are moving a lot of product out of the Secret Garden downtown."

I knew the gang. The Fat Cobra Society had branched out from San Francisco in the seventies. It found Canadian homes in Vancouver and Toronto, and its tentacles had gripped Hamilton sometime in the last decade. The Fat Cobra Society wasn't a punk street gang. It was organized and hostile. It ran women, drugs, and black market goods to the Asian community, and business was good. Hamilton was home to a large Asian population, especially after Columbia University opened its doors in West Hamilton.

Columbia University was a boarding school for immigrant kids from all over the world who needed time to acclimatize to Canada before attending nearby McMaster University. Most of the students were Asian, and most of them got their illegal shit from someone with a familiar face.

"The police are watching the place?"

"No, I just found out from a CI. No one knows but me."

"Why haven't you told anyone?"

"I wanted to see how I could spin it. I like Chinese food, Chinese women, I figure I'll like their money too. But money's worth as much as rice if my ass is in jail. Word is the place is full of cash — full of it. Product and guns too. So you and your guys hit the Secret Garden tonight, take the slants by surprise, and you get your payday. With your crew, there will be enough manpower to get the job done fast and quiet."

"No crew, just us."

"Us? Fuck us. I can't have no part in this. This is your problem, your show. Why can't you use your guys?"

"If Sergei is after me, as you say, then they will be after me as well. They will be looking to kill me so that they can have my spot. It is common practice."

"I can't rob the triads outright. They'll kill me, if I don't get arrested first."

"I will do the robbing; you will just help me get inside by thinning the ranks. Don't worry, all will appear legal."

The two men spent an hour hashing out a plan to hit the Secret Garden. If they cared about the dead body lying in front of the stove, it never came up. I waited, listening, until Miller left and Igor went back upstairs. I slipped out back and got to the Volvo unseen. I left Igor at his house and drove back to the motel. On the way I thought about what Miller had said. Morrison left him in the dark about the reasons behind his search for Igor. That meant whatever bond they had was being stretched. He still hadn't found Igor, so he had no way of knowing how corrupt Miller was, but a few more days of off-the-clock hunting would be enough time for him to find Igor's house. Luckily for me, Igor didn't have a few days. I got back to the motel and dove straight onto the lumpy bed. I needed sleep if I was going to be having Chinese for dinner.

CHAPTER THIRTEEN

I slept for four hours, put on my clothes, and went for a late lunch at the Secret Garden. It was a hole-in-the-wall place on Main Street, just down from a few really good Chinese food restaurants. I walked the streets and noticed the same three faces outside the restaurant each time I was nearby. They never noticed me because on each pass I was farther and farther away. The first pass was in front of the building. The second, ten minutes later, was from across the street. The third pass was done in a cab. We rode by twice, the first time watching the men I saw, the second eyeing the area for what I would need.

The three Chinese men were in their forties with tall bushy hair and tight leather motorcycle jackets. Two of the men stood near the entrance of the restaurant — one in front of the door, the other fifteen metres away in the mouth of an alley. Both had black hair that they had let grow long in the back. They accentuated the mullet with wisps of hair combed over one of their eyes. The men were similar in height, weight, and style. The only difference was the tattoo that showed on the neck of the man in front of the alley. The third guard was on the opposite side of the building. His hair was bleached and sculpted high on his head. The hair was very white, and I saw no roots, meaning the job had been done recently. The heavy leather made it impossible to tell if the men were carrying — I figured it was a safe bet that they were.

"Never guess anything that will make your life easier. The world has a way of making sure things stay as shitty as possible, remember that." My uncle's voice was still as loud now as it was when he was alive.

The three men were a constant; customers were not. On every pass, I never saw anyone getting any food from the Secret Garden. There was an old woman behind the counter wearing an apron, but it was white — too white to belong to a cook. Miller's intel had been good. He knew about the three men out front, making me think what he had said about inside was probably true too.

On my fifth pass, again on foot, I walked inside the Secret Dragon. The old woman behind the counter looked at me, then into the back, then at me again.

"I help you?"

"An order of rice and sweet and sour chicken."

"We no have sweet and sour chicken."

"Just the rice then."

"No rice."

I blew out a bit of air and put my smile on. "Okay, just get me a plate of whatever you have."

"Food cost a lot of money."

"That's cool."

"Food take a lot of time."

"I'll wait."

The woman disappeared into the back and was gone for five minutes. I used the time, and the small spaces between the lettering on the window, to look out at the men out front. They were tense because of my arrival, but they never left their posts; they stayed on duty outside the restaurant. The woman came back with a small Styrofoam container that cost ten dollars. The container was cold to the touch, and when I opened it across the street, and around the corner, I saw that it was some kind of meat in brown sauce. They had added a live cockroach for flavour too. I chuckled at the move and left the container open on the concrete. Birds descended on the open container, eager for a free meal. They got close enough to the container to see what it was, then left it alone.

The front served expensive, shitty food with service that paralleled the worst orphanage cafeteria line. People got the message to stay away in rude stereo. Miller had explained that the men out front were the primary security force. The men inside were mostly money counters. There were only three other armed guards behind the counter. The men outside watched who came in and out; if you tried a stick-up, they would be behind you waiting in the streets. If you took a run at any of the three men out front first, the money would be run out back by one of the armed guards, and the other two gunmen would back up the men in the street. The Secret Garden was a good front with satisfactory protection and not a lot of overhead. The main deterrent was not the men but the triad's reputation.

Igor was going to take money from a well-sourced, dangerous group of people, and he had to do it without help too. His own crew would be as dangerous to him as the Fat Cobra Society, but worse than that, if someone figured out that Igor worked for Sergei, pride would dictate a gang war. Then it wouldn't matter if Igor got the money back. Sergei would kill him ten times over for stirring up the Asian hornet nest.

I waited around the corner for just the right kind of truck. There weren't many big stores downtown that operated outside Jackson Square Mall. Most of the shops were mom-and-pop run, and they got stock in via the family minivan every week or so. I had to wait the better part of an hour for a U-Haul, the largest the company supplied, to lumber down the street. Traffic was slower than usual because of the people driving back home to their apartments in the core or driving through to their nicer homes on the fringes of the city. I let the U-Haul pass me and jogged into the temporary cover it provided as it rolled down the street. The angle of my body behind the U-Haul made seeing me impossible for the three men in front of the Secret Garden. The truck hit each pothole with a thunderous explosion of metal on worn out shocks. People ignored the sound and looked at something other than the orange and white truck with the large squid painted on the side that showed off the majesty of the aquatic life of Newfoundland. All of the U-Haul trucks had been painted recently. They each had images on the sides of the cabs that represented the different wild animals of Canada. The pictures were hideous, and they kept even more eyes off the truck in the same way a large facial mole forces people to look but not look.

Three storefronts up from the Secret Garden, I hooked, unseen by the guards, into a vacant storefront. The dark doorway was sunk two metres in, and the glass door still advertised a foreclosed decorative bead store called Bead Craft and Beyond. The smaller print underneath told me that the store was once the city's jewellery and decoration headquarters. The previous owner left notices up in the window about how-to beading classes and custom work that could be done to clothing. The store was like most others in the city — alive for a minute, then gone. The storefront would flicker with life a few more times over the next couple of years, I expected, until it finally became something more palatable to the city. When the vacancy was replaced by a Tim Hortons or a dollar store, it would finally stay occupied longer than a couple of months.

The doorway went back enough to keep me out of sight while I waited for Igor to show up. On either side of me, display windows went out to the sidewalk. I was able to look through the panes of glass beside me to see the Secret Garden. Miller had told Igor that the money came every day around lunch. It was counted, bagged, and picked up by eight. There would be a lot of cash, according to Miller, because this was the only money-counting front the Fat Cobra Society had in the city. Igor planned to show up just before eight. That way, the money would be together and already set up to move.

I spent a few hours in the darkness until I saw Igor, duffel bag in hand, walk past the Secret Garden. The leather-clad security out front didn't look at him more than once as he passed. Igor, on the other hand, stared openly. He even stopped in front of the restaurant to look for the third guard, who was standing out of sight, on his own doorstep, just up the street. When Igor was done his shitty scope, he crossed the street and took a spot on a bench four storefronts away from where I stood. The vacant storefront was perfect camouflage — he never saw me. Igor pulled out his phone and dialled a number. He said a few words before closing the phone and putting it back into his pocket.

I watched Igor sit for ten minutes until a wave of red light stabbed into my hiding place. An unmarked police car rolled down the street behind a large SUV. The SUV pulled to the curb, and the cop car pulled in behind, right in front of the Secret Garden. A huge man rocked his way out of the driver's seat of the cop car. Sergeant Miller was doing a traffic stop downtown.

Igor waited for Miller to get to the window of the SUV before getting up off his bench and crossing the street towards the Secret Garden. The three men out front saw him cross with the bag and enter the restaurant, brushing the arm of the fat cop as he walked over the sidewalk. Each guard stayed where he was, staring at the police lights and the fat cop. I could see through the window of the Secret Garden enough to make out Igor holding a gun. The guard closest to the restaurant saw it too, because he pulled a phone from his pocket and spoke into it using a walkie-talkie function. I watched the other two guards use their phones in a similar fashion. A rapid discussion broke out in Chinese. I knew what was on their minds. To stop the robbery, they would have to pull guns and rush past a cop to get inside. The cop would try to stop them, and that would cause them to break one of the only rules criminals have — never shoot a cop. You break that rule, and the whole weight of the police force will roll over you. Cops hold the line between the shit and everybody else, but if you go and make it personal, you'll find out they play dirtier than anyone on the street. They'll fuck you and make sure you get charged for not saying thank you. Everyone knows this, and it froze the Chinese men out front.

Inside, Igor had pistol whipped the old woman in the clean apron. Miller stood outside, with his back to the restaurant, holding the SUV driver's ID. He was moving the licence back and forth as though he were trying to focus his eyes without his glasses. Miller's stall kept the men out front, but they weren't standing still. One was still on his phone as he slowly approached the other two men and the restaurant entrance. Miller saw the men coming and went so far as to put his back against the glass for support while he wrote the ticket.

Igor had worked fast. He had an arm around the woman's neck as he headed towards the back room, gun pointed forward. He was following the plan he and Miller had devised back at his house. Igor would use the woman as a human shield while he took the money. Once he had the money, he would force everyone out the back door. He would lock them outside and then bolt out the front while Miller covered him with his bullshit traffic stop. As I crossed the street, Igor got a shoe inside the back room. When my foot crossed the median, I put three bullets, in one second, into Miller's unmarked police car.

The heavy .45 spit the slugs 250 metres per second, and the bang chased after the lead, shrieking a warning to everyone around. The sound of metal repeatedly piercing metal was obscured by the gunshots from across the street. Everyone looked around for the source of the sounds except Miller and Igor. Miller dropped the ticket pad from his hands and took cover behind his car while Igor spun his human shield around to face the street. I put two more bullets into the unmarked car's tires before letting three more rounds chew holes into the Secret Garden's windows. Drivers ducked their heads below their dashboards and stomped on the gas. Cars crashed into one another, and traffic ground to a halt all around the restaurant. I used one car — its occupants screaming on the floor — to crouch behind as I reloaded. As I took cover I pulled a fresh magazine from my pocket. The spent clip slipped into my hand, and I slid its replacement home. I pushed the spent magazine into my pocket, racked the slide, and came out from behind the car. The four seconds I wasted reloading gave the leather-clad Chinese men time to cross the street towards me. A bullet starred the windshield of the car I was behind as I stood. Another bullet, from a second shooter close to the first, shattered a window across the street behind me. I went to one knee and took a two-handed grip. Another bullet whizzed over my head and found the hood of a nearby car.

The man in front of me was trying to pick me off without getting any closer. He was probably used to shooting at new-to-the-life kids or ambitious junkies taking a shot at a refund. He expected me to run away from the bullets and straight into one of his partners. He had no way of knowing that this wasn't my first rodeo. I came up fast, sighted the man, and pulled the trigger once, then twice. Two heavy slugs punched him off his feet. The first hit centre mass, the second impacted high in the chest near the collar bone. As he fell, a mist of blood and bone fragments stained a white car behind him.

I turned and moved along the car, looking for the other guard who had taken a shot at me. Through the rear windshield I saw the man with the neck tattoo approaching. He held his gun in two shaky hands as he wove through the petrified gridlock. Terrified heads lifted enough to see the man moving, gun in hand, and then disappeared back below the windows. The guard was staying low and waving his gun with stiff movements in front, behind, and under each car he approached. I watched him advance on a small hybrid and waited for him to check the space in front of the bumper when gunfire got my attention. Thinking it was the third guard, I ducked back behind the car, but the shots weren't at me — a firefight had broken out in the Secret Garden. Flashes could be seen from behind what was left of the starred and broken glass. Some of the shots came from an automatic, making me think that in the confusion Igor lost control of the situation and the men in back had enough time to get to a weapon. Within seconds of another burst of automatic chatter, Igor came running out of the Secret Garden — without his bag. His grey shirt was bloody, but he still managed a speedy getaway down the street. The guard near the hybrid saw Igor running away in his bloody shirt and turned his stiff-armed stance away from my direction towards Igor's back. I rose off my knee, aiming just above the tattoo, and put a bullet into the side of his head before he could pull the trigger. The top of the man's head came off, his scalp parting like leaves of cabbage.

Igor ignored the shot and kept on running. He turned down the first side street he saw and vanished from sight. I turned back to the store front and saw Miller on his feet, police pistol in hand. His feet were spread wide, and one eye was closed. I dove left as the muzzle flash erupted. Behind the car, I felt my chest for any wet spots, but I found none. I shuffled back and tried the door handle to the car I used for cover. The handle moved, but the door stayed closed. I swung the heavy barrel of the Colt into the window and was showered by pellets of glass.

"I'll get out. I'll get out. Don't shoot!" the man inside the car shouted.

I ignored his screams and came off the concrete enough to put my elbow on the glassless window ledge. The small white-haired man inside tried to slip out, but my left hand found his throat, and I held him up. The man gagged and went stiff; his pants became wet as he pissed himself. Over the shoulder of the human shield, and through the windshield, I saw Miller approaching with the same two-handed police combat stance. Miller hadn't seen me behind the man in the car. I aimed wide and let three bullets go. The gunshots rang inside the car and etched a network of spider webs into the windshield. I let the white-haired man go, and he put his hands over his ears, sobbing wordlessly with pain and fear. When I came up from behind the car, Miller was out of his combat stance. He was hauling his fat ass back to his squad car and his radio.

I kept my head down and ran down the street. I made the first left and opened the door to the Volvo. I had left the car under the cover of a low-hanging tree. The branches covered the car like probing fingers, making it hard to see from more than three metres away. I reloaded the gun using bullets I had packed in the glove box — and kept my eye on the corner for Miller. I saw something else entirely. The third Chinese lookout, the blond, rounded the corner in his tight leather jacket. In his hand he held a black pistol.

Only two of the guards had made an appearance in the gunfight. That meant the third man ran either for cover or for a phone. The fact that he was here looking for me meant that he must have gone for the phone. A coward wouldn't follow someone who had put two of his associates down; he'd stay put and cook up a story. The blond man didn't let emotion or pride colour his actions. He let his friends get carved up in the street while he protected the front. He did what he was trained to do, and now he was making up for lost time. The blond was a pro who kept his head in a fight. That kind of man would get the make and plate of a car that sped away. I had to get out of the area before Miller's backup showed up and the whole neighbourhood was locked down. I also had to keep anyone else from putting me on their shit list. That meant the last sentry had to go.

I reached up, turned off the overhead light, then eased the door open. The blond guard had started down the middle of the street, gun in hand. He checked each car with a cautious lean from a safe distance. He never totally turned his back on anything he hadn't already checked. This guy was by the numbers and dangerous. I opened the car door wide and stepped behind the tree trunk.

The blond saw the door ten seconds later and slowly approached. I took the gun by the barrel and got ready to slip out from behind the tree. Too many gunshots had rung out; more from this direction would make it harder to slip away in the commotion and confusion. When the trigger-man bent to look under the branches and into the car, I rolled out from behind the tree and closed the distance between us. The blond saw me coming at the last second. His gun was useless pointed inside the car, so he bent his head forward and turtled, trying to take the impact and stay conscious. The butt of the .45 glanced off the back of the Chinese man's head with enough force to send him to his knees. I pivoted and swung the gun down on his wrist, sending his pistol into the darkness of the Volvo. My elbow drove back towards his face, but a kick met me halfway. The kick connected with my knee and hyper-extended the joint. I staggered back, using the car to stay up before awkwardly lunging back in. The blond was off his feet coming to meet me.

Part of me expected kung fu. What I got was a boxer's stance and a haymaker starting somewhere near the blond's back pocket. I shuffled forward and erased the gap between us, making the haymaker ineffective. My hands took fist-fuls of shirt and pulled him towards me. His hands were still set up for the haymaker when my forehead connected with the bridge of his nose. He grunted, and readjusted, sending an uppercut between my hands on his shirt. The punch grazed my chin, and my teeth cracked together. I was dazed, but I stayed in tight. Boxers need a certain distance to remain effective. Eliminate the distance and the referee separates you. When there's no ref, the boxer is left somewhere unfamiliar. I introduced the blond to the new place by pulling down on his shirt with my left hand. His head came forward into my right fist. My knuckles compressed the soft cartilage of his throat, creating a gag and then no sound at all. The blow interrupted the flow of air and startled the blond. The effect was visible from head to toe. He was no longer fighting me; his body was instead fighting for air. My left hand pulled him in again, but my right hand stayed away. My head collided with his nose again, and it flattened like a balloon deflating. His body bounced off mine, but my left arm reeled him back in. My elbow came across my body and caught the gasping face in the jaw. I didn't let his body fall, I shoved him into the car and got in behind him.

I drove out of the neighbourhood in the opposite direction of the commotion. Miller's call had gotten out fast, and the response was even faster. Ahead of me, I could see flashing lights; seconds later, I heard the sirens of the approaching police cars. I let my right foot sink to the floorboards and felt the Volvo purr in response as though the engine were thanking me for the chance to run head first at the police cars. The odometer hit seventy as I leaned across the seat and pushed the passenger door open. The emergency brake flatlined the odometer and sent the car into a long skid. I turned the wheel and released the brake, pulling out of the controlled 180. The blond's body hit the pavement and rolled. Each limb flailed out straight like spokes on a tire as the body tore down the street at ten over the speed limit. Eventually, the broken limbs made slow, fluid, limp arcs as the body careened to a stop on the asphalt.

The lights, now behind me, had a speed bump to deal with, and the cops inside had protocol to follow. Procedure dictated that they had to stop and help the body in the street before they followed in pursuit. The Volvo was already purring again as I made use of the diversion and wound around a corner to a side street. Two turns later, the sound of police sirens was barely audible as I drove away from the crime scene. I slowed the car down and became just another downtown car on its way out of the core.

CHAPTER FOURTEEN

I drove out to Igor's house but found the driveway empty. I parked the car and moved around the back of the house. All of the lights were off inside. Through the window, by the dim light given off by the digital displays on all of the appliances, I could see the burned and beaten dead body of Tatiana still on the floor.

Igor had a head start and nothing else to lose. Holding up the Secret Garden had been his fourth-quarter Hail Mary. The plan failed, and now there was no way he could recoup what he had lost. I needed to catch up with him before he went to see his boss. If he got there ahead of me, he would disappear without a trace, and so would my chances of keeping my face out of the news. I didn't know where Sergei Vidal operated, and I couldn't ask Morrison. After he heard about Miller getting shot at, his conscience would force him to come after me. Morrison was the type to bend the rules to get the job done, but no cop would let a murder attempt on one of their own go. I had to find Igor on my own.

I left the house and drove to my only other lead, the Steel City Lounge. I drove by the entrance and saw Igor's car double-parked out front. The car was empty, and the engine was still ticking. I did a drive around the neighbourhood to make sure Morrison wasn't still hanging around the club. His car was nowhere to be seen. I figured everyone played dumb when he first came to the club and he struck out. He wouldn't have wasted more time on a dead-end lead, he'd have decided to go after Igor another way.

I parked on a side street and waited under a burnt-out streetlight for the right moment to move. At 12:15 a.m., the street was bare. If Igor was watching his back, he'd see me coming. After twenty minutes, my patience was rewarded. A Hummer limousine pulled up out front and belched out a rowdy bachelor party. The groom had a jail-striped shirt on and a foam ball and chain around his ankle. The group chanted "Whores!" as they walked into the club. All of them were too drunk to notice that their party picked up one more member at the door. I broke from the party inside, took a corner table near the bar, and scanned the room for Igor. He wasn't hard to find.

The Russian was on stage screaming at one of the girls. The music still pumped as Igor's words put a look of terror onto the girl's face. Spit left his mouth as he screamed; it arced high in the stage lights before nose diving into the topless dancer's hair. The floor staff, each wearing a T-shirt with SECURITY printed on the back, all turned their backs to the stage. Igor ran the club, and they knew better than to try to control him; they focused their attention on the audience. The crowd, drunk and horny, did not know how to deal with the spectacle. Many turned their attention to another dancer or their drinks; others got excited. There was part of the crowd that liked watching the intimidation and humiliation of the girl on stage, and there was a murmur of appreciation from the men still watching. The groom from the bachelor party screamed, "Hell, yeah!"

He broke free from the party he was with and approached the stage.

"You tell that bitch, man."

Igor took a fistful of hair and pushed the stripper to her knees. He pointed to the pole she had used and screamed more words in her face. Igor backhanded the girl onto her ass, and the groom jumped. Both his hands were in the air, and he cheered loudly. I heard his hoot, over the bass, from my table. He clumsily pulled out a camera phone and held it high in the air as Igor slapped the girl again.

Igor's body blocked the groom's shot, so the fake jailbird drunkenly climbed onto the stage for a better angle. He stumbled around Igor and forced the camera towards the girl's tear-stained face. Igor was surprised by the camera and even more by the presence of the man in the jail stripes on the stage with him.

The groom slapped Igor's back and nodded to him. Igor looked around the club, squinting to see beyond the stage lights. More people had looked away, trying to pretend the degradation on stage wasn't happening. The bachelor party at the bar was still all eyes, watching their captain. Igor slapped the camera away and sucker-punched the groom. His drunk body went down all at once, and Igor was on him. Igor mounted the groom's body and began pounding down onto his face. His fist jackhammered into flesh. At first, he just broke skin and bruised flesh, but each successive punch did more and more damage. Blood began to spurt into the brightly lit air on the stage. More and more of the fluid shot into the air like liquid rubies. As the groom's face gave way to becoming pulp, teeth skittered away from the limp body.

The bachelor party rushed past the floor security and hit the stage after the twenty-seventh punch. The groom was convulsing when a member of the bachelor party finally tackled Igor. A crowd formed around Igor on stage as everyone tried to get a shot in, but the VIP section upstairs was on stage before Igor got hurt. A brawl broke out between Igor's men and the bachelor party. The twenty-something kids were all completely shit-faced, unlike Igor's men, who were hardened toughs. Igor's men had been drinking all night, but alcohol was an everyday thing to these men. The booze only dulled them enough to silence any morality that might try to speak up. They weren't drunk; they were ice-cold numb.

The bachelor party was thrown off the stage one by one until none was left but the groom. Igor spat on the still shaking body and walked upstairs to the VIP lounge with his crew. The audience that had been ignoring Igor's abuse of the stripper had taken notice of the fight and cleared their chairs. Everyone was on their feet trying to stay clear of the men being thrown from the stage — no one wanted to be mistaken for a member of the bachelor party. The floor security did double duty holding the crowd back and dragging the bodies of the bachelor party out the door one by one. There were murmurs and scared looks from the faces in the crowd until a new dancer hit the stage. It was amazing how fast a new gyrating naked woman on stage lured the crowd back to their seats.

Upstairs, the lounge was comprised of black leather, chrome tables, and neon lighting. Igor and his men sat on the shiny leather couches watching the action below. The lights made their angry faces demonic and made the roped-off area look like a modern circle of Dante's *Inferno*. The hours that followed were full of binge drinking and sexual assault. Women went up the stairs with trays of drinks and ran back down with torn clothing. Igor screamed and yelled at the stage, and more than once he came close to falling over the railing to the floor below.

Igor left at three, opting to drive himself home. I followed him out and stood ten feet away while he tried repeatedly to open his door. Igor had lost everything: his girl, his money, his job, all of it was gone. What he hadn't lost yet was his usefulness. Igor could still get me off the hook with Morrison. He'd lost Sergei Vidal's money; Sergei would not let that slide. The day's grace Igor said he needed was three hours over. Igor was late, and now Sergei would come collecting. I had worked for a mob boss for a long time. Money drives every action, and pride keeps everything in line. Igor had fucked with both. It would be time to pay up very soon.

Igor got home in one piece. His tires dragged against the curb more than ten times, and he dinged the side mirrors of a whole row of cars on a side street, but he survived the trip. He parked diagonally in the driveway and walked towards the house, making only two detours into the flowerbeds before he managed to get to the door. Covered in dirt, Igor managed to fall into the open doorway.

I parked across the street and watched the house. No lights came on, and no curtains moved. I gave Igor five minutes before I opened the trunk and pulled out the cash I stole off him the night before.

I lugged the bag across the street and let it rest beside the front door. I unholstered the .45 and took out the house keys I'd stolen from the kitchen drawer earlier. I used my left hand to quietly ease the key into the lock. I turned the key to the right, but the mechanism offered no resistance — Igor had left the door unlocked. I crept inside, letting the black eye of the .45 lead the way. Tatiana was still in the kitchen, and Igor was nowhere in sight. I covered the first floor and then moved up the stairs. The second step responded to my weight with a groan, so I put my next step closer to the wall. The wood was more stable there. Halfway up, I saw a black shoe dangling over the edge. At the top of the stairs, I saw that Igor had done my work for me; he was sprawled out on his stomach — unconscious. His chest rose and fell at a regular rate, and his mouth pushed out puffs of air in measured gusts. Igor was alive, for now.

I went back down the stairs, opened the door, and pulled the duffel bag inside. I put the bag on the welcome mat and quietly unzipped the double zipper. I took eight of the paper-bound bundles of cash and walked into the kitchen. I ripped the bands and spread the money over the kitchen table, the counters, the floor, and Tatiana's body. The bills landed on her blistered face and lay on top of the crusted blood. I took the rest of the money into the basement and used an old chair to stand on while I pushed free some of the ceiling tiles. When there was enough space, I put the bag up in the ceiling. The weight of the bag pushed some of the other tiles out of place and made an obvious lump in the ceiling. I left the chair in place below the money and walked back upstairs. Igor never stirred when I opened the door — he was dead to the world, just the way the rest of the planet wanted him.

I slid back behind the wheel of the car and got comfortable. Igor had been drugged and then had gone on his own bender — he would sleep for a while. I dry chewed more caffeine pills and chased them with warm soda while I watched the house. My plan would only work if the Russians responded in the same way every other gangster I'd worked with would have.

At 9:30 a.m., a black Hummer pulled to the curb in front of Igor's house. The windows were too tinted for me to see inside, but I knew whoever was inside worked for Sergei Vidal. I memorized the plate while I waited for something to happen. Both the driver and passenger side doors opened, and I saw that I was right. Nikolai and Pietro, Nick and Pete, Sergei's personal security, got out. They looked around the neighbourhood before taking a step away from the cover of the vehicle. They were not anywhere as big as the man they had replaced. Ivan had been six and a half feet tall and at least 300 pounds of beef. These men were unlike Ivan; they were compact — five-ten, maybe 200 pounds. They had bodies built in the military. Running with heavy packs and relentless days of body weight exercises had left the men with hard, wiry physiques. They would be fast, tough, and relentless — like wolves. Wolves weren't large, that would conflict with their purpose. Wolves hunted prey almost twice their size, and they always came home with dinner. They ran their prey down in relentless pursuit, then hit them where they were weak. These two men had the same feral look I saw every time I looked in the mirror.

The military campaigns in Afghanistan would be a problem. You shoot at some corner thug, he runs. Maybe he shoots back at you over his shoulder as he goes. Army is different. Combat veterans don't lose their heads, and they don't run unless there is a tactical reason for it. They will take cover and shoot back, and not over their shoulders. Most of the veterans who took a job in the streets were adrenaline junkies who got spoiled in the service. Pulling the trigger for a paycheque was a high they couldn't shake, and normal life didn't have an equivalent.

The blond, Nick, unholstered a gun and held it against his thigh between the Hummer and his leg, while Pete walked to the door. The light reflected off Pete's scalp as he crossed the driveway. His hair was shaved so short that it was hard to tell what colour it was without squinting. He kept a hand behind his back while he peeked in the darkened windows. He finally tried the doorknob, and when it worked he motioned Nick over with a single hand gesture. Nick hid the gun inside his leather coat and walked up the driveway. On the porch both men looked around one more time before drawing their guns and nodding their heads.

The two men entered the house in a professional two-man formation keeping their shit tight. Their guns went up in two-handed grips, and Pete went in straight. Nick followed, covering Pete before angling off to check the front room. I saw Nick cross the doorway, and then the door closed. I pulled the Colt from my shoulder holster and put it in my lap. Igor had never noticed me parked across the street, but he sucked. Nick and Pete might have caught sight of me from the tinted Hummer. They could have decided to scout me out from the house and use the back door to come at me from a spot I wasn't watching. I rolled down the window and slouched in the seat, making as small a target as possible. No bullets came. Instead, Nick and Pete came out the front door with Igor. Both had a hand on a shoulder, and Igor's face was bloody — Nick and Pete had asked some questions with their hands. Igor didn't struggle, he just got into the back seat with Pete. Nick threw a grocery bag into the front seat and got in. I figured the bag had some of the money I'd spread around the kitchen.

The Hummer slipped away from the curb and headed into the city. I gave the boxy vehicle a head start, but I kept it in sight as I followed behind.

Morrison's CIs had done their job. Sergei Vidal heard through his twisted grapevine that Igor was stealing, and the proof came when he was late with the money. Sergei had sent his two best to pick up Igor — that meant Sergei was focused. I had come across Sergei's focus once before in an office building belonging to a bunch of computer programmers. In broad daylight, in a crowded neighbourhood, Sergei sent a crew to execute more than ten men and women. He sent his right hand after the most important man in the office. Everything would have gone down according to plan if I hadn't gotten there first. I put a bullet in Sergei's right-hand man, three more a day later. I didn't deal with the rest of Sergei, and now he was back with two new right hands.

They worked fast and by the numbers. There was no sloppiness or rust on Nick or Pete. Whatever Russian military outfit they bounced out of left them with good habits. Good habits made moving on Sergei tough — not impossible, just tough.

We drove down Main Street until it turned into King. We kept on King going out of Hamilton into Stoney Creek. Stoney Creek was famous for ice cream from the Stoney Creek Dairy and for a battlefield where some soldiers mixed it up during the War of 1812. Around these sights, a town for the upper middle class sprang up. The town was an appendage of Hamilton. If Hamilton was a diseased body, Stoney Creek was the manicured hand.

The Hummer stayed on King until it pulled across traffic to the curb in front of an off-track betting building. I kept my distance, double-parking a couple hundred metres down the street. It was just later than a quarter after ten, and the Jackpot OTB looked closed; its patio was empty, and the white plastic outdoor chairs were still up on the tables. Nick and Pete got out of the Hummer, bringing the money and Igor with them. Nick and Pete stopped at the door. Both men scanned the street with their arms just inside their jackets. Satisfied with what they saw, Nick pulled the door open and ushered Igor inside. I drove past the OTB, circled back, and parked across the street.

Inside the OTB would be at least five people plus Igor. Nick and Pete I saw, but Sergei would have two others at least. They weren't going to kill Igor right away; if they wanted him dead, it would have happened at his house. They brought him back because they were told to do so. When Sergei saw the money, he would send men back to find the rest. They would tear the house apart until they found what I left in the ceiling. Once the money was recovered, Sergei would have Igor killed and disposed of. It would always be money first, blood second.

I pulled out my cell phone and dialled a number I knew never changed. When I finished my call, I called another number I heard on the radio the day before. I was dialling a number I could see on a sign a block down the road when two different men left the OTB. I spoke into the phone as I watched them get into a Cadillac sedan and drive away. The two men were in suits. The jackets looked to be a size bigger than the pants, probably to conceal the weapons underneath. Muscle often never thought about tailoring a coat to conceal a gun the way I had done — they just wore bigger clothes. The two men were not like Nick and Pete. Their bodies weren't the same; these men had the bodies of bruisers. Each had to be 250 pounds of muscle. The Cadillac seemed to wince as they got inside and began adjusting the mirrors and seats. Both men were bald by choice; they had shaven their heads completely, leaving nothing but razor burn and glare. Most would think that the two huge men were Sergei's security, but I knew better. The two bruisers were like guard dogs — big and scary animals who kept most people away. Nick and Pete, the real killers, looked nothing like those men, but that was the point. They were sleek like matadors — they let you get in close before they drove the sword home.

I finished my call, then dialled Detective Sergeant Huata Morrison's private number, the one left on the back of his card. He picked up right away but said nothing. I listened to the silence and matched his with my own.

"What do you want?" he asked.

I let a bit more of the silence run down his battery before answering. "It's time to move."

"No."

"No?"

"We're done," he said. "You went too far, and now we're done."

"What happened?" I asked, knowing the response.

"What happened? What happened is you took a shot at a cop, that's what happened."

"What are you talking about?" I lied.

"Enough! You thought you could play me with all of your lies, and I'm telling you it's done. You're done."

"What cop got shot at?"

Silence answered me.

"Morrison, I can prove to you I didn't do it — just tell me what cop it was."

"Miller," he said. It sounded like it came out through clenched teeth.

"When?"

"Last night." I heard teeth grinding in my ear.

"Where?"

"Outside some restaurant downtown, the Secret Garden. Like the fucking Springsteen song."

"And why do you think it was me?"

"You got a hard on for Miller, and we both know it. You asked about him too many times for you not to be involved."

"You know what the Secret Garden is?" I asked.

"A shit restaurant and a bad fucking song."

"It's a front for the Fat Cobra Society. Their drug money goes through it."

I got no answer.

"Why was Miller there?"

Still no answer, so I repeated the question.

"Traffic stop," Morrison said.

"That normal for the Lieutenant? Pulling traffic stops? Or did he just feel like going above and beyond the job yesterday because that is the kind of outstanding cop he is? He can't let even the smallest infractions to the law go? Was this upholding of the law a day or night event?"

"Night."

"Miller work nights in the city a lot?"

Silence answered me.

"So you got Miller doing a traffic stop at night, in the city, outside a Chinese drug front, and you think I shot at him? You think I'm dumb enough to make enemies of the Chinese *and* the cops? You're a fucking detective, look at the facts and detect something from them. 'Cause if it looks like fire and smells like fire, it's probably a fat crooked cop."

"Why did you call?" Morrison asked.

"We made a deal. I'm giving you something, but you'll need to do some detecting. Can you handle that, Columbo?"

"Tell me."

"I told you about a name — Igor."

"I remember."

"You need to get to his place right now. It's right by…"

"Bayfront Park," he said, finishing my sentence. "I'll know the place because there will be a yellow car parked out front."

Morrison was even faster than I had thought he was. He was stalking me using the one clue I let slip, and he was now just a step behind. If I had taken any longer, he would have found me staking out Igor's house. Then the game would have changed to something bloodier. "You've been there?" I asked, knowing he hadn't.

"I just found out about his house last night. I planned to go there today."

"You need to get there now. Inside you'll find two men, drug money, and a body. If you put your thinking cap on, Holmes, you might get a good lead out of the two men." I hung up the phone and looked at the man approaching the OTB with his arms full. The pizza I had ordered was right on time.

CHAPTER FIFTEEN

The Pizza Pizza delivery guy showed up eighteen minutes after I called with three sets of twins and an order of wings. Sergei was on the hook for $78.34. It took two minutes for the body of the delivery guy to come bouncing out the door. Nick had thrown him out with one hand; the other held a slice of pizza.

Pete threw the full boxes of pizza and wings at the delivery guy and walked back inside with Nick. The pizza guy picked himself up, flipped off the window, and walked away from the mess on the sidewalk. He made it three steps away before Nick was outside again. He screamed at the delivery guy and started towards him. The pizza guy put two hands up in appeasement and walked back with his head low to clean up the mess. He worked fast under the watchful eye and foot of Nick.

The mess was gone, and Nick was back inside when Pizza Hut arrived with ten medium pizzas. Sergei owed $124.18 to the Hut and its teenaged, acne-scarred, red-hat collection agency. The kid didn't even get in the door. Nick and Pete opened the frosted glass door before he could put down the pizza and open it himself. The door came at the kid fast, and it knocked him on his ass and sent pizza everywhere.

I had the window down just enough to hear the commotion.

"Who sent you here?" Nick demanded. He had an accent that was unmistakably Russian. "Who?"

The kid crab-walked back from the door and the blond man, scrambling to get to his feet. Pete passed Nick and planted his right foot on the kid's chest. The kid fought against the foot, but Pete just put more weight on him. The kid gave up and fell to the pavement, cracking his head.

Nick picked up each box and lifted the flap. When all he found was pizza, a rain of bread, cheese, and sauce fell on the kid. This happened nine times. Nick pulled a slice from the last box and let the cardboard fall to the ground. He told the kid to clean his shit up, and the kid nodded as best he could while still cradling the back of his head. The crack against the pavement had cut deep, and blood seeped through his hair and fingers. Nick and Pete went back inside, leaving the kid to clean up the mess one-handed. When he left, his hands and shirt were red from the sauce and the blood. I could see his confusion as he looked from hand to shirt trying to figure out how much blood he had lost. He stumbled away never knowing what was his and what belonged to Pizza Hut or why he had to give up either to the pavement.

By the dashboard clock, it was eight minutes until Domino's showed up. This time it wasn't an acne-speckled kid, it was a middle-aged man with a thick moustache. He wore a light blue golf shirt adorned with black-and-white checkerboard sleeves, navy shorts that gave everyone a view of his inner thigh hair, and old Velcro-strap running shoes. The untrimmed moustache, the clothes, the shitty job all led me to believe that this was a guy who was a joke to everyone he met. He wasn't in on the joke, and he never would be. Worse, he was in front of a door that led to two men with zero sense of humour.

Fortune smiled on the man with the moustache. Nick and Pete met him at the door and told him "No" too many times to count. The delivery guy pointed to his receipt, proving that he was in the right, but Nick and Pete didn't move. They shook their heads until Nick exploded in moustache's face. He screamed, "No, not ours! Now get the fuck out of here!"

The delivery guy saw the Russian was serious and backed away. Nick and Pete didn't watch him go like they did with the others, they just turned their backs and went inside.

I got out of the car and caught up to the Domino's guy on the street. The thirty bucks in my fist would cover the $24.18 bill with enough for a good tip.

"Hey! Hey, Domino's!"

He turned to face me, and I put on what I guessed to be my best apologetic face.

"I'm sorry about the boys. We bring a lot of cash in in the mornings, and they get too protective sometimes."

"They didn't have to yell. I don't appreciate being yelled at. I wanted to work things out, but they wouldn't let me speak. That's not how you treat a delivery guy. I just go where they tell me. When people don't pay, I gotta prove it was a crank call, or my boss will think I screwed up. Then I gotta eat the cost myself."

"Let me make it up to you," I said, showing him the money. "I'll take the pizza. How much is it?"

Domino's looked around. "We're not really supposed to do it this way. Store policy is very clear. I'm not supposed to sell the pizza on the street. Business should only be transacted at the customer's place of work or business."

"We can go back to the store if you want. I'm sure the boys will be nicer this time."

He thought about it for a second. "No, no, no. I'm just saying for next time. Next time you should pay at the door. It'll be twenty-four eighteen."

I gave him the thirty dollars and told him to keep the change. I waved him goodbye and watched him get into his Ford Taurus. When he was out of sight, I put two of the boxes down and pulled the .45 from my jacket. I zipped up the coat so my shoulder rig was invisible and put one of the pizza boxes over the gun. The Colt was in my hand, under the flat bottom of the box, invisible from view so long as I kept the box tilted forward.

I left the other two boxes on the ground and walked, bill in hand, towards the OTB. I didn't just walk straight up to the front door — that had gone badly for the three other delivery men. Nick and Pete saw them coming and never let them get inside. I waited for a few minutes, three stores down, until a city bus came down the street. Traffic was slow enough that the bus crept along the street in the right lane. When the light turned red, the bus blocked the OTB's view from at least half of its windows. I walked into traffic along the side of the bus facing away from the storefront and hooked around the back bumper jogging as though I was trying to cross the street before the light turned. I rounded the front of the bus and jogged straight in the front entrance.

I got five steps inside before Nick and Pete blocked my way. The OTB had an area with several windows for business as well as a bar surrounded by tables underneath huge mounted flat-screen televisions. This wasn't a walk in, walk out, kind of place; it was a gambler's paradise.

"No, no, no, no. No pizza. We order nothing. Leave now!" Nick yelled. Pete said nothing.

"Whoa, whoa, guys. Let's look at the order," I said, pulling out the Domino's bill. "One medium pizza for Igor."

"No pizza. No!" Nick screamed. His breath was warm in my face.

"Igor?" Pete asked. I marked him as the smart one, Nick as the violent one. Nick looked at him, confused, then looked back at me after he figured it out. "Did you say Igor?"

I checked the bill and nodded at Pete.

"Who told you that name?"

"No one told me anything—it's on the bill along with the cost. You owe me thirteen forty-nine."

Nick closed the distance between us, taking over the conversation again, ready for violence. "You will tell me who told you that name." He slapped the pizza box, trying to knock it out of my hands, but it didn't fall. He grabbed the box and tried to wrestle it away from me, but it stayed in my hands. We locked eyes for a second as he groped for the pizza and I grinned; Nick didn't understand. He got it a second later when the .45 took his knee off his leg.

The big slug scrambled patella and cartilage and sent Nick to the floor. His scream was silent at first, but he found his voice fast. I turned on Pete, but he was already running towards the bar. Pete didn't waste any emotion on his partner. He was surviving, just like he had been trained to do.

The .45 spat loud, obscene shots at him, but they all came up wide. Each spasm of the gun was just a little off. Pete jerked up, down, left, right, making him a hard target. He threw himself over the bar, and I moved in his wake. I heard the metallic crunch of a shotgun loading. Pete came up with the shotgun levelled at his shoulder ready to shoot through whatever cover I took, but I wasn't where he thought I was. I was like him — a survivor. I had been shot at before, and it didn't spook me anymore. It scared me as much as it always did, but I stored the fear away while I worked. The .45 was in my hands, three metres away from where I had been standing when Pete went for cover. Pete caught sight of me, out of the corner of his eye, and realized that he had misjudged where I would be. He turned at the hips to correct his aim as I pulled the trigger. The first bullet hit Pete in the left shoulder, spinning him and the shotgun away from me. The second shot punched a dark hole into his back. Red hit the bottles behind the bar as the lead ripped through the wiry flesh. Pete went down behind the bar, and I heard the shotgun hit the floor, I heard it for a second, then a bullet ripped through my right ear.

I dove left and hit the floor hard. The wind went out of me as I hit the floor rolling. A second bullet whizzed over my head from Nick's direction. Pete had moved so fast that I never got the chance to put Nick all the way out. I crawled behind the bar and saw Pete's prone body. He had managed to roll himself over. His hands covered the hole in his shoulder and the exit wound on the front of his body. I crouch-walked closer and pulled a pistol from his belt — a 9mm Heckler and Koch USP. I put the gun in my coat pocket and kept moving.

"He is hard to kill," Pete said to me, nodding over the bar towards Nick.

"Aren't we all."

I grabbed one of the bottles that hit the floor when I shot Pete and lobbed it over the bar. It landed with a crash. I lobbed a second and a third. With the third bottle came a grunt — I knew where Nick was. I picked up the twelve-gauge Mossberg and put my back against the wall. I put five more bottles in the air; each landed with a crash near the spot that produced the grunt. As the fifth bottle left my hand, I stood with the Mossberg and pulled the trigger. I racked the slide and shot again as I stepped away from the bar. The bottles I had thrown landed near the dining area where Nick had taken cover. The shotgun was aimed low, and it caught the edge of a table and the back of a chair as it let loose. None of the spray from the shotgun caught Nick; he had sensed what was coming after the bottles and had managed to drag his mangled leg across the floor. The barrel of the Mossberg followed the trail of blood on the floor towards the booths on the wall where Nick had taken cover from the bottles. Nick had burrowed in like a tick behind the vinyl in a spot that might have offered him a chance at surprising me if there wasn't a crimson trail ratting him out. I racked the slide again and shot at the furniture hiding Nick from me. The twelve gauge punched a hole through the back of the booth and toppled the table.

"Okay, okay," Nick screamed.

I put another shot in Nick's direction.

"Stop!"

Two hands came up from behind the aerated seat, empty. I walked towards Nick and saw a matching H and K pistol two feet away from his body. His face was pale under his sweaty blond mop.

"Put your hands on your leg before you bleed out," I said.

Nick nodded and sat up. He groaned with the effort and screamed when he put his hands to his leg. His eyes were looking glassy, and I figured shock was setting in. He didn't even flinch when I put the butt of the shotgun between his eyes.

The OTB was suddenly quiet. I looked at my jacket and saw blood soaked into the sleeve. I took a handful of napkins from a dispenser on one of the tables still upright and put them to my ear. The sting took me by surprise, and I closed my eyes for a second. My ear didn't feel right under the napkins — the lobe hung too low. The napkins came away red and damp, so I pressed them harder to the side of my head again. I managed to pack the tissue paper around my ear, using the blood to hold the thin white material to my head. The rest of the napkins were used to wipe down my coat. The waterproof material kept the blood from absorbing, and the napkins soaked up the beaded fluid and became heavy. I put the napkins in my pocket and took the shotgun down a single hallway leading away from the betting windows and bar. At the end of the hallway was a small backroom with an office and an emergency exit. The exit had a sticker on the door explaining that if opened the mechanism would set off an alarm. The deafening silence told me that no one had used the door.

The office door was closed, and when I tried the lock I found the handle didn't move. I crossed to the other side of the door, closer to the exit, and knocked. No one answered.

"Nikolai and Pietro are down and bleeding to death as I speak."

"I care not," a voice I remembered as belonging to Sergei Vidal said.

"See if this makes you care. I got the shotgun from behind the bar in my hands. You don't give me what I want, I'm going to fire through the walls. Twelve gauge like this should spread enough to pulp everything. You know what pulp means, Sergei?"

"I know pulp. What do you want?"

"Send Igor out. That's all. Send him out, and we leave."

I heard a hushed conversation and a few loud "No's" from Igor. I racked the slide on the gun for effect and let a shotgun shell fall to the concrete floor.

"Ten seconds, Sergei, then I just let the shotgun sort it out."

"Nine, eight, seven, six, five..." I shouldered the gun and got ready. If I bluffed once, Sergei would find a way to exploit it. At three, the door opened, and Igor walked out with his hands up. When Igor was beside me, I pulled him away from the doorway. I looped the shotgun under his chin and snaked my left arm around the barrel. My left hand found the back of Igor's head, and the choke compressed. The hard metal gun on Igor's throat clamped his carotid artery, and blood stopped flowing to Igor's brain. Igor left his feet as I arched my back. Eight seconds later, he was unconscious.

"Set-up was just like you said, boss. Let's get you out of here," I said to Igor as he went limp, loud enough for Sergei to hear. I shouldered him quietly and kicked open the back door. The alarm screeched to life as my feet touched the alley gravel. I hustled Igor around the corner and onto a side street that connected with King. I was on the busy street in thirty seconds and in the car thirty seconds after that. I wasn't worried about Sergei following me; he had to get the alarm off before someone showed up and found the bodies in the OTB. I didn't kill Nick and Pete, because live bodies present more problems than dead ones. Dead bodies get carted off, buried, and erased. Wounded men, if they are found by the authorities, go to hospitals and get questioned. Nick and Pete would never talk to the cops, but they would still bring all kinds of heat down on Sergei unless they were dealt with quietly. Sergei couldn't outsource this problem to anyone else — there was no time. If Sergei wanted to stay out of custody, he would have to do something about his men — and that meant giving me time to get away.

Within the hour, Igor was taped to a chair in the motel room next to mine. His clothes were in the bathroom, and the folding knife was in my hand.

CHAPTER SIXTEEN

The bullet had torn through the lower half of my ear, leaving a section of undamaged ear hanging. I used the knife in the bathroom to take the wrecked part of the ear off. It took two rolls of toilet paper to stop the bleeding and a piece of duct tape over some more of the cheap motel toilet paper to cover the wound.

The motel room next to mine was just as tight. Igor's chair was at the foot of the bed, and it took up all the space between the bed and the wall. To get behind Igor required a trip over the mattress. His feet were taped to the back two legs, and his wrists were fastened to the metal frame behind his back. Over his mouth, a piece of tape kept him quiet. His eyes weren't on me, they were on the knife.

"Feels like we've been here before, eh? Except last time you had *me* tied down."

Igor thrashed his head, the only part of his body that he could move, and grunted at me.

"I've been reading *I'm Okay, You're Okay*." Igor's eyes peeled away from the knife and found mine. "I figure you thought of your own solution to get that closure you want-ed. One that wasn't in the book. You figured I'm not okay, and neither are you. But you thought that if you killed me you could get okay. Sort of take out half of the equation, and everything will sort itself out." I chuckled. The sound made Igor's lip quiver under the tape. "I hate to break it to you, Igor, but killing never sorts anybody out. If anything, it turns you inside out even more. The more you do it the less it will help, because you keep turning off a bit more of yourself. It's like burning nerve endings one at a time. You feel it for a minute while it dies, but pretty soon you can't feel anything no matter how hard you try. Way I see it, you got it all wrong. We'll never be okay. Okay isn't for people like us. We've done too much wrong to too many people. Okay went out the window the first night you rode with a gun in your pocket and violence in your heart. You can never come back from that. The most you can hope for is alive. It's not what we deserve for what we've done, but it's what we get. It's all doing wrong earns you, if you're good enough at the bad. That was always your problem. Try as you might, you never had the gravel in your guts, but some-how you managed to defy the odds and stay above ground. Now stay put."

I went outside and walked into my room. I powered up the cell phone and dialled Morrison while I cut through the decades-old yellowed drywall with the knife. I winced when the phone touched the ear damaged by Nick's bullet and quickly switched the cell to the other side of my face. Morrison picked up as I finished my first cut into the wall.

"Morrison."

I dragged the knife a foot down the wall, turned the blade, and made another long cut. "Where are you?"

"The house you told me about. It's a fucking mess."

"You having crime scene techs go through it?" I turned the knife again and started a cut back up the wall.

"No, I got some uniforms with some mops. They're just gonna wring 'em out back at the lab."

"Not all of the blood belongs to the girl; some of it belongs to Igor. If you compare it to the blood left on the bed in the hospital, you will find a match."

"He good for it?"

"I didn't kill the nurse. He was the last one to see her alive. Either he did it or the girl did after she let him loose. She was a hard one; don't let the skinny legs fool you."

"This is a start, but where's Igor?" said Morrison. "I have to have someone to tie all this blood to."

"He's in the wind, but I'll have him soon," I said. "What happened with the two men on the scene?"

"We found them in the bedroom fucking with the mattress. Put a big slit down the centre. They don't speak English though. Only word they seemed to have a grasp of was 'lawyer.' That was one word they knew real well."

"You know who they are?"

"I know they're Russians."

"They work for Sergei Vidal."

"No shit."

"No shit," I said.

"Why were they here?"

"You're the detective. I'm sure you can piece together a motive if you put your mind to it," I said as I put the phone on my shoulder so I could use both of my hands to pull the drywall free.

"So," Morrison said, "I have Sergei Vidal's men at the site of a brutal slaying with shit thrown all over the house like someone was searching for something. Something they didn't find yet, because there was nothing in the car or on them. What am I gonna find in the house?"

I ignored the question. "Is Miller there?"

"Why?"

"I want you to tell him something."

"I told you he's clean," Morrison said, still clinging to his badge brother.

"Why do you stick up for him when you know he's dirty?"

"And how do I know that? Because you told me? You think your word means anything to me? I know your type — I've been schooled on people like you since birth. My brother is like you. He's a meth addict 'cept back home on the island we don't call it meth. We call it P. He's twelve years older than me, so he was my idol growing up. Problem was he lied all the time so he could get high. He'd say we'd go to the park after school, but he'd never come get me because he was high. He'd tell me we'd go to a rugby game, but I would sit home all night in my jersey because he went and got high. When he got worse, he'd steal from me to get high. He stole my bike, my Nintendo, one time he sold my new shoes. Every time he came down he'd swear it would never happen again, but it would because he was a junkie, and lying is part of being a junkie. See, to me, you're just like him. You'll say anything you can to get what you want, but it will always be a lie because you're a junkie just like him."

I pulled some cheap insulation out of the wall and dropped it on the floor. The other wall of Igor's room was now visible through the square hole I'd made.

"You're not on P like my brother, you're a criminal addicted to something stronger than meth; something much more addictive — staying out of jail. I don't really need to explain to you how hooked you are on staying out of a cage, do I? It's only been a few days since I turned you loose, and you've already killed a man with my gun and blackmailed me with it to avoid doing time. What other things have you done, that I don't know about, to get your fix? Who else had to die so you could walk the streets?"

"Let's cut the shit. You and I are both bent. You set me loose, Morrison. Everything that happened was because you saw fit to use me as bait. And what was I on the hook for? You just wanted a bust you could attach your name to so you could get ahead, so don't try to pretend that you're Dudley Do-Right. You're just an opportunist with a badge — a different kind of junkie who gets off on his pay grade."

"You're right about that, mate. There's definitely some dirt under my fingernails. Most cops are a little dirty. No one trusts a guy who doesn't have a little stink on him. And maybe Miller has dirtier hands than me, but I'm not turning on him on your say so. I know you're running game, mate, I've been lied to by better, and it won't work."

"Maybe I am wrong about Miller," I said. "But you set me loose to shake the trees. You wanted me to find you a bigger fish to arrest, and now you're changing the rules because the fish I found stinks. You need to get okay with what I have because there is nothing else on the menu. You want a big bust with a lot of press? Then you need to accept that Miller is involved in some way. Deep down you know I'm right. You have to admit, things just seem to have a habit of happening when he's around."

Morrison sighed. "Yeah," he said. "They do." He paused, and I heard him taking a deep breath. He let it out slowly, then said, "What do you want me to tell him?"

"You just tell him that Sergei is taking a run at Igor. Tell him that you heard it from a couple of your sources on the street while you were looking for Igor. Tell him Sergei almost got him, and you're sure that Igor will be turning up dead any day now. Tell him your CIs are saying that whoever brings Igor in will be set for life. Get that? Set for life."

"Is it true?"

"Enough of it is."

Morrison sighed and told me he'd pass it along.

"You need to do it fast," I said.

"He's been hanging around for the last hour. He's real interested in the scene. I'll tell him now."

"How did it end with your brother?" I asked.

Morrison paused, and when I heard his voice again it was serious. "I arrested him the day I became a cop, and I broke his arms so he couldn't shoot up anymore."

I hung up and listened with a motel glass against the single sheet of drywall separating me and Igor. I could hear him grunting clearly enough, then I heard a crash. I walked back inside the other room, gun in hand, and found Igor toppled in his chair. He had rocked back and forth too hard and had sent the chair over on its back. I righted the chair and rested the blade of the folding knife between Igor's legs. I understood Igor. He worked out of a strip club, kept a woman he never touched, and beat her regularly because he was emasculated. Everything he did was meant to seize some part of the masculinity he felt he was lacking inside. Igor was empty, but he still had the right useless decorations. I slid the knife forward until it met resistance. His head thrashed, but the rest of him stayed frozen. Igor couldn't afford to move because of the knife against his balls.

"Igor," I said. His eyes were shut tight. I pushed harder and said it again, "Igor." He looked at me, and I leaned in closer. "You're already a fucking joke. Everyone sees through you. Those who don't think you're gay. What will they say when they find out you have no balls? Will they still let you run the strip club if they know you can't enjoy it?"

Hitting Igor where it hurt was never going to be physical. If I cut him, he would give up and accept death. If I pierced something inside, something deep and emotional that was already rotten and festered, I would have him.

"You can get out of this, Igor." I showed him the red knife. "You want out?"

Igor nodded vigorously.

"All you have to do is make a call and say what I tell you to say. One call and we're done. Sound good?"

Igor nodded.

"Stay put."

I sat on the bed and wrote out what Igor was to say on the inside of a red palm Bible left inside the night stand. When I finished, I capped the pen and got Igor's cell phone out of his pants on the floor. I powered the phone up, pulled the tape on Igor's mouth free in one pull, and asked, "What's Miller's number?"

Igor looked at me puzzled for a moment. "Miller?"

"This isn't about you, Igor. You're just too stupid to realize that."

"I'm not stupid."

"Then tell me the number."

Igor told me, and I dialled. I put the phone between his shoulder and ear and rested the knife back against his balls. Igor grunted and then started reading.

"It's me. Listen, I'm in some shit, but I can bring it around. I just need some help. Sergei's trying to fuck me, and nothing can make that change, so I'm gonna fuck with him first. I'm gonna give you some places that he uses, dirty places. You're gonna bust 'em. You'll have enough to take down Sergei, then I'll take over."

I pulled the phone a few inches away from his ear so I could listen to Miller backpedal. He wanted no part in taking on Sergei. I had prepared for this.

Igor read on, "If I have to take you down with Sergei, I will. Remember, I have tapes, you cocksucker. I want you at the Escarpment Motel, Room Thirteen, in one hour, or we're done."

I took the phone off Igor, hit end, and closed the knife.

"That plan — it will never work," Igor grunted. "Miller will not help me go up against Sergei — it's suicide."

I nodded.

"You son of a bitch cocksucker. I am bait? You want Miller to tell Sergei so he can kill me. You motherfucker!"

Igor was getting loud, so I shut him up with a right hook. I didn't put much into the punch, just enough to feel teeth break. Igor spat blood on the floor and kept his voice down. "How did you know about the tapes I had on Miller?"

"I heard you tell him about them."

"When?"

"Right after you killed Tatiana in your kitchen."

Igor's mouth hung open. "You did this? All of this? You were the one in the street. You stole the money and shot at me in the restaurant. This is all your fault. You cocksucker, I'm going to…"

My fist hit Igor on the side of his rib cage on a spot where there was no muscle protecting the bones. This time I didn't hold back. His body, taped to the chair, went rigid with the impact, leaving the other side open for the same treatment. I felt bones break against my fist once then twice.

"Igor, you did this, not me. You opened up something that was dead because you couldn't let what happened go. Getting shot warped you when it should have just taught you something. You want to live in this life, you have to accept the risks. You want to live by the gun, you have to expect to die by the bullet."

Igor didn't answer me; his ribs were broken on both sides. Moving was agony and would be almost impossible. He forced out a few words in an almost soundless whisper. "You're dead, Moriarty."

I understood the threat. He would never be able to understand my response. I grinned at his fluttering eyes. "I'm not dead, Igor; I barely even exist. Death doesn't know my name, but he keeps searching for me, and I keep moving. I know he'll catch up one day; just not today. Today is your day."

I put him the rest of the way out with a fist and then untaped his wrists and ankles. The ribs would confine Igor to the bed. He'd barely be able to breathe enough to stand, let alone run. I left Igor's pistol on the corner of the night table just out of reach from the bed, propped Sergei's shotgun in the corner, and called Morrison.

"Miller leave?"

"Yeah. He got a call and took off."

"You free?"

"I can be, mate."

"Get in the car and drive to Whitney Billiards. It's near a restaurant in the West End called Greece on King."

"I know it."

"Get there and leave your phone on."

I hung up on Morrison and went to my own room. Everything was in motion now. What I cooked up would either work out or end in a bloodbath.

CHAPTER SEVENTEEN

The thin mattress in the room had two guns on it. The Glock police pistol, already on the hook for a murder, and the Colt .45. I wiped the guns down, making sure to get everything, even the brass cartridges. I didn't want to leave anything behind. I put the Colt in the shoulder rig and the Glock behind my back. I had to be careful about which gun I fired and at who. One wrong bullet would destroy any hopes I had of walking away.

I tore a piece of thin pillowcase off and wiped down every surface in the room. I put the rag in my pocket, turned off all of the lights, and stood by the door using the peephole to watch the parking lot. Time went by, and every few minutes I moved from the door to the hole in the drywall. Igor made no sounds at all from next door.

Eventually, an unmarked police cruiser rolled past the peephole, parked in the rear corner, and killed its engine. No one got out of the car. The bedside clock had only counted thirty-five minutes since I hung up Igor's phone. In the dark car across the lot, I saw the flare of a lighter, then the small circle of a cigarette. I knew it could go two ways with Miller. He could decide to kill Igor himself in an "attempted" arrest, earning himself a commendation, or he could trade up by selling Igor out to Sergei Vidal. I bet Miller wasn't going to try to kill Igor in an arrest attempt. There was too much chance an investigation into Igor might turn up his name or Igor's tapes. It would be better if Miller took care of Igor off the books. And if he was already freelancing, why not trade up for a better partner? Miller was corrupt already; why should he settle for being in bed with mid-level muscle when he could get in bed with upper management?

Miller sat quietly in his car while Igor lay silently in his bed. I watched Miller and listened to Igor, but neither man moved. I watched for nineteen minutes until a black Mercedes sedan pulled into the parking lot. The unmarked car flashed its lights once, and the Mercedes pulled in beside it. The two cars were snug together in the adjoining spaces. They stayed like that for a few minutes, probably talking through lowered windows, until Miller squeezed out of the police car. The man in the Mercedes followed — it was Sergei Vidal.

I waited, watching the Mercedes for more bodies, but there were none. Sergei had come alone. Sergei and Miller together must have been a result of a battle of wants and needs. Sergei needed Igor dead because he believed he was turning on him. Sergei was four men down, and Miller was the only way to get to Igor right away, so he had to work with him. Sergei needed Miller. Miller wanted the money working with Sergei would offer, but more than that he wanted to live. He must have insisted that Sergei come alone. That way, no one would kill him too. Miller needed Sergei alone to get what he wanted. Wants and needs had brought them together to kill a man in Room Thirteen.

Both men walked wordlessly across the parking lot. Whatever they had to say had been said when they were parked. Miller raised a fat arm and pointed to the room next to mine. Sergei, a man in his fifties with salt and pepper hair and wearing a black turtleneck and black pants, scanned the parking lot. He saw something to his left and said something I couldn't hear, or lip read, to Miller. Sergei broke away from the other man and strode across the parking lot towards whatever he saw. As he walked, he reached inside his coat and pulled out a knife. He opened the knife and let it hang low in his left hand brushing against his thigh as he walked. The only thing in front of him would be the manager's office. I remembered the glow of the television splashing out onto the puddles on the pavement as the kid inside working nights watched Romero movies — he'd never see the Russian coming. Sergei was beefy; his chest was barrel shaped, and he walked proudly with his shoulders back. His form told me he was powerful as a young man and surely now still stronger than most. His bulky frame left my view.

I used the time the murder in the office would take to concentrate on Miller. He had taken a spot to the left of Igor's door. His fat back was so close I could have touched him from the open doorway. I took a few steps back and pulled out the .45. Sergei would know the room was occupied when he killed the manager. The info would be in the logbook. If he decided to try to do the occupant of the room like he did the manager, he would find the black eye of the .45 instead of a punk kid. If that happened, I would have to work on the fly. I backed up to the hole I had made in the drywall and listened with my eyes, and the gun, trained on the door. After a few minutes, the door inside Room Thirteen creaked open and shut.

There was silence while Miller and Sergei approached the body. I took a few steps away from the wall, out of earshot, and powered up the phone. I got Morrison after one ring. "Escarpment Motel just up the street. Room Thirteen. Now!" I hung up the phone and put my ear back to the wall.

"Wake up, motherfucker!" Miller said.

There was a murmuring that must have started somewhere inside Igor's broken ribs.

"What's that? Speak up."

Another murmur.

"He's fucking high or something. I told you he was on the stuff. He doesn't even know where he is, but we know, don't we?"

"Finish it and let's go," Sergei said.

"Go ahead, Sergei. Do it."

"*Nyet*. You want in? This is the way. Otherwise, I will never trust you. You want to work for me? Fine. Do your first job."

"I work for money, not for free."

"Fine, fine. You will be paid, now do it."

"Well, I do like to make a good first impression. Tell ya what, Igor. I think the grief of killing your wife became too much for you to bear. You ran, got high, and then shot yourself with your own gun."

There was some grunting and rustling before Miller said, "Stand back. You don't want any brain matter on you. The spatter on the wall and ceiling has to be perfect, or someone will know there was someone standing near the body. Plus, that shit never gets out. We caught a body one time…"

"Do it!"

BANG.

"Take the shotgun," Sergei said.

"Is it yours?"

"You work for me now. We are not partners, so shut the fuck up and get in the car. *Da?*"

"Yeah, yeah. I mean *da, da.*"

I got away from the wall and back to the peephole. A new car was parked in the middle of the lot. Detective Sergeant Huata Morrison was walking from the car to Room Thirteen. I eased the door open a crack so I could hear what went on outside.

Morrison drew his gun and screamed "Freeze!" when he saw Sergei leave the room. In his hands was the same squat revolver he had aimed at me in the cemetery.

Sergei said nothing.

"Hands where I can see them!"

If Sergei moved, I couldn't see it.

"It's all right, Morrison. I got this handled."

"Miller?" Morrison was confused — his voice gave it away.

"Yes, sir. I've been on this Rusky for months now, and I finally got him red-handed."

"What happened here, Miller?" Morrison lowered his gun, keeping two hands on the revolver; it was a textbook safety procedure.

"Single gunshot to the face inside the room. Sergei Vidal shot and killed Igor Kerensky."

"And you caught him?"

"Yes, sir."

"How did you know he would be here?"

"CI, sir. Tipped me off an hour ago at the scene. That's why I left. I'm sorry I couldn't tell you, but these bastards have ears everywhere. There's dirty cops everywhere on the force."

"So you caught Sergei Vidal with that shotgun?" Morrison's head gestured to the gun I couldn't see from my spot behind the door.

"Yes, sir."

"That is some good police work. My only question is: why is the suspect not cuffed? Why is he free to walk with you a few feet behind?"

There was no answer, at least not in words. A bullet took the back of Morrison's skull off. The big cop stumbled back, as his body figured out what his brain could no longer tell it, and fell to the pavement.

I wasn't surprised. Morrison was in a dark parking lot with a bent cop and the head of the city's Russian muscle, and he never thought to keep his gun up. I wasn't sure if Morrison was still trying to believe Miller over me or if he had no idea how deeply corrupt Miller really was. Whatever his reasons, Morrison died with his hand on his gun. He should have seen it coming like I did through the crack in the door. I made no noise as I adapted to the situation by holstering the .45 and slipping out the Glock police pistol.

"Sorry I took so long to get out there. When I heard Morrison's voice, I went back for Igor's gun. New story is Igor killed his wife, got high, shot a cop, then turned the gun on himself. Tragic story — film at eleven."

Sergei laughed, "I think you have Russian in you."

If Miller did, the Russian in him was all over the pavement a second later.

I opened the door and pulled the trigger of the Glock. Miller caught the movement of the door, turned his head, and brought Igor's gun up. He was a second too late. Three bullets went into his chest. I pivoted to gun down Sergei, but he was already moving. Instead of going for a gun, he put his body behind Miller's staggering form and went for the shotgun still in his hand. I put a bullet in Miller's thigh, and his huge body lurched back into Sergei. The Russian gave up on the shotgun in favour of keeping the obese cop from falling on him. Sergei didn't hesitate; he used a shoulder to prop the fat man up while he went for the police pistol still on Miller's hip. The grope under the cop's cheap jacket took a few seconds as Sergei held Miller up while stretching his arm around the massive torso; it was enough time for me to shoot Miller's other leg. Sergei wasn't strong enough to hold the 300 plus pounds of dead weight up. Miller fell forward, leaving Sergei standing unarmed.

"Evening," I said.

"You were the one who came for Igor."

"Yes."

"But you do not work for him."

"No."

"Who do you work for?"

"No one anymore."

"He said someone was after him. A James Moriarty. Is that you?"

"It's who he thought I was."

"I know that name, Moriarty. It is a fake, *da?*"

"Yes."

"He was the nemesis of the detective Sherlock Holmes."

"You read the books?"

"Pah, books. Those books were not party approved. I learned the name when I came to Canada. I heard it on *Star Trek.* The robot fought Moriarty, the master criminal. Is this what you are, the master criminal? If so, you should come work for me. I need good criminals."

"I'm not a master criminal, I'm just one of the bad guys. The one who doesn't get caught. I don't want a job. Way I see it, you'd just string me along until you had a shot at killing me. You tried it before, and you would again."

Sergei's eyebrow rose, and he looked at me with a hawk's peering gaze. "I know you?"

"We never met, but I knew Ivan and a man named Mikhail. They were both on their way out when I met them."

Sergei's veined fists clenched the air, and he said, "I know you."

"Did the robot on *Star Trek* catch Moriarty?" I asked.

The question caused Sergei to falter. He thought about it. *"Nyet,"* he said.

"So what chance do you have?" The Glock erupted

twice, and Sergei went down. I pulled the cloth from my pocket, wiped the pistol down, and put it in Morrison's dead hand. Death was everywhere, but enough of the wrong people were dead to make it a quiet case. Two cops shot and killed each other along with a mob boss and his trusted lieutenant. Morrison and Miller would be branded as corrupt, and their deaths would be whitewashed. Whatever Morrison had on me would be branded as tainted by corruption, deemed unusable, and probably destroyed or "lost" forever. The top brass would want it that way out of fear that Morrison's corruption becoming known would call into question every case he had ever worked.

I got in the Volvo and left the parking lot dialling a 911 call as I got onto the road. When the call ended, I took apart the phone and let each piece fall on a different stretch of road.

CHAPTER EIGHTEEN

Outside Sully's Tavern, I took the Colt apart and fed it to several sewer grates. The shoulder rig and belt holster went inside a garbage can chained to a light post down the street from the bar.

Inside were the same bunch of regulars I'd seen two years before in the same seats. I sat at the bar and ordered a Coke. Behind the bar, Steve filled a glass and walked it over to me.

"Still in town?" Steve spoke as though I hadn't been gone for years.

"Leaving now. I just wanted to stop by to see how you and Sandra were."

"Sandra will be sorry she missed you. With the baby on the way, she goes to bed early."

I smiled and grabbed a hold of the shaggy-haired man across the bar. We hugged, and Steve actually laughed.

"Someone was looking for you," he said.

"Who?" My neck was hot all of a sudden.

"Said she was a friend of your uncle's."

"What does she look like?"

"Small, dark hair, Asian, in her fifties. Pretty lady. Always alone."

"You sure?"

Steve's look said he was.

"She coming back?"

"Been coming 'round every couple of days for the past few weeks. She said she knew you were in town and that you would probably stop in here. Guess she was right."

"When was she last in?"

"Two nights ago."

I wanted to know what Ruby Chu wanted, and I had no reason to run anymore. Everyone who wanted me dead was cold. I had no illusions that Death would learn my name eventually, but he could get in line when the time came. I stayed on the bar stool for a few hours, then I went looking for the woman who knew my uncle to find out what she wanted with me.